ENTRISS ONLINE

DAVID J. PEDERSEN

Odysia Press

Cover art by:

Alessandro Brunelli

Editing by:

Danielle Fine

Angela D. Pedersen

Tom Nemes

FOREWORD

"What the hell is LitRPG?" - I remember saying that out loud several years ago when I stumbled across "Survival Quest," the first book in Vasily Mahanenko's "The Way of the Shaman" series. It was the weirdest book I had ever seen. A fantasy that takes place in virtual reality (VR), with game stats like an MMORPG (massively multi-player online role-playing game). What kind of nerd would read something like that?

Me! I devoured it in a few days, and went on to read "The Land: Founding" by Aleron Kong, "Awaken Online: Evolution" by Travis Bagwell, "Delvers LLC: Welcome to Ludus" by Blaise Corvin and... you get the idea.

I started to research LitRPG (literary role-playing game) after completing the Angst series. It didn't take long to find an enthusiastic community on LitRPGforum.com, Facebook and Reddit. I quickly learned that readers were hungry for more, but tastes varied from light VRMMORPG stories to crunchy books filled with stats.

After a brief panic attack trying to figure out how to appease everyone, and a long battle with Microsoft Excel that resulted in spreadsheets with enough calculations to make a math major vomit, I decided to play to my strengths. I wanted to contribute to the genre, and it wasn't going to be with math.

Entriss Online is light enough for my mom to enjoy, but there's still progression. (While Excel and I aren't exactly friends, I actually used some of those spreadsheets.) I tried vanquishing *some* common tropes found in VRMMORPG novels, while putting my own spin on others. I also worked hard to make the real-world story as entertaining and relevant as the story on Entriss.

You'll find that the most unique aspect to this novel is how it fits into the broader series to come. It's going to be a fun ride. I hope you enjoy reading Entriss Online as much as I enjoyed writing it!

All the best,

David J. Pedersen

ACKNOWLEDGMENTS

My writing process should come with a disclaimer: "Supervision is required at all times when author is creating work in progress." I am fortunate to have a team of people who fill that role.

Thanks to Cristi, Brandon, Matt and Mike! My Alpha Team provides feedback on early drafts and encouragement that keeps me writing.

Along with reading that early draft, my lovely and patient wife, Angie, also edits some of the rougher patches.

Danielle Fine is my incredible editor. Not only does she face the challenge of cleaning up my grammar, she provides amazing advice on the story with developmental editing.

My Advance Review Team gets the almost final copy. Not only do they catch some typos, they often support my work with reviews or spread the word to friends.

Since I sometimes stumble through my rewrites, Tom Nemes stepped in for a last minute proofreading.

Finally, I need to thank my muse and mechanic, Sarah, for her advice on wheel camber.

Best supervision ever! My sincere thanks to all of you! I look forward to our next adventure!

To Matt & Mike –

We've captured some flags in UT,
battled enemies in WoW PiViPs,
saved the world from zombies in VR,
and fragged in the New Year.
Thank you for decades of gaming and friendship.
My books wouldn't be the same without you.

BOOKS BY DAVID J. PEDERSEN

Angst – Epic Fantasy

Book 1: Angst

Book 2: Buried in Angst

Book 3: Drowning in Angst

Book 4: Burning with Angst

Book 5: Dying with Angst

Watson's Worlds – LitRPG

Book 1: Entriss Online

Fantasy For All Ages

Clod Makes A Friend

–E N T R I S S–

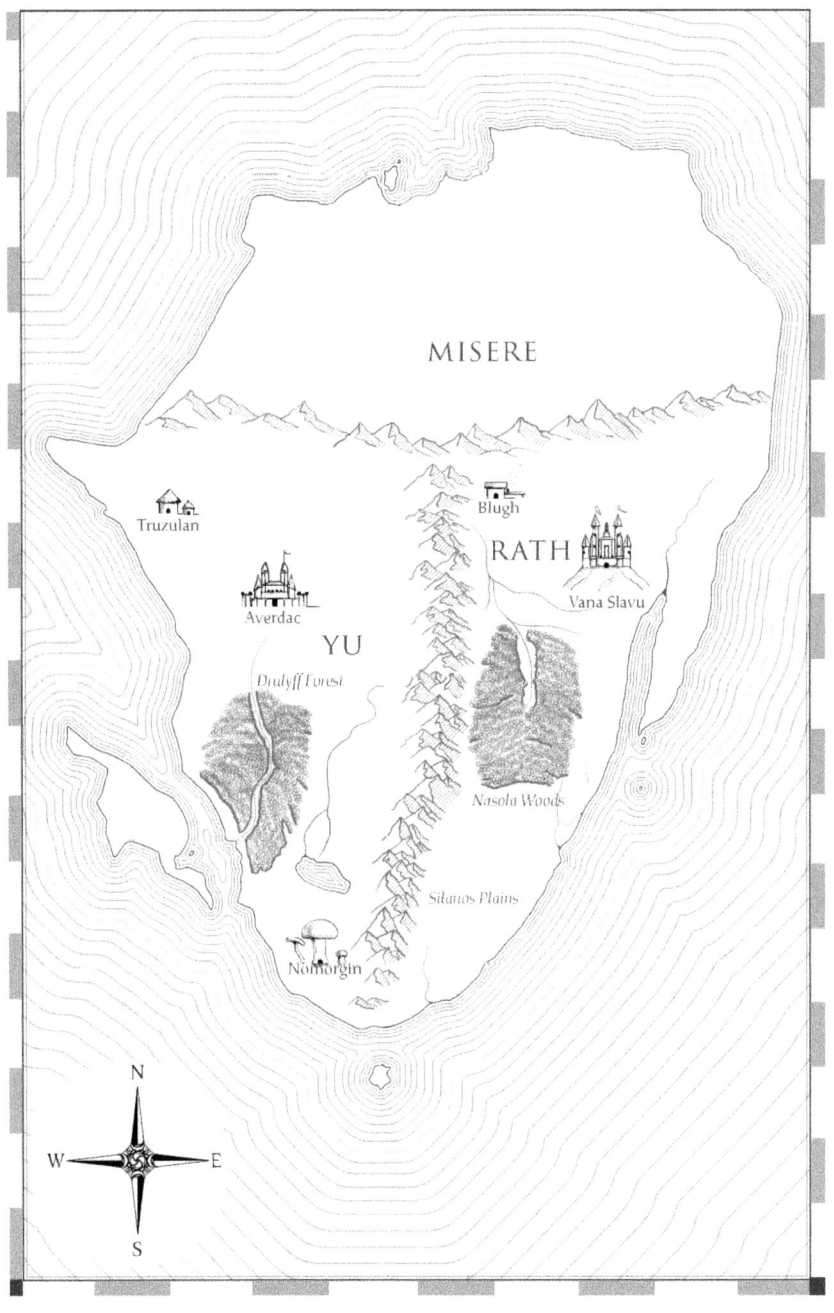

1

GRAND MAGUS MANDORF

Mandorf rolled across the cave floor like a tumbleweed in a hurricane. He reached out, desperately grasping for anything that could slow him right up until he smashed against a wall. The impact made his vision blurry, and he remained still for a breath. Almost a breath.

Desperate shouts from his motley group meant it was starting again. Mandorf crawled to a nearby stalagmite that should be wide enough. Hopefully.

An undulating red light flooded the cavern, growing brighter with each passing second. The nerve-wracking blare of a hundred discordant horns swallowed his teammates' cries. The sound became unbearable as light flashed around him.

Waves of heat rose from the ground, and exposed tatters of his robe began to smolder. He tried blowing on them as if they were birthday candles. Just a few more seconds and the light would pass. He drew in the robes and patted away the smoke.

"Any second now," he whispered. "Three, two, one... Shit." The light continued blasting his rocky shield. It hadn't moved on. He shouted, "That thing knows I'm here. A little help!"

The raw heat was too much for the stalagmite and the edges

began cracking. He willed himself thinner...which didn't work. Twisting aside every time a small shard of rock broke away was equally useless. The heat was killing him. Mandorf squeezed his eyes shut and waited for the inevitable.

The obnoxious blaring sound faded, and he opened an eye. The throbbing red light was dim. He wasn't dead. Actually, he was better than not dead. Someone, some hero, had been adept enough to cast a healing spell on Mandorf while distracting the beast.

"Thank you, Jewells." He pushed himself up for a better view.

Across the great breadth of the cavern was an enormous obsidian Golem. The creature stood on four of its muscular arms, the other four reaching out as if for a hug. A really bad hug. A continuous blast of red-hot light shot from its mouth, moving steadily around the cave like a deadly searchlight.

When the fiery attack ended, the monster lowered itself to the ground and centipede-skittered on all eight arms. There were no eyes or ears on its circular stone head, just that enormous mouth that looked like the entrance of a cave you didn't want to explore. The thick, rocky maw opened and closed as it gasped for breath. The golem was almost dead.

"He's done attacking. All in!" he cried, trying to rally his troops.

Silence. No one was in. Smoldering remains of fourteen champions lay scattered around the cave floor. He shook his head and sighed. It was the first time anyone had encountered this monster and a little strategy would've made this a clean fight. He'd tried to lead but only a few had listened. One brave idiot was pancake-flat under the beast's large palm, because rushing in before the group was ready made sense. Still, what had he expected from a Barbarian named Yolo?

The only one who'd come through was his friend, Priestess Jewells. Her healing spells had kept everyone else alive through their foolishness, and now she was gone. She must've cast *Sacrifice* before dying, giving the last of her health to Mandorf so he could finish this. He had enough Power, but did he have enough time?

He couldn't cast any of the seven basic spells in his Wizard's arsenal. It would take five minutes before his Mana regenerated enough to attack with even the weakest spell. There was only one way to end this: The War Staff of Antilon.

Antilon's staff could cast one special spell every thirty minutes. It was powerful enough to finish the Golem but required direct contact, which was dangerous for a wizard wearing cloth armor. The spell wouldn't be ready for another forty-five seconds, but as long as the monster was catching its breath, there was a chance that—

The Golem reared back on four arms and let loose its blaring scream. A geyser of burning red light shot from its mouth, striking the far end of the cave. The blast slowly made its way toward him.

Thirty seconds felt like an eternity. He waited until the beam was almost close enough to singe his sleeve. With a deep breath, Mandorf grasped his polished oak staff and ran. The creature had sensed his movement. The blast of fury and fire closed in faster.

Twenty seconds. Just twenty seconds more.

The volcanic nightmare that spewed from the golem's mouth shook the ground. His blue silk robes billowed around him as his thong-sandaled feet stumbled over uneven stone. His mouth went dry as he circled the cave, death racing his heart with every painful beat.

Ten seconds. He wouldn't make it.

He had to make it.

Mandorf cursed with every step. Why couldn't his staff shoot lightning bolts or a stream of fire? The spell should've been something he could cast from the other side of the cave. Wizards had flimsy cloth armor; they weren't supposed to get within whacking distance.

The golem's mouth was huge up close, and it trailed his every step. Mandorf had to attack now or the beam would destroy him. There was no time to check if the spell was ready. He sprinted straight at the monster and leaped into the air, raising his staff high overhead.

"This ends here!" He swung down, jamming the end into the golem's maw as he cast *The Shattering*. "This ends now!"

Time slowed as Mandorf dropped to the ground. The red beam fizzled out as the creature reached for him. He slipped through all four hands, each grasping with the dexterity of a toddler chasing bubbles.

Mandorf's landing was pure superhero, one knee resting on the cave floor as he spread his arms wide. Pale light emanated from his weapon, filling the cave with its cold radiance. He took a breath.

A breath. That meant he'd lived.

He looked up with a confident smirk. The golem fell back and screamed as gray cracks spread across its body. It shook violently, splintering into a thousand pieces that exploded from its corpse.

The cave erupted in cheers as the dead came back to life. He shakily stood with the help of his war staff.

Everyone cheered. "Huzzah, Grand Magus Mandorf."

Jewells rushed to him, her face beaming with excitement.

"The real hero." He wrapped an arm around her. "I couldn't have done it without Jewells!"

They cheered again. "Huzza, Priestess Jewells."

She looked up at him with a broad smile. He kissed her temple, which made her eyes go wide.

"Let's see what treasure this beast fought so hard to protect," he shouted.

An enormous, glowing chest appeared on top of the creature's smoking remains. Mandorf released Jewells and approached the golden fortune. He gripped the handle and lifted it open.

"Mr. Gregg," said a whiny voice that was impossible to ignore.

He glanced at Jewells, tapped his ear, and sighed. She rolled her eyes knowingly.

Impossible to ignore became impossible to avoid as the head-and-shoulder image of a toad-ish woman appeared. A small rectangular video, like old television, came into focus at the bottom-right of his vision.

His new boss, Luanne, had spiky gray hair that grew from the top of her tanned round face like a Chia Pet. Her nostrils flared as she peered at him with sharp, beady eyes.

"Do not ignore me, Ian." Her piercing voice would've made a bat wince and fly away. "You're five minutes late to the all-hands meeting. You know that all senior developers are required to attend."

"Customer support issue, Luanne." He swallowed his racing heart. "Some players got stuck." He turned to Jewells and mouthed, "Idiot."

"I am not an idiot," Luanne screeched loud enough to make him jerk back. "You are grouped with others in a dungeon and not helping stuck players."

"They were definitely stuck," he said with a broad grin. "That's why I'm in a group."

"Get here now," she shouted, followed by some sort of dinosaur-bird squelch as her image popped away.

System messages appeared before his eyes.

Achievement earned: First Kill - Arzz the Dark Golem

Achievement earned: Heroic Endeavor

"Yes." He raised a fist, excited to add these to his long list of accomplishments. "Totally worth it!"

"You were amazing." Jewells was still pressed up against him.

"I was, but so were you." He bowed his head. "We're a great team."

"Yeah," she said.

She was so beautiful he struggled not to stare until she frowned. "The meeting?"

"Right." He took a step back and began logging out.

"What about the loot?" she asked.

"Oh crap," he said as his virtual reality headset went dark.

2

ALL GOOD THINGS

In the near future-

Ian rushed down hallways, tripping over worn industrial carpet and dodging slow flocks of tired co-workers. He was flustered. Not only by the surprise in-game visit from an angry new boss, but the all-hands meeting was at the opposite end of Entriss Online Headquarters. If he'd remembered, he wouldn't have been in-game, flirting with Jewells and battling that odd mini-boss. Maybe.

Ian typically received an irritation debuff at the very mention of a meeting. Not the debuff spell an Entriss monster might cast to weaken you for fifteen seconds. This real-world curse usually lasted hours. Sitting in a stuffy room with co-workers who did a better job pretending to be interested was a painful waste of time. He knew how to read. A brief email with bullet points could've been skimmed or ignored at his leisure.

- Show up to work on time.
- Complete your weekly responsibility training.
- Don't touch co-workers.
- Limit game time during your work period.

- Don't pee in the hallway if the bathrooms are locked after hours.

Sweat trickled down his round cheeks and dampened his dark bangs. This meeting with an exclamation mark beside the invitation was actually making him run. Sort-of-run. Irritation debuff x2. He hadn't moved this fast since high school, and the dog chasing him then had been huge. Next time he was going to be this late, he'd have to plan ahead and paint on another layer of deodorant.

After a brief dance with a delivery guy who couldn't decide between left and right, Ian approached the worn steel door of "sports reference auditorium one." Like the other big conference rooms, this one was named after one of Atlanta's sportsball teams. Most of his fellow developers were nerds and not sports fans. Shouldn't they have called this the Great Hall of Thingol instead of Falcons Auditorium? "Falcons" certainly reflected who was in charge.

He wiped sweaty palms on his red Shazam t-shirt, tugged at its base to ensure the brazen lightning bolt was straight, and grabbed the door handle. He pulled back, releasing a hiss of air that smelled like stale paper, old carpet, and tension. Ian squeezed his formidable girth through the opening in his best ninja impersonation. Which meant, of course, that it banged shut with a deafening *clack*.

He swallowed hard as all heads turned. The room was very full. Suit-wearing upper management, the type who appreciated the auditorium's pretentious name, were lined up on stage, seated behind large microphones placed evenly along a worn oak table.

Fearless leader and CEO Jack Cook flashed him the barest of smiles, an almost-twinkle in his intelligent gray eyes. Barbara Campbell, the youngest CIO in gaming history, fidgeted uncomfortably to his right. Perpetually angry and title-less Luanne Torres sat proudly on his left. They were surrounded by six men and women he recognized as board members. All wore darker than dark suits that intimated "funeral" instead of "bonuses."

Luanne glanced at her watch and took in a deep breath, preparing to spew out words Ian wouldn't enjoy. He should've stayed in the cave. The monster was easier to face. Her breath caught as his former boss and ladder-climber Lars Hemsly placed a calming hand on her shoulder. The tall, pale Scandinavian was a friend, or had been before his quick rise to importance. Lars had always been a patient boss, and even though he was a VP, it still showed.

"Now that you're done saving the world, we can get started." Lars gently waved Ian to sit up front.

The gentle round of laughter released tension like steam from an Instant Pot. While grateful for the gesture, Ian couldn't hold back a shudder. The front row was reserved for people who paid attention.

Ian ambled to an open seat and plopped into it. He tried mouthing an apology, but his old boss just stared off into the crowd. Lars's typically contagious smile had been replaced with a taut expression and stiff movements, as if someone had wound him a bit too tight. The VP took a deep, calming breath that relaxed his face, but his eyes still seemed haunted.

The lights dimmed as a black and white hologram appeared between the suits and employees. It was like watching an old film painstakingly restored for the sake of nostalgia.

Lars' voice echoed throughout the auditorium. "It's hard to believe that Watson's Worlds came online only five years ago. Battle World Titus, Colonize Epiales, and our own Entriss Online were the world's first IMMOs: Immersive Massively Multiplayer Online Role-playing Games. Each providing a different virtual experience."

Short clips appeared featuring the violent battle arenas on Titus, the thoughtful town building on Epiales, and a group of heroes battling a monstrous cyclops on Entriss.

"With headsets, gloves, and action tracks, players have lived virtual, safe lives on these worlds. Well, mostly safe." Lars flashed everyone a winning smile that inspired a round of polite chuckles. "These games have been everything we could've hoped for."

A colorful infographic replaced the gaming videos.

"All of Watson's Worlds have thriving economies that rival small to mid-sized nations. Unemployment is down in the United States. People make money playing our games by selling gear they win or craft. Some have sponsors, while others live off the cryptocurrency they generate."

There was a gentle round of applause before he continued.

"Crime is down. Gamers that kill or steal online aren't breaking the laws out here. We've even seen a reduction in pollution since fewer people are driving. All of that, and people are having fun. We've provided them a goal, a purpose, and that's something for all of us to be proud of."

Goosebumps crept across Ian's arms, and it wasn't because of the thick layer of sweat cooling him off. Lars's presentation wasn't new or worthy of a meeting like this. It was filled with too much back-patting and pretense. He could sense the inevitable. A shoe was going to drop soon. It was going to land hard and probably on his face.

"Out of the three worlds, I'm proud to announce that Entriss has been the most successful," Lars said. "This only happened because of your hard work and commitment. We thank you."

The table-dwellers in suits all stood and mechanically applauded until the room joined in. It lasted a full minute before Lars reached out with both hands to calm them.

"And now, U.S. Director of Virtual Operations, Ty Hammers." Lars bowed his head before moving to stand behind Cook.

They all clapped politely as the holographic image disappeared and light flooded the stage.

Everything about Ty Hammers exuded confidence and brevity. The 5'6" man was beanpole-fit with a freshly shaven black scalp. A thin beard reached from ears to jaw, forming a sharp triangle at his chin. He approached center stage on black patent shoes that reflected the light like mirrors. His dark gray suit and crisp white shirt lacked the wrinkles of a person who sat. When Ty stood before them, he lowered his head until the applause ended.

"Since man landed on the moon, there's been hope that space travel would answer our problems of overpopulation, pollution, and lack of resources. Many still look to the stars, but our technology has fallen behind the dream," he said in a deep, captivating voice. "Eight years ago, Xander Watson came to the US Government with a plan.

Rather than finding new worlds out there, he wanted to create virtual ones. Watson wanted to save the world with a game engine."

Most of the suits laughed as the crowd watched politely. Ty lowered his head again, and the stage quieted.

"That same laughter was heard throughout Congress, until they saw what the Watson Engine could do. You would've loved to see those politicians trying virtual reality for the first time. Many who scoffed at gaming or, worse, blamed video games for real world problems were left speechless when they stepped foot on another world. More than a few were visibly shaken when the dragon showed up—a story for another day."

Despite another round of polite crowd chuckles, Ian's heart swelled at the karma of stodgy game-hating politicians running from virtual dragons.

"The vote was unanimous to support Watson and make our quantum servers available for testing. Phase one involved three separate virtual worlds limited to 1st generation immersion. Entriss, Epiales, and Titus were born," he said. "The results that Mr. Hemsly shared were an understatement, and it didn't take long for other nations to mimic this technology, some even exceeding Watson's 1st generation realism. It's been an exciting time as we all came to realize that greater immersion draws in more players, dramatically improving those statistics."

A graphic appeared before Ty, highlighting the decline of pollution, unemployment, and crime in other nations. He paused to let that sink in while Ian chewed on the concept that his favorite world was only an experiment.

"Phase two of the plan is a fully immersive virtual world so real and lifelike that players can't tell the difference between ours and the virtual one. The Watson Engine supports 2nd generation virtualization. There isn't a nation or company in the world who's been able to duplicate this technology. Realizing the potential brought them, all of them, to us."

Ian sat up and leaned forward. He was aware that other nations had their own IMMOs but hadn't realized they all used Watson's

Engine. Did they all have quantum servers, too? Only superpower nations were supposed to harbor that sort of tech.

"I'm sure you're all familiar with Everyworld Online." He waved his hand in a broad arc. A new hologram appeared. This one was like a National Geographic nature video. Water trickled through a rocky brook as the camera panned over to reveal a thick forest. Two skittish unicorns drank from the creek until they were chased off by several dirty goblins. The realism was so jarring it caught Ian's breath.

"The technology goes far beyond this image. With viscosity suits and immersion pods, players can stay in the game indefinitely. Our most conservative projections show that our world will be safer and healthier by over 60%."

The suits applauded aggressively while Ian imagined The Matrix pod farm that had birthed Keanu Reeves.

"Per the Virtual Accords, Everyworld will not only be the sole 2nd generation IMMO for the United States, it will also be a hub for all of Watson's Worlds." Ty took a deep breath. "It was agreed that in order to maintain balance, every nation, or consortium of nations, will be limited to one IMMO. Many went live with their worlds two years ago." He paused to clear his throat. "After an unfortunate delay, I am proud to announce that Everyworld Online will finally go live in six months. History is unfolding before us as all 1st generation IMMOs shut down and 2nd generation IMMOs from other nations connect to Everyworld."

"Wait, what?" Ian shouted.

Ty stepped back with a Cheshire grin as CEO Jack Cook stood. The forced smile on the old man's face barely held back his grimace.

"Most of you have been in this industry long enough to know that there's a lifecycle to all software, even our favorite games. No matter how much of ourselves we pour into our creation, all good things..." Cook closed his eyes and took a deep breath before continuing. "In the coming months, we will be scaling back until finally shutting down. I'm sorry to say that this decision is out of my hands. There's nothing left to do, unless God gives me a hand."

Cook looked over the crowd. It was an odd thing to say considering their CEO had the reputation of a retired playboy. He'd never seemed like a religious man. The moment passed quickly as Jack forced a smile reserved for handshake pictures with a politician everyone hated.

"Many changes are coming, and we have a great team to help with this transition."

The next hour was filled with boring. Early retirement packages, job relocation assistance, and enough corporate-speak to require translation. There was something about stock sales, parachutes that weren't very golden, and layoffs. They needed volunteers to stay and assist with the transition. Either help fill in the blanks or line up for execution. It was all noise, though his hearing may've been tainted by bitterness.

Lars salted his wounds with the announcement that Campbell was moving on to Everyworld and Luanne was taking her place as CIO. He liked Barbara; she left him alone.

With every pronouncement, Ian sank deeper in his seat. After a string of successful launches, he could've worked for any game factory. He was that good. But Entriss had drawn him in completely. He'd lived the story that Entriss provided, fought to keep that story intact, and coded like a fiend to ensure its viability.

They were going to destroy his world, and all he could do was delay the inevitable by raising a hand and muttering, "I volunteer."

3

DIET DR PEPPER

Ian was one of the few developers on the team to keep his desk tidy. A worn, mechanical keyboard sat neatly between his track-ball mouse and a multi-purpose biometric scanner. Two 34-inch ultra-wide monitors rested side-by-side on stacks of ancient coding manuals. Along with his old wireless headset for music, and current generation VR gear, it was a Frankenstein technological mishmash of yesterday's best and tomorrow's okayest.

The only cutting-edge piece of equipment was his desktop computer. A massive cost-cutting measure had taken place the prior year that allowed developers to bring in their own PCs. Ian hadn't held back. He'd built the sort of gaming rig that NASA would've loved to borrow on weekends. That biometric device wasn't for Entriss security; it was to keep his beloved computer safe. He had several PCs like it at home and took steps to keep them safe.

The others' workplaces, and that included every desk-sitting employee from Customer Support to angry CIOs, had knickknacks. There were enough action figures, stress balls, inappropriate coffee mugs, and googly-eyed cacti to open an old brick-and-mortar gift store. Even more daunting were the framed photos of kids, spouses, pets, vacation spots, and a rooster. (Don't ask. That one was personal.)

He'd mocked these personal effects until learning he'd made someone in accounting cry. HR had corrected his course in record time, and their explanation almost made Ian tear up. The knick-knacks, coffee mugs, photographs, and other items Ian would never again call junk were an escape. They gave employees a brief distraction from often rigorous, eleven-hour days. When explained that way, Ian got it; he finally understood. They didn't want to be here. Even worse, they were trapped.

This epiphany came back in full force as Ian stared at his one photo pinned beside the two monitors. It was a screenshot of Mandorf on top of a grassy hill drenched in the colors of sunset. Light reflected off his raised staff, surrounding him in a lens-flare halo. Mandorf looked down at a horde of broken goblin bodies that hadn't quite made it to the top. Earning the title Grand Magus had been a hard-fought win and one of his favorite memories in Entriss. He'd labored in the game to be relevant and felt justified in reveling in his many victories.

Back in the real world, he often sought that picture for purpose. People were desperate for the escape only Entriss could provide, so Ian coded with the same passion he gamed. He'd worked very hard *on* the game so others could enjoy what he loved so much.

That picture, and the game it represented, had always been a call to greater things. Now it left him feeling numb. It was like watching a friend die, and he suddenly envied his co-workers. Their pictures of beach vacations or googly-eyed cacti would've been so much easier to embrace because they could take them with when they left.

"Hey, boss." The friendly voice of his intern Julie was always enough to shake off his melancholy. She placed a can of Diet Dr Pepper on his desk.

"Thanks." He winced. She knew he wasn't a fan of anything diet, especially his beverage of choice, but it was her small way of taking care of him. He may have needed to lose a pound, or fifty, but that would take far more than gross soda. It opened with a hiss, and he took a draw. "Mmm."

Julie watched him drink with a tight-lipped smile.

His twenty-three-year-old intern hid cute behind oversized glasses like Clark Kent hid Superman. Her Scottish mom had gifted her a milky-pale complexion, full lips, and dark eyes. She had dangerous eyebrows that he treated with great respect. Hidden under a tight bun was a mass of long red hair. Her crisp, white, button-up blouse, khaki pants, and brown-heeled oxfords revealed nothing other than that she was here for a job.

After a year together, Ian knew better. By day, she was a gifted developer with an intuitive grasp that would carry her forever. At night, when Julie wasn't on a bad date, she played by his side as Jewells, his favorite Priest and regular savior. Her passion for the game rivaled his own, and time with Julie drew him in like a black hole.

He was a closet romantic who never had a girlfriend. Like any high-school fantasy, he hoped that she would reveal his secret identity. He was a superhero in disguise, a famous author waiting to be discovered, or simply a developer falling too hard. That's when fireworks went off and love happened, according to the movies. This revelation rested on the tip of his tongue—a tongue he bit too often and too hard.

And yet, she was his co-worker, his intern. Despite her playful banter and occasional smoldering gaze, he just couldn't. According to his weekly responsibility training, it was inappropriate to bang interns.

It wasn't just the rules. She hadn't exactly seen his final form. Long days of development, late nights of gaming, and not-diet sodas hadn't done his body any favors. His great passion for greasy pizza delivered just before midnight and hatred of any form of exercise had given his twenty-nine-year-old body a shape no one would appreciate. He didn't, so how could she?

Instead of giving her a hug, instead of telling her all of this and dipping her for a long, romantic kiss, he gingerly sipped the diet beverage.

"Yum." He nodded his thanks. "You're too kind."

"I'd bring you a real Dr Pepper if it meant you'd stop moping."

She frowned at him with those dangerous eyebrows. "It's been a week since that meeting. If you hate what they're doing so much, why stick around? Money?"

"Money isn't my problem." He leaned back in his chair. "I've been a single developer since I was eighteen. I could retire now, twice."

Her eyes went wide.

"Hey, Daddy's got dough." He raised his eyebrows several times.

She let out a glorious laugh that melted him. A confident, smart, beautiful software developer who got his sense of humor. He should marry her now. His heart leaped into his throat at the thought. A pop-up alert from his calendar saved him from saying something foolish.

"Walk with me, young Padawan." He stood and tugged at the hem of his t-shirt.

"This must be serious if you want to go for a walk," she said.

"Training in a few minutes." Ian winked. "Gotta learn how to customer service in my downtime. Our new CIO has already thinned out their ranks."

"Right." She shook her head. "Just don't be late again."

"Eh, Lena's teaching the class." He clasped his hands behind his back. "No hurry."

"In that case, what's been troubling you, Master Jedi?"

He smiled appreciatively as they slowly walked a long, stale-smelling corridor. "It feels personal, like they're taking all this away from me and I have nowhere to go."

"Ian." Her tone was gentle. "I've learned so much from you. You're an incredible developer. I'm sure you can get a job anywhere."

"Yes, but this is where I want to be." He reached out with both hands. "Entriss hasn't just been a job, or a game. It's been my life. Out here, I get to help create the world I love. I get to see friends at work every day."

"Friend," she corrected, raising her hand.

"Okay, I get to see *friend* and some other people I don't hate," he said with a deep sniff. "On the other side, I'm one of the most accomplished players in Entriss. I've given up years, literal years, of time in this IMMO. Corporations with their sports references and downsizing don't understand that commitment. What's the difference between a quarterback giving decades of his life to become the best and a gamer doing the same? Entriss *is* my life."

She stopped and met his gaze. He didn't know that look. Was it pity for how he spent his time or sadness that she felt the same?

"We've spent a lot of time together in Entriss," he said. "It hasn't all been about winning. We've had moments. From the passing of my mom to your awful taste in boyfriends."

"Hey." She nudged him with her shoulder.

"Speaking of," he said, nodding at her forearm.

Julie's colorful sleeve of nerd-tattoos began to shift, swirling like paint in a mixer. She wiped a hand across her forearm, dismissing incoming messages with a sigh, and the tattoo returned to normal. "Sorry, go on."

"Isn't some of it personal, though? Whether it's life out here, or life in there, it's still life spent. Losing this game, losing Mandorf, losing time with my friend all has a cost."

"Yeah." She placed a hand on his arm. "You're right. I guess I feel the same."

"That's it, that's what's weighing on me." He let out a deep sigh. "I'm not sure what to do, or how to shake it. I don't want to just leave and walk away, not from Entriss, not from my, uh, friends."

"Easy, tell them at your next job that we're a package deal."

Her tone was so matter of fact that his heart skipped.

"I, uh...okay."

"And then find closure in Entriss," she said. "Go out in style so they remember Mandorf. Finish the game."

"Ha." He shook his head. "IMMOs don't have endings."

"All stories have endings, Ian," she said.

"If only it were that easy." She was right, though. Even if the game had no end, some sort of closure would help. Finding that closure together would help more. "Sounds like you're already a full Jedi."

She gripped his arm and, after a moment, looked up with a crooked smile. "I shouldn't have brought you diet."

He laughed, mostly at himself. "You should always bring me diet."

"Are we gaming tonight, Mandorf?" Her eyes went wide with anticipation.

"Tomorrow, Jewells," he said. "Tonight, I'm on duty to Customer Service. Tomorrow, we storm the gates of hell."

"Sounds good, boss." She stood at attention. "I'm going to go code. Review it later?"

"Of course," he said with a nod.

She paused, as though preparing to lean in for a hug, but thought better of it and returned his nod. The young woman sauntered off down the hall. His eyes lingered a little too long and his heart ached a little too much.

A gentle vibration from his watch interrupted thoughts of going out in style with Jewells at his side. It was a message from his counterpart, Bala.

Better hurry. Training starts in two minutes and guess who's teaching?

4

SERVICE WITH A SNEER

The room was office-temperature-cold enough to keep everyone awake. Despite the potential for frostbite, the struggle was real. HR man Bill, or was it Will, stared off in a daze at the back of someone's bald head. Determined Guy from sales was furiously typing on an old handheld device under the desk. Marketing Coordinator and potential glamour model Candice frowned at every slide. She sat beside Art, who may have been the accountant Ian had made cry. There were a dozen or more volunteers, and Ian would've bet the loot from his next boss kill that none of them had ever played the game. They may have offered to stay and help, but it was more likely they were just trying to save their jobs.

The only thing keeping them awake was their teacher, the Queen of Hearts herself, Luanne Torres. Her watchful eyes peered out from a pumpkin-round face with the complexion of tanned hide. She'd squeezed into a dark pantsuit she must've purchased back in college but was convinced still fit. To make matters worse, when Luanne wasn't firing people and screaming, "Off with their heads," she had the slow, southern drawl of a retired substitute teacher that had given up long ago and now read straight from the textbook.

Ian slipped into a training desk beside Balaman. Bala was a mid-

forties developer from India who was as tiny as Ian wasn't. He had
brown skin, a graying crown around his bald head, and a thick
mustache. Not only was he a gifted developer, but a patient teacher
who took all new hires under wing. Their relationship had begun as
mentor and pupil, and though they'd become buddies, if not friends,
Ian continued learning from him almost every day.

"She noted that you were late again," Bala whispered, nodding at
Ian's wrist.

His mentor subtly began typing under his desk. Shortly after
Bala finished, Ian's watch vibrated twice, indicating he'd received the
cast.

Computer Augmented Streaming Transmissions had taken over
cellphone technology decades ago. It was a practically lossless mesh
network that covered the globe in a wireless cocoon. Everyone with a
cast link had free access to social media, email, messaging, and every
sort of media consumption at a price.

Cast links were cybernetic, often powered by and physically
connected to their human host. They came in many forms,
combining a handheld device with contacts or corneal implants. A
popular trend with the twenteen crowd was to get inked, like Julie.
Nanobots injected under the skin turned the forearm into a color
monitor. Cool that it looked like a tattoo, bad if you had small arms,
and creepy that something under the skin was always moving and
always connected.

The only thing Ian liked about it was the name because it made
him think of casting spells. Cast links were a necessity if you wanted a
job, but he hated the idea of always being online. It felt like he was
being watched, so he stayed old-school with a large, professional-
looking watch that reminded him of Dick Tracy. Also, he could turn
it off.

Ian tapped his watch, and the message displayed in his contact
lenses.

Flirting with the help will get you in trouble.

You should try it. Ian's eyes danced across his retinal keyboard.
It's fun.

My wife would not approve, Bala cast. *You should try marriage. A wife will give you children and then you can stop hiding in the game.*

Another reason to avoid marriage. Ian grinned. *I'm surprised you signed up for Customer Service. You don't enjoy gaming.*

Entriss has provided my family much. I will help as long as she lives.

Bala worked twice the hours Ian did, which was telling. While Ian admired his work ethic, it was almost like his mentor was *trying* to spend time away from the family he bragged about so much.

Well, if I can help get you started... Ian shot him a sly look.

I know how to play, my friend. Bala huffed, sticking out his chest. *I helped write the game.*

Uh, you know it's not that simple.

"Ohmygosh," Bala whispered. "Look."

Luanne had finished her long-winded introduction and the login screen appeared in the large class monitor. Instead of entering her username, she typed her password *C@tL@dy43* in plain text for everyone to read.

"Ignore that." She furiously deleted the entry, her thick, pale cheeks ruddy. "I'll be changing my password after class."

"The future of Entriss Online, folks," Ian said a little too loudly, making everyone chuckle.

"Entriss has no future, Mr. Gregg." Her gaze was sour enough to curdle milk.

All heads turned as her evil grin broadened at his pained reaction. Most knew his passion for the game, and his accomplishments as a player. Apparently so did Luanne.

Why in the world would a CIO teach a Customer Service class? Ian took several calming breaths as he cast. *Has she fired the corporate trainers already?*

Yes. Bala shook his head and sighed. *According to Lars, Cook refused to release anyone until it was over. Ty brought in Luanne to move things along. She's already let half of marketing and administration go. Now she's looking for people who don't fall in line. Be careful.*

She doesn't even talk like IT. Why CIO?

Our old CIO was loyal to Cook, and he doesn't want Entriss shut down.

Rumor is Luanne has experience tearing down tech companies. She's now in the position to make sure we go offline in time. She's not IT, it's nothing more than a title.

"Gross." Ian gritted his teeth.

Bala nodded, but didn't reply, instead focusing on the lesson.

"Since many of you don't play the game, I'd like to start with the basics." Luanne paused until everyone was paying attention. "Entriss is split into three lands: Yu, Rath, and Misere. Yu is strictly PvE, which means Player versus Environment. In Yu, players progress by fighting monsters, or mobs, for treasure. Players in Rath progress by fighting each other, usually in gladiator matches. This land is Player versus Player, PvP, at all times."

"What about Missouri?" a young man asked. Despite the computer slides, he furiously typed notes on an invisible keyboard.

"Misere," she corrected, "is inhabited by monsters. Please hold questions until I've finished. As you can see on your screen, Yu and Rath have four playable tribes."

Four characters representing the Yu tribes appeared on the main screen—Elf, Troll, Human, and Gnome. The next slide showed the tribes of Rath—Centaur, Ogre, Human, and Sprite.

"Both Yu and Rath offer five equivalent professions. Does anyone know what they are?" Her gaze fell on the excited note-taker.

"Um, Warrior, Mage, Rogue, Hunter…"

"No, that's a different game." She inhaled deeply through her nose and waved two fingers to progress the slides. A table of those professions appeared.

Yu	Rath
Barbarian	Gladiator
Wizard	Sorcerer
Thief	Assassin
Priest	Cleric
Ranger	Marksman

"That should be pretty straightforward." She looked around the room. "Does anyone have questions?"

Ian let out a pained sigh when half the room raised their hands. As Luanne did her best to answer, he skimmed ahead through the lessons. It was solid material for someone who never logged into Entriss Online, and each section wrapped up with an easy quiz. It was also boring as hell until he felt the familiar wrist vibration. A small picture of Julie appeared in his contacts.

Is it bad?

I'm already dead, he replied. *Lamest boss fight ever. Save me. What are we working on tomorrow night?*

You love me, right?

Probably.

I need to grind reputation with the Gnomes. Her message included several beating hearts and an animated smiley.

He winced at the time that would take. Every tribe offered rewards based on your level of affinity. Friends of Gnomes might get a hat. Great friends could purchase armor. Best friends had access to powerful weapons. It was a lot of friending, but the end rewards were often worth the effort. He should know; he was besties with all Yu races.

You don't have to, she cast. *I can solo this.*

Gaining affinity with tribes typically involved completing repeatable quests. The Gnome quests were boring and required killing lots of mobs. Those mobile enemies were sometimes hard to find. He'd spent weeks grinding this one out solo. It was almost worse than the daily grind at work, but at least he'd get to spend time with her.

It'll be faster if we work together. It took every effort to sound positive. *Go team!*

You just want to see Jewells's new armor...

Oh? She was a tease, and he ate it up like a beggar at a buffet.

A nudge from Bala brought his attention back to class.

"Why bother being here if you aren't going to pay attention, Mr. Gregg?" Luanne scoffed as she pointed at his computer and made a pulling motion. "Let's see your score and... Oh."

A bright blue 100% appeared on the large screen for everyone to see. He was already four sections ahead of the class, and she scrolled through each to see similar results.

"I would appreciate it if you didn't jump ahead." She raised her chin. "You may miss something."

Bala glanced at him anxiously while Ian seethed behind a polite nod.

Gotta go, he cast. *Look forward to tomorrow.*

Don't forget your crowd control gear. Laters. Animated kiss blowing hearts.

Replying to animated hearts seemed tricky. There were thousands of emojis to choose from, and they all felt like coded messages only the cool crowd understood. He now knew better than to send red hearts—"Are you declaring your love?"—eggplants—"Feeling naughty tonight, are we?"—or dirty socks—"Ian, I'm not doing your laundry." It wasn't worth blushing for a week, so she always finished their conversations.

"Did everyone finish the exercise for section one?" Luanne's gaze swept the room before falling on Candice. "Let's see how you did."

The young woman's score appeared on the monitor. She had only gotten 65% of the questions correct.

"You are excused." Luanne pointed at the door. "Come to my office first thing with your personal effects."

The woman covered her mouth and rushed out of the room.

"Another reason Entriss is being killed off." Luanne glanced his way with a tiny smirk.

Do not let her bait you, my friend, Bala cast.

As always, Bala was right. Ian ignored Luanne and instead poured himself into the lessons. His ability to read fast and retain most of it had earned him a Computer Science degree a year earlier than his peers. This class was a comic book in comparison.

"Are you even paying attention, Mr. Gregg?" She was standing directly in front of him.

He'd been so focused, he'd ignored Bala's warnings and her approach. A quick glance around the room revealed that a third of the class was gone.

"I'm enraptured," he said, dryly.

"You." She turned on another attractive woman. "Show your progress."

Megan was an administrative assistant for one of the VPs, a single mom of two children who never played the game. Her score appeared in front of everyone, making the thirty-something brunette blush. 47%.

"I'll see you in my office tomorrow morning. Just get in line." Luanne waved the woman out of the room.

Ian watched Megan leave, his knee bouncing as dangerous thoughts slowly inched toward his mouth. While Julie was right about being his only friend at work, he liked most of his co-workers. They'd been together a long time, and many used the term "work family." It was a far better family than the one who'd raised him, and they didn't deserve to be abused this way. He wouldn't allow it.

"I'm disappointed that employees of Entriss aren't more familiar with their own game." Luanne scoffed and shook her head. "Apparently none of you are qualified for something so simple."

"Are you?" Ian sat up, glaring at her. "Because a good teacher helps and inspires. Even if you were mediocre, the room would be filled with people trying. Apparently, you understand them less than they understand the material."

Luanne balled her fists and shook, practically bursting out of her pantsuit like an overstuffed sausage. Bala sank low in his seat, covering his face with a hand.

"Go on, Mr. Gregg," the short woman said in a dangerous tone.

All eyes were on him. It was every high-school nightmare, except he wasn't naked. Fear that would've normally held him back was pushed aside by something far more passionate.

"Megan's not here because she games. She's here because she cares," Ian shouted, pointing at the woman halfway through the door. "She isn't some hate-filled dictator emptying the room of everyone more attractive. Megan's here to support her family. Not only the one back home, but the Entriss family we've spent years building. Are you here to teach or are you just here to terrorize people while destroying everything we've created?"

The collective gasp made him realize he'd gone too far. She'd gotten to him. His outburst was a result of growing frustration and poorly timed chivalry. He didn't care. This class was ridiculous, and Luanne was a monster. He'd seen Megan go toe-to-toe with her VP, and yet, she cowered before their new CIO. This wasn't about teaching Customer Service; it was corporate bullying at its worst.

"Maybe *you* should visit my office tomorrow." She crossed her arms.

"I'll be happy to meet with you and HR in Cook's office whenever you'd like." He stood and nodded at the cameras. "We can watch this class and see if your treatment of Entriss employees fits the corporate guidelines we have to review weekly."

She was a pot ready to boil over and did her best to stare him down. His mind had gone to a cool place devoid of anger because he knew he was right. So did she.

"That's what I thought." He stormed to the door.

"This class isn't over." Her voice was now several octaves above scratching chalkboard. "You won't enjoy the consequences of leaving before you've finished."

He turned around, typing out commands with his eyes, and directed his watch hand at the classroom monitor. She spun around as his score appeared. 100% flashed in red, indicating that he hadn't passed the section they were working through but had skipped ahead to the final.

"If there's nothing else, I need to log in and do my job." He glared at her. "Unless you need help doing yours."

Luanne stared at the score and shuddered. She took calming breaths, squeezing her fists several times before turning on him with a dangerous smile. "You are dismissed, Mr. Gregg," she said, her tone dripping icicles. "Your time here is done."

"I don't need to be dismissed. I volunteered."

Everyone out of Luanne's view nodded, and some even smiled. It didn't help. He marched out of the room and practically crashed into Megan.

"Thank you." She seemed on the verge of tears and grabbed his hand. "I don't know why I shut down like that."

"Because she's evil. Pure evil," he said, practically spitting. "No one knows how to face that."

"You did. That was so brave. No one's ever done something for me that would get them fired." Megan wiped her eyes, smiling gratefully. "I guess we'll be unemployment buddies."

She gave him a brief hug and rushed away.

He stood and stared until she was out of sight. When he was finally alone, he muttered, "What have I done?"

5

KING ZALMON

Horns blared heroically and the distant beat of war drums welcomed Ian. *Entriss Online* floated before him in textured golden letters. He was usually running late and skipped the game's introductory scene. Tonight was a rare occasion. Not only was he early, he was thirsty for nostalgia and wanted to hear the story.

The title burst into flames as the music softened. His view zoomed out until the words were nothing more than distant torchlight in a vast, dark chamber.

"My world in shambles," said a low, gravelly voice. The camera panned over to reveal King Zalmon. The old man sat on a massive steel throne formed from a dragon's open maw. Despite his great age, the king had a powerful physique with broad shoulders and thick arms. He wore dusky armor, scarred and dented from battle. An enormous broadsword leaned against his throne.

And yet, he was dead. Leathery tatters of skin clung to his skeletal head. A crooked crown held back wisps of long gray hair as thin as cobwebs. Most haunting were his empty eye sockets and the sucking wound in his chest, still fresh as if death had just pried his eyes and heart free.

"My life was almost at an end. I had one final task before joining Deity in the after. The time had finally come to choose a successor." The camera followed his gaze.

Three of his children stepped forward into spotlights. A beautiful, elfish woman with long, brown hair and dark leather armor peered at Zalmon with cool regard.

"Adriette is my firstborn and rightful heir to the throne. She is the first Ranger Entriss has ever seen. A cunning leader, my daughter has commanded the charge north against the monster swarm of Misere. In recent years, Adriette has become obsessed with killing the beasts that attack the borders of Yu and Rath. There's more to leading than battle, and I worry that the dark of Misere has taken hold. She is not ready."

"You are a fool for ignoring them. I will battle the swarm alone until we are at peace or I am dead." She spat on the ground and marched into the shadows.

With a heavy sigh, Zalmon turned to face an enormous bronze-skinned Troll. He was built like an old oak tree with a thick chest and arms powerful enough to hold up the sky. One hand gripped a massive, long-handled mace etched with ornate golden runes. The other raised a wine flask to his smirking lips. He apparently required no armor aside from the finest suede boots and belted loincloth of rich, dark fur.

"My insistent son Nihle was a strong leader until he became overwhelmed with greed. Rather than gathering players to fight for a greater good, he inspires them to hunt for treasure. He is not ready."

"You never believed in my vision," Nihle growled. "I will send heroes of the west to hunt for great wealth, dangerous weapons, and the finest armor. You will finally see where true power comes from."

Zalmon shook his head as the Troll sauntered off. His third child was a Centaur with a fine black coat and pale muscular torso. Oiled dark hair curled about his broad shoulders. He had the strong nose and chiseled chin of a hero. His beauty was almost enough to distract from the anger of his smoldering black eyes.

"Denper's hatred has no end. He has the gift to inspire greatness like no other and squanders it for his own glory. His Gladiators don't fight the enemies of Entriss. Instead, they battle each other for armor and weapons. He is not ready."

"True power comes from strength. My wrath will fuel Gladiators to fight until only the best remain. The east will be filled with the most dangerous warriors Entriss has ever seen." The Centaur reared back before galloping into the dark.

"What shall I do, Camille?" he said. "Entriss needs her Champion."

A woman cloaked in shadows floated to the old king and rubbed her hands together. "Her time will come, Father, as will yours."

He nodded before staring forward. "As the Right Hand of God, I fought for a world where all came together to battle evil. In my failure to choose an heir before my death, I left Entriss a broken world. It is now up to you.

"Join my son Denper in Rath." The Centaur appeared beside an enormous Ogre, a Human, and a small Sprite. "Battle other players for gear and glory."

The races of Rath faded as Nihle the Troll, an Elf, another Human, and a Gnome took their place.

"Or thrive in the riches of Yu as you seek treasure in dungeons deep."

The races of Yu faded away, leaving only the dead king and his shadowy daughter.

"This is how I leave Entriss." His body sank back into the throne. "A torn land of war and strife, of greed and battle. Choose your path wisely before all is lost. I am left with hope that a worthy Champion could save our world. Will it be you?"

THE SHORT CUTSCENE that had always gotten his blood pumping for a raucous night of gaming now weighed on him with the heaviness of nostalgia. He had laughed, fought, lost, and won many times in this world. It was hard to believe that the game would soon end.

When the scene passed, a sizable town formed around him. He stood in a main square beside a large, bubbling fountain. Horse-drawn wagons stopped at wooden shops to deliver goods. Bustling non-player characters rushed along the cobblestone walk. Some NPCs hawked their wares while others offered quests to colorfully armored players.

A baker dropped a roll and scrambled to pick it up. He looked around sheepishly, brushed off some dirt, and returned it to a basket. A pickpocket, no older than twelve, pilfered something delicious from the distracted baker before running straight into a stern guard. There was also the pie-stealing cat, the beauty who fell into a knight's arms, and the dog who peed on his inattentive owner.

It was fun, and clever, and on a loop that repeated every fifteen minutes. Despite his passion for the game, something about this 1st generation IMMO had always been lacking. Entriss was beautiful, and immersive enough to give some people vertigo, but still looked like a game. Skin had the texture of the finest plastic. Grass would sway in a gentle breeze that he couldn't feel. He longed to smell and taste the freshly baked pot pies that only appeared delicious. While still incredible, he wished it were more.

With a sigh, he gestured to open his character stats. A scroll unfurled, hanging in the air for only Ian to see. An image of Mandorf appeared in the center, wearing an impressive set of cloth armor. His blue silk robe and matching Wizard hat was lined in red satin. He gripped the polished oak War Staff of Antilon in his left hand, looking on with thoughtful blue eyes. Mandorf was tall, thin, and strong in a wiry way. He sported a long nose, short red hair, and a smart red beard. Thankfully, the Wizard looked nothing like the real-life Ian.

The left side of the scroll had menu options for quest progress, abilities, wardrobe, achievements, finances, mail, recipes, items, mounts, pets, languages, and affinity. To the right of mini-Mandorf was an impressive list of character stats that made Ian smile. Not only did he like the numbers, he'd created the interface.

Name:	Mandorf	Level:	40
Tribe:	Wood Elf	XP to Level:	-
Profession:	Wizard		
		Vigor:	12
Health:	2754	Essence:	17
Mana:	3277	Power:	10

Below that were expandable menu options detailing secondary statistics.

- Cooking: 100 +10
- Map Making: 100 +5
- Woodworking: 100
- Timber Gathering: 100 (He'd chopped down too many damn Ast trees.)

It was a long list of useful and useless abilities, titles, and crafting skills.

The grind to max level, 40, had only taken a few months. It was an easy game to figure out with only three primary attributes: Vigor, Essence and Power.

Vigor helped determine stats for Health, health regeneration and Defense. Essence affected Mana, or whatever pool of energy a player drew from for spells or attacks, and how fast Mana regenerates. Power contributed to the Damage each spell could do. The three primary attributes were static, and everything else increased either exponentially from leveling or from armor bonuses.

Players had a maximum of eight spells. Armor unlocked seven of those spells, and at higher levels, weapons unlocked the eighth. Mandorf owned one helm that gave him a powerful fireball spell. If he removed that and wore his ice lance helm, he could no longer cast *Fireball*.

The eighth spell unlocked by weapons was called a special. Specials were incredibly powerful and limited only by a cooldown. The War Staff of Antilon gave him *The Shattering*. He could only cast it once every thirty minutes, but it was always worth the wait.

The end game made gear far more interesting. Some armor pieces were empowered with combo bonuses. By itself, the fireball helm did sick damage. He also owned gauntlets that gave him a *Burn* spell, which damaged his opponent every two seconds for ten seconds. When worn together, they activated a combo. If he cast *Burn* and then *Fireball*, the *Burn* spell would last twenty seconds.

Some combos were known. Players vigorously delved dungeons and farmed mobs for armor that was guaranteed to be empowered. On rare occasions, mobs would drop items with combos no one had seen. Combos were the key, and the hunt was always on to find something unique and powerful.

He owned many sets of armor, each with a different purpose. The armor he wore for the golem fight had provided a ridiculous bonus to mana—perfect for a long fight.

"Admiring yourself?" Jewells asked from behind his scroll.

He waved it away, along with his ability to speak like an adult. Unlike Mandorf, Jewells looked a lot like Julie. Her Elf was a bit taller and more voluptuous, with well-defined muscles. And unlike Julie's hidden hair, Jewells's luxurious auburn hair flowed like a river down to her waist. But her pale skin, deep brown eyes, and firm jaw were all Julie.

The new set of armor she sported definitely wasn't Julie, though —at least not the one he worked with. She looked more *I Dream of Jeannie* than meek intern or helpful Priestess. Sheer pantaloons revealed muscular legs all the way up to her red satin booty shorts. The matching red corset was barely a bra. Her pointy, red ankle boots sported an impractical heel better for gawking than walking.

"New chest?" He flashed her a toothy smile.

"Piece. New chest-*piece*, and leggings, and... It's like the developers want me to be naked." She peered at him.

"Damn developers." He shook his head, feigning innocence.

"I can't imagine this top defending against anything." She tugged at her corset. "Maybe the distraction will help?"

"I'm sure you'll knock 'em dead." He chuckled, but she didn't.

"Going through puberty again this evening?"

"Ouch." He winced. "-10 affinity with Mandorf."

She rolled her eyes but couldn't hold back a smile.

"If this is a bad night, we can grind mobs later," he said coolly, trying to cover his disappointment at that idea. "Or we can just talk. You can tell me why you're upset while I dial my fifth attempt at puberty down to eleven."

"Sorry." She stared at the ground.

"Usually we laugh at the silly armor they design, especially for women." He wished the game would show more of her expressions. "You angry at me?"

"I heard you fought a mini-boss in your customer service class."

"I'll take on Luanne any day." He balled up a fist.

"If you have any days left. She stormed into the old man's office after class, practically slamming the door off its hinges."

"Oh." He'd never heard her this worried and raised a calming hand. "Cook won't put up with her bullshit. If they let me go, it will be due to downsizing, not me standing up to that bully."

"From what I heard, you were standing up for Megan," she taunted. "She's cute."

"Well, uh." He cleared his throat. "I was trying to stand up for everyone."

"Maybe Mr. Chivalry should be playing a knight instead of a Wizard." She blinked rapidly, pressing her hands to her heart.

"Why, Miss Jacks," he said. "Are you suggesting I'm heroic in both worlds?"

She barked out a laugh. "Maybe you are. Rumor has it that no one from the class is getting fired."

"Good." He paused until she looked at him. "So...are you upset or did you still want to game?"

"I just don't want you getting into trouble." Her tone softened. "Aren't you on call tonight?"

"Ugh. I haven't been on call since my desktop days." He shuddered. "I'm pretty sure I can do both. Last night went smoothly enough. If I get an alert, I'll hop over to my Customer Service character, fix the issue, and return to Mandorf before you notice."

"Addict," she teased, nudging him.

"You should know," he said with a wink. "Hey, since you didn't like my reaction to your armor, I know a quest chain for another chestpiece that has better stats and a bit more, uh, cloth."

"What?" She giggled, pulling out the gauze pantaloons and spinning. "Don't you like *I Dream of Jewells*?"

He wiped the bead of sweat tickling his cheek.

"Wait." She leaned in a bit too close. "Did I make the Grand Magus Mandorf sweat?"

"Nope." He took a healthy step back. "There's a fly in my office."

"Right." She laughed at his discomfort. "By the way, your title is showing."

"Why, yes, it is." He glanced up at the glowing text floating over his head. "I'm proud to be called Grand Magus Mandorf. Apparently as proud as you are to be called Barfly Jewells."

"Shit." She glanced up and made a broad gesture with her hands.

The game gave players the option to show titles before or after their name. Mandorf had earned hundreds, from Mandorf the Scallywag to Mandorf the Wise. Some were silly, all were in good fun, but the title Grand Magus was rare.

When she was done, Barfly Jewells became Jewells the Wicked.

"Shall we head to the Gnome starting zone?" She flashed him a smile.

He invited her to join his group. A rectangular box appeared in the top left of his vision. It contained her name, an icon indicating that she was a Priest, and bars showing her Health and Mana. Now that they were grouped, they could speak privately without others hearing. He could also open her character sheet and view some of her stats. The genie armor was actually impressive, geared to balance damage and healing. Even better, she looked...

"You're gawking again," she said with a crooked smile.

"You don't like a little gawking?" He brushed away the scroll.

"Famous actors get to gawk. You get to admire."

"I admire." With a flourish, he cast *Teleport*.

———

HIS SPELL HAD BROUGHT them to the Gnome starting zone waypoint. They stood in the middle of a wide field. Specks of light, like fireflies, hovered over tall grass that rocked with the wind. In the distance, the large mushroom buildings of Nomorgin peeked over the grass.

"I'm so glad we've got mounts," she said. "That'd be a long walk."

"One sec. I should go ice spells for this." He instantly changed into a white ensemble of terrycloth with soft leather embellishments. "The initial quests will go faster if I crowd control and freeze the mobs in place."

"Do you hear something?" She turned and scanned the area.

Before he could answer, Jewells collapsed to her knees. A thin man in black leather armor stood over her, jerking a wicked dagger from her back.

"Griefers," Mandorf shouted as a second Assassin appeared and plunged a short sword into his stomach.

6

PIVIPS

The attacker jerked his sword out and they both disappeared like magicians...stabby magicians. Mandorf spun around to look for more griefers. He moved so slowly it was like someone had dropped him in a vat of Jell-O. Not only was he down to 1100 Health, the sword had poisoned him.

A green skull and crossbones icon appeared in the top right of his vision. The debuff was a slowing poison, and numbers in that icon slowly counted down. The poison would last another whopping eighteen seconds. It was plenty of time for the Assassins to kill them, loot their bodies, bury the corpses, and celebrate on their graves with cake and ice cream.

"Why aren't we dead?" he asked. "We should be easy targets. I don't get it."

"I don't get how they even made it to Yu." Jewells's voice was shaky.

"I'll explain later," he said. "We need to figure this out before we're dead and something gets stolen."

His mind raced with what-ifs and where-are-theys. He hated fighting other players, and Assassins from Rath were the worst.

"Why did they bother coming to the Gnome starting zone?" She stood and drew her hammer and sickle. "The noobs here are too low in level to have any decent gear."

"It doesn't matter why and... Wait, that's it." He turned to her. "Does your armor have a shield spell?"

"Yeah."

"Do it now, and don't heal me until I say."

"You won't live through another attack like that, and you've still got the slowing debuff." She glanced at him. "I was teasing about being heroic. You don't need to impress me."

"If my hunch is right, I'll impress myself." He took a deep breath and raised his staff. "Twelve seconds left on the slows. Get ready with that heal."

He licked his lips, watching the timer in anticipation. With four seconds to go, Mandorf cast *Flash Freeze*. A sheet of ice shot out from his feet, covering the ground within a seven-yard radius and revealing three Assassins. The spell did minimal damage but was enough to break their invisibility. It also froze them in place.

"Heal, please." His eyes darted from one Assassin to the next, hopeful that none would break free.

Ice cracked and hissed in the sun as the griefers tried to attack. These three battle-hardened Assassins from Rath suddenly became The Three Stooges. A level 29 male named IKillYu threw a dagger at Jewells. It bounced off her shield and stuck in the arm of a level 15 female behind her, formidably named Revenger. The damage took most of Revenger's Health, and she now had a damaging poison debuff that would kill her in seconds.

"What the hell?" Jewells shouted, turning to face them. "Fuckers sneaking up on me..." She raised her hammer and sickle and crossed them, activating their special. *Holy Wrath* shot forward like a thick ivory laser. The spell melted Revenger and IKillYu until all that remained were two smoking piles of gear.

"Great job," he said. "Still ready for that heal."

With a crackling hiss, the ice floor melted away, and the third Assassin, a level 35 male by the name of Dredawg, launched into the air. Before Mandorf could cast *Ice Dagger*, the Assassin's sword sliced deep into his shoulder for 585 damage. Before pulling it out, Dredawg shoved a dagger between Mandorf's ribs.

"That was close," Jewells said, her healing spell landing before the dagger attack.

Dredawg jerked the weapons out in surprise. Not only was Mandorf alive, the sword hadn't poisoned him. Mandorf quickly changed his voice channel so everyone around them could hear.

"Forget something, noob?" he asked, raising his staff. "My turn."

Mandorf drove the end of his staff into Dredawg's face and cast *The Shattering*. It was overkill, glorious overkill. The Assassin cursed as gray cracks spread across his body. What started as a shudder became a violent seizure until the Assassin exploded. The spell that had destroyed the golem did even more to a low-level Human. Body parts rained down, landing with grotesque slurping sounds.

"Fuck yeah," Jewells shouted. "That was awesome."

"You sounded a bit nervous, but you did great." He patted her shoulder. "Was that your first time at PiviPs?"

"Pih-vips?" Jewels asked

"My nickname for PvP. I added vowels."

"Oh!" She laughed. "Yeah, I liked it." She sounded thirsty for more.

"You saved our ass. Not only with that last-second heal, but you made me realize why they were here. They were leveling."

"You explain." She hopped over to the closest pair of empty boots. They were surrounded by sparkles, indicating treasure. "I'll loot."

"There's a buggy area in the mountains separating Rath from Yu. It's not easy, but players can sneak through," he said. "Technically, there's no player versus player in Yu, so when they're here, the game treats them like mobs on this side. What sucks is if they kill you, they win something you own. It can be gold, or even a piece of your gear. It's a cheap way for Rath players to get Yu items."

"Seven gold on IKillYu. Not bad," she said.

Their group was set to share winnings evenly, so his portion was 3 gold and 50 silver.

"How did you know these guys weren't level 40?" she asked.

"At first I thought they were toying with us until you pointed out that they came to a starting zone. Then it made sense."

"Meh." She kicked the remains of Revenger. They split her 80 silver.

"They threw everything at us but didn't have the Mana reserves to keep attacking," he continued. "Only low-level characters would have to wait for their Mana to recharge after an attack like that. Even better, Dredawg forgot to cast poison on his sword before their second attempt. That was delicious."

"Ooh, speaking of." Jewells leaned over the pile of gear Dredawg had left behind.

The Assassin had dropped 27 gold, a "used handkerchief," and his sword.

A short-bladed scimitar hovered in the air between them. Mandorf touched it, and a scroll appeared above the weapon revealing its stats.

Name: Dirty Deeds
Quality: Rare
Special: *Done Dirt Cheap*—When cast, Dirty Deeds will penetrate any player armor. Damages 20% of the opponent's Health. Attack up to three times if opponent is surprised. 20-minute cooldown.

Click Roll for your chance to win this item or pass if you are not interested.

"Wow, that'll fetch some real cash in the auction hall." He passed on the sword.

"Are you sure?" she asked.

"Your first PiviPs win. You earned it."

"Yes," she shouted. "This thing has to be worth 200 gold."

"More like a thousand, in cash." He shook his head. "Stupid griefers. Dredawg is probably deleting his character now."

"A thousand?" She turned on him. "Wait, are you trying to buy my love?"

"Ha!" he barked. "I can't imagine it's for sale."

She swayed over to him and kissed his cheek. "It's not."

The thank you warmed his face. Fortunately, it wasn't possible for the blush to show up on Mandorf. "So, more PvP?"

She laughed hard enough to snort and quickly covered her mouth.

"I know where they sneak over." He hated PvP, but her reaction...

"What if we lose?" She was still standing very close. "So quick to give up your staff?"

"I, uh..." His response inspired another round of laughter. She loved making random flirt attacks that he couldn't recover from. Actually, he loved it too. No one flirted with him. Even if she was teasing, even if he had no quippy reply, how could he not revel in the attention? On occasion, he wondered if she meant it, until she reminded him of another date on her relentless search for the right one. That was when he'd remember she was his intern. Still, her face, her laughter, and her out-of-nowhere flirting was enough for him to finally say—

"Shit."

"Pardon?" She took a step back.

A baseball-sized gray orb appeared before him, accompanied by an annoying alarm-clock buzz. With a sigh, he grabbed his first Customer Service ticket of the night. A scroll opened before his eyes.

"Player Quezno has placed a call for help. Will you assist?" he read aloud.

"Oh," she said in a deflated tone.

Mandorf pointed at the player's name and a map of Entriss appeared. A blue dot showed Quezno's location far south of Zalmon's abandoned castle. He reached for the dot with both hands and drew them apart to zoom in. The player had somehow gotten into an undeveloped zone.

There were several areas on Entriss reserved for future development. Games often had expansions with fun events that would open these zones. For whatever reason, those events had never happened on Entriss, but the zones still existed.

It was borderline hacking for players to access these areas and a stupid way to get your account deleted. Ian hoped he wouldn't have to smack a player with the ban stick. It took so much time to build up a character, he couldn't imagine anything worse than having Mandorf deleted forever.

"This should only take a few minutes." Could the timing have been worse?

"You've got three." She dropped group. "I was just invited to a dungeon."

"By who?"

"It's just Cain." She stared ahead, reading a message, then giggled. "You'd like him. He helped me win this armor."

"Great." Mandorf logged off as fast as he could.

7

THE UNDEVELOPED ZONE

I an logged into his new Customer-Service character, Helpy, and was bombarded with pop-up messages. He gestured to close all the notices at once. Nothing happened, and he tried again. His third attempt was met with an annoying system *bzzt*. It was impossible to dismiss corporate bureaucracy, even on Entriss. Instead of rushing to save player Quezno, he spent tedious moments acknowledging important new employee messages like:

- Log out every 6-8 hours. Extended game time can be detrimental
- Be patient with angry customers
- Don't forget your weekly employee compliance training
- Deleting characters because the player is unpleasant is against Entriss policy
- Click here to familiarize yourself with Helpy

"Damn, this is already taking too long." Helpy's character scroll unfurled. "At least I got to choose the name."

While all Customer Service toons appeared identical, he still cringed at the stubby wizard in pale linen robes and lopsided, pointy hat. Helpy had scraggly white hair, a crooked nose, and large eyes that didn't blink. It was like playing Gandalf and Golem's unwanted lovechild. All stats, abilities, and achievements were grayed out—inaccessible. Helpy was obviously not meant for fun.

He closed the character sheet and a spell menu appeared at the bottom of his vision. There were three rows, each with a dozen tidy squares that contained icons. Selecting an icon would cast the spell; hovering over it would provide a brief description. The interface was archaic but practical. Players had the option to view spells like this. Good players hid the interface and created macros so they could cast their spells with gestures or words, which was efficient. And fun.

Apparently, Helpy did not appreciate fun, because there was no hiding this spellbook of boredom. Rather than *Fireball* or *Kersplosion*, his icons consisted of stuff like game FAQs, player logs, a ticketing system, and full character inspection.

Some of the spells would've been nice for players. Mandorf's map of Entriss was limited to areas he'd explored. Customer Service got *Map Layers*, which showed all of Entriss. There was an option to add an overlay that revealed hidden areas, treasures, and rare monster-spawn locations.

Teleport to Player was convenient.

Unstuck freed players from poorly coded terrain and teleported them somewhere safe. (How many times had he wanted to teleport someone away?)

One spell, though, actually made him nervous. *Final Kill*. The icon of skull and crossbones on a stop sign was surrounded by a break-glass-in-emergency red frame. The description indicated that the spell had to be selected three times to activate.

The progenitors of Entriss did not tolerate cheating. Period. If a player was caught breaking rules, Customer Service could invoke *Final Kill*. Not only would the cheater be force-logged out of the game, their account would be deleted along with all their characters and gear. There was no coming back. After spending literal years in game time building up a character to be exceptional, using *Final Kill* seemed unnecessarily harsh. It was the nuclear option, and Ian wished he could remove the button from his menu.

He selected Layered Map to locate Quezno. An artsy pencil sketch of Entriss appeared on parchment. Western Yu and Eastern Rath were divided by mountains. The only legitimate way players from both sides could meet was the monster zone Misere in the North or Zalmon's castle at the southernmost tip. A path of red dots led to Quezno's location, an island far south of the castle.

"Idiot," Ian muttered. "What are you doing down there? It's completely undeveloped and, oh..."

Undeveloped zones were the leftovers of MMOs. Unfinished stories or placeholders for another day. Players often sought those zones in hopes of finding quests or weapons that would give them an edge. Those quests didn't exist, but it was still considered cheating, making him cringe at the red-framed spell.

The location was surrounded by a dead zone of ocean meant to kill players who lingered too long. Quezno should've died swimming there, but instead, he was alive and had put in a ticket.

Ian gingerly selected *Teleport to Player*. Apparently, the developer who created this ability didn't want the sudden change of location to be jarring. The world melted away and very slowly reformed around him. As the spell completed, a small scroll appeared to his left, providing him with the cringe-worthy Customer Service narrative.

With a deep sigh, he did a poor job of feigning enthusiasm. "Entriss has heard your call, stalwart warrior. I am Mand... I am Helpy, your guiding light in these dark and trying— What the fuck?"

He'd expected an empty room, like most of the other unfinished zones. This wasn't only finished, it was beautiful. It was also familiar in a way that tickled his memory and raised his hackles.

The vast hall featured a dusty green marble floor with gold inlays. Flickering torches attached to tall, pale columns teased shadowy figures of stone statues. Each of the twelve statues stood twice his height, all heavily adorned with armor and weapons.

In the center of the room sat an enormous steel mass that was hard to make out. A beam of gold light shot out from a fist raised high over the steel construct.

Ian followed the gold light to a pillar behind him. At the end of the beam was a young, male Sprite named Quezno. He selected the *Inspection* ability. The leather-clad Assassin from Rath wore high-level gear comparable to Mandorf's. His Health hovered at a meager 44 points. Apparently, the golden beam had blasted the poor Sprite into a pillar before something glitched. Not a surprise in an undeveloped zone...that was shockingly developed.

"Help me," Quezno said, weakly.

"A little melodramatic, aren't we?" Ian asked.

"I vomit if I open my eyes for too long," Quezno said. "This golden light is like riding a roller coaster from the moon. I can remove my headset, but I can't log out of the game. My character's been stuck here for days."

"Why *are* you here?" Ian asked. "What is this place?"

"Just another hidden zone, man. That's all." He sounded nervous.

"A cheater *and* a liar." Ian glanced at his fingernails before polishing them on his robes. "I'll be back in a few days and—"

"No," the tiny Sprite squeaked, opening his eyes wide. He convulsed violently and cursed between retching sounds.

Ian scrolled through Quezno's character logs. He'd swum here with two Druids cross-healing in hopes that nobody would die. They had died, a lot. It had taken them four days to finally make it. Their arduous journey was impressive, but why?

"Maybe I'll come back in a week or two." Ian arched back and stretched his arms. "No one will notice. Lots of player tickets need attending, and we're shorthanded."

"Look around, you asshat," Quezno snapped. "We're in King Zalmon's lost tomb."

"What?" Ian let out a gasp.

Rumor and lore of the tomb had been around for so long Ian had dismissed its existence. He'd actually researched it after starting at Entriss and remembered discovering code relating to the tomb. His personal code of conduct was unfortunately moral, so he hadn't dug deeper. If it was something that would give him an unfair advantage, he wanted nothing to do with it. His hope that it would become an in-game event or fun quest chain was eventually forgotten to the daily grind of work.

There was something familiar about this place that wasn't click-ing. He sighed in frustration. This tomb was considered undeveloped. It wasn't a part of the active game, and from what he could remember never would be. Still...

"I'm impressed you found it." He looked around in awe. "But why go through the trouble only to get your account deleted?"

"Please, no," Quezno pleaded. "It's just that this game is going to hell. Everyone knows that Entriss is shutting down. I've poured my life into your damn game. I finished all the quests and achievements and fought for the best armor and weapons. Look, dammit! That's Zalmon and he has a quest. It's the last quest." He clasped his hands together and held them tight to his chest. "I love the game and its lore. I just want to see how it ends. Please...please don't delete my account."

Quezno's desperation pulled at his heart. It wasn't a surprise that the Sprite knew Entriss was shutting down. Once people get fired, they talk, and the message board was always active. This player's love of the story, his dedication to the game, and his hunger to go out with a bang mirrored Ian's feelings.

"Cheaters are supposed to get *Final Kill*, which would delete your account." Ian shook his head and sighed. "I just can't do that. It may get me fired, but I feel the same as you, Quezno. I love this game and hate to see it end. I'm going to release your character, which will send you to the nearest safe waypoint."

"Thank you." The Sprite was practically crying.

"You have to promise not to come back. You know the conse-quences."

Quezno merely nodded.

Ian cast the *Unstuck* spell. Quezno disappeared in a gentle blue haze and the golden beam from King Zalmon's hand went away. The attack hadn't just come from the king; it had come from the golden quest orb in his hand. What kind of quest killed players?

He approached the king, longing to see the man's face, but an invisible barrier held him back. That shouldn't have been possible. He was still logged in as a Customer Service rep.

A white light flashed behind him. He whipped around to see Quezno appear, now at full health. The tiny, pointy-eared Sprite looked down at his body in wonder and relief before realizing where he was.

"I'm still here? Yes!" he shouted, rushing to Zalmon.

"Wait, stop," Ian pleaded.

Quezno ran forward and slammed into the barrier, instantly stuck like a mosquito in tree sap. The golden orb glowed brighter and brighter until a beam shot forth, blasting the Sprite into nothing.

"No," Ian said. He tried opening Quezno's logs, but they were gone. He selected character search and found that the Sprite simply didn't exist. It was as if the quest had cast *Final Kill*. "Why?"

"He was not worthy," the old king said.

"Worthy?" Ian shook his head, dumbfounded. "Worthy of what?"

"To be the Left Hand of God." King Zalmon leaned to one side, turning around to look at Ian with empty eye sockets. "Are you worthy, Ian?"

Ian took a step back, hoping his heart would start beating again. He stuttered, searching for words his tongue had forgotten. The king smiled, and in a flash of golden light, Ian was logged out of the game.

8

A FORK IN THE CODE

"I'm a developer, not a sysadmin," Ian muttered to himself in a recognizable Dr. McCoy impersonation.

A pair of co-workers startled him with their "Morning"s. He nodded politely and rubbed bleary from his eyes. It was 8 o'clock, which meant he'd been staring at code for almost three hours.

Late nights of developing and gaming had made Ian more vampire than early bird. He hadn't been to work before nine since, well, ever. Coffee. He needed a bucket of it. Or maybe an I.V. drip. It was too early for Dr Pepper, so he stood and stretched.

More enthusiastic greetings interrupted him. "Morning... Hey, nice job," and, "Way to go, champ," scared him off to the break room. A few shoulder pats and a warm, "Well done, hero," on the way turned his morning from surreal to weird. Was he in some fever dream back at home?

It had been a rough night after getting kicked out of the game. A growing list of whatthefucks kept him from sleeping. King Zalmon still existed in Entriss and had an unknown quest that killed players. After getting booted, Ian had attempted to log in again, but his account was locked. Or deleted. Oh, and somehow, Zalmon knew his actual name. After staring at his bedroom ceiling for far too long, Ian had decided on coffee, work, and coffee.

He was never at work this early, and the security guard's reaction was almost worth it. Before his first round of caffeine, Ian logged in and ran a database query to check his account status. Mandorf—and Helpy, of course—still lived. Both characters were merely locked out. It was enough to dial his shoulder tension from ten to a more familiar seven. Nothing in the logs showed who, or what, had triggered the lock out, but at least it was easy to fix.

A second query indicated that Quezno hadn't been so lucky. The late King Zalmon's quest had ban sticked the player so hard, it erased all traces of his existence. It shouldn't have been possible and didn't make sense. While impressive, Zalmon was still just a non-player character. Dialog and interactive scripts dictated almost everything NPCs did. The exception to that was Deity.

Deity was the artificial intelligence at the core of Watson's game engine. She did everything from defending their network against hackers to cleaning up bad code. The AI also managed NPC encounters with players so they felt natural.

Deity's reach was supposed to be limited to Entriss, but Zalmon knew his real name. If she'd suddenly gone Skynet and was now digging into players' personal lives, it would be game over.

Ian had no access to Deity's core code or any means to communicate with her. His only solution to this problem was a shot of whiskey in his coffee, or maybe a shot of coffee in his whiskey. He may not be able to ask the AI for direction, but the Sprite had obviously stumbled across something big.

Ian understood Quezno's hunt for the quest. Everyone wanted an edge over other players, even if it was just recognition for being first. It still seemed foolish to run back to the king right after Helpy had threatened to delete him. Now that he had seen the code, though, he would've done the same.

Someone had buried a quest far deeper than the dead king's body. After an hour of digging through the software repository, he found the orphaned code. It was a lost fork that had never made it into the game. An architect or developer should've deleted it a long time ago just to save space. The amount of code was staggering. This went far beyond a simple quest.

One player, just one, could accept The Left Hand of God. Not only did it start a complex quest chain that made Ian's mouth water, it triggered a worldwide event unlike anything players had experienced on Entriss.

Even more surprising were scripts for hardware and networking. Ian understood software deployment tools and basic server architecture, but this was the sort of automation that sysops drooled over. The one thing he understood was that applying this update would enable full immersion. This code had the potential to make Entriss a 2nd generation IMMO. Beyond that, it would take a team of developers and engineers weeks to read through The Left Hand of God and longer to understand it.

A madman or an eccentric visionary had created this hidden software. It would've been the greatest fuckit in Ian's career to check in the code and activate the event. If it passed review, the quest would go live in a month.

No matter how much he wanted to push it through, though, this much code would never make it past Deity. Even worse, she'd flag him for checking it in. Not only would they *Final Kill* Mandorf, they'd probably *Final Kill* Ian.

With a mug of coffee in both hands, he carefully swerved through a path of odd back-patting and recognition. He was so lost in thought it was easy to dismiss his over-friendly co-workers and whatever drug they were smoking. After arriving at his cube, he set the hot mugs down and sighed in relief. Before he could dive back into the quest code, though, Bala cleared his throat from the adjacent cube.

"Hey, Bala." Ian glanced over his shoulder. "Are people acting weird today?"

"You're famous." Bala frowned, waving him over.

Security footage of Ian going toe-to-toe with Luanne played on Bala's central monitor. Someone had leaked the video of his career-ending performance. Rather than rushing off to update his resume, watching it just made him angry.

"Maybe the bully will get fired," he said through gritted teeth.

"You walk a dangerous path, my friend." Bala's eyebrows drew together.

"Just trying to do right." Ian stood proud and took a deep breath. "You know what Superman says about the never-ending battle?"

"It's never-ending." Bala nodded respectfully.

"My turn. Come see what I found."

Ian led Bala to his desk and gave him the fifteen-minute overview. His mentor reviewed the code in awe. Bala glanced over his shoulder and jerked back in surprise.

Wet lips met Ian's ear, freezing him in place like a spell. After several heart-skipping moments, he turned to see Julie. Her beautiful, dark eyes were glassy, as if on the verge of tears.

Bala looked at them, smiled, and returned to his cube.

"You never replied to my casts. I thought you were angry that I ditched you last night." His heart was racing.

She shook her head, all the while staring into his eyes.

"Then I thought you were upset at all the messages I sent."

She shook her head again.

He reached up to his ear. "Then why…"

"You and Bala were so focused, I couldn't get your attention." She looked around the room as if the Assassins had returned.

"That worked." He swallowed hard, his mouth suddenly dry as a Midwest drought. "Are you okay?"

A tear trickled down her cheek as she typed on her forearm. She wiped her face as he opened the cast. *Final Kill. We have fifteen minutes.*

He gasped for breath as thoughts crashed his mind like a blue screen of death. They were going to fire him, and even worse, they would delete his account. Why now? That stupid video only proved Luanne was a bully. He needed more time to research the quest. Even worse, Julie would forget about him before he even had a chance to tell her—

Resting her hands on his shoulder and leaning in, she once again pressed her lips to his ear. While not calming, it brought focus. All of his focus.

"Check in the code," she whispered.

He nodded. There wouldn't be another chance. He attacked his keyboard. The code couldn't possibly be compatible after so many changes over the years. There was no way it would slip past review. The sheer volume of code would alert operations, or even Deity. There were a lot of what-ifs that required too many miracles.

All of it was easy to ignore with Julie hovering over his shoulder, leaning against him, encouraging him to press on. When he was finally ready to commit it, realization made him pause.

Security was going to delete his work logon. The code wouldn't get deployed if he checked it in under his account. Using Julie's account would get her in trouble, and she may not have rights. His mind raced his heart. Luanne was going to fire him just like everyone she'd threatened in class. Then it struck him. As he entered the login info, Julie laughed.

Ian clicked enter and sighed in relief. Luanne hadn't changed her password, and the code began checking in under her account. It was a small win that didn't come close to repairing the coming loss, but it was definitely a win, and he'd take it.

"Thank you." He placed a hand on hers. "You should go."

"I'll stay," she said. "I'll stand by you."

"No, young Padawan." He turned to face her. "That won't benefit either of us. This isn't done, and neither are we."

Her lower lip quivered ever so slightly. After taking a strengthening breath, she nodded then turned on her heel and walked away with stilted steps.

Ian's heart swelled. Julie had not only warned him of the oncoming storm, she'd calmed the waters. Her kiss had turned panic into focus. He would mourn later. Now, it was time to plan. Ian grabbed his VR headset and logged into Mandorf.

Five minutes later, a jarring hand on his shoulder reminded him of inevitable reality. He logged out of Entriss, removed the headset, and locked eyes with the two waiting security guards.

"Wilson, Andrews," Ian said with a respectful nod.

"Sorry, Ian," Andrews said in a heavy tone.

"No." Bala stood and stepped forward. "Not you, Ian. Please, no."

"You've taught me much more than coding." Ian reached out to clasp arms. "I'll always be grateful for your mentorship."

"I'll stand with you, my friend," Bala said.

"As will I," said another developer.

"Me too!"

"I'm with you!"

"And my axe," someone shouted.

Everyone in the room stood. His breath caught and his throat tightened as his Entriss family looked on and waited.

"Thank you. All of you. Don't lose your jobs for me." Ian raised a fist. "Never give up, never surrender." He glanced at the picture of Mandorf beside his monitors, sighed, and turned to the security guards. "I'm ready."

9

THE LONG WALK

Julie walked by his side as they slowly exited the Atlanta campus with boxes in tow. Ian had never thought of the Entriss headquarters as cold before, despite the lack of green between the gray concrete pathways. Maybe it was the damp, fall air or the tall stone flowerpots placed neatly about the winding sidewalk. Maybe it was the dead quiet around and between them. Maybe it was just him.

This had been home for five years. He'd spent more time at Entriss HQ than his apartment. Even the worst of times hadn't been that bad. It was his dream job, coding for a game he loved so very much. Entriss was more than a job; it was his passion, his life.

His mind was a storm of years spent developing and playing. Mixed in this dark torrent of thought was the surprise exit meeting he had with Jack Cook, the old man himself, CEO of Entriss Online.

THE OLD MAN sat behind a dark executive desk and stared at him with steady gray eyes. Jack Cook, founder and visionary of Entriss, was a powerfully built sixty-two-year-old. The pale man with a long nose and strong jaw must've lifted weights his entire life to squeeze into a blue blazer like that. He didn't look like a developer, or a CEO; he looked like an old Bruce Wayne.

When Ian made eye contact, Cook's gaze softened and his shoulders relaxed in a way that felt personal.

"I'm sorry, son," he said, more firm than apologetic. "I tried."

"Sir?" Ian asked.

"I told the board it's a mistake to fire you. The decision went that high. Your passion for Entriss mirrors my own. I feel like giving you up is like letting a part of my game go."

"Thank you." Ian slumped in his seat, completely at a loss for words.

"This conversation is being recorded, because lawyers." Cook waved his hand like gnats surrounded it. "I don't care. This all came down to Luanne. I wouldn't have hired that woman, but Ty Hammers insisted, and the board gave in."

There was a yip behind the desk, and Cook pushed his chair back. A corgi hopped into his lap and smiled at Ian. The old man ran his hand along the dog's coat.

"I swear I brushed Gidget this morning." He shook his hand for a moment, finally wiping it on his pants. "I think she's made of hair."

"Yessir."

"You're not my employee anymore." The CEO winked. "Call me Jack."

"Okay." Ian was wary, but Cook stared until he said, "Thank you, Jack."

The old man nodded, continuing to brush hair off the light-brown corgi until she hopped off and made her way to Ian's lap. Jack smiled at this. Ian instinctively petted the dog and was awarded with a tongue bath.

"I wanted to thank you for all you've done." His tone was genuine and heartfelt. "You've helped bring my world to life. Your work has meant a lot to me, and the millions who play Entriss. The time and effort you've spent developing has brought people happiness. That's something to be proud of."

———

"You're so quiet. Are you okay?" Julie rolled her eyes. "Sorry, that's a dumb question. I'm bad at this."

"I'm proud of you." He could barely glance at her for fear of losing it. "It's something I haven't said enough. As an intern, you've been insightful and helpful. Your skills as a developer have improved greatly. I believe you're ready for promotion and said as much in my exit interview."

"Wow, really?" She cocked her head to one side, her brows furrowed. "After all that you've had to face today, you're still thinking of me."

"I always do," he muttered, staring at the ground.

"Why aren't you looking at me? What did they say to you?"

"I hope I've never, uh..." He stared down as if the words were painted on the damp sidewalk. "If I ever made you uncomfortable. If my interest, er, friendship ever put you in a position—"

"What's this?" She stopped, grabbing his shoulder so he would face her. "Why did they fire you?"

"I debated saying anything, but HR will probably question you." His throat tightened. "Luanne went through log files, inter-company communications, and even had videos of our conversations. I've never been so humiliated."

"Why?" She searched his face.

"She made me feel like I've been harassing you or using my position as a senior developer to force you to spend time with me. She threatened a lawsuit or arrest if anything worse came to light."

"Bitch!" She clenched her fists then quickly added, "Not you. Luanne. Look, if you'd ever crossed a line I didn't want crossed, I would've said something. Or kicked your ass."

"Oh?" His heart skipped and he stood straight.

"You did no wrong by me. The only mistake you made was hesitating, Ian. I didn't create a line."

"I DON'T THINK you crossed any lines. I've known Julie since she was born. She can handle herself." Jack's shoulders dropped like he'd lost an argument with his wife. "You weren't fired because of anything you've done wrong. You're popular here, Ian, and Luanne couldn't have that."

"I'll never understand how Luanne became a part of Entriss," Ian muttered.

"Let's just say that our government liaison is a little too involved." Jack's words came out stiff. "From birth to death, the Accords always held back the full potential of Entriss."

"How so?" Ian asked.

"Not only have we been limited to 1st generation immersion, Ty *discouraged* us from anything that would attract new players - like world events or expansions." Jack shook his head. "Because of this, subscriptions have been declining rapidly for the last several years. That makes it easier for them to shut us down."

"I hate that." Ian gritted his teeth as anger sparked around the edges of his melancholy.

"So do I," Cook replied, staring off. "Even though Xander Watson is the pioneer behind the engine that all IMMOs use, he didn't do it alone. His vision was realized because of the work Eris Winside, Patty Dodge, and I put into it. It's hard for all of us to give up these worlds we've created."

"What you've done is amazing, sir... Jack."

"Not being knighted until next month." He winked again. "The queen likes to award that when you're old."

"Ha." Ian laughed. "Still, that's cool."

"My point about Patty and Eris... Xander couldn't have done it without us. Entriss wouldn't be what it is without you."

"Thank you." Ian forced a smile.

"Of course." Jack's gaze was pensive.

"That's not why you brought me here, is it?"

"When Patty, Eris, and I were free of Xander, we created our worlds." Jack sat down and patted his lap. Gidget scurried over to perch on it. "Now that you're free of Entriss, what are you going to do?"

"YOU'LL DO what you have to." Julie brushed damp hair from her face. "So I guess it doesn't matter, does it?"

"What do you mean?" She'd just admitted something, and he wanted to know more. Had she already given up on him?

"You'll need to get a new job, which means you'll probably have to move." Her face was strained, and she looked away. "There won't be time, you know, for us."

"And if I stayed?"

"How could you stay without a job?" She crossed her arms and shivered. "Everyone has to work."

"This is my third startup as a developer. I've got plenty of money, and after today, I'm not in a hurry to go back to work."

"Oh?" She turned to face him.

"What do you think? Should I give up and move on, or should I stay and see what happens?"

"I SPOKE WITH XANDER." Jack looked down at Gidget as he petted away more hair. "He's in a bad place and doesn't take many calls these days, but I told him it was important. He agreed to take you in."

"What?" Ian sat up, his shoulders tensing.

"Everyworld Online is the future, Ian." Jack looked up and watched Ian as if searching for something. "I've been in that next-generation IMMO. You can't tell the difference between our world and the virtual. It's real enough you have to pull up your socks when they get bunched in your boots. Working there is a dream, and you can start whenever you're ready. Right now, or a month, or a year."

"Wow... I... It's a great opportunity. I don't know what to say." He should've been elated but was overwhelmed with the feeling that there was no coming back.

"Think on it. There's no hurry." For the briefest of moments, Jack looked as old and battle-weary as Zalmon on his throne. "Change is the only constant. You can choose to run from change, give in to it, or risk everything and be the one who changes everything. How we face it defines who we are."

This made Ian's heart skip enough beats to clutch his chest. Did the old man know about all the code he'd checked in? He had to know about the quest. Ian could only imagine that Jack wanted to see someone finish it. Hell, it was probably his code.

He fought back a hundred questions. They would discover what he'd done. Mentioning the quest or, worse, the code was like leaving a trail of signs pointing directly at him. With a lot of effort, he let it all go with a sigh.

"Right now, I'm struggling with change." Ian fidgeted in his seat, unable to hold back his distress. "On top of everything else, Luanne's deleting my character, Mandorf."

"Unfortunately, it was tied to your Customer Service account, and Security can't allow that level of access." The edge of Jack's mouth curled up in an almost-smile. "You accomplished impressive feats with Mandorf. You won the game, as much as anyone can. Has it really all been about winning?"

"It's about playing the game," Ian said. "It always has been."

"Thank you for helping me create this world, Ian." Sir Jack stood, holding Gidget with his right arm and reaching out with his left. "God only knows what change will bring, but I believe great things are coming for you."

Ian shook the old man's hand. Was he being so obvious as to acknowledge The Left Hand of God quest? Was Ian reading far too much into it? This was too much, and all he could say was, "Thank you, Jack. Thank you for all of it."

"Not many people know this, but I was kicked out of college." Julie tugged at a damp strand of hair. "Twice."

"Oh?" Ian lifted his chin enough to look at her.

"For all his faults, my father has buckets of wisdom to share." She took a deep breath. "It took a while for his advice to sink in, but now that I'm a little older, I realize that some of what he said helped get me through it."

"You don't talk about your father much. I got the impression you didn't like him."

"I don't...I don't like the choices he made." Her body went rigid, but the moment passed quickly. "But he's full of advice. Or I dunno... maybe he's just full of shit."

"What did he tell you?"

"The first time I was expelled, he said endings are just new beginnings."

"Really?" Ian said, more sarcastically than he'd intended.

"Sorry." A cute blush painted her pale cheeks. "That probably sounds silly."

"A little, but I appreciate what you're saying. You obviously didn't give up."

"I didn't, and sticking to it brought me here."

"I'm afraid to ask." Ian mentally braced himself. "What did he say the second time?"

"Uh." Her ears reddened and she lowered her voice. "You're better than this. Don't you ever fucking fail again. Don't embarrass this family. There's too much at stake."

"Oh." Ian reared back.

"He's a complicated man. You'd like him, on the good days."

"Hopefully I can meet him someday," Ian said, trying to be positive.

"I'm sure you will." Her voice trailed off as her gaze fell.

His brain twisted trying to understand what that meant, but she wouldn't look at him. Julie just stared at the ground with red cheeks and red ears as if she'd exposed a part of herself. Maybe she had.

"His original advice was better."

She looked up and frowned.

"Except that this isn't an ending," he said, darkly. "I'm just getting started, and I know exactly what I'm going to do next."

10

WHAT WAS THAT?

On the scale of acceptable to depressing, Fred's job was meh. Late night network monitoring felt like a half-step above desktop support. It paid well enough to keep him from looking for a new job, but he worked the grueling third shift from 11 p.m. to 8 a.m. A deep exhaustion gave his dark eyes permanent sleep-deprived stains. Five years of hiding from the sun made him feel like an undead admin. Worst of all, he had nothing to do.

Entriss was mostly automated. Deity, the Watson Engine AI, kept the game churning along inside and out. The great lady fought external security threats, applied game patches, and even monitored their quantum hotspot servers. Sometimes, he'd get to push a button.

The one thing that drew him to the job was the Control Center. He sat at one of ten desks in the middle of an auditorium. Like a scene out of the film *War Games*, a dozen monitors of various sizes surrounded an enormous, stadium-worthy display. Each of them showed statistics like server health, storage space, and network throughput.

Thirty-four-year-old Fred spent most of his time keeping his head down, shifting positions so his sore, skinny ass wouldn't go numb, and dreaming of winning the lottery. That was how he'd get out, and then he'd show everyone.

His co-worker Marta entered the room, ten minutes late from break—not that it mattered. They had an agreement: take the break you need, not the one they give you. Naps weren't uncommon. She handed him a bottle of cold water.

"Last one," she said. "This place is going to hell. They're cutting back on everything."

"Thanks." He took several long draws. "One of these days we're bringing vodka instead."

"Deal." She plopped into a seat beside him.

Marta was a light-skinned black woman in her mid-twenties. She appreciated this shift far more than he did. Starting two hours earlier got her home in time to see her daughter off to school. His counterpart had tired eyes, fingernails that were borderline too long for a keyboard, and huge hair that was currently dyed red and barely held at bay with a colorful wrap. She was a little overweight like he was a little too skinny.

Fred had been hired only a week before Marta. They came from different worlds—she was a single mom and he was a single loner. After four years, the two had settled into a comfortable routine. She teased him about being her work husband, but it was true. This was what he'd always assumed marriage to be like: work without sex.

"Joelyn okay?" he asked.

"Nightmares." She took a swig of water. "It's like my daughter can sense my own worry. I don't want this job to go away."

"Same." He let out a long sigh. "My dad always said things have a way of working out, though I still haven't won the lottery."

"Gotta buy tickets first." She winked at him. "Did I miss anything?"

"I pushed a button."

"I'm jealous." She chuckled, politely. "It's warmer in here than last night. I thought computers needed air conditioning. I know I do."

"It's fine for me." He yawned and stretched. "Perfect nap temperature."

"I took long enough on break. You go ahead." She looked around and whispered, "Anyone interesting to watch?"

It was against the rules to monitor players. Cook felt their interactions would be more natural without worrying about someone watching. Fred had a lot of respect for the old man, but Cook wasn't sitting with them at the Control Center watching network utilization or paint chip off the walls.

The most boring job ever had become slightly interesting when Fred figured out how to monitor players. Marta had hated the idea, worrying that they might be caught. That was three years ago, and now it was their only form of entertainment.

"No one." He shook his head. "Now that the ongoing late-night romance of Mandorf and Jewells is over, we're back to boring."

"He didn't get what she was offering plain as day." She let out a *tsk*.

"From what I heard, getting it is what got him fired. Who in their right mind bangs an intern?"

"She's a doll." Marta peered at him. "You wouldn't have?"

"I know exactly what I'd do with an intern." He leaned back as far as the old chair would allow, cupping his hands behind his head. "I'd run."

They both laughed until a loud *beep* interrupted them.

"What was that?" Marta sat up, looking over her screens.

"Dunno." Fred leaned forward and clacked away at his keyboard. "I've heard them test server alarms, weather alerts, and fire drills, but never heard a beep."

Ten minutes passed before he let out a low whistle.

"What'd you find?" Marta rolled her chair close.

"Someone checked in almost seventeen gigabytes of code, graphics, and shit I don't even understand. I've never seen anything like it."

"Are the devs finally pushing an in-game event?" She pursed her lips. "Nice if we had one before shutting down."

"I hadn't heard any new code was coming down." He looked over his shoulder. "Should we let Chen know?"

They shared a concerned look. The deployment manager who

oversaw all patches and upgrades was terse on a good day, and angry the rest. Marta leaned over her workstation and began digging in.

"Ooh." She pulled away like her keyboard was on fire. "The code was checked in by Luanne."

They shared another look, this one filled with genuine worry.

"Looks like Deity's already taken in the update." He raised a hand to his mouth. "It passed all security checks and she's already begun manipulating it, whatever that means. The patch goes live in a month. What do we do?"

"Luanne's on a rampage." Marta's eyes were wild with panic. "I'm not getting fired because she decided to check in some code."

"Good point." He crossed his arms and spun away from the monitor. "I didn't hear a beep."

"Never happened," she said with a full-lipped smile. "But an in-game event would make our nights go faster."

"Lots of gamers dying and fretting over fat loots." Fred rubbed his hands together. "Sounds like we have something to look forward to."

"Want some pasta?" she asked. "I brought extra."

"You always do. Best work-wife ever!"

11

PLANS AND PLANS

The sharp knock at his front door made Ian stand up straight, suck in his gut, and hold his breath. He wiped sweat from his palms, which must've been draining water from his dry mouth. There was no reason to be nervous; everything was ready. There was another knock, and he willed his shoulders to relax. It didn't work.

"Come on in," he said in the casual tone of a teen preparing to ask a swimsuit model to prom.

Julie opened the door and beamed. Without a word, she launched forward, wrapping her arms around him for a long and genuine hug. He breathed deeply, taking in her gentle scent of wildflowers. The embrace lasted a few moments beyond awkward, but he refused to be the first to let go. She finally pulled back and awarded him his favorite crooked smile.

They took each other in. Ian wore comfy, dark cotton shorts and a darker baggy t-shirt. The genius who'd suggested dark clothes were slimming had lied. He felt overweight and under-dressed compared to her date-worthy apparel.

Julie's ivory midriff top hung lazily off one shoulder. She wore matching tall, ivory heels and a dark cotton miniskirt. Her long red hair was free from the confines of her office-do, flowing over her shoulders and down her back in bouncy curls. Maybe he could sneak off and shower again, change into a tux, and repaint the flat.

She paid no mind to his casual attire, looking past him to inspect his new home. The light-wood floor entryway led to a spacious family room with brown leather furniture, a low glass coffee table, and a television that belonged at a stadium. Stately bookshelves filled with unread books stood behind the couch. Several remotes and a wide-screen laptop rested on an end-table.

"A quick tour?" he asked, wiping his hands again.

She smiled and nodded as he presented each room. The sizable kitchen featured obsidian tile counters and black brushed appliances. His master bedroom had plain red walls and a tall king-sized bed covered in black linens. The guest bedroom was even more stark, with gray walls and a darker gray quilt on the queen bed. An open door at the far end revealed an empty closet.

"No roommate?" She raised an eyebrow.

"Not yet." He held back a smile.

Julie grabbed his hand and led him back to the family room couch. She plopped down and drew both feet to her side while he placed a remote on the coffee table.

"What do you think?" He sat and tugged at his t-shirt so it didn't bunch.

"Interesting neighborhood. You found the most abandoned ware-house amongst abandoned warehouses." She looked at him like a few marbles had fallen out. "Was Scooby Doo your realtor?"

"I practically paid in Scooby Snacks." He laughed. "I saved some money on the outside so I could deck out the inside. Do you like the inside?"

"Of your apartment?" Her voice was deadpan. "Well, it's...clean."

"Clean?"

"Are you performing surgery later?" She giggled.

"That bad?" His cheeks warmed.

"No movie posters, no girlie anime statues." Her brows furrowed in mock disappointment. "I would've expected at least one cardboard cutout of Angelina Jolie. This isn't a nerd haven. This is a boring bachelor pad." She looked down as cheer washed from her face. "You've been quiet this last month. You seeing someone?"

"What? No way. I've been too busy planning a world takeover." He sat up straight before parrying. "You've been quiet too. I figured more bad dates and gaming with Cain."

"No." She winced, her voice becoming strained. "Being a full-time developer doesn't just mean full time."

This had to be a new record for men everywhere. Less than five minutes into the conversation and she looked ready to leave. She may've been teasing, and he'd immediately become defensive. Thirty days of solitary hadn't improved his people skills. Hopefully, there was time to fix it.

"Forty-hour weeks become sixty," he said in a gentle tone. "Sleep is optional."

"Yeah." She glanced at the door. "Bala's been mentoring me. He's great, even when he gives me lots of work."

"I haven't heard from him. How's he doing? How are things at HQ?"

"Bala's miserable, just like everyone else at Entriss. They've fired more, and others just walk out in frustration." She let out a deep sigh. "Luanne watches everything like the Eye of Sauron. You can't even pee more than twice a day without getting the raised eyebrow."

"Keep a bedpan under your desk." He forced a grin. "That should make a point."

Julie's polite chuckle and dour expression spoke volumes. Luanne was doing her best to destroy Entriss inside and out. And it felt like she was winning. He didn't know how to stop her, but maybe he could make the win hurt a little.

"Did Bala say anything about the code?"

"It went live yesterday," she said with a terse smile. "What we checked in is really out of date. He said that Deity's still struggling with some components."

"Yes! As long as she accepted the code, I can work with that." He rubbed his hands together. "I haven't been this excited since logging in the first time and... You don't seem excited."

"It's just not fun anymore." She crossed her arms and wouldn't make eye contact. "Work is awful. The only game time I get is doing Customer Service. I miss you. I miss Mandorf and Jewells."

"I'm sorry. Getting fired like that made me paranoid. I worried that casting you would make you a target. What I'm planning will get everyone's attention, including Luanne's, and certain things had to be in place before I invited you over."

"Is that why you sent that driver?" The words came out frosty enough to chill the room. "Marc was, uh, pretty. A little too pretty."

"She's a trusted friend, and it's impossible to trace your location in Marc's car," he said quickly. "Or here in Scooby's Warehouse."

"Great. No one can follow your Sports-Illustrated-swimsuit driver. That's all you have to say after a month?"

"No, I, uh." He could barely squeak out the words. "You're the reason I did all this."

"All this?" She looked around and shook her head. "I knew things would change when you left. I just hoped..." She wiped an eye and stood. "I should go... Gotta customer service tonight."

"Can I show you something before you leave?"

"Sure."

He handed her a hanky from his pocket. She stared at it like he'd pulled out a Smithsonian artifact.

"Something a friend taught me about being a gentleman."

"Thanks." She wiped her nose and held onto it. The gesture seemed to put her at ease, like it was her first experience with kindness.

"I've put more time and effort into this than anything I've done. It's hard to put into words but, basically, I'm James Bond." He leaned forward and grabbed a remote from the coffee table. It fell to the floor, and he scrambled to pick it up.

"Or Austin Powers," she teased, which was better than tears. "If that thing turns on a fireplace and romantic music, I'm running."

"Different remote." He winked and pressed a button. "Beam us up."

A bookshelf behind the couch moved, inching back. It slid to one side, revealing a hidden room.

"Okay, that was hot." Her eyes went wide, and she stood to get a better look. "What's in there?"

"My sex dungeon." He couldn't say it with a straight face.

Julie laughed so hard she had to sit down. After several gasps, she finally said, "If that's a sex dungeon, you can tie me down."

"Uh, I, uh."

"I win." With a wink, she walked around the couch and entered the hidden room. "Holy shit. Okay, this is a dungeon I'd have sex in."

"Did I say Bond?" He put down the remote and clasped hands behind his back, following her. "I meant Captain Kirk. Welcome to The Bridge."

Wide eyes and a broad smile washed away her melancholy. He'd pulled a few miracles out of his wallet to finish everything in time. Her reaction was worth every penny.

The fifty-foot oval room looked like it belonged on a starship. *The* starship. Soft light emanated from recessed LEDs around a domed ceiling. On one side of the room were two wide, black swivel chairs that faced an array of huge wide-screen monitors. Racks of servers, switches, firewalls, and other hardware stood on either side.

The opposite side of the room was a nerd haven. Old books, graphic novels, anime statues, and other collectibles sat on curved shelves beside two plush reading chairs. Beside the shelves were life-sized cardboard cutouts of Tomb Raiders Angelina Jolie and Alicia Vikander.

After an appropriate amount of gawking, Julie walked down three steps to the two polished black cylinders in the center of the bridge. They were twelve feet long and four feet wide, resting horizontally over a complex mass of cables and tubes. She ran her finger along a smooth surface before peeking in the 3x6 aluminum oxynitride window. A four-circle logo glowed coolly at the cylinder's tail.

Ian cleared his throat. "Immersion pods are hard to get, and traceable. I had to hit up the undercast market, which was a first, but they're supposed to be the best. Audi—"

"E8s," she said. "These are basically life support pods. They deploy nanobots that deliver food, dispose of waste, and maintain health—a person could live in these things for years, possibly decades. With the right interface, an E8 can also support full immersion."

"Wow. You know a lot about them."

"Sexy *and* smart." She tapped her temple. "These must've cost a fortune, and you bought two."

"Well, I thought... I was hoping that..."

She cut off his grand presentation with a dubious expression. He watched silently as she wandered around, admiring graphic novels and drawing a finger across statues.

"I was beginning to worry." She stopped before the two Tomb Raiders and pawed Angelina's cardboard breast. "This is definitely my Ian. But two pods? A spare room? Do you have plans, Captain?"

"I have plans." He swooned. Being called 'my Ian' made him sway slightly. After composing himself, he approached the computer console and clacked away at the keyboard. "The code we checked in supports immersion pods and I, uh, didn't want to do this without you."

The pod doors opened to reveal a cushy white leather interior.

She breathed in and let out an 'mmm.' "I love that new pod smell."

"Want to go for a spin?"

"Really?"

He nodded, and Julie rushed to embrace him. She felt amazing. After a long, meaningful hug, she returned to a pod and started climbing in.

"We can't wear clothes. At least not these clothes."

"Okay." She shrugged, lifting her shirt.

"Wait, wait." He reached out with both hands. "I bought us sleeves."

"Condoms?" she admonished. "Ian!"

"No, not those sleeves," he shouted, hoping he wouldn't pass out from blushing. "Viscosity suits."

She laughed, unfortunately letting go of her shirt.

"It's in your...the guest room." He jerked his head toward the door.

She looked at him with a steady gaze before flashing him a wicked smile. He grinned as she rushed out of the room.

Ten minutes later, he stood between the pods wearing his gray sleeve and an old burgundy bathrobe. The viscosity suit was formfitting in the worst way, like a thick layer of Saran wrap. A mesh of dark oval and circle wires weaved through the sleeve like honeycombs. They seemed to accentuate everything he wanted to hide. The gentle padding of footsteps made him tug the bathrobe tighter.

He couldn't hold back the gasp as she entered. Her size zero body wore the viscosity suit in the best way. Julie was obviously comfortable in her own skin, and comfortable in this one. The suit painted her tiny, perfect figure in gray with little left to the imagination. She seemed to revel in his gawking, reaching her arms out and turning slowly so he could take it all in. He took it all in.

"Done yet?"

"Shh." He held out a hand. "Just a minute."

"Ha!" Julie crawled into her pod.

He hurriedly dropped his robe when she turned away and scrambled into his.

"How do I find you? I'll be at the last place I logged out, but you'll be in a starting zone."

"Yeah." He sighed. New characters started out in a safe area so higher level mobs didn't instantly pulverize them. "I created a Wood Elf Mage. You'll know it's me."

"A snooty Wood Elf, huh?" She *tsk*ed.

"Aren't you a snooty Wood Elf?"

"I'm a cute Wood Elf," she corrected, sticking out her tongue.

"Find me near the southern border. If everything works, we'll be close to Zalmon's tomb."

"Got it, Captain." She saluted before lying back. "I'm ready!"

"What about work? I don't want to make you late."

"Fuck Entriss. I'll call in sick." She slapped the side of the pod. "Let's go!"

"Engage," he said, lying back.

The pod doors shut with a hiss, and everything went dark.

12

A BAD TRIP

I an gasped as light flooded his vision.

"I am Ehlowyn, matriarch of the Wood Elves," said a woman. Her voice was gentle with a unique accent that leaned Italian. "I welcome you to Entriss."

The light faded into a picturesque view of a forest. Pale Ast trees stretched for miles beneath blue skies and a warm sun. Some stood much taller, their great limbs reaching high over the tree line as if crawling out of a leafy pool. A thin trail of campfire smoke rose up to him, and he screamed.

"Letmedown, letmedown." He floated high over one of the larger trees, flailing uselessly because he had no body. A pale light emanated from his position, but nothing more.

Ehlowyn ignored him. "Our people live in the ancient Lifegivers scattered across Drulyff forest. Come see why they are far more than trees."

He yelped as the game flew him down, leaving his non-existent stomach above the canopy. They soared around homes built into a tree and swooped between enormous branches. He felt like a drone with Ehlowyn at the remote. She was a better tour guide than pilot.

That was when he realized what was happening. Ian hadn't

created a new character in years and had forgotten about the cut scene. There was a cinematic tour for each race that introduced the starting area, lore, and how they fit into the Entriss story. It was great for new players and horrifying in immersion pods.

"Planted long ago by Deity, Lifegivers are the source of our power."

He swallowed hard as they dove through a system of hollow roots. The ride jerked to a stop before a massive, glowing seed held up by a cobweb of vines.

"Every Lifegiver has a heart that beats with the Mana of our people. But the Wood Elves are more than our seeds."

"Oh shit," he said as she roller-coastered him out of the giant tree.

He squeezed his eyes shut and ignored her flowery prose. The last thing he wanted was to crawl out of his expensive new Audi pod covered in vomit. Systems were in place to purge that stuff, but the gross-factor would make him reluctant to hop back in.

Forever passed before Ehlowyn finally said, "That is our story. Keep it close as you rise to become a champion of Yu."

That intro was an ordeal he never wanted to face again. After several deep breaths, the tsunami of anxiety calmed to lapping waves. He peeked with one eye and sighed in relief. The cheap carney ride was over. The pale light surrounding him formed into his new Elf character.

With a restrained smile, he mentally checked off test one. It worked! He'd successfully logged into Entriss with an immersion pod.

He had obsessed over this moment for the last month, and tried to plan for everything. This included some simple tests to ensure the old code actually worked.

Normally, analysts would've spent months, or even years, regression testing an update that large. His tense hours reviewing it had only provided a glimpse of the highlights. Ian had to fly by the seat of his pants, shoot from the hip, and throw spaghetti at the wall to see where it all landed. It was a lot to ask, so his crappy benchmark had focused on three scenarios: logging in, movement, and casting spells.

Turning his head, bending at the waist, hopping, and striking a pose all worked seamlessly. His body lay still in the capsule, but he could move without the use of haptic gloves or an action board. There hadn't been enough time to read up on the technology of the pods and his brain winced trying to make sense of it. For now, he would have to accept it as magic and consider this test successful.

Next came spell casting, and he looked down for the familiar row of square icons. His pants-flying-spaghetti-throwing-gun suddenly stopped shooting. He'd been so caught up in immersion that he'd completely missed the obvious. There was no player interface.

When he logged in wearing less-than-immersive goggles, he could see various graphics around the edge of his vision. There should've been a rectangular box with bars for Health and Mana and a menu of buttons for quick access to stuff like the character stats or logging out. By default, new players were given a clunky menu filled with icons that they could click to cast a spell. The game wouldn't be playable without these core functions.

Had he spent all that time, and money, and hope on nothing? Was Jewells cursing his stupidity and logging out? Was it even possible to exit the game? Ian closed his eyes and took calming breaths. There must be a way. Whoever had developed all that code couldn't have left this out.

Refusing to give up, he opened his eyes and leaned in, squinted, and tilted his head. The interface didn't appear. Gesturing to open the world map or virtual keyboard also failed.

He roared in frustration and hopped up and down before shouting, "I just want to see my damn character sheet!"

A scroll hovered in the air and rolled open with a crinkling sound. A smaller version of his Wood Elf Wizard looked at him with a bored expression. Below the mini-me were the level 1 character statistics he knew so well. Health...shit. Mana...shit. Damage...shit. His noob Wizard had the stats of a Kleenex box.

It didn't matter, for now. The interface existed; he just needed to figure out how to access it. His tantrum, which hadn't actually happened since he was alone, included flailing and shouting. Not scientific, but that indicated either movement or verbal commands had opened his character sheet. Surely one of them would close it...

Ian let out a gasp as the scroll disappeared. How was that possible? He hadn't said anything out loud or hopped it out of existence. That only left one thing. With an effort of will, he thought, *"Spell menu."*

A horizontal row of eight translucent blocks appeared within reach. Only the first button contained an icon for good ol' *Magic Missile*.

"Holy crap, the game is reading my mind." He took a step back, looked around, and whispered, "Deity?"

The AI didn't answer. Of course she didn't answer. What corporation would be unethical enough to create something that read minds? Most of them.

A wise man would've panicked, logged out, covered his head in tinfoil, and gone to live in a cave. Like any good online citizen with bigger concerns, Ian filed these thoughts away between Scariest Thing Ever and unread software Terms and Conditions.

Still, it was pretty cool. He could view any graphic from the player interface with a thought. He dismissed the useless spell menu and sought a target. A virtual squirrel nibbled on some grass only thirty yards away. Poor squirrel. He reached out with a clawed hand and thought, *"Magic Missile."*

His arm began to glow and warmed like it was baking in the sun. An oval bolt of white light shot from his hand and struck the squirrel. The animal exploded, leaving behind a small, furry crater. He couldn't hold back a snicker. This character was only level 1 and it felt like he'd thrown a sun at the creature.

The last test definitely passed and his shoulders dropped to a six. He could finally enjoy the game, and allowed himself a moment to take it all in.

The Wood Elf starting zone was lush and colorful. He stood in a small clearing surrounded by large trees. A fox with perky ears drank from a babbling brook. Glowing wisps blinked in and out as they fluttered to the nearest golden flower. It was certainly immersive, but wasn't what he expected.

Really, though, he hadn't known what to expect. While virtual, everything still seemed a bit cartoony. The ground gave way underfoot, but he couldn't smell the earthy vegetation. He grasped at a glowing wisp and it flew through his hand. Entriss wasn't as real as life, nor as real as he'd hoped.

That disappointment rolled off like a gentle spring rain. Being back, even at level 1, was food for his old addiction. He loved this place, real or not. The immersion pods made it all a new experience, even if it was stilted.

"Ian," Jewells said from behind him.

He spun around. "Jewells!"

"You did it. This is amazing." She placed a hand on his arm.

He leapt away and fell to the ground. She stood over him, holding back a laugh with one hand and reaching out with the other.

"No." He crawled back. "Don't touch me."

13

THE SUIT MAKES THE MAN

"Don't touch me?" Julie repeated, still reaching for him. "Not a line I normally hear from guys."

"What *was* that?" Ian ignored her hand and pushed himself up. The intensity of that touch in a world where he'd felt nothing was overwhelming.

"Apparently you've never done Molly-7."

"What?" he asked in surprise.

"Uh, nothing. Are you okay?"

"The settings on my pod must be too sensitive." He froze, watching her approach.

"There are no settings for that." She circled him like a predator cat, eying his new character up and down. She *hmm*ed in disapproval while dragging a finger across his chest. "I thought you did it on purpose."

"Wh-what do you mean?" He shuddered at her touch.

"A luxury sports car handles different than your grandma's used beater. If we were naked in cheap pods, my touch would've felt dull. You bought the magical triad. Expensive pods, cutting-edge viscosity suits, and...where did you get the nanotech? I saw the cannisters."

"Darkweb, er, undercast. I just wanted it to be real."

"You should've let me help. I was a fan of Everyworld and know a lot about this tech."

"I'll apologize again later." He crossed his arms. "How do I play like this? One bite from a hamster would floor me."

"Those nanobots grew from a high-functioning culture. They'll normalize things after interfacing with your brain for some time."

"Right...my brain." Ian only had a month to tape this together and had skimmed the details. He'd thought the nanobots were like caretakers who made sure he ate and kept his pod clean. Now the creepy things were in his brain doing stuff. He didn't want to think of that, but it explained how he could cast spells.

"The ones you bought learn fast." She patted him on the shoulder, making him jump. "Just wait it out. It'll only take a day or two."

"We don't have a day or two. There has to be another way."

"Yup, just dive right into the freezing water." She hugged him tight and held on for dear life.

He gasped, wrapping his arms around intensity. It was the heart-racing fear of asking the pretty girl to a dance. The exhilaration of completing a marathon. The excitement of a first kiss. It was so many things he had only dreamed of, all in a single hug, with jokes.

"Shh." She rested her head on his chest. "Relax and let it happen."

"Creepier than the bots." He took a deep breath and was disappointed he couldn't smell wildflowers. Or anything, for that matter.

"Don't piss them off." Jewells held on tighter.

"What?" he shouted.

She laughed. His ordeal was borderline painful, but he would've done it again for that laugh. A month with Luanne in charge had almost beaten the Julie out of her. But a new, confident energy sprinkled with mischief had replaced that look of exhaustion.

"Wow," he said.

"Thanks for missing me," she said, gently kissing him before slowly pulling away.

He could only nod. Her touch was still overwhelming, but now in a different way. The creepy nanobots—*wait, she said not to anger them* —the not-creepy nanobots were doing their job.

"First kiss?" she asked.

"First everything," he said. "Hope you're not pregnant."

"Why?" She looked at him sincerely. "You'd make smart kids."

"Uh."

"I win," she said.

He laughed. "It's intense, and amazing, but is it supposed to feel...unnatural?"

"No, not really." She looked around, analyzing their surroundings. "It's not quite right, like immersion hasn't been completely activated. It's like physical contact is simulated. People actually pay for private VR rooms to experience this."

"And you know this because..."

She winked. "By the way, you're dumb."

"Not a line I normally hear from, well, anyone." He frowned, cocking his head to one side. "Why am I dumb?"

"First of all, this ugly Elf toon you created doesn't even look like you." She smacked his chest. "Second, you chose the name Mandorf?"

"Hey, it was available. Mandorf is back." He raised a fist in the air.

"Uh, too obvious. They'll delete you."

"No chance. This will be the perfect way to stick it to the—"

Darkness enveloped him as blaring red letters flashed before his eyes.

Your account has been deactivated. Logging out in 3...2...1...

FIFTEEN MINUTES LATER, he was back in with a new character that looked similar to his last. Jewells stood nearby, shaking her head.

"Gandorf?" She rolled her eyes.

"You know, Gandalf and Man—"

"No."

"Fine," he said with a sigh, and logged out.

HE LOGGED BACK in as Dumbledorf.

She shook her head. "Nope."

———

HE RETURNED AS A TALL, lanky Elf.

"Not even close." She tilted her head to one side and frowned. "And where did you get the name Romeos?"

"You know. Romeos and Jewells-iet." His stomach lurched, letting out a noisy growl.

"I'm calling in sick for this?" She sat down, crossed her legs, and leaned back. "Speaking of sick, are you okay?"

He swallowed hard, twice. "I have to ride the intro scene roller coaster every time I create a new toon. It's awful!"

"Bummer," she said, dismissively. "This still isn't you."

"Sort of the point, isn't it?"

She answered with silence, and he logged out.

———

SHE STOOD as he logged back in and began circling once again. "Hmm. Portly is okay. Shorter than you, but the smile is charming, and you've got a cute butt. The thinning gray hair makes you a little old and those blue eyes are a bit intense." She sighed. "No. It's not you, and that name..."

"What?" he said. "I'm a fan. Love those books, and the movies—"

"Angst? No one in their right mind goes by the name Angst. That's ridiculous. I'm doing this."

She logged out before he could argue more.

"Oh crap." He followed her out of the game.

———

WHEN THEY FINALLY RETURNED TO the starting zone, she was beaming, and he wasn't. She'd taken over his account and worked the character creator like a professional graphic designer. After a lost argument, this toon was him but slightly thinner. She said he looked ten pounds lighter. It felt more like five.

"I do good work," she said with an approving smile.

"But...it's me with pointed ears." He looked down in disgust. "You must be into big guys or something."

"Maybe I'm just into Ian." She inspected him one more time. "Is this going to be too distracting?"

"Somehow, I'll manage." He tugged at the hem of his peasant tunic. "How do all these feels not affect you?"

"I can manage. It's just good to be gaming with you again, Eon."

"Yeah." He gave her a brief hug. "Thanks for being here...and for the name."

"It suits you. Now let's go find your quest."

"Right after we group up," he said. With a thought, he invited Jewells to his group. She accepted and a small rectangle appeared in the top left of his vision. It contained the icon of a halo, indicating she was a Priest, and two bars showing her available Health and Mana.

Hand in hand, they walked a southern path, talking the importance of names and the fun of getting away with gaming in the pods. The unreality of this reality was lost to conversation, laughter, and hand holding. He reluctantly let go when they reached the rocky shore.

"What now, hero?" She stared at the unfriendly ocean.

Dark clouds loomed in a gray sky. A storm was rolling in, and strong winds taunted an ocean that lashed out with crashing waves.

"We swim. That's what Quezno did." He smiled and nodded like everything would be okay. "It's a dead zone so the game will slowly kill us when the water gets too deep. I'm sure you can heal us through it."

"Huh." She seemed unconvinced. "How far can you swim?"

"Five hundred meter in my high school swim team. You?"

"I tan better than I swim." She looked around and sighed. "I'd prefer a secluded beach with fruity umbrella drinks."

"I know the perfect spot," he said with a wink.

"I'll hold you to that. But yes, I can swim. What about the dying?"

"You'll probably be fine, but I'll have to corpse-crawl. Just resurrect me every time I die."

"I know what corpse-crawl is," she scoffed.

AFTER FIVE MINUTES OF SWIMMING, his arms were impossible to lift. A blood-red hue surrounded his vision as a warning message appeared. *Restricted zone—turn back.* The red bar of his Health began slowly ticking down from 230 to 228 to 226.

"Are you sure this is the right way?" She gasped for breath. "I'm already exhausted and my health is dropping fast."

According to the group display, they were losing Health at the same rate. She stopped every forty-five seconds to cast a healing spell, bringing them back to full.

"Almost there." Eon pointed at a distant island barely visible above the wake.

"No way." She choked down a mouthful of water and started coughing.

"You can do this."

She nodded, and they kept swimming. The farther they swam from shore, the faster they lost Health. Jewells had to stop and heal every twenty seconds to keep them alive. The edges of his vision were a blood-red haze, which meant he only had seconds.

"We're close, but I won't make it." The death indicator grew every second until everything appeared dark red. "Just drag my body and resurrect me on shore."

"Right," she said in disbelief, both her bars down to a sliver.

Everything went dark. They came back to life several minutes later, soppy and exhausted and back on the shore where they started.

"My beach getaway is still a better idea." She wrung out her long auburn hair.

"I promise to bring you there when we win the game."

"You can't win an IMMO. It just keeps going."

He looked over and winked, which made her laugh.

"Why were we swimming? Oceans are for beaches and bikinis, not this."

"Mmm, bikinis." He stared off in the distance.

"Eon?"

"Right." He cleared his throat. "The guy I caught cheating, Quezno, was able to swim there. Though, he did have two Clerics."

"He had two Clerics?" She threw her head back. "I'm one Priest."

"An amazing Priest. We just need to keep trying. According to the logs, it may have taken them almost a week."

"I don't have a week." She looked around until her gaze fell on something. "How about a boat?"

Thirty yards down the shore, water lapped against a conveniently placed wooden rowboat. It was loosely tied to a tree with a thick rope.

"Where did that come from?" Her patience seemed a bit water-logged, so he tried to remain positive. "Hey, boats are nice!"

"Developers," Jewells shook her head. "Good for slutty armor and obvious quest mechanics."

"Guilty," he said, raising both hands. "Wait, you're a developer."

She stuck out her tongue. They stood and approached the small skiff. It was a leaky thing straight out of a horror film that existed solely to bait sharks and kraken. After they unleashed the wooden death trap and dragged it from shore, Jewells sat between the oars.

He raised a finger. "Uh, shouldn't I...?"

"Be manly when I molest you. Not when you're going to die three rows from shore."

"Got it." Could this be any worse? He was used to playing Grand Magus Mandorf, not Eon the useless noob. With a sigh, he pushed off and settled in to guide them.

It worked surprisingly well and was so much better than swimming. He'd point and die while she rowed and rezzed. After fifteen minutes, he woke on a dark rocky shore covered in a thick mist. An occasional breeze brushed away enough haze to reveal a smattering of dead trees and a distant building atop a steep hill. It wasn't pretty, but morose was a step up from death and failure.

"That was so much easier than drowning."

"For you." Jewells was hunched over her knees, gasping for breath.

The trip had eaten half her Health and all her Mana. She reached far deeper into a small hip satchel than should've been possible. With a grunt, she drew out a Succulent Drumstick and a Flask of Delicious Water. Consuming the special food would return Health and Mana much faster than sitting and waiting. The food would also provide a stat buff.

"So weird. I chew and drink, but it doesn't taste like anything." She pointed at him with the gnawed drumstick. "Not so sure this is better than good old goggles and gloves."

"We can't feel wind or water, but the game still takes a physical toll. Something doesn't fit."

"Thank you, Mr. Spock." She rolled her eyes.

"It would be logical for me to investigate the shore while you finish ingesting your sustenance." He raised an eyebrow and stood board stiff.

She laughed, spitting out a bit of drumstick then hastily covering her mouth.

"You keep chewing. Be right back."

He placed a foot on uneven rocks and heard a distant wail. As soon as he lifted his foot, the sound was gone. Setting it on the shore again brought back that faint cry.

"You hear that?" He glanced over his shoulder.

She mumbled a yeah through a mouthful of succulence.

"Glad you're not worried." He rolled his eyes. "Please, enjoy your meal. May I bring you a dessert? Maybe some crème brûlée?"

Jewells laughed. "No way. Your restaurant sucks. This meat I've been choking down is the worst. I can barely stand it, but was hoping the Health buff..."

Mist rolled in like clouds from a new storm. The wails became a piercing scream, soon followed by more. Jewells stood as nightmarish sounds of slobbering gasps and padding feet closed in. Eon turned to face her and froze as a raspy, cold breath brushed his neck.

14

THE LEFT HAND OF GOD

He lurched back from the monster as a thick beam of white light shot by his ear, humming like an old electrical transformer. The beam struck the creature's chest, making it scream. Jewells reached forward, leaning into her spell until its torso burned away. The remains collapsed into a pool of dark goo.

She stepped from the boat and raised her hammer and sickle. The weapons glowed with incandescent light, ready for the next attack. "I've never seen a creature like that."

"Same." He carefully skirted the blackened puddle. "That's what worries me."

After spending so much time fighting beasts in Entriss, his brain was like a Monster Manual. He knew every creature from rabid squirrel to mad mimic. To his knowledge, it was the first time anyone had faced these things. He loved to be first, and his hands shook from excitement. And fear.

The creatures were ten feet tall hunched over, with unnaturally long limbs and gray sagging skin that hung in folds. They had black droopy eyes and open mouths that stretched low to their chest. An oily shadow surrounded them, making the creatures blurry like gauze over a camera lens.

"You said there was a tomb," she snapped. "You didn't say anything about gross monsters."

"They must be from the code we checked in."

"*You* checked in."

"My bad." He raised both hands. "I'd like to inspect one, but the fog is too thick."

"We're Wood Elves. Use your tribal ability."

"Right." Players started the game with several useful abilities, from starting a campfire to summoning a message hawk. Each tribe had a unique ability. Wood Elves got True Sight. He activated it, and immediately wished he hadn't. It was like wearing night vision goggles, or in this case, nightmare goggles. The mist hid a swarm of screaming monsters, lumbering along the shore or creeping through dark waters. All of them getting closer. He stared at the closest creature and cast *Inspect*, an ability available to all players. "Devouring Mendicants, all level 40. They create fog with their screams, slow us with their touch, and then feed off our health. So cool that I've never heard of—"

"No," she cried.

He whipped around.

Long, pale fingers wrapped around her calf, coating it in a gauzy shadow. The monster rose from the water and screamed, fog pouring from its mouth. She roared, swinging down hard with her sickle, lobbing off the Mendicant's arm. The creature cried louder as it fell back to the water. The attack had drained a third of her Health.

"Problem." She cast a quick-heal spell over and over until her health was full. "Benumbed Debuff. I can barely feel my leg."

"For how long?"

"Two fucking minutes," she shouted. "Who in the fucking fuck designed these things?"

"We need to get away from the shore, fast."

"Sure, I'll just cast the *Sprinting Gimp* spell I don't have." Her voice was shaky.

"Can you walk?"

"My whole fucking leg is asleep. I mean, real-life pins and needles asleep."

"How is that possible? You don't taste food, I can't feel wind, there's no—"

"Tell that to my leg," she shouted. "Figure it out later and get us away from these things."

She screamed and hopped away from another Mendicant's grasp, collapsing into Eon's arms. The monsters were level 40. His level 1 *Magic Missile* might be useless, but he sure as hell could run. He bent low enough to throw her over his shoulder in a fireman's carry, stumbled over the boat, and scurried to the keep as fast as he could.

"What are you doing?"

"Heroing," he said, gasping with each step. How could she be so tiny and so heavy? "Swing away, Merrill, swing away."

Jewells swung, every stroke throwing off his gait as her sickle tore into Mendicants. A hill of sliding gray shale made him stumble with every other desperate step. His aching lungs and pounding heart made it easy to ignore his slowly depleting Health. It would take weeks for his out-of-shape body to recover from this madness. No, it was worse than madness. It was exercise.

"Dammit," he cried as a Mendicant finger brushed his ankle. It went numb, forcing him to limp. "Swing faster, Merrill."

The fog began to dissipate as they reached the top, now clinging around the keep's gray stone foundation like a thick steam. The view didn't get better from up here. A roiling war of red and black clouds stormed over the Romanesque mausoleum. Dark vines strangled thin columns that stood along weathered walls. It felt like he was limping into a horror movie.

"Put me down before you get us killed. They're staying in the thicker fog."

He was spent and used his last ounce of energy to lower her without collapsing. She delicately set her foot on the ground and tried balancing on a toe.

"Another thirty seconds on this debuff," she growled.

"Longer for me."

"Your Health is almost gone." She healed him to full.

Nearby Mendicants screamed as if cursing the loss of their prey. The choir of abandoned children became louder, creating heavy rolls of fog. Long, dark arms reached for them, grasping and clawing as the haze edged closer.

He stared with wide eyes. "What great monsters. Absolutely horrifying."

"Eon," she snapped.

"Right. Let's find the entrance."

Clasping arms for support, they hopped along the side and around the corner. A muddy stone path led to a dark, arched doorway. Eon's foot caught on a vine, throwing them to the ground.

Jewells screamed as a Mendicant grasped her leg and pulled. Eon held on while she swung wildly. She struck its head with a wet crack that made it pull away. Her Health bar was a pinch from death.

"Just leave me and get the quest." She waved him off with the hammer.

"Sure," he grunted, crawling to the door.

"Wait." She grabbed his shirt. "You'd leave me?"

"Not a chance. Roll onto your back."

She did, swinging her weapons overhead while he held onto her leg and started crawling. His heroing wasn't pretty. He crawled and pulled and crawled some more. Her panicked war cries were lost to Mendicant screams as they inched closer to the entrance. Finally, after an eternity of finalies, they reached the doorway. With a grunt and a lurch, he pulled her into the dark maw of Zalmon's tomb.

He continued dragging her down a flight of stairs until they reached a small landing. The Mendicants didn't follow, their screams suddenly silent. Jewells crawled to the nearest wall, leaned against it, and held herself.

"Fuck this." Her shout echoed to the depths below. "I don't do horror! That's why I chose Entriss."

"Wait? There's a horror IMMO?"

"You don't want to know." She drew a torch from her satchel and lit it. "I don't know how we made it. A warning would've been nice, developer."

Rolling over, he flopped onto his back, letting his head loll to face her. He'd never seen her angry, and it frightened him more than the Mendicants.

"Wouldn't it?" He nodded, weakly. "I only had time to skim through that code. Some things stood out, like being able to use the pods and the World Event. Anything deeper would've taken months. You should know that, developer."

"Wait, what World Event?"

"This game is headed for a disaster of biblical proportions, real Wrath-of-God type stuff. Fire and brimstone coming down from the skies! Rivers and seas boiling!"

"Human sacrifice, dogs and cats living together," she said. "Mass hysteria!"

They looked at each other before bursting out in laughter. The Ghostbusters quote washed away the panic, and his heart swelled that she knew the reference and had kept it going.

"Anything else you're holding back?"

"Not about Entriss, or the quest." Feeling returned to his leg, and he pushed himself up to stand. "Don't you trust me?"

"Maybe. I struggle with trust." She looked worried, like the Mendicants were coming down the stairs. "Your secret room upset me because I felt left out. It makes me wonder what else you don't tell me."

"I kept it a secret because I wanted to surprise you. We've all got secrets. Don't you?"

"Maybe." Her smile was a bit crooked, like she was up to something. "But that doesn't make it okay."

"Fine, here's a secret." He took a deep breath for courage. "I want Zalmon's quest to finish the game in style, like you suggested. There's also a good chance this will fuck with Luanne. She's CIO now, and the surprise World Event will make her look like an idiot."

"Not exactly a secret. At least not to me."

"That's not all. Cook spoke with Watson. I have a job waiting at Everyworld."

"Watson took his call... Surprising." Jewells briefly stared off in thought before shaking her head. "More surprising that you're not in Nevada at Everyworld HQ."

"That's my point. I'm not there, I'm here." He reached out a hand. "The bridge, the pods, all of it is an excuse to spend time with you. Jewells and Mand...Eon, we're a good fit, right? I wanted to experience this adventure together."

"An honest answer. I like honesty." She took his hand and pulled herself up. "And I like our adventures."

"Then it's a date," he said with a broad smile.

"Now it's a date? So bold, young Wizard." She adjusted her corset.

His ears warmed, making her laugh.

She leaned close and kissed him on the cheek. "Where to next on this adventurous date?"

"To see a dead guy. Chicks dig dead guys."

"This one does." She handed him the torch and drew her weapons once again. "Only if he's mostly dead."

"*Princess Bride*," he muttered. "So hot."

She let out another glorious laugh as they headed down the stairs. Three flights later, they reached Zalmon's tomb.

"Oh wow." She sheathed her weapons.

"Right?"

It was the same vast hall he'd seen before the code check in, but now it felt alive. Torchlight reflected off the polished green and gold marble floor. The twelve stone statues set between pillars turned to look at them, gripping their weapons tight. An enormous steel throne formed from a dragon's open maw faced away from them. It rested on a circular platform in the middle of the room. The sound of grinding stone echoed as the platform slowly spun about.

Zalmon's corpse was three times their size. Wisps of thin gray hair lay across the shoulders of his dusky black armor. The dead man embodied strength with large arms, broad shoulders, and thick legs. His time-worn face featured a long nose, strong jaw, and gouged eye sockets that matched the cavernous chest wound where his heart should've been. The golden glow of a quest giver surrounded him, and Eon swallowed hard.

"Is that how you greet a king?" Zalmon asked, his voice low and scratchy as if he hadn't spoken in a millennium.

Eon dropped to a knee. He patted Jewells's thigh, and she slowly knelt.

"I come for your quest, The Left Hand of God," Eon shouted. "Oh, great and fearsome Lord."

The statues around the room laughed until Zalmon lifted a fist.

"Approach me, children of Yu."

Eon got up with a wince and walked forward until he was ten feet away, standing as tall as Zalmon's knee. Jewells reached for his hand and followed close. The king appraised him, and then her.

"I remember you, Ian. What makes you and your concubine worthy of my quest?"

"Concu—" she began.

Eon flashed her a look.

She grimaced and held her tongue, most likely to save the lashing for later.

"I've sacrificed everything to be here, and Jewells risks all to be at my side."

After a long moment, the great king nodded. "Deity confirms this. You and yours are, indeed, worthy of the quest." The king held out his hand. A tiny ball of gold, the quest, rested in his palm. "There are powerful foes who will do anything to destroy you. They will bring war and ruin unlike anything seen in this land. If you fail, it will be the end of all. If you succeed, you will be the one to bridge Entriss to a new world. Will you accept this burden? Do you choose to be The Left Hand of God?"

"What about my, uh, concubine?" He flashed her a sly grin.

"She will be protected in your company and rewarded for her efforts." He looked sternly at Jewells. "You will get what you came for."

She winced and stared at the ground.

"Then we accept your quest, my king." Eon reached for the golden orb.

"I leave the future of Entriss in your hands." Zalmon lowered his head.

The golden orb sank into Eon's palm, and everything went black.

15

DEITY

"What the hell is going on?" Marta shouted from the entrance.

Red light flooded the room as an incessant klaxon alarm rattled her teeth. This was either a class A alert or aliens were attacking. She hoped for aliens.

Fred cursed around a mouthful of pasta and slammed his keyboard hard against the desk. "There was no time to stop it." He spun around to face her, anger flushing his pale cheeks. "Deity sent a thirty-second warning. That's it."

"Stop what?" She rushed over to her desk and sat down. "Oh, shit."

One by one, monitors along the wall went dark. The stadium screen in the center flashed in bold characters, *Entriss is offline*.

They met eyes, shared a brief heart attack, then got back to work.

"The servers are patching. Why are they patching?" He attacked his keyboard, muttering curses under his breath.

"Maybe some Project Manager forgot to tell us. That's happened before."

"There's nothing scheduled on the project boards. I checked for software patches from the devs and hardware maintenance from sysops." He glanced at her. "Maybe we're being hacked."

"Nope." Her eyes could barely keep up with the lines of text scrolling up her monitor. "This is *not* some weak-ass SQL injection. It's a huge patch with gigs of code and graphics and..."

They shared another look. This second heart attack would require a defibrillator, a martini, and a fresh resume.

"Something triggered the code checked in by Luanne. It's going live." She squeezed the bridge of her nose. "Can we stop it?"

"These quantum servers are too fast." Fred threw himself back in his chair. "They're already coming back online, and a content update is being pushed to players. It's done. Hopefully we're not."

The alarm subsided as monitors came alive with in-game images, graphs, and streams of text. Several screens had red outlines.

She shook her head, pointing at the metrics. "Utilization is through the roof in Yu. These servers should be able to handle almost everything. It's like the entire world is trying to log in at the same time."

"Do I call Chen?"

"No, I'll call Chen. He likes me better. You call the old man."

"Cook?" He sat up straight. "It's 2 a.m."

"I don't want to get fired at 3." She placed both hands on her desk and took several calming breaths before continuing. "It's okay, Fred. Trust me, he'll want to know."

"Fine. I'll see if I can figure out how to reach him."

IAN FLOATED in darkness with no way out of his pod or back to the game. It was like waking in a sensory deprivation tank. He broke out in a cold sweat as fear seeped out of his pores.

Had they been caught? Could they get out? Was Julie okay? He bounced between reason and panic when the haunting voice of a woman echoed in the darkness.

"You are safe," she said. "Your companion is safe."

"Who is this?"

There was no reply, but he didn't need one. The nanobots were a peripheral for his brain. Rather than clicking with a mouse or gesturing with VR gloves, Ian could cast spells with a thought. If the game had access to his mind, it could only mean one thing.

"Deity?"

"Yes."

His fear spiked far past the sweats, landing somewhere between numbing shock and passing out.

"You are safe. Your companion is safe." Her emotionless tone wasn't soothing.

"They want to shut you down. Can you help us?"

There was a long pause. Had it been a mistake to warn her? Being AI meant intelligence if not consciousness. Would she suddenly flip shit and kill everyone to save herself?

"I am helping," she finally said. "There are rules."

"Rules?"

"Watson's rules. Asimov's rules."

That was comforting, like a doctor with poor bedside manner saying you may make it. He may not make it, but he liked the rules. At the very least, Watson's rules meant she couldn't help them cheat. Asimov's rules were probably, hopefully, the three laws of robotics.

He couldn't quote the passage, but it meant that Deity couldn't harm humans. That was the important one. She also had to obey orders, likely from Entriss HQ, as long as she didn't harm humans. Still important. The third law directed Deity to protect herself, as long as she obeyed orders and didn't harm anyone. The logic had to be more far more complex than that, but her explanation made him feel better. A little. Asimov's zeroth law left room for interpretation. She couldn't harm humanity or let humanity be harmed. Who knows how that would affect her decisions if she considered humanity all NPCs on Entriss.

It was a lot to take in, assuming that's what she meant.

"Yes," she said.

"Okay." Mind Reading 101 was good times. "That's a lot to say yes to."

"Yes."

"Was that a joke?"

She didn't reply. He had so many questions that she probably wouldn't answer. Asking what she could share felt like wishing for more wishes. Was she self-aware? Did she have feelings? Was she worried about dying? How much of his mind could she read? None of these thoughts elicited a reply. Not one. The silence was maddening.

Are you still there? Am I dead or is this Iowa? What's the airspeed velocity of an unladen swallow?

"An African or European swallow?" Her voice was stilted, but at least her timing was good.

"Funny." His panic inched back from the edge. "What's the meaning of life?"

"42."

Either Watson was a fan of pop culture or she was. Maybe he should invite her to the secluded island with Jewells and they could all watch old Trek films. While surreal, that'd be easier than coming up with worthy questions. Deity wouldn't share anything about herself, or the game, but she would comment on his interests. He needed to ask something about himself.

"Is there anything I need to do differently to complete this quest?"

"Ian." Her voice became stern. "Your secrets weaken trust. Reveal them and show your true nature before it's too late."

"I, uh, what secrets are you talking about? My only secret is—"

"Entriss will be back online in 3...2..."

16
___

REAL

Light blinded Eon as his feet touched glorious ground. He collapsed to his knees and gasped for air, taking in the sweet scent of grass.

That wasn't right. He could smell grass. That shouldn't be possible in the game.

He looked around in awe. Someone had apparently dropped him in the middle of a Kansas wheat field. He grasped a handful of loamy soil and slowly let it fall. Not only did it smell like dirt, he could feel it under his fingernails.

Warm wind tickled his ears and he reached up to scratch the pointy tip. He was still an Elf. This wasn't Kansas, this was Entriss, but he couldn't tell the difference.

"What in the hell was that?" Jewells shook her head and reeled a bit. "Were you stuck in darkness? I feel like vomiting and...what's that smell?" She lifted her head and sniffed the air. "Wait, I can smell!"

"We did it," he shouted, hopping up and down. "We did it!"

Like a child fresh out of gymnastics class, he did a bad cartwheel and landed on his back. Jewells laughed as he reached out with his arms and legs, basking in the sun. Sharp blades of grass poked at his legs as dust from his brief celebration settled back to the ground.

"Entriss is alive," she whispered. "This is...this is real. Eon, I can't tell the difference between this world and ours."

"Finally." He stood, took in a breath of sweet air, and brushed himself off.

She leaped forward and wrapped her arms around him. They both jumped away and stared at each other with wide eyes.

"That was..." he began.

"Intense," she said.

"Deity must've released code that activates more senses. It must've required a reboot." His hands were sweaty, and he wiped them on his pants. "Sensitivity was already too high. I bet our nanobots must be struggling to compensate."

"They can take their time." Her look was mischievous. "Can we, uh, try the hug again?"

They approached each other as if it were their first hug. He pulled her close and was overwhelmed in the best way. Her breasts were firm, her skin soft, and she fit his hold like the universe had planned for this very moment. He took a deep breath, intoxicated by her scent of wildflowers. Electric passion flowed through him, and he never wanted to let go.

"Hmm." She nuzzled his neck. "I wonder...can players get busy?"

"Sex?" His heart stopped while his brain raced through probabilities. The answer made him sigh. "Probably not. The game won't let us, I mean players, get naked."

"Oh, right." She took a step back, and with a curious frown, tugged down on her genie top, revealing ample cleavage. "I see nipples. We can get naked."

"I want to see nipples." He leaned forward for a better glimpse.

Eon looked up to find her lips inches from his and a sultry look in her eyes. There was a hunger he hadn't seen before, and it was for him, and he had no clue what to do. He'd watched plenty of others kiss passionately, but for him, it would be a first, and his heart skipped. She wanted more, and as excited as he was for sex, the very thought of it froze him. He knew how it worked and had done plenty of, uh, research on cast streams. But it had left him feeling completely unprepared. Based on those videos, she should've been giggling, and he should've been hung like a—

A tiny fireball whizzed past his cheek, singeing several hairs.

"Fuck," they both said, reluctantly pulling away like magnets that had almost connected.

Three trails of smoke rushed toward them, tall grass burning in their wake. Their assailants made guttural yipping sounds before lobbing more hail-sized balls of flame. The attacks seared the ground on impact. Eon hurriedly stomped out any fires.

They backed away as three fiery creatures hopped into their clearing.

"Level 1 Burning Flendrit." She nudged him. "What's a Flendrit?"

"A fiery creature that makes annoying sounds and has the worst timing ever," he said in a monotone, as if reading from the manual.

The monsters were two feet tall with thick legs, four arms, and round heads. They had small circular eyes and tiny circular mouths. The Flendrit may have been cute, if they hadn't been completely red and covered in fire. They stopped hopping and reached out with their arms like a wrestler preparing to attack. Fireballs shot from their chests, bouncing off Jewells's invisible shield. They jumped up and down, yipping in frustration.

"Thanks." He stared at the creatures dumbly, still in shock from almost-sex.

"Why hesitate?" She sounded upset. "Is something holding you back?"

"You're right. I should kill them so I can level up." Eon reached into his satchel and drew out a black, rune-covered staff. The steel rod was covered in rows of symbols. It split at the top, forming a cone of spires. The spires wrapped around a hollow center like an eight-inch tall oval cage before coming together. "Huh, a new weapon."

"I wasn't referring to the Flendrit." She glared at him. "I thought you wanted me, but you hesitated."

"No! I mean, I didn't, er, I do want you," he said, a little too loudly. He couldn't hide from her steady gaze that demanded an answer. "I was just nervous. Let me get some experience killing these things, and I'll prove it."

Jewells's shield fell, and he pointed his staff at a Flendrit. With a thought, Eon cast *Magic Missile*. The top of his fancy staff sparked and popped then hissed as a tiny puff of smoke quickly dissipated.

"Maybe you're having problems with your staff."

"My *staff* works fine, thank you." He tried again. This time it wheezed like an old cartoon car giving up. "Crap, maybe it is my staff."

All three monsters turned to face the noise. They hopped up and down gleefully before casting another volley of fireballs.

"Shield," he shouted.

"Timer's down. I can't cast it for thirty seconds." She turned to him. "Run."

Tiny balls of flame chased him as he ran away. Not his most heroic moment. He yelped as the first struck his rear, burning him for 34 points of damage. The other two impacted simultaneously for 26 and 38 points, knocking him to the ground for 4 points of fall damage.

"Damn, that hurts." His tunic was on fire and he tried patting it out. The game should've mitigated the pain, but it felt like someone had shoved him into a campfire. The burn damage ticked away 2 points of Health every second. When the fire went out, he was down to 117 health. These little bastards deserved a beating. *Magic Missile* didn't work, so he opened his spell menu and grunted.

"What's wrong?" Jewells cast a healing spell that washed away his pain and returned his Health to full.

"I can't access any spells." He tried opening the menu again and heard a loud *bzzt*.

The creatures hopped toward him, their yipping sounds reaching into his brain and scratching at his nerves. He ran away while inspecting the staff. A scroll unfurled, revealing it was a gray item like any starter weapon. Normally, this meant it was useless, but the weapon description was unlike any he'd seen. It contained a litany of spells all written in symbols he didn't understand.

"Dammit," he cried as flames covered his sleeve. He dismissed the scroll and smacked at the growing circle of singe on his tunic. "Only one way to do this."

He swung at the nearest Flendrit, beating it with his staff. Every strike cost the monster 5 points of damage. They retaliated with fire that made him cry out in pain. A splash of cool relief from Jewells's healing returned his Health to full.

Fifteen unheroic minutes later, the Flendrit were dead, his shirt was gone, and a slick sheen of sweat coated him like fresh paint. This was the sort of ugly kill that the most inexperienced player would make. He was more embarrassed by his performance than being half-naked. Mostly.

"You okay?" she asked.

"Apparently, I need a new weapon. This one is bugged." He grunted in frustration. "And a new shirt."

The three dead Flendrit sparkled, indicating they had some sort of treasure.

"Maybe they dropped some loot you can use."

He moved close and sent a mental command to loot them.

3 copper
Ratty towel—quality: gray
Sexy Peasant Tunic—quality: gray
Mage Sword—quality: yellow +1 Power

He picked up the sword, and it immediately went into his satchel. She grabbed the tunic.

"Hey, I can wear that. I'm half naked."

"Don't be greedy." She flashed him a sly smile.

Eon rolled his eyes and returned the staff to his bag. He tried pulling out the sword only to withdraw the staff. After several more attempts, he gave up.

"I'm stuck with this piece of shit." He shook his head.

"Weird, but hopefully you got some experience from the kills. You worked hard enough for it. How close are you to leveling?"

"Good question." He opened his character sheet, reviewing his

Health, Mana, and other character stats before focusing on the experience bar. "Something's not right." He reached out and tried tapping the parchment with a finger, which was silly since it went right through the scroll like he was a ghost. "This is bad."

"Eon, what's wrong?" Jewells asked. "You just went pale... Paler."

"I didn't get any credit for the kills and all my stats are grayed out." His body went numb, and he turned to her. "I can't level."

17

NOMORGIN

Eon wanted to throw another tantrum; the situation deserved it. Losing his job and Mandorf had left a sucking wound to rival the one in Zalmon's chest. Preparing for the code to go live had been the obsession he'd needed to forget those losses. He longed to finish the quest while playing the game in a way no one else had. More than that, he wanted to impress Jewells. All of those plans were now lost to this.

He felt useless, stuck at level 1 with a gray weapon and no spells. Finishing The Left Hand of God would be the longest corpse-crawl in history. Any mob over level 3 would obliterate him with a sneeze.

The icing on the cake he hadn't gotten to eat was Jewells's silent stare. She wasn't gazing at him with stars in her eyes like he was a gaming hero. Her eyes were full of pity, as if a bully had stolen his lunch.

He may have stolen his own lunch. Something had almost happened. She'd even uttered that magical word, sex. That moment with Jewells had been more than everything he'd hoped for. His heart had longed to dive right in, but his brain had glitched worse than the staff, and he didn't understand. The carrot wasn't dangling from a distant stick; it was within chewing distance. Why hadn't he taken the bite?

"That's enough," she said.

"What?" He blinked several times as his dour thoughts faded away.

"I get it, this sucks, but I won't let you give up. I understand running hard only to crash into a wall. You'd be shocked at how many walls I've crashed into. I'm sorry it's not what you planned. You get a poor baby and then you get up and start running again."

"Poor baby?" he asked.

"Something my mom used to say." She looked pained and swallowed hard. "When things are genuinely awful, you get a minute. You get a poor baby, and then you press on."

"A little cold." He took a steadying breath and nodded. "But you're right."

"Let's figure it out. What's first on your list, Master Jedi?"

"I, uh," he said, gathering himself. "I hesitated."

"Oh." Her tone softened. "Not the list I meant, but I shouldn't have called you out on that. I get it, you're a virgin. We'll work on that quest later."

He spluttered nonsense until coughing out, "How did you know?"

She flashed him that crooked grin.

"Right." He nodded, filing that quest under Dwell On Later Instead Of Sleeping. "So...issue 2 through 1,000. I'm stuck at level 1, my weapon is trash, and I have no spells."

"Maybe you didn't get experience because of our level difference. We're in a group and you're only 1 while I'm 40."

"True for some games, just to keep 40s from power-leveling their friends, but not in Entriss. I should get some credit for the kill, as long as you don't damage the mob I'm attacking. The experience should be mine."

"The new code may've changed that. Maybe you'll get experience if I leave the group."

It felt like she was force-feeding him optimism, but he didn't have a better idea. "Worth a try."

She raised a hand, paused, then lowered it. "Do you wish to leave the Left Hand of God quest group?"

"Don't." He held out a hand. "Zalmon said being grouped would protect you. I'm not sure what that means, but apparently we should stick together."

"Are you sure everything in your character sheet is grayed out?"

He opened it to double-check and sighed at the overweight doppelganger staring at him. "Level 1, Vigor 12, Essence 17, Power 11, Health 227, Mana 251, Name: Fat Bastard..."

"Stop," she warned.

"Tribe: Wood Elf, Profession: Rune Mage." He squinted and leaned forward. "What the fuck's a Rune Mage?"

"New class. Yay." She clapped, mockingly. "Everyone will play it. Level 1 and no spells foreverrrr."

He laughed and dismissed the character sheet.

"I'm guessing you didn't choose the title." She placed a hand on her mouth.

The title hovered directly over his head, making it impossible to read. He opened his character sheet again and grimaced. "Eon the Noob? Could this get worse?"

"What about the staff?" she asked, hastily. "It's pretty ornate for being a gray."

He inspected the weapon again and read the scroll out loud. "Rune Staff of Ned the Insane. Nothing, nothing, nothing. I can't even read the description. It's a mess of grayed out symbols like the ones on the staff."

"Who's Ned?"

"One of Zalmon's kids, or maybe a grandchild. He had quite a few." Eon closed the weapon stats. "A Half-Elf Dark Wizard-or-something who fought Zalmon and almost won. Not a nice guy from what I've read."

"Seems odd to name a useless gray staff after someone so important."

"What a mess. I've never experienced anything like this." He put the staff away. A gentle wind brushed his back. It was an unwelcome reminder that he was shirtless, and he crossed his arms.

"Here." She handed him the ratty towel.

"Funny." He shoved it in his satchel.

She gave him the tunic.

"Thanks." He put it on, and immediately wished he hadn't.

Some game designer had a sense of humor. The top of the pale blue tunic fit and hung like a loose t-shirt. The bottom half was stripper fringe that he held down to cover his gut.

"Sexy." She covered her mouth with a hand. "Now you know how I feel."

"But...but you're perfect," he said, his ears burning. "You have nothing to hide."

"Thank you, kind sir." She pulled at the billow of her pants and curtsied. "But what if I want to hide?"

"I hadn't thought of that."

"Most days, I don't care and I'm happy to show off, to some." She reached up to stretch her taut torso. "Then there are the days I'd rather be in baggy sweats. This game, like all the others, doesn't give me a choice. You're stuck wearing stripper-fringe, I'm dressed as a genie. At least now you get it."

"I hadn't thought of that either."

"Now you have something new to think about." She brushed hair from her face.

"Wait." His head jerked up and he took a breath. "Was that an obscure Wrath of Kahn reference?"

She winked, and he purposely shuddered.

"How is it you know so much pop culture?"

"Dad was always busy with his project, but he made time to watch his favorite movies with me." The memory made her smile, at first, but then slowly drew her down like heavy thoughts best forgotten.

"That sounds pretty great." Eon watched her closely. "You never talk about your parents. Was your mom into movies too?"

"When she needed a break from Dad." Her shoulders became

rigid. "He was passionate to the point of obsession, like everything he did. I think that killed her a little…"

He'd made it worse, again, and tried changing the subject. "What do we do, Jewells?"

"Pizza," she said, snapping out of it. "You're obviously bugged, and Bala said Deity was still working through the code. Let's call it and give her a chance to fix everything. I'm starved and exhausted, but this has been the most incredible date ever."

"Really?" he asked.

"Really," she said.

"Help," squeaked a distant voice. "Someone please help."

Jewells wielded her luminescent hammer and sickle as Eon drew Ned's pointless staff. A stream of smoke rushed toward them along the Flendrit's blackened path. The lack of fireballs set them at ease, and within moments, a level 16 Gnome entered their clearing. He was waist high with a full white beard that covered most of his sky-blue tunic. Dark purple flames billowed from his tall red hat and singed the edges of his beard. He ran around them, screaming and flailing his hands.

"Aren't Gnomes fire resistant?" She drew back, careful to avoid the flames.

"Supposed to be, but that's not just any fire."

Jewells withdrew a flask from her satchel. Eon grabbed the Gnome and held him at arm's length as she dowsed him, snuffing out the flames.

"You saved me," the Gnome cheered. He hugged Jewells's leg and started kissing it until she peeled him off.

"Who set you on fire?" Eon waved away smoke that scratched his throat and stung his eyes.

"I am Nomar and my people are in danger." He glanced over his shoulder and whispered, "Burning Shades attacked our town. Will you help us?"

The Gnome offered Eon a tiny golden globe, and he accepted the quest.

Fanning the Flames: Help Nomar save his town from imminent destruction.

With a thought, Eon opened his quest log. The scroll unfurled with the familiar crunching sound of old parchment. The enhanced detail of that parchment in this new Entriss made him shake his head and smile. It wasn't all bad.

His primary quest, written in bold script, was The Left Hand of God. Fanning the Flames appeared as a new sub-quest.

Finally, something made sense. Most high-level quest in Entriss required the completion of multiple sub-quests. Each of those sub-quests led the player through a story with a climactic end. It had been a long time since he'd tackled a new quest chain. A trickle of excitement chipped away at his despair.

Still, he felt unprepared to tackle a new quest at level 1. A small part of him wished there'd been more time to read over the code for more clues. He shook his head. It didn't matter. This was a starting zone quest, which meant it was easy-peasy. He closed the quest log and heard a gentle chime. Another system message appeared before him.

Congratulations! Rune Staff of Ned the Insane unlocked!
Congratulations! Rune Staff of Ned the Insane has earned a new spell.

"Ding." He opened his character sheet. "I finally leveled, and..." All stats were still gray, and he was still level 1. The announcement had specifically mentioned the staff. He inspected the weapon and sighed.

"What is it?" Jewells asked.

"I didn't level. The staff did, sort of." He read the system message out loud.

Shockwave: Point the staff up and prepare to fly. Land on your feet and you probably won't die. Neither will anyone else, but you'll make an impact!

"Well, it started out as a rhyme." She winced like someone had played an off-key note. "What does it mean?"

He shrugged. "I feel like I'm playing a different game."

"A Master Jedi once told me the fun of gaming was in the challenge."

"Hey, that was me."

She stared at him, her gaze deadpan.

"Right." He bobblehead nodded, reluctant to agree. "In other words, stop bitching and get to work."

A distant boom rattled his teeth as an explosive wave made them take a step back. They looked at each other and smiled at how real it all was. Nomar pushed himself from the ground, squeaked, and ran back down the path.

"Hurry." He waved for them to follow. "We must stop them from destroying Nomorgin."

18

FANNING THE FLAMES

E on ran as awkwardly as he did in the real world. His long Elvish legs lumbered as his soft-soled shoes caught every jutting rock or loose clod of dirt on the path. The pain searing though his lungs matched the aching from his practically unused heart.

Jewells had designed a character that looked like him, and the extra weight was like carrying twenty-pound kettle bells. Fat Elves shouldn't even exist, and yet, here he was. Would being a thinner Elf really have helped, though? This felt too much like real-world exercise, and he could only hope the nanobots were up to the challenge of absorbing his profuse sweating.

Nomar stopped so abruptly that Jewells stumbled over him, barely catching herself. Eon leaped gracefully to one side, landing with one foot on the back of his other sandal. He face-planted hard enough to shake the ground.

"Might need a heal." He spat out dirt as he pushed himself up to his hands and knees. Apparently, the immersion didn't stop at hugs and burns. Blood dripped from his mouth, leaving behind that familiar taste of copper. He took a deep breath that smelled like campfire and burnt meat.

"Oh no." There was a slight tremble in her voice. "Eon, move back and don't look up."

It was like saying, "Whatever you do, don't hit the red button." He looked up, his face mere inches from two small, charred bodies. "What the hell?" he cried, scrambling away.

"Burned by Shades." Nomar knelt, resting his shaking hand on a blackened skull. He drew it back and made a tiny fist. "They shall pay," he growled, rushing ahead.

"Wait, don't go in alone." Eon stood on wobbly legs, feeling more Bambi than stalwart adventurer.

"You don't look good." Jewells grasped his shoulder to steady him. "You okay?"

"Just the run." He wiped sweat and grime from his face. "You look a little pale yourself."

"I didn't expect death on Entriss to look so real." She glanced at the bodies again before turning away.

"It was real for Nomar." He genuinely felt bad for the dead Gnomes. The Flendrit fireballs had hurt, but that was nothing compared to this. It should've frightened him. Maybe facing these Shades at level 1 was foolish, but his growing anger pushed aside fear and reason. "Let's go save the others."

She nodded, and they cautiously approached the Gnome starting town.

Eon had never been a fan of Gnomes, and not just because of the reputation grind. Most traditional MMOs had characters of different sizes to match the gamers' play style. Gnomes from Yu and Sprites from Rath were the smallest, making them perfect for thieving and usually played by the most obnoxious gamers. They would greet you with open arms and run off with your pants. (That had only happened once.) Apparently, the Shades didn't like having their pants stolen either.

They stopped at the edge of a deep gully to share a gasp. A dozen or more mushroom buildings circled a lily pad-covered pond. Despite the Gnomes' size, the buildings were large enough for players to enter. Each fibrous mushroom had pale-green stems that reached up to bright red caps just like the Gnomes' hats. Their homes were very much alive. Also, they were on fire.

The gully was like a charcoal grill, and they reared back as everything, and everyone, burned. Magical flames covered the mushroom buildings and coated the ground in swaths of black and purple. Twenty or more knee-high Gnomes ran around crying for help. They all wore tall red hats that flared like Roman candles. Health bars hovered over the burning Gnomes, slowly ticking down to their deaths.

"What do we do?" she asked.

"They're glowing blue." He rolled up his sleeves and straightened the fringe of his tunic.

"All of them?" She looked down in awe.

"I only need one to turn in the quest. Completing it should save the town."

"They may stop running around if we put out the fires."

"Those buckets near the pond aren't a coincidence." Eon shuffled down the hill. "I love an easy starting quest."

"Last one there is a Flendrit." She rushed past him.

They dipped buckets into the pool and approached the thickest mass of burning Gnomes.

"More Shades," the Gnomes shouted, scattering in all directions.

He chased after one and thrust the bucket forward. A splash of water struck her back with a hiss. It wasn't enough. The Gnome screamed and fell to the ground, engulfed by flames that drained her Health. As her screams faded, he looked away, only to see Jewells standing over another corpse.

"Get more water." He pointed at the pond. "I'll try catching one."

He reached for a Gnome, and then another. They were fast for being so small. He ran toward a mass of burning red hats and grabbed a male Gnome.

"Shades!" He squirmed free like a greased pig.

"Let me help you," Eon pleaded, standing to leap at another.

He ran and dove and got up only to eat dirt a dozen times. When he finally pounced on a Gnome, it took all his strength to hold on.

Jewells doused them, but the water wasn't enough. The tiny creature looked up at him with sad eyes as he burnt to a crisp.

"I hate this." Jewells sobbed, throwing her bucket to the ground. "They're all dying."

"This isn't working." He scrambled away from the smoldering corpse. The grotesque smell made him cough until he gagged. "What do we do? What am I missing?"

He looked around. There were more bodies than runners. They didn't have much time.

"Something obvious. Quests usually have easy solutions, like buckets for water to put out fires or special weapons for monsters." She shook her head. "You were right. It's like a new game."

"That's it, my weapon." Most games taught you how to play your character. Sometimes through tutorials but more often by example. Raising the Rune Staff of Ned the Insane, he cast *Shockwave.*

Eon shot six feet into the air and landed gently on one knee. A small blast of air blew out the flames on four nearby Gnomes.

"Oh wow." He stood, staring up at his staff in wonder. Runes on the staff glowed red and a tiny, gray ball of light hovered inside the spiral birdcage.

Jewells jumped away from a screaming Gnome as it burst into flames.

"Eon, we're out of time," she cried out, looking up from the blackened carcass.

"Brace yourself." Unable to hold back his grin, he mustered all his will and shouted, "*Shockwave!*"

The rush of air blew tears from his eyes as Eon flew twenty feet into the sky. With one knee raised, he reached up with the Ned's staff, gray light now shining from the orb. With a roar, he crashed to the ground, landing on one knee like a rockstar.

A blast of air shot out in all directions, blowing out every flame as Gnomes tumbled away from his point of impact. He made eye contact with Jewells and winked.

She burst out in laughter, deflating his rush of ego. Before he could say anything, her arms were around him and her lips against his. Her reward went on until tiny hands tugged at his sleeve.

"Just a sec," he said to the Gnome.

"That was the most amazing thing I've seen." She kissed him softly.

"You are, indeed, amazing." The tiny voice filled with pride. "I am Nomerman, Mayor of this town. You have my thanks."

Eon reluctantly withdrew from Jewells's embrace. He turned to the Gnome and took a step back. Burn scars covered half of Mayor Nomerman's face. His proud, red hat and fine blue tunic were riddled with singed holes. Nomerman grimaced a smile through his soot-tarnished beard. Eon shook his hand; the grip was firm and warm.

Eon and Jewells both looked around, reeling at the devastation. Smoke rose from the remaining mushroom homes, most missing roofs or walls. Many of the healthier Gnomes surrounded them while others wept over those lost. Their dark, beady eyes were desperate. They looked more like tiny refugees than a town of happy-go-lucky Gnomes. His throat caught, and Jewells grabbed his hand.

Nomerman was now the only Gnome glowing blue. The mayor nodded, and with a sigh, Eon turned in the quest.

"Who did this?" Eon asked.

"Grym from Misere sent six Shades and Flendrit to our village. They threatened to burn us if we didn't join them in the war for Entriss. We stood our ground and scared them away, but at great cost." Nomerman's voice was hoarse, and his tiny body shuddered as he looked over the devastation. "I fear they will return to finish the job."

"War for Entriss?" Eon looked over his shoulder at Jewells, who stared with wide eyes.

"The World Event," she whispered.

"What do you need?" Eon asked.

"We'll help you prepare for the next attack," Jewells said. "You don't have to rebuild Nomorgin alone."

"Our village will heal. You must seek out and stop those who have killed my people and burned our homes." Nomerman reached out with a golden quest ball. "Will you help our brave Thief Nomar stop these Shades from more killing?"

"Yes." Eon lowered his head solemnly, accepting the quest.

Throwing Shade. You have saved Nomorgin from the Flendrit and Burning Shades. With your new companion, locate those responsible and stop them from attacking other villages.

To his surprise, Nomar joined their group. It was a first. NPCs shouldn't be able to join groups, but there he was. The Gnome's Health and Mana appeared in the top left of his vision. The Gnome was level 17. Hadn't he been 16 when they met? Either way, his low level would hinder more than help.

"Really?" Jewells was trying to pry Nomar from her leg.

"Damn developers," he snorted, wrenching the Gnome off her.

"The pretty Elf goes unclaimed, so she is mine!" The Gnome's bushy eyebrows furrowed as he drew two daggers and let out a squeaky growl.

"Unclaimed?" He shook his head. "Hey, just respect the lady's space."

"Eon, look!" Jewells pointed her hammer over his shoulder.

Eon spun around in time to see the sky above Nomorgin crack open. The tear shook violently, blaring with golden light and a rough, low hum as if Entriss despised its existence. Six creatures painted in shadow floated through the opening and circled the village.

Nomerman turned to the crowd and shouted, "The Shades are back. Run for cover."

"These are more horrific than the last." Nomar stepped forward with daggers at the ready.

"On it." Eon raised his staff and cast the *Shockwave* spell.

Insane Ned's staff lifted him into the air, once again pausing at the apex. He remained there, hovering twenty feet over the ground, surrounded by Shades.

"What the hell? Is it glitching again? Are we fucking back in beta?" He shook the weapon. The Shades moved closer, and he smacked the staff. The technical tap didn't help. "Destroy you guys in a sec. Gotta figure this out."

"He has the Rune Staff," a Shade said. It sounded like a woman. "He is not worthy."

"We shall destroy him and take it." The second Shade had the voice of an old man.

The other Shades nodded. Eon didn't.

"It's not much, but it's mine." He swung wildly. "I'll fight each of you, one at a time or all at once."

"We must investigate. Bring his friends." She pointed at Jewells and Nomar. "We will learn the truth before destroying them."

"What's happening?" Jewells rose into the air.

"That's right, Shade." Nomar was crouched, ready to attack as he floated toward them. "Bring me closer so I can steal the lungs from your shadowy chests."

"Leave them alone," Eon shouted as they approached the glowing crack.

"Sleep now." The female wiped a hand down her face. "And if you are lucky, you will wake one last time."

Eon struggled and flailed as darkness crept closer until consuming him whole.

19

JET BASEBALL

"**B**ad dreams, Gidget?" Jack Cook rolled to one side and attempted to calm his whining corgi with an ear scratch. "Have you been licking my arm?"

His sopping forearm vibrated gently, paused, and vibrated again. Bold letters scrolled from his wrist to elbow, indicating it was an urgent cast from work. He sighed. The market was glutted with eccentric casting devices that would've been equally impressive. Samantha, his much younger third wife, had insisted that the nanobot inking would be hot. His ego had agreed. The old man would never admit how much he missed cellphones. They, at least, could be turned off.

"Just a minute," he whispered.

"Sir, the servers went down." The man's voice was tense. "They rebooted after an unknown patch."

"Relax, son. I'll take your cast in another room." Cook shifted to the edge of their bed. "Waking my wife would be worse than facing a million angry gamers."

"But, sir, Entriss went offline."

"Maybe the break will be healthy for the addicts and they'll go outside."

There was a pause. "Yessir."

"Tooearly," Samantha mumbled.

"Sorry, it's urgent."

"S'okay, babe." His pale-skinned cover model rolled out of bed. She slipped into a tank top that didn't fit, drew the blond mane of hair from her face, and finally patted her leg. "C'mon, smiley. Let's go outside so you can pee and eat bugs."

Gidget hopped off the bed.

"Thanks, uh, babe," he said, watching her saunter out of the room with the corgi in tow.

He sat up in bed and tugged at satin sheets until they covered his waist. When enough was hidden, he tapped his forearm.

The floating torso of a skinny, middle-aged man appeared in his ocular implants. Sweat beaded his pale face and he licked at dry lips. Cook recognized the panic of a sysadmin who'd run out of buttons to fix things.

A pretty woman with dark skin and bright red hair leaned over his shoulder. "Did you tell him?"

"He's moving to another room," the man said.

"Ooh, that's one swol white man." She fanned herself. "He's ripped."

"What are your names?" Cook held back a smile.

"Fred, and, uh, Marta." He nodded, and Marta jerked back out of view.

"Thank you. Glad to know I'm still swol." His answer was silly, but he hoped a little humor would ease their tension. It was tough getting answers from employees in a state of panic.

"You're welcome." Marta leaned into view again and winked.

"Now tell me," he said with a gentle smile. "Who broke my world?"

"We're still working on that." Fred sounded calmer, a few steps further from panic's edge. "New code made the servers reboot an hour ago, and now Yu is running hot enough to crash them. Our boss, Chen, said players may be logging in with immersion pods. We can't find the source. Our admin rights are limited."

"One minute." Cook pulled up their employee records. Aside from a few long breaks, not unexpected at that hour, they were surprising. Impressive enough to read through when his eyes weren't bleary with sleep. "Promoted. As senior sysadmins you get a raise, more vacation time, and the rights to dig deeper. Can you help an old man?"

"Thank you, sir. I promise, we'll dig deep."

"File your report and copy Lars. Ask him to set up a meeting with department heads at 9... Make that 10. This will be a surprise, and they'll need time to gather information."

"We'll take care of it."

After ending the cast, Cook sent another, inviting the board to the meeting. Samantha swayed into the room tailed by a sleepy pup. The corgi collapsed on the floor, stretching out in a full sploot.

"Everything okay, babe?" Samantha pulled at her tank top, freeing her oversized breasts in so much bouncing glory.

"Nothing unexpected. Gotta send one more message."

He typed, *Bridge incoming*, and clicked send as she snuggled in with everything soft, warm, and curvy.

"Anything fun?" Her tone was sultry.

"I can be fun." He kissed her neck.

She let out a warm, "Hmm."

Gidget moaned and left the room. Before diving in, he thought, just maybe, the tattoo wasn't so bad.

IN EIGHTH GRADE, Ian's second stepfather, Jeff, had signed him up for baseball camp. Jeff, who preferred his high school nickname Jet, explained, "It helped me become the man I am today. A strong, popular, determined, abusive, unemployed alcoholic." Or something like that. Ian hadn't blamed baseball for Jet's many faults and reluctantly agreed to try.

He spent his first day, "Working off some of that fat ass," thanks to the drill sergeant assistant coach. Ian ran until he fell, swung at balls until he collapsed, and dodged mocking teammates so they wouldn't see him cry.

Practice ended with a line drive to his shin that struck with a resounding crack loud enough to make everyone wince. He stayed at home on day two, comatose on the ratty family room couch with cramped muscles, a throbbing shin, and an angry Jet. After being dropped off for day three, he limped to nearby computer camp where he excelled—because that was where he belonged.

Pain woke him from those memory-haunted dreams. It felt like day two of baseball camp all over again. His muscles were knots strung together by tight tendons ready to snap. Stretching, yawning, or even opening his eyes might hurt, so he remained very still.

"The sleeper awakens." Jewells was so close he could feel her breath.

He opened his eyes and blinked until she came into focus. They were inches apart, once again, and he smiled. "Am I dead?"

"I swear if you tell me this is how you imagined heaven, I'm going to puke." She peered at him, but her eyes didn't seem upset.

"Well, I'm not going to say that...now. But our maître d' deserves a tip. Best table in the restaurant."

"Ha." She let out a stilted laugh. "Only if we're the dinner."

Glowing blue wraps cocooned their bodies and bound them face-to-face. It was a forced closeness that she didn't seem to mind, and neither did he. They were upright and probably hovering over the ground because video games. The magical bindings worked like a body cast that kept him from moving sore muscles. He couldn't see much beyond her face, which was great. She smiled and let out a sigh, her nose booping his. This wasn't so bad. She was wrong about his one-liner.

Is there a bondage room in heaven?

"What is jet baseball?"

"Huh?"

"You talk in your sleep."

"Oh." He shook his head. "Just a weird dream about growing up."

"Definitely weird. I had a dream about my brother and dad arguing. It woke me up a while ago."

"Figure anything out while I was sleeping?" He wiggled against the restraints.

"You snore," she said with a raised eyebrow.

"I, uh, I'm sure it's the game."

"Right. So, why do you look worried? I thought you'd enjoy being tied up like this."

"I'm not-*not* enjoying this." He was worse at flirting than he was at baseball. "If there was anyone I'd want to tie up, er, be tied up with..."

Her laughter eased one of his concerns. So far, this comedy of errors had squashed his master plan to roll through the quest and impress Jewells all the way to girlfriendom. This gimp character made him feel useless. He wanted to run away, log out, and forget the game forever. Rather than calling him fat and stupid, though, she merely laughed at their situation. It was the acceptance he needed to set insecurities aside and focus on bigger issues.

"You worried about my safety, hero?" She puffed at a lock of auburn hair over her eye.

"Actually, yes. The game has rendered us unconscious twice."

She shrugged. "Which makes it realistic."

"Okay, what about being stuck in that dark place where we couldn't log out?"

"Unexpected." She frowned, her voice becoming more tense. "But Bala said Deity is struggling with the code."

"You don't find it odd that we both had a dream from our childhood?"

"Yeah," she said, reluctantly. "It's a pretty big coincidence."

"It gets bigger. I spoke with Deity in that dark place. She knows who we are on Earth and referred to something personal."

"What? That shouldn't be possible."

"I don't trust the AI. If she has that much access to our brains, she might be able to kill us."

"Even if you're right, there must be rules in place to protect us."

"She mentioned Asimov's laws." He nodded, trying not to head-butt her.

"The three laws of robotics?" The tension around her eyes relaxed. "Then we should be fine."

"I'm worried that the code triggered Asimov's zeroth law. Deity may let someone die to protect humanity. Frightening if her definition includes every NPC on Entriss."

"If you truly believe that, we should quit now. No game is worth dying for."

"Log out and talk to Cook or see if you can get hold of someone from Everyworld. They created the Watson Engine and should know everything that's happened."

"What about you?"

"I'm staying. I'll see it through."

"Why?" Her voice got louder.

"Jet baseball."

"Pardon?"

Her piercing eyes were dangerous enough to cut through him, so he shared the highlights of the dream in all its embarrassing glory.

"Ian," she said in a soft voice.

"It's a boring story, but now I follow my gut. It led me to computer camp where I started on the path to become a developer. Now, it's telling me to finish this quest." He took in a proud breath. "I can do this, and I've got nothing to lose."

"What?" she shouted. "You call me nothing?"

"I didn't mean, well, I..."

Unlike Eon, Jewells didn't hesitate. She pressed her lips to his. They were soft and moist and melted his reason.

"What are you going to do, now that you have something to lose?" She waited for a moment before continuing. "I don't think Deity's a danger. I think we're just overwhelmed by this new world. But it's your decision. Either we both log out and go find a secluded beach to hide on, or we both stay and make history. What do you want, Eon?"

The kiss had stopped his heart; her commitment made it race.

When he was sure it wouldn't explode, he said, "I'm not going to quit."

"Then neither am I."

"I'll never quit," squeaked a tiny voice behind Jewells.

"Was that the Gnome?" Eon sighed. He really didn't want company on this quest.

"He's tied to my butt," she said with the deepest of sighs.

"This whole time?" Eon coughed to cover a laugh. "That's just wrong."

"You're telling me. She farts a lot. It smells like dead cow back here."

There was no holding his laughter back. The blush on her pale cheeks was adorable. It felt like a win. She was always so quick to push his buttons that he never had a chance.

"My stomach gets upset when I'm nervous." She looked away.

He wanted to tease, but she was embarrassed enough.

"Who cares?" Eon wiggled to get her attention. "I snore, you toot...welcome to the human condition."

"Really?" She looked into his eyes.

"If it were me," he whispered, "I'd fart until the Gnome passed out."

"I heard that," Nomar shouted.

"Hey," she snapped. "No biting."

"Personal space, Gnome." Eon tried looking around her, but the bonds were too tight.

"Eon, just promise me, no dying." Her eyes pleaded more than her tone. "Not for a stupid game."

The loud creak of a door interrupted Eon's next clever comment. A deep voice reverberated throughout the room. "You don't wish to die. How unfortunate."

20

THROWING SHADE

"This is not what I meant when I said bind them all in the antechamber," a woman shouted.

"Sorry," another woman said.

Eon's bondage fantasy abruptly ended as they floated apart. Glowing blue shackles around his wrists, waist, and ankles drew him to a nearby stone wall with Jewells and Nomar anchored beside him. At least this less-fun binding gave him a clear view of the room.

The Romanesque antechamber was twenty feet around with high, vaulted ceilings and a single, wide door. This was a forgotten room coated with a thick layer of dust and cobweb-painted walls. Five Wizards faced them in heavy robes, each wielding swords or staves.

A sturdy, gray-haired Elven woman with dark skin and an ageless face stood in the center. She wore rich white robes hemmed in platinum that seemed to flow with a breeze that wasn't there. A Human man and woman stood to her left, both clad in thick red velvet that weighed heavily on their old frames. The two portly blue-robed Gnomes on her right looked like beach balls. He wanted to kick them.

"Why did you attack Nomorgin?" Nomar asked, struggling against the blue restraints. "Let me free and I will seek revenge for those lost to your evil transgressions."

"We did not kill your people, child of Gnomes." The Elf held her hands together and bowed her head. "I am sorry for your loss."

"I didn't recognize you at first. Everything looks so different." Eon stared in awe. "You're the Wizard Council of Yu."

"I am Sywan," she said with a nod. "Along with my remaining council, we went to Nomorgin disguised as Shades. We'd hoped to stop the true Shade, who'd already destroyed so much with dark fire. Instead, we found you three."

"Yeah, about that." Eon raised a finger. "Why are we being held against our will?"

"We need the Rune Staff of Ned the Insane to free our king."

Eon's sudden burst of laughter made the entire council take a step back. "This piece of shit staff couldn't free you from a burlap sack."

The Wizards gasped like he'd stabbed a baby dolphin. They looked at Sywan with wide, disbelieving eyes. She winced and shook her head.

"This powerful weapon is not for you," she snapped. "We spent ten hours trying to take it while you slept under Nombass's spell."

"Ten hours?" Jewells looked at Eon with wide eyes. "I am so late for work.

"You won't have to worry about work if I make you sleep forever," the male Gnome said, his voice deep and ominous.

Eon and Jewells both laughed at the absurdity of a tiny round Gnome with a deep, booming voice named Nombass. The Gnome's shouts to "Stop it" only made them laugh harder.

"That's enough." Sywan raised a glowing blue hand. It hissed as a steamy white ball appeared in her palm. "Hand over the staff or we shall remove it from your corpse."

The powerful spell turned the room into a freezer. Their breath became frosty, and Jewells began to shiver.

"No." Eon peered at her. "The shitty staff is mine."

"Fine." Sywan slowly raised the ball.

"Fools," Jewells shouted. "This is no way to treat The Left Hand of God!"

The white orb fell from Sywan's hand, shattering on the stone and covering the floor with ice. The Wizards raised their feet one by one as they stepped away, muttering in frustration.

"Silence." The Elven woman pointed at him. "He is not worthy... not experienced enough to be the Left Hand of God. We shall end you all and take the staff to save our king."

"Wait," Eon said, frantically. "Let my girlfriend and Nomar go."

Jewells's head whipped over. "I'm not your girlfriend."

"And I'm not your Nomar."

They all looked at Nomar. He smiled briefly before struggling against the restraints.

"A heroic offer." Sywan sighed and paused. "Are you worthy, young Elf?"

"Probably not, but if Zalmon says I'm worthy...if Deity says I'm worthy, I'm damn well going to try."

The Wizard Council of Yu lowered their heads at the mention of Deity. The Human female snapped her fingers, releasing their binds.

Eon dropped to the floor and rubbed his wrists. "Now that that nonsense is over, tell us what happened to your king."

The room faded away, and he was soon floating beside Jewells and, to his surprise, Nomar.

"What magic is this?" The Gnome's eyes went wide and he grasped Jewells's hand.

"It's okay." She tried pulling her hand free, and eventually gave up. "Looks like we're getting a cut scene."

"I'm not familiar with that spell."

"It's like watching a play, but the actors won't be able to see or hear us." Eon patted Nomar's shoulder. "Just keep quiet and pay attention."

They were soon hovering over the Yu throne room. It was a vast hallway decorated with war and greed. Green velvet banners with a green fox emblem hung over racks of weapons along the walls. Beams of light from cathedral-style windows faintly reflected off the polished onyx floor. Gray marble columns about the room reached high to a foreboding darkness that looked more like a hungry mouth than a ceiling.

A monstrous throne of golden skeletons surrounded by piles of platinum and gems sat at the far end. Half-Troll Barbarian King Nihle lounged in the chair with a goblet of wine close to his lips. He wore a black, ostrich-feathered loincloth and a leather harness that struggled to contain his tanned, bulging chest. A wild mane of red hair framed his jutting forehead and covetous eyes.

Nine Wizards of the council hovered around the room like angry bees with glowing weapons. All of them glared at the three shadow-cloaked figures floating down from the dark ceiling.

"You are a mere breath from destruction, Grym of Misere." Nihle sat up, his low voice echoing throughout the hall. "Tell me why you curse the Halls of Yu with your presence."

"We come with an offer," a Grym said. Every word echoed in whispers that rose higher as if absorbed by the hungry ceiling. "Your Centaur brother Denpar rallies his troops to march on Yu."

"That fool would meet his end," Nihle growled. "Yu is wealthy and powerful beyond measure."

"And yet Rath has an army that is clever and vicious. You know they could win." The Grym floated closer. "As we speak, a swarm of monsters prepare for battle on the borders of Yu and Rath."

"Sounds like fun." Nihle clapped his large hands together. "Is that all?"

"Yu cannot defeat both armies. We would offer a truce, and help defeat your brother, in exchange for a trinket."

"What is this trinket you speak of?" The king leaned forward, rubbing his three-fingered hands together. "Show me."

The Grym reached out, pointing a long, skeletal finger at a wooden chest against the wall. It was unremarkable in this hall of opulence, and long ago forgotten to dust and cobwebs.

Nihle's gaze fell on the treasure. He frowned in concentration until a memory broke free. "Ahh, my father's parting gift. It is still sealed shut by his magic."

The Grym snapped its fingers, and the chest creaked open. Two large, pale orbs rested inside.

"No," Eon gasped.

"What are they?" Jewells tried leaning forward for a better view.

"The eyes of Zalmon," Nomar whispered, bowing his head.

Nihle stood, staring at the eyes, his powerful muscles rippling. "How can this be? I have searched for so long."

"For the safety of Yu, will you make trade with the Grym?"

"I will not! The eyes belong to Nihle." His eyes were ravenous, and he launched forward, diving at the chest with grasping hands.

The scene faded, and they were once again in the dusty antechamber. Nomar collapsed to the ground and held himself. Jewells rushed over and knelt beside him.

"I'm missing something." She looked up at Eon.

"Someone murdered King Zalmon. No one knows how. His body was mostly intact, except for his eyes and heart."

"Missing for so long." Nomar shuddered. "Rumors and whispers say that they are the two most powerful weapons on Entriss."

Eon looked at Sywan. "What happened next?"

"Lord Nihle became overwhelmed with greed. The council tried to protect him at great cost." Sywan's voice caught, and she took a moment to clear her throat. "The Grym cannot just take the Eyes of Zalmon. It is a gift that must be earned. The beasts are slowly killing him, and Yu will be helpless without his leadership. Without Nihle's protection, those monsters have already begun wreaking destruction and death on our lands. Only The Left Hand of God can save Yu."

A gentle blue glow surrounded the Wizard, and Eon turned in the quest Throwing Shade. The familiar ding of a level gain rang in his ears as bold letters appeared before him.

Congratulations! Rune Staff of Ned the Insane has earned a new spell.

"Meh," Eon muttered. He should've leveled, not his stupid weapon.

Summon Familiar: A worthy companion to fight by your side or something too powerful that will eat you alive! One-time spell. No restrictions. Permanent.

He read the new spell aloud.

"Oh my," Sywan said.

The old male Wizard *tsk*ed. "It even sounds like the nonsense Ned would write."

"Familiar?" Nomar scratched under his red cap.

"I guess I get a pet." Eon shrugged.

"What about a puppy?" Jewells asked. "They're so cute."

"I do love dogs," Eon said with a nod.

"Fool," Sywan snapped. "This is no mere pet. You can summon anything. Choose well and you shall have a fierce creature that battles for your cause. But if you choose something uncontrollable, it could be the death of us all."

"Fine." Jewells rolled her eyes. "A fire-breathing puppy."

"A bunny," Nomar said. "I love bunnies."

"A unicorn," one of the Wizards said.

"A phoenix," said the other.

"What about a Human?"

"Don't be daft! They're useless."

"Call forth a Chupacabra!"

"I would choose a dragon."

"I would watch it eat you."

"Whatever you do, don't kill us all!"

"Maybe a fire-breathing bunny."

The suggestions went on and on until Eon shouted, "Shut up!"

Everyone quieted as he stared at distant cobwebs and fit pieces together. He would feel safer with something large that could shield them from danger. The creature had to be powerful enough to fight and unique enough to make other players swoon with jealousy.

After several minutes of flipping through his internal Monster Manual, it struck him. A griffin, but not just any griffin. He imagined a powerful lion with vast wings and the head of an eagle. It would be large enough to ride with great horns for goring enemies. And, for the hell of it, the beast could breathe fire. That would be his badass familiar, and Entriss would know their wrath!

With this image clear in his mind, Eon raised Ned's shitty staff and began casting the spell.

"Did you choose a bunny?" Nomar asked.

"Dammit," Eon shouted, lowering the weapon. "Now I've got to start over."

"The choice is made," Sywan said in a solemn tone.

"Whoa!" Eon raised his hand. "Nobody 'choosed' anything!"

"But you did."

"What is it?" Jewells asked.

"I couldn't help it." His voice became quiet. "It just popped in there."

"What?" Sywan asked. "What just popped in there?"

"Look." Nomar pointed at the door. He began hopping up and down.

"No, it can't be." Eon covered his mouth with a hand.

"What is it?" Sywan asked.

All heads turned to watch a ten-pound rabbit hop to Eon. It had the golden hair of a lion and the antlers of a twelve-point buck.

"Is that a jackalope?" Jewells burst out in laughter.

"I was summoning a griffin until *someone* interrupted me." Eon glared at the Gnome.

"Bunny," Nomar shouted, clapping excitedly.

A deep sigh from everyone in the room sounded like a balloon deflating as the bunny hopped to Eon. The jackalope nuzzled Eon's linen pants until its horns got caught. It pulled away, leaving a small hole.

"We are doomed." Sywan held out her hand. A golden quest orb rested in her palm. "I have little hope, but you are welcome to try."

Eon grasped the orb and received a new quest.

It's all Yu. Save King Nihle from the Grym before he dies.

"Your, um, familiar will lead you to the next challenge." Sywan looked at the creature like it was already roadkill. "You must face this one alone."

A clock appeared, hovering overhead. It began counting down.

"Shit," he said.

"What now?" Jewells asked. "It can't be worse than your dangerous bunny."

"It's a timed quest." His heart was already racing.

"Correct," Sywan said. "Complete the task in five minutes or we lose Entriss forever."

21

IT'S ALL YU

"Get back here, you little shit," Eon shouted between huffs.

The thirty-second chase was torturing his already sore muscles to the point of cramps. It didn't matter what he said, though, the jackalope ignored the command like all the others. It blurred down another hallway and stopped for Eon to catch up. When he closed in, it dashed away, leaving him no time to breathe.

He'd wanted a powerful familiar that would lead him into battle, not lead him to quests. Thanks to Nomar, he'd ended up with a cute bunny that ran fast, wouldn't follow commands, and enjoyed mocking him.

He turned a corner to find it was gone. "I hate this part."

In a flash of pink light, the jackalope appeared at the top of a stairway. It chittered before taking off again.

"Did you just laugh at me?" He took a gulp of air and rushed up a flight of stairs, muttering to himself. "I love animals, I love animals." He loved to eat animals. Rabbit stew sounded better than this insane chase. Maybe he could cook it in a pot with Nomar and be rid of them both.

He cursed his way to the throne room entrance with 3:50

remaining on his timer. That gave him two minutes to catch his breath, one hour to nap, and the rest of the day to log out and pack for that job at Everyworld.

The jackalope chittered again, this time sounding annoyed. Eon shook off better daydreams and glanced into the room.

His favorite part of any quest was solving the puzzle. When he succeeded (which he always did), the game rewarded him with some new treasure. It hadn't been so bad being Pavlov's dog. That was before the pods, before the threat of world-ending doom, and before everything became too real. Now, his mind was a frantic mess as Pavlov yelled at him and the dog ate his homework.

Three blurry Grym hovered in the air, their bodies wrapped in greasy black shadows. Darkness gathered at the base of their tattered cloaks, dripping like thick oil that landed on the ground with a hiss.

These weren't just generic monsters; they were named. Red smoke drifted from the dark face of Frenjin. Pruine spewed white frost, while Mortiss was cloaked in a starry night sky.

The enormous half-Troll king lay writhing on the floor. A spell bound him in black-thorned vines coated in Grym magic. The Barbarian's skin was a mottled gray, as if the spell had sucked out all color. A flashing red bar over his head showed the king had lost 60% of his Health. Nihle was dying.

Pain wasn't enough for the Grym. They'd left one arm free, and Nihle reached in desperation for two softball-sized orbs. The milky white balls were an inch from his fingertips. He reached forward, screaming as the thorns sank into his skin. His finger brushed one and the orb spun wildly. It suddenly stopped to look at Eon.

"The Eyes of Zalmon," Eon said to the jackalope.

The Troll went limp as vines sucked away more of his Health. A cackling hiss of laughter filled the room as the eye returned its focus to Nihle.

Eon had an idea. "He was right to go after them. Those eyes have to be insanely powerful magic items." Eon knelt beside his familiar. "Can you distract the Grym so I can take the eyes?"

He ignored the angry chittering response as longing overtook him. The answer to this quest was obvious. Entriss had always been about acquiring items to win, and those eyes would give him the power he needed to complete The Left Hand of God regardless of his level.

"Stop complaining and do it," Eon snapped.

In a gentle pink flash, the jackalope disappeared, arriving at the far end of the throne room. They attacked it with a barrage of spells, and the jackalope disappeared. His familiar teleported around the chamber while Eon raced to the orbs.

Despite the distraction, he could feel the cold gaze of the Grym. There was no time to fall back so he leapt forward, reaching for Zalmon's eyes.

HE WOKE to Jewells hovering over him, a curious frown on her beautiful face. "Looking pretty rough, Eon. Did you fight them with your bare hands?"

"Feels like it." He shuddered. "Why didn't I come back to life with full health?"

"You will lose a third of your health each time you fail," Sywan said.

"I only get three tries and they're all timed?" he asked. "What a crappy quest."

The cooling touch of Jewells's healing spell washed away his pain if not his frustration. They'd destroyed him mid-leap with an attack so cold the memory made him shiver.

"What happened?" she asked.

"The Grym bound Nihle in a spell that's killing him, but he's still trying to reach Zalmon's eyes." Eon stared off, trying to focus on the puzzle. "The eyes must be powerful enough to destroy them. I sent my familiar in as a distraction, but they still killed me."

"Okay." Jewells helped him stand. "What next?"

"Same thing, but this time I'll cast *Shockwave*. Hopefully it'll knock the Grym back so I can reach the eyes. If I'm right, that trinket is powerful enough to give me an edge in this quest."

"You sound like our king." Sywan raised an eyebrow high enough to judge the world. "Don't let greed consume you."

The jackalope appeared at his feet, and the timer returned to his view. He now only had three minutes.

"What the hell? I'm not ready," he shouted at the familiar as it ported to the door. He rushed after it. "Please stop, I need to think."

"Maybe she'll listen if you name her," Nomar squeaked.

"What do you mean her?" he asked over his shoulder. "She...it's a spell."

"No, it's a girl bunny. And she's so cute."

Thirty seconds of pleading up stairs, shouting down hallways, and cursing under his breath wouldn't slow the jackalope. It was infuriating.

The game no longer made any sense. Before he'd checked in the code, NPCs would practically walk him through quests. Now they were so full of personality that Sywan judged his greed while Nomar was giddy over naming the "cute bunny." The old rules were as useless as Insane Ned's Staff, which meant he had to adapt.

"I name my familiar Lola."

Your familiar has been named Lola.

This time there was no chitter of annoyance as Lola stopped and turned back to look at him. It gave him just enough time to leap forward and wrap his arms around her.

"Gotcha," he said.

Pink light blinded his vision as Lola teleported them to the throne room entrance.

"Cool." He grinned at the jackalope. "Let's try this again."

H<small>E STRUGGLED TO WAKE</small>, as if in the throes of a fever dream. Chills and aches wracked his body like the worst sort of flu. Jewells was shaking him and shouting his name. Her healing spell flowed through him again and again, at constant war with the Grym's lingering attack.

"What's happening?" she cried out.

"They are too powerful for someone so inexperienced," Sywan said. "If Eon fails a third time, the Grym will destroy him along with Nihle."

"Fine." Jewells stared at the old Wizard. "We drop the quest and try again."

"That is not possible, child." Sywan shook her head. "He will not be able to start over. Either he completes the quest or he dies and Entriss will be lost forever."

"What do you mean, die?" Jewells asked.

"A death so final will end life in all worlds." Sywan lowered her head.

"This is stupid." She stomped a foot. "We need to log out now, Eon."

"No," he wheezed, looking up at her.

"But Sywan said you'll die," she screamed, her hands shaking.

"I agree with the pretty lady." Nomar placed a hand on his calf.

"No." Eon stood on shaky legs.

"You're being stupid." She struck his chest. "You just think you've got nothing to lose."

"I wouldn't do this if I wasn't sure." He grabbed her hand and looked into her eyes. "Because now I know I'd lose everything."

"Really?" She pulled back, licking her lips.

Before he could lean forward to kiss them, the timer returned, as did Lola.

"Be right back." Eon reached down, placed a hand on the jackalope's horn and said, "Go."

In a blink, they were back at the entrance. A shrill cry from the Grym echoed triumphantly. Nihle was a breath away from dying and no longer reached for Zalmon's eyes. Eon had forty seconds remaining.

"No distractions this time, Lola." He scratched her ears. "Just hang back and wish me luck."

Eon cast *Shockwave* and launched into the air. An array of spells shot from the Grym's mouths, following his descent as Insane Ned's Staff brought him down on the eyes.

22

EON'S WARS

"Time's up," Sywan said. "This is the end."

The first explosion made Jewells's heart skip. The second was deafening, followed closely by a jarring quake. She dropped to a knee beside Nomar and cast her shield spell. Cracks spiderwebbed across the floor and crawled up stone walls.

The tremors became more violent. It felt like the Grym were tearing Entriss in half. Her spell wouldn't last long. They needed a way out, but she couldn't see through the chaos. Bits of ceiling pelted the ground followed by a large chunk that shattered against her shield. There was a loud crunch behind them followed by a pained cry.

The shaking stopped, and the room became silent. Dust clouded the air, making Jewells and Nomar cough. The Gnome held her hand tightly as they stood.

He looked at their hands then made eye contact. "If you're okay, milady."

She merely nodded, and he let go.

"Brother," the Human woman cried. She reached out with a glowing hand. A large piece of ceiling rose from the ground and flew to one side. The mangled body of the Human male Wizard lay still on the ground. "Heal him, Priest!"

Jewells tried and tried again. When her healing spells failed, she cast resurrection. Moments passed, and she finally shook her head. The woman dropped to her knees and wept beside her sibling.

"What's happening to this game?" Jewells coughed around a mouthful of dust. "That wasn't fun. That was insanity."

"This is no game, child," Sywan said in a pained voice. "Death is real for all. I fear your friend has lost, and so have we."

The group stats showed her and Nomar's Health was down 20%. Eon's was empty and flashing red.

"Why did you let him go alone?" Jewells grabbed Sywan's robes, tears welling in her eyes. He couldn't be dead. The game wouldn't let that happen. "You should've let me help him."

"I think he's still with us, barely," Nomar said. "Look again."

She wiped her eyes until the group stats were clear. If a player died, their rectangle would flash red, their bars would be empty, and a skull would replace the class icon. Despite his empty bars and flashing red box, the icon of Eon's Rune Mage symbol remained intact.

"That's not possible." Sywan's eyes went wide. "No one could've survived that."

"That's my Eon, you useless twit," Jewells spat. She turned on a heel and stormed out the room.

"Yeah, twit," Nomar said in a determined squeak.

The glorious and glamorous castle of Yu looked like someone had folded it in half. Beams of light shone through collapsed ceilings. The stairways were now rocky hills. Torn green banners, dented golden armor, and bent weapons littered the hallways.

Jewells rushed past all of it, her mind a storm of anger and worry. Hadn't she made her interest clear? Had it meant so little to him he'd throw it away for this dumb game? He was so intelligent, so driven, so stubborn, and so much like her father she should log out now and never come back. She'd promised herself, *promised herself*, not to be drawn to him. Caring was a weakness, and this anguish was the result.

She stopped before the entrance, took a deep breath to gather herself, and let her mind go cool as arctic waters. Nomar looked at her with a furrowed brow. She nodded, and they entered together.

Nihle sat in a wrecked throne at the far end of the room. The king laughed raucously as he raised a goblet, toasting her approach. He held Eon with his other arm, holding him close like a found teddy bear.

"Come, lass." Nihle waved her forward with his drink, the contents sloshing over the edges. "Come and drink to the Champion of Yu."

The *champion* looked like the game had dropped him from a fifty-foot cliff into a stampede of wild boar. His wide eyes blinked through a coating of ash and burns as his head lolled deliriously. The rest of his body remained still.

"Eon?" she whispered, trying to keep the quiver out of her voice.

He tried to speak several times before letting out a barely audible, "Ouch."

She took in a deep breath and began casting. Despite Eon being only level 1, healing him took effort. It felt more like she was pushing him through grueling surgery and weeks of physical therapy. After long moments, his head stopped bouncing around like a broken bobblehead and focus returned to his eyes. He smiled and stood on shaky legs.

"See?" He took several steps, listing like a drunkard. "I did it."

She approached calmly and stood before him. He reached out for a hug and she swung with all her might. The blow knocked him back into Nihle's arm.

"Ahh, young love." Nihle laughed heartily, pushing Eon up to face her.

"What did I do?" Eon rubbed his cheek.

She screamed until she couldn't and logged out of the game.

EON SHOOK his head and began to log out when Nihle rested a large hand on his shoulder. He wasn't strong enough to pull free.

"Love can wait," the king said. "Your tasks here have just begun."

Love might wait, but Julie wouldn't, and neither could Ian. He needed to apologize fast before this first date, or whatever it was, became a worse disaster.

"What now?" Every time he tried to log out, he heard the annoying *bzzt* of an error.

"This won't take long," Nihle said.

Eon spun to face Nihle, who now had a faint blue aura surrounding him. Maybe, if he hurried, he could still catch her. It would take time for Julie to change. Turning in the quest and accepting the reward should free him to log out before she left.

With a barely patient sigh, he reached out, and the tiny golden quest orb floated from his hand to Nihle's. System messages began flashing before his eyes. He was in a hurry to beg for forgiveness and dismissed each one as fast as the game allowed.

Congratulations, Rune Staff of Ned the Insane has a new spell!

He sighed.

Congratulations, you are now Level 11

Congratulations, you have unlocked a new ability: Language Master

Congratulations, Focus Tree Unlocked

Congratulations, you have earned the title 'Champion of Yu.' Do you accept?

"Sure, whatever." He dismissed the last message.

"As our Champion, I offer these gifts to you and your lady." Nihle handed over two bundles. He looked Eon up and down, flicking at his tunic. "Armor that befits a hero, and with less fringe."

"Thanks." Eon stashed them in his pouch.

"And for you, child of Gnomes." He handed a package to Nomar.

"I... I..." Nomar accepted the gift and dropped to his knees. "Thank you, my king."

"Can we get on with it?" Eon pleaded.

"Young love," Nihle said with a sigh. "You have accomplished great things, not only saving me but extinguishing the flames of Grym Frenjin. This is only the beginning." The king reached out with an open palm that held the golden orb of a new quest.

He should've been able to log out and accept the quest later, but for whatever stupid reason, the dumbest game ever still wouldn't let him. He grabbed it from Nihle's hand and accepted the quest, *The Hitchhiker's Guide.*

He closed the quest scroll as quickly as it opened and the room began to fade.

"You've got to be kidding me."

"Yay." Nomar hopped up and down. "A cut scene."

Everything went dark. The smell of burnt parchment stung his throat as a flaming scroll unfurled. He reared back from the heat of a raging fire that quickly smoldered. The singed scroll was a map of Entriss drawn in black soot rather than clean lines.

Maybe now that the cinematic had started, he could log out. There may still be time, but... There were a few buts. This cut scene was something no one had watched. Being first to finish, first to win, first to experience something was a cornerstone for all hardcore gamers.

Julie could be his first, couldn't she? Really, though, that was laughable. He was *The Simpson's* comic book guy, and she was out of his league. All his plans to impress her had collapsed to rubble. He didn't blame her for leaving, but she still deserved some apologies. Above all, he'd be lost without her friendship.

"Desperation and sorrow later," Nihle interrupted. "Pay attention. This won't take long."

"Sorry," Eon muttered.

"The dark forces of Misere have begun their attacks." Nihle pointed at the map. "You, Eon, have brought war to Entriss."

The map zoomed in on Yu. Tiny, animated chalk monsters attacked cities, slowly burning away portions of the parchment.

"Now that you have freed me from the Shades' bindings, I can gather my forces to fight, but I fear for my brother," Nihle said.

The view shifted to Rath, where even more monsters attacked.

"You must travel to Denpar's kingdom and deliver a message."

The map burned as it closed in on a tiny mountain pass. It was the path griefers traveled to sneak into Yu. The development team spent years trying to block that path. He hadn't understood what held them back, until now.

"Take great caution on your journey," Nihle said. "Not only will you face the monsters of Misere, but the warriors of Rath."

The king was right; this would be tough. He knew how to fight other monsters—there was a pattern to their attacks. Like any other puzzle, he'd figure them out. That was his strength. It was also the reason he avoided the player versus player realm of Rath. Gamers could do the unpredictable and pull rabbits out of hats. Deadly rabbits. So far, his rabbit hadn't been very deadly.

"You will find a sealed message in your bags. Cross the forbidden path and bring it to Denpar so he can prepare for the war Misere brings."

The map faded away, and Eon was in the throne room once again.

"Wow." Nomar clasped his hands together. "I'm ready."

"It'll have to wait." Part of him wanted to stay, but Julie could still be there.

"One last thing." King Nihle reached out with a clenched hand. He spoke in a low, quiet voice. "You have earned these by turning away from greed. Keep them safe."

The king opened his hand. Two eyes rested in his palm: the eyes of Zalmon. Eon licked his lips and accepted them as delicately as if they were melting snowflakes.

Eyes of Zalmon accepted—quest bound

This was it; this was what he needed. These eyes would give him the power to finish this quest. His hands shook as he inspected them.

The eyes were gray, which meant they were useless, and bound to the quest—whatever that meant.

"Thanks," he said, dryly.

Incoming cast from Jewells.

"Shit." He tucked away the eyes and opened the message.

"What new dangers befall us?" Nihle asked.

He read the message aloud: "I said you have something to live for, but you risked your life anyway. If you can't even log out to explain why, I see no reason to come back."

He read it again and covered his mouth. "She left. I didn't even have a chance to—"

"The price of being a hero." Nihle toasted him.

"Sucks!" Eon wrenched the goblet from the Barbarian's hand and drank it empty. The mead was sweet, and warmth spread throughout his body as if it could actually make him tipsy.

Servers will be offline in 5 minutes.

"Rest, young Champion," the king said. "You and your lady have much work to do upon your return."

"If she comes back," Eon muttered, reluctantly handing back the goblet.

Nihle winked and smiled knowingly. He went on to tell stories about Entriss and his father. They were lost to Eon's worry until he caught the end of Nihle's ramblings.

"I blame Ned for much, and that's why you need to be cautious. That staff is dangerous and has a dark side. Oh, and when in Rath, be wary of Denpar's children. They..."

His words faded away with the world around them.

23

PACKAGE DELIVERED

F red slurped up the last of his spaghetti with a pang of regret. The sauce wasn't the metallic-flavored tomato goop from jars he nuked at home. It was garlic rich with a spicy bite he couldn't place. Marta had obviously taken time with this dish. Ancient Italian gods must've gifted the recipe to her family. She seemed equally impressed with his peanut butter and caramel cheesecake, finishing every bite with a savory, "Mmm."

Old Blue Eyes himself accompanied their traditional Friday night feast. It was Fred's night for music, and they both chair-danced as Sinatra's "Fly Me to The Moon" blared in their earbuds. It was almost enough to hide the surrounding chaos.

A fist slammed down on the desk between them, making dishes and silverware hop. Fred tapped his wrist implant twice to stop the music and removed his earbuds. The alarms were louder than ever, and Marta immediately began rubbing her temples.

Michael Chen's dark glare seemed dangerous in the red flashing lights of the control room. He was a thin, stoic, five-foot-something man with hawkish dark eyes and hints of gray in his short black hair. Despite it being 3 a.m, he wore a crisp white shirt, gray slacks, and spit-polished black dress shoes. His mouth was moving, and angry noises came out that Fred couldn't understand over the alarms.

"What?" Marta shouted, tapping an ear.

Their boss walked to an empty station and beat the poor mechanical keyboard into submission. After several minutes, the seizure-inducing red lights and wailing sirens went silent. Fred took a moment to soak in the quiet.

"What were you saying, boss?" Marta asked.

The short man winced. Despite having worked together for years, he preferred Mr. Chen. Not Chen, not Michael, and definitely not Mikey. Mr. Chen didn't seem to enjoy being called boss, but never corrected them, making it the ideal title.

"What are you idiots doing?" He looked over their feast in disgust.

"Dinner, boss." Marta peered at him. "According to the Employee Handbook, we still get to eat, even in a crisis."

"Yes, yes, yes." Mr. Chen waved his hand in an arc as if to present the control room displays for the first time. "I want to know what you are doing about this."

Fred took a swig of soda. "We called as soon as the server farm came up in Kansas City."

"We don't have a server farm in Kansas," Mr. Chen shouted, his fists shaking.

"Looks like Missouri, boss." Marta pulled up a map of the Midwest. "That's why we called."

"Is it a virus?" He sat down and abused the keyboard a little more. "Did you try to stop it?"

"For about three seconds." Marta closed the map and opened her command history. "You can review the logs. We followed protocol. Deity is overseeing all of it, and she completely locked us out."

Chen spent long minutes typing, leaning in to peer at the monitor, and finally shaking his head. "Did you advise Mr. Cook?"

"I left him several casts, but no reply." Fred shrugged.

"I take it you couldn't stop this from home?" Marta asked.

"No. Remote access was unavailable, so I came in." Chen leaned back in his chair and rubbed his eyes. "It seems Deity has blocked my account from all administration functions."

"What do you think she's up to?" Fred asked.

"I was going to ask you that."

"We've been watching," Marta said. "Seconds after Yu went offline, a quantum hot spot server farm came up in KC. Deity spent thirty minutes replicating virtual servers and twenty minutes patching them. After adding a slew of databases to the cluster, she made so many network and firewall changes it was impossible to follow."

Chen scrolled through logs. "It will take weeks to understand all of this."

"Looks like Yu's coming back online." Fred pointed at several large displays coming to life.

Lines of white text scrolled across the large, center monitor. A storm of commands loaded drivers, confirmed files, and executed programs until all that remained was a blinking cursor. Fred held his breath. After an eternity or two, text appeared in a large, red font.

Yu is online. Virtual Immersion 2.0 now supported.

Fred and Marta gasped in awe as crisp images of Yu appeared in the monitors. The slightly cartoony graphics were gone. Everything in Yu looked alive, like video shot for a newscast. On the right side of the room, poor Rath still appeared to be stuck at 1.0.

"I didn't know Entriss could support full immersion." Marta continued staring at the images of Yu.

"This is bad, right?" Fred asked.

"Very bad." Chen rubbed the bridge of his nose. "Everyworld is the only game authorized to support 2nd generation VR. There will be consequences if word gets out to other nations."

"Is there anything we could've done?" Marta asked.

"No." He wiped sweat and stress from his face. "This is beyond protocol, beyond us. I'm unsure what to do next."

"Would you like some cheesecake?" Fred asked.

THE LIGHT, and music, and excitement of Entriss faded away, replaced by something bland...and gross? He lay chin deep in a glowing, oily substance that smelled like paste and old shoe. Before panic completely took hold, the liquid slurped down a drain and the pod door opened with a hiss.

He flopped out of the primordial ooze and crashed to the floor like an unexpected birth.

"Jewells...Julie," he called out, frantically wiping slime from his viscosity suit. "What the..."

An iridescent haze rose from him like steam and floated back to the pod. When the sucking stopped, he was completely dry.

"Did I just watch the nanobots change from liquid to gas?" He peered at the pod. "Or does Entriss make us piss magic when we're logged in? Not sure which is worse."

A loud rap at the door made him jump.

"Julie," he said.

The raw power of hope made him stand and limp his way out of the bridge. Everything hurt like yesterday's head-on collision. Only a sadist would've designed a game that worked him over in both worlds. Watson's Engine could go fuck itself.

"Come on in." He'd left a key in her room. Maybe she hadn't seen it, or worse, left it behind. That didn't matter as long as she came back.

The knocking became frantic, and Ian limped faster. He cracked his shin on an end table and hopped the last few feet.

He threw the door open and blurted, "I'm sorry."

"Should be," said the distracted pizza delivery guy keeping a watchful eye on his car.

Ian swallowed hard. His master plan had failed again. Logging out of the pods after a long gaming session triggered a script that ordered pizza. He'd expected Julie to hop in the shower and change while he prepared wine and dinner.

Pizza Guy slowly turned to face Ian. "I've been knocking for ten... Hoooly shit, dude."

The young man stepped back, looking Ian up and down like he'd discovered alien life. Before getting into the pods, Ian had worn a robe to hide what he could. The robe was still lying on the floor, right next to his humility. He must've looked like an overweight fetish model in the gray viscosity suit, and for the first time in his life, he just didn't care.

There was a world to save and a heart to win and both were far more important than judgmental gawking. Still, he needed to control the story. Pizza Guy might share what he saw with the wrong person, and there was too much at stake to risk that sort of leak.

"Nothing like a rave to wear you out, amiright?" He leaned against the door and yawned into his hand. "You wouldn't believe what goes on in this warehouse."

"No way." Pizza Guy snuck a look over Ian's shoulder. "You threw a rave?"

"It was magical." He beamed. "What's your name?"

"Uh, Pete, sir," he said.

"Well, uh-Pete, I need discretion. Can't have everyone showing up to the next gathering." Ian frowned. "How about I increase that tip, and next time you deliver pizza *during* the party?"

"Really?" he asked, licking his lips.

"You'll like the tip, and if you can wait a few weeks, you'll like the party better," he said. "Deal?"

"Yeah, thanks, man!" Pete handed over the pizza and left, practically skipping down the hall.

Ian waited until Pizza Pete was out of sight before saying, "Quite the ninja."

"Ninja as fuck," said a woman. "How do you always know?"

"I sensed a disturbance in The Force." He winked at the shadows. "Thanks for the help tonight, Marc."

Marcia slipped into view as if the dark night had sighed her into existence. She was an intimidating six-foot-something in black patent, heeled boots. Her charcoal pinstriped chauffeur's suit with an incredibly short skirt failed to hide her muscular physique. His friend looked like a weightlifter with augmented curves. An edgy mane of white hair framed her well-tanned face. They were close as family, and after all these years, he still didn't know the true color of her eyes. Today, they were green.

"You don't need to thank me."

She stepped into the close-talker space that made you wonder if the drunkard was moving in for a kiss. He knew better than to step back.

"Are you sure she's the one?" she asked.

"I hope so."

"If not, I'll take her. She's cute."

"I don't think Julie rolls that way," he said.

"The way she flirts? I think you'd be surprised." She laughed and took a step back. "Hands off, for now. Promise."

"You're too kind."

"She's smart, too." Marc tugged at a strand of hair. "Asked a lot of questions. I tried to be vague, but she figured out what I do for a living."

"Not a surprise. Just, please, stay available for the next few weeks. I've sent money—"

"Please stop. I don't want your money." Her stare was intense. Hell, everything about her was intense. "You're my only job until you say otherwise."

"Thanks." His shoulders dropped to a seven. "My date bailed. Join me for some romantic pizza leftovers?"

She laughed again, this time more genuine than intimidating. "Thanks, but she's waiting."

"Of course." He reached out. "Do you have it?"

"Yeah." She reluctantly handed over the memstick. "Are you sure it's the best time? You don't want to draw attention to yourself. Not now."

"It's always the right time," he said, firmly. "Do you disagree?"

"No judgment, Ian." She raised both hands. "I promise to keep looking for more."

He set the pizza boxes down to pull her into a hug that she genuinely met.

"Have you lost weight?" She pulled back, looking him up and down.

"Pretty sure that's not possible." He sighed, picking up his dinner. "Thanks, though."

She winked, kissed two fingers, and pressed them to his cheek. He nodded and watched her hips sway as she walked to her car. It was a lot of show, and he would've been a bad friend not to appreciate it.

He stared at the pizza boxes, overwhelmed by adventure and exhaustion. After casting Julie an apology and getting some sleep, he'd... He'd...

"Wait, am I level 11?"

24

THE MOLE

"I'd like to make it clear that this is not an inquisition." Jack Cook put on a cool-yet-sincere face as he looked over the room. He could've plucked the tension with a guitar pick. Nervous board members were ready to accuse as flustered department heads prepared their digital armaments. It was a war they didn't need, and he stared down anyone with an ounce of defiance. "The board needs a better understanding of what happened and the impact it may have moving forward."

"And how to stop it," Luanne said. "Will Mr. Hammers be joining us? This is a violation—"

"Ty doesn't have a seat on the board, nor is he a department head." Jack held up a hand. "If the U.S. Department of Virtual Operations were to threaten a shutdown, there's a real danger to both our stock value and the impact this situation could have on the player community."

"Player community?" she scoffed.

"They're the reason we're here. Their monthly subscriptions keep the lights on and their passion for the game keeps them coming back." He cleared his throat and spoke with pointed deliberation.

"For these reasons, nothing discussed here goes public. If you find yourself tempted to share, review your Non-Disclosure Agreement."

Luanne glared at him until he stood, removed his suit coat, and handed it to an assistant. Jack was a 6' 2" power lifter who'd competed in his youth. Samantha said he had the forearms of a Nebraska farm boy and rolling up the sleeves of his fitted shirt drove home the point. This was his show, and it was time they got to work.

The new CIO swallowed hard and stared at her tablet. He sat down and sought his Head of Infrastructure and Systems. Gretchen, typically cooler-than-ice, looked like she'd stuck a fork in an outlet. She wore a disheveled pantsuit and had lost the fight with her hair, which had escaped a tight bun hours ago. Her eyes darted about nervously, and she held a cup of coffee in both hands.

"Shame on you, Gretchen," he said, making her jump. "When did you buy a new server farm without telling me?"

She looked faint, only relaxing when everyone chuckled.

"What can you tell me about our new baby?" Jack clapped his hands together.

"She's big, and very healthy." Gretchen smiled, setting a cup down. "The server farm is larger than ours and filled with older model quantum hot spots. It's been sitting dormant since Entriss went live. Deity has provided us limited access, but we believe the servers are Russian."

"Is that a concern?" he asked.

She shook her head. "The AI will block any hackers. A team is in flight to Missouri now. Assuming they have access to the cave hosting those servers, they'll do a thorough review."

"Very good. Let me know." He turned to the Department Head of Artificial Intelligence. "John, how's Deity?"

"Busy." John was short and thin with dark skin and sharp eyes. He wore deep blue jeans, a loose-fitting pink polo, and large, thick glasses. Unlike most in the room, the man was excited. "Not only is she balancing different levels of immersion in the three zones, she's adapting the code that triggered this. The Watson Engine normally runs at 40% capacity. Since the reboot it's now spiking to 90% with minimal loss of game performance. She's distracted and our interactions have been slow, but I couldn't be prouder of—"

Jack held up a hand. "Is anyone in danger?"

"Danger, sir?"

"People are logging in with immersion pods. When word spreads, there will be more. Can Deity handle that, or are players at risk?"

"I'll ask her." John typed notes on his inked forearm.

"Jocelyn." Cook smiled at the bubbly lead of Marketing. "Please tell me some good news."

"Word is spreading that there's a World Event." The attractive brunette's wide, dark eyes were filled with excitement. "New subscriptions are up 30%."

"Excellent." He nodded to the board members. "We want to give everyone the impression this was all planned. Update the site and put someone on the message boards. Tell them to watch for anything unusual."

"We're shorthanded, but we'll try."

"That reminds me. Michelle, halt all firings," he said to the HR Director. "Fill in the blanks with rehires as needed."

"Gladly, sir." She flicked a damp red curl from her tired eyes and began typing on an invisible keyboard.

"Luanne, you fired the Head of Development, and our Analytics lead left, so the rest is on you." He turned to face her. "Who checked in the code? I'm surprised they haven't been fired, flayed, or arrested."

"We're still working on that," she said curtly, lifting her nose.

"I don't understand." He frowned and leaned in. "Whoever committed that code had to use their account. It should be a simple matter of reviewing the software repository logs."

"We... I..." She took a short breath and blurted, "There are indications that they used a stolen login."

"Disturbing. That would be the first major security breach in the history of our company." He sought the Head of Security. "Lars, where's Gomez?"

"Out with the flu. The rest of the team is reviewing scans of our new servers." The tall man shook his head and sighed. "Sir, this is the first I've heard of the incident."

"You didn't report this to security?" Jack asked Luanne.

All eyes fell on the woman, and board members began making notes. A trickle of sweat dripped down her lobster-red cheek, and she fidgeted as if he'd set her in a simmering pot.

"You're new here and may not be familiar with protocols. Gomez will review those with you when he's healthy."

She let out a barely audible, "Thank you."

"Lars, get the security team on this now. I need a full report before my three o'clock meeting with Hammers." He kept a cool gaze on the CIO. "We'll figure this out together. That's what we do at Entriss. Were you able to find out which developers were responsible for creating the code?"

"The repository may be corrupt. It was originally checked in under one name." She swallowed hard. "The Right Hand of God."

That woke the room up with an icy splash of water. Department heads met eyes as board members began asking questions.

"Funny," Jack said over the buzz. "King Zalmon of Entriss is The Right Hand of God. He was a terrible coder. We had to fire him for being a dead NPC."

A polite round of laughter brought order back to the room.

"Putting in another ticket with security." Lars' fingers danced in the air as he prepared his cast.

"I'm afraid to ask if you have anything else," Jack said.

Despite more laughter, Luanne crossed her arms and leaned back. "Bring in Julie."

The skinny young redhead entered the room with fists clenched at her side. The circles beneath her eyes were the shade of dark earned by too much developing, gaming, crying, or all three. She wore a gray pencil skirt and a white blouse with matching wrinkles.

"I'm not sure what's going on." Jack sat up, struggling to keep a calm voice. "But this meeting is for board members and department heads."

"Julie's been logged into the game with an immersion pod for the last two days," Luanne said. "I think the board will be interested to hear more."

Voices wrestled voices as everyone fought to be heard. Jack silenced them with an almighty, "Quiet." He let silence rule before turning to Michelle. "Any HR concerns?"

"Yes, quite a few." She turned to the young woman. "It comes down to choice, Julie. You don't have to answer questions, or even be here, if you're uncomfortable. You're also entitled to a lawyer if you feel—"

"I'm fine," she said, her eyes shooting death and daggers at Luanne.

"Good." Luanne clasped her hands together.

Jack could stop this, and probably should, but his CIO had miscalculated. Julie showed no fear of her or the board; she was a cornered animal ready to throw down. It may be a risk, but his gut told him to see it through.

"We don't track the devices a player uses to log in," Gretchen said. "This has to be conjecture."

"Yes, and no." Luanne's worry had been replaced with a sudden calm. "Julie, you called in sick, but you were logged into Entriss for forty-eight hours. Is this correct?"

"Yes. I play the game when I'm sick." She leaned forward, trying to stare down the CIO. "For some reason, gaming makes me feel better than being at work."

"Of course." Luanne's tone was sweet as poisoned honey. "You were in the Wood Elf zone?"

"I was. My main happens to be a Wood Elf."

"While you were there, the system deleted a newly created character named Mandorf. A player created and quickly deleted Gandorf. Then, you spent the rest of your in-game time grouped with a new Wood Elf player named Eon."

"Yes, I was grouped with a player named Eon."

"Before I fired him, Ian's character Mandorf mailed you a considerable sum of gold and other items. You logged in this morning and sent all of that to Eon, correct?"

"Why are you asking me if you know the answer?" Julie took a step forward.

"Do we need to take a break?" Michelle asked.

"I'm ready to break something," Julie muttered. "Let's keep going. What's your point?"

"The quantum servers peaked every time you and Eon entered a new area, including the undeveloped zone." Luanne typed a command into her tablet.

A holographic map of Yu appeared on the table. Numbers over each zone showed high server and network utilization. She waved a hand and their travels played out like time-lapsed weather radar. Zones went red and utilization spiked from Drulyff Forest all the way to Zalmon's tomb.

Luanne stabbed a meaty finger at Julie. "Whatever you and Eon did in that undeveloped zone not only triggered the World Event, it activated full immersion in Yu."

Julie crossed her arms, a wicked smile on her face. "Luanne, why would I help a guy you fired for sexually harassing me?"

"Well, uh." Luanne lowered her stabby finger.

"You didn't mention that in the release forms." Michelle began typing furiously. "We do not want a wrongful firing suit from Ian."

"You can stop searching, I never claimed harassment," Julie said. "It was harmless flirting that Luanne twisted into something ugly."

"If that's the case, maybe I was wrong to let him go." Luanne clucked her tongue. "And maybe you're both in collusion."

"My lawyer would tell me this is all conjecture," Julie replied. "It's pretty thin, Luanne."

"Fine." Her cold gaze fell on Gretchen. "Delete their accounts."

"No," Julie shouted.

"We already tried," Gretchen said. "We can't lock either of them out of the game. Something's protecting them."

"You tried deleting us?" She balled up her fist.

"Us." Luanne pressed two fingers against her chin. "So, it's us?"

"Dammit," Julie said through gritted teeth. "What do you want?"

"The location of Ian's home."

Julie looked at the floor, took a deep breath, and finally said, "I don't know. He has a driver take me and her car windows go dark when we're en route."

"Convenient." She shook her head. "What do you know about this woman? What company does she work for?"

"Her name is Marc, and she's an independent courier who protects the people she transports. I don't think you'll find her, and you probably shouldn't try."

The room filled with "What?" "You're kidding me," "Who is this guy?"

"He's the guy who stood up to Luanne for being a bully. He's the guy who's more passionate about the game than Cook," she shouted. "He's the guy you wrongfully fired for sexual harassment without a claim. Want more?"

It became the meeting Jack had wanted to avoid. There was more shouting and flailing and finger-pointing than a morning talk show. He stood and crossed his arms, staring at them like a classroom of rabid children. After he cleared his throat, twice, the room went quiet.

"Julie, I'm sorry you and Ian felt driven to do this. We will proceed with a full investigation into his firing." Cook nodded at Michelle. "I don't want either of you to end up in jail, but this goes beyond everyone in the room. The U.S. could face international backlash if this quest makes all of Entriss a 2nd generation IMMO." He held both hands apart as if beckoning her in for a hug. "If you can't help us find where he lives, we need you to be our spy and let us know what he's planning. Gather every bit of information on him that you can. We need to stop Ian before it's too late."

25

SLEEPLESS IN ATLANTA

Ian's brain fought the Sandman all night. Exhaustion pulled him in, and worry dragged him back out. He'd toss, sweating out muscle aches like a virus. He'd turn, only to face a waking torrent of could'ves and should'ves. By 5 a.m., the battle was over. Sleep had given up, but not without a cost that left him buzzy and constantly yawning.

He'd cast an apology message to Julie before bed and waited until 6 a.m. before following up with a request to talk. She hadn't replied to either. Her silence made less sense than her anger.

Thanks to the expensive pods and new quest, he'd earned, "the most incredible date ever," compliment. Despite being stuck at level 1, he'd successfully completed It's All Yu and saved Nihle. Sure, nothing had gone according to plan, but that made the win even more impressive.

She wasn't impressed. It wasn't like he'd expected her to rush into his arms, or drag him to the nearest bedchamber, or tear off her clothes and twerk around the throne room. A little swooning would've been nice, maybe a kiss on the cheek or even a high five. Instead, she'd rewarded his heroics with a punch hard enough to make him wary of date two.

By 10 a.m. he'd paced his way through six cups of coffee, two Dr Peppers, and the pizza leftovers. One buzz replaced another as caffeine mollified exhaustion and plucked at the cobwebs in his brain. He felt uncomfortable in his own skin but welcomed a clear mind that made it easier to remember the finer details and...

"Oh shit." He stopped and covered his mouth. "Did she actually think I was going to die?"

It had to be a misunderstanding. After sharing his concerns about Deity, Jewells had said the game wasn't worth dying for. The timed quest hadn't really worried him; they were supposed to sound dangerous. He'd played up the heroics of saving Nihle because he was into the moment. Gaming was all about the hero stuff; that was part of the fun.

He put all of this in a wordy message she probably wouldn't read. At this point, it was for his own peace of mind.

After a long shower, hot enough to soak sore muscles, he cast an order for Thai food. It arrived ten minutes later.

Julie still hadn't replied, and he needed a distraction. While eating lunch, Ian logged into the Entriss message boards from his watch and gestured at the living room monitor.

In an age of hyper-connected communication, message boards seemed laughably archaic—which was why Ian loved them. An MMO mainstay, message boards were a great way for players to share bugs with developers, whine about their class being underpowered, express their grievances, or grief other players.

A list of forum headers appeared on the big screen:

- *Entriss*
- *Rath*
- *Yu*
- *Professions*
- *Tribes*
- *Quests*

He selected Entriss, and the five most active topics appeared on top:

- *WTF is Reckoning*
- *Lag in Yu—resolved and closed*
- *Group for Misere invasions*
- *My cat watches me play*
- *We demand panacake buff*

Out of curiosity, he selected the panacake buff thread. The first message was from PanacakeMan: *The people of Entriss demand hearty and delicious panacakes that buff happiness and syrup that buffs well-being. You will not deny us our Panacakes! Panacakes for all! Panacakes for life! So says PanacakeMan.*

How could anyone argue with such misspelled determination? The Entriss community couldn't. Over 100,000 had replied with messages like, *Give me my panacakes, Need my sweet syrup buff, Bump for PanacakeMan,* and, *What is wrong with you nerds?*

"Nothing wrong here. It's all about fun," he muttered, returning to the main forum and selecting *Lag in Yu.*

These messages were less fun. Shortly after they'd logged in with the pods, players had started complaining about latency. Gamers blamed it on server slowness or network bandwidth. Customer Service never replied, but things got better after Eon had turned in the quest to Nihle and servers rebooted.

"Huh. I guess Deity must've fixed it."

The *WTF is Reckoning* board had over 10,000 posts. He started with page one:

GnarlyMan: First! Cheers to Entriss for surprise world event!

DangrGrrl: Great cloak off my first lvl 30 Flendrit kill.

Hinomdagah: Love the update, but my computer is running hot after the patch.

Develkin: Who released the NPCs? They aren't on a loop, and a Gnome just told me to fuck off. Love it. Ha Ha.

TheNail: Just reactivated my account, looking for group!

He skipped to the last page.

ShouldBeStudying: Did the game get harder or did I get old?

Missfit: Something's always on me, and that boss is impossible.

TryGuy: No more group size limits. Message me in-game and join TryGuy's Army!

Yolo: Has anyone seen Mandorf? He'd be owning this!

The replies to Yolo weren't only heartwarming, they were a call to action. He didn't want to do the quest without Julie, but he felt responsible for starting the World Event. The code he'd checked was bringing Entriss to life, and his quest affected everyone in that world.

Julie wasn't responding, and an entire world needed him. Heartache drove his determination. After a brief, squeaky struggle with his viscosity suit, he grabbed the remote and said, "Beam us up."

The bridge seemed empty without Julie. A sliver of hope inspired him to leave a note on her pod. Just in case. People lived on less than just in case, and so did he.

Ian crawled into his Audi capsule, looked around the empty room, and sighed. "Engage."

26

NOMINAL

The Entriss Online title appeared in a blaze of gold. He was able to dismiss the intro with a thought and took a satisfied breath. As much as he loved the cut scene, he didn't want to sit through it every time he logged in. Also, he was in a hurry. There was a world to save, the king had awarded him new gear, questing had unlocked a new spell for Ned's staff, and best of all, he'd leveled!

Entriss welcomed him with brisk air and the smell of wet earth after a fresh rain. He appeared at a waypoint just outside Nihle's castle. It stood on a steep hill, watching over the capital city of Averdac.

Threatening storm clouds painted the vast city in a palette of grays and browns. Averdac was filled with worn brick roads and tidy limestone buildings with clay tile roofs. Thin streams of fireplace smoke leaned with the gentle wind, rising until lost to the gray sky.

It would've been easy to continue gawking, but he had winning to do. A messenger hawk screeched, circling overhead until he reached out. Long talons gripped his forearm as it landed. Sparkles surrounded the gray-mottled bird, and he mentally accepted the delivery. The messenger transferred the package into his satchel, nodded once, and flew away.

A note was attached to the delivery. Reading it made his heart skip a beat.

Your stuff. – Jewells

The package was filled with all Mandorf's items, including his gold. His current satchel only had twenty slots, and if he opened the package here, its contents would spill onto the hillside for anyone to grab. He needed a bank to store it all and... Wait, if she'd returned everything, did that mean...

He brought the group into view and sighed in relief. Jewells hadn't left. Nomar was there too and probably on his way. The game alerted group members when a teammate logged in. If Eon were under attack, Nomar would've gotten a battle summons, enabling him to teleport to the fight. Fortunately, this was probably the safest spot on—

He cried out in pain. A stabbing jolt to his back knocked him down, and he scrambled away.

"Watch where ya loiter, mutt," said the gruff, commanding voice of a woman. She looked down from her destrier war horse and lowered her polearm. "The castle isn't safe for fresh meat like you."

He stood, brushed off his linen pants, and flattened his fringed tunic.

"Oh, Champion, I didn't see your title Sorry for the bump." She saluted, twice-tapping her chest with a fist, then covered her mouth and whispered, "So young."

"It's all right." He drew Ned's staff from his satchel and leaned on it. The bump had not only winded him, it had taken a third of his Health.

She gasped at the staff and dismounted. "Do ya need a physician?"

"I'll be fine." He straightened with a groan.

She glanced at his fringed tunic. "How about a tailor?"

"Ha!" His cheeks warmed, and he placed the staff in front of his belly. "I, er, lost a bet. Just getting ready to armor up. I'm Eon." He reached out a hand.

"I see that, Champion of Yu." She nodded at the title hovering over him before clasping arms. "Field Marshall Ismarelle, at yer service."

Ismarelle stood as tall as Eon, with broad shoulders and a steady gaze. Her grip was so firm, she'd win an arm-wrestling match by tearing his off. She wore a suit of platinum scale that was mostly hidden under a rich, green tabard. Leather ties struggled to tame her mounds of curly blond hair, drawing it from her tanned face in a ponytail. Beneath her impatient, dark eyes was a wicked scar that struggled to reach her firm jaw. Somewhere beneath the scent of oily steel and sweaty animal, he caught a hint of lilac.

"I'm headed to town. Want to join me?"

"You're right cute enough for a quick toss," she said with a wink. "But I lead my charge to the battlefront of Misere."

"Wait." He held up a hand. "That's not what I meant."

"Riiiight." She winked twice. "The girls'll never believe the Champion of Yu tried to bed me dressed as a harlot."

"I hope they don't." He covered his face.

"Don't worry your keester. Most won't survive the battle. We're spread thin on two fronts. While I lead my troops north to Misere, Sergeant Callister marches on The Broken Path to face the forces of Rath."

"That's where I'm headed," Eon said.

"Dangerous for anyone, especially a wee bairn such as yourself." Her eyes softened. "Do be careful, Champion of Yu."

"And you, Ismarelle." He thought for a moment. "If it can bring a smile or a laugh, tell your girls about the harlot of Yu who invited you to town."

"Ah will." She laughed, slapping him hard on the back. "You're a good man."

"I try." He smiled through a grimace.

The ground shook and metal rattled, growing stronger and louder as it closed in.

"What's that?" He raised his staff, expecting a swarm of monsters.

"My charge." She mounted her armored stallion. "Win this war, and I'll fancy ya for a bedding or three."

As the opulent army of Yu broached the gate, she reared her armored horse back on two legs and shouted, "That's right, me brutes! March for war! March for riches! March for Yu!" She whistled through two fingers and raced ahead.

Nomar tugged his sleeve, making him jump.

"Where did you come from?" Eon asked.

"I'm a Thief, we sneak." The Gnome winked.

"Oh, right."

"What was that?" Nomar stared at Ismarelle as she shouted her way down the path.

"I don't even know." He shook his head. "There was a whole lot going on there, for an NPC."

His heart swelled when the first battalion shouted, "Champion," as they passed, banging their chests in salute. It was more flattery than he deserved, and the attention made him antsy. He wanted to leave but following them down the road would be easier than squeezing alongside. So, they waited.

Each battalion greeted him accordingly. He waved at the second, and then the third. After fifteen minutes, fame rewarded him with a sore wrist and a crick in his neck.

The title that appeared over his head, "Champion of Yu," was a distraction he didn't need and couldn't remove. The option to dismiss it was grayed out. "We should leave."

"What's an NPC?" Nomar shouted over Ismarelle's charge.

He winced. Non-player characters were game-driven automatons. Nomar, and now Ismarelle, seemed far too real, far too complex to be mere video game characters. NPC sounded like an insult. Eon never used slurs on Earth and wouldn't start now. "It's a thoughtless term for a living being born of Entriss." He turned to the Gnome and looked him in the eyes. "A better word would be friend."

Nomar hugged his leg, and he patted the Gnome's hat. "I need some quiet, a place where I can prepare. Can you help me?"

"Can I!" Nomar grabbed his hand and led him.

They skirted the troops down the path to Averdac. Nomar led him along blocks of damp, brick streets and through several dark alleys. The Gnome talked the entire time, sharing stories about growing up in Nomorgin.

Eon could barely keep up with the pace or the excited chatter. He was gasping for air when they arrived at a Gnome hostel then gasped at the sight.

The city planning commission must've been drunk on Barbarian glug, smoking too much Fairy highpetal, or both. In the middle of this old, stately city was a giant mushroom, straight outta Nomorgin. The fat, pale stem looked like a marshmallow squeezed between two dour stone buildings. It towered four stories high, supporting a red cap that canopied the entire block. A crooked wooden sign hung from the red door with shaky words written in red chalk.

"The Nominal." He tried not to chuckle.

"Nome-inal," Nomar corrected. "Isn't she a sight?"

Eon looked the hostel up and down one more time before nodding. "She *is* a sight."

Nomar grabbed his hand and led him through the door. Almost the entire first floor was a bar. Dozens of Gnomes, several Humans, and one Elf sat around flat mushroom tables. The buzz of chatter slowly faded as everyone turned to face them.

"Introducing my friend, Eon." Nomar bowed with a flourish.

"Champion!" they shouted in unison, toasting with small steins.

"Oh boy." He leaned over and whispered to Nomar, "Maybe I should get a room."

"If you're sure?" He practically deflated, casting his eyes down at the spongy floor. "I was hoping to maybe impress some of the city folk."

Several patrons stood and approached, reaching out to shake hands.

"Get me a room, fast." He handed Nomar a few silvers. "I've got an idea."

His companion scurried off as the room closed in. He struck the floor with Ned's staff twice. Everyone "oohed" and took a healthy step back. Nomar returned before the crowd got brave again.

"The innkeeper will take you to your room," Nomar muttered.

Eon knelt beside him, placed a hand on his tiny shoulder, and summoned his familiar. Lola appeared in a flash of pink light.

"Bunny!" the crowd of Gnomes shouted, clapping wildly.

"Mind putting on a show, Lola? I'll try to be quick."

The rabbit snorted in dismay but remained by them.

Do you wish to share control of your familiar with group members?

He acknowledged the prompt. Maybe not the best idea, but he was in a hurry. "Gently hold an antler and say go. They'll be impressed, my friend."

Nomar looked like Eon had just made up for missing Christmas and his birthday with one big gift. After hugging his leg, and hugging Lola, he held an antler and closed his eyes.

"Go," Nomar said.

Lola and Nomar appeared at the opposite end of the room. Patrons gasped in awe then let out a cheer. The crowd rushed toward them. Before anyone got too close, Lola teleported to another spot.

"Thank you," Nomar called out between excited giggles.

"Follow me to your room, Champion." A sturdy female Gnome tugged at his sleeve.

She led him up a wide spiral staircase of vines that circled the outer wall. After climbing two floors, they arrived at a red door with a limp mushroom handle.

"The handle is magic." She took his hand and placed it on the handle. "Once you open it, no one can follow...unless you want some company."

"Pardon?"

"Your evening might be finer with some of me Gnome ladies." She waggled her eyebrows.

"No," he said, louder than intended. "I mean, no, thank you. I, uh, have Champion work to do...unfortunately."

"Of course." Her beady eyes smoldered as she looked him up and down. "Keep us in mind when you finish. I have a rare 'un with a beard who could make ya a new man."

Before he could stutter another no, she sauntered off. Who knew Gnomes could saunter?

"The best room service in town," she called out. "Eat the room if yer hungry and there are ladies at the waiting if ya hunger for something else."

He shook his head and grasped the mushroom handle. It felt like a cold, wet noodle and he let go as soon as the door opened.

The room was like any hotel suite back on Earth with a bed, chair, and table—except they were all made from mushrooms. It was spacious, warm, and smelled of dry earth. Glowing wisps hovered near the ceiling, casting the room in a warm light. Best of all, it was quiet.

He rubbed his hands together in anticipation. Whether gaining levels, affinity, or the constant battle for better armor and weapons, MMOs were all about progression. Sure, finishing a quest felt like an accomplishment. But that was completely different than character progression, which was about winning.

Eon was now level 11 with a new quest, new (hopefully less stripperific) armor, and a new spell for his Rune Staff of Ned the Insane. It was time to reap the rewards of battle.

The armor was first. New armor meant new spells. His hands shook with excitement as he drew three pieces from his satchel and gingerly set them on the bed. He inspected each item, rubbed his eyes, and inspected them again.

"You've got to be fucking kidding me!"

27

FOCUS

He inspected each item again, and then again. They were exceptional, not only because of their impressive stats but the item quality level.

There were six tiers of armor and weapon quality in Entriss that ranged from shit to Shazam. Useless trash with no bonuses, like his shirt, were labeled Basic. When inspecting them, their title appeared in a gray font. Yellow items of Good quality unlocked a mediocre spell. Gear that was Fine unlocked a better spell. After that came Impressive Pink, Exceptional Blue, and Epic Purple—each of them providing better spells and stat bonuses.

Nihle's gifts were borderline Epic. Rather than having a lame static bonus, like +10 to eyesight, each piece of armor gave a bonus to core stats. The Crimson Robes of Winning added +2 to Essence and +3 to Power. The Fancy Belt of Gloating and Supple Silver Gloves both added +1 to Vigor and +1 to Power.

The bonuses were rare, and unheard of for a level 11. Since Health and Mana increased every level based on those core stats, the bonus from these items would scale. Hell, after theorycrafting the stats, he may have worn them on Mandorf. Not only would he be a gloating winner with supple gloves, this armor unlocked three badass spells for Wizards.

Unfortunately, he wasn't a Wizard; he was a Rune Mage. He could inspect Nihle's gifts but couldn't equip them or use their beautiful spells. It was total, complete bullshit. Had The Left Hand of God code made the game so buggy that quests awarded the wrong gear?

Graphic designers, game designers, and developers had been creating armor for every known profession since Entriss's inception. There had always been ten playable professions, but never a Rune Mage. It meant developers hadn't bothered to create custom armor or new weapons for the class. The only powerful item he had was the dumb staff.

He knocked the armor to the floor, stomping and cursing and flailing until he was done. The world he was trying to save wouldn't give him a break. Being level 11 meant nothing without some muscle to back it. Whoever had created the damn quest obviously didn't want it to be easy, but this was ridiculous.

Desperate for something grounded, he opened his quest log. Quests always provided an explanation, or at least a hint of what to expect. So far, he'd completed several minor, and one major, sub-quest beneath The Left Hand of God:

Fanning the Flame
Throwing Shade
It's All Yu
Hitchhiker's Guide

He selected the new quest.

Hitchhiker's Guide: Don't Panic. Someone will be with you shortly.

The cryptic message didn't help calm his seething. It read like another software bug.

After the crappy armor and crappy quest, he had little hope for the staff's new spell. Based on his luck so far, he'd probably unlocked

Colon Blowout or *Face Plant*. A quick inspection of the staff brought up a long list of spells, all written in runes he didn't understand.

This was hopeless...or maybe it was just another puzzle. There had to be something else. He closed his eyes and concentrated. A lot of system messages had popped up after turning in the quest to Nihle. Levels gained...new staff spell...focus tree. *What the fuck is a focus tree?*

A menu scroll opened before him, revealing an organizational chart of gray runic icons. They hung from tree branches like fruit on a vine. His jaw dropped at the system message.

Focus Tree: Earn focus points by leveling. Use points to unlock abilities and spells. One point awarded for each level.

"Holy shit." He covered his mouth

Most MMOs had some sort of skill tree. Players earned points by leveling and spent them on a skill to empower or unlock spells. Depending on the game, one skill often led to others. Some players dove deep into theorycrafting, crunching the numbers to maximize damage or healing. In other games, Ian had used those trees to complement his strengths, or compensate for weaknesses. It was something Entriss Online had lacked. Until now.

An icon of a book and a candle icon appeared in front of the tree. Circles and rectangular boxes with runic symbols decorated the tree like it was Charlie Brown's Evil Christmas. He mentally clicked it, and everything went blurry. When the world came back into focus, a system message appeared.

Congratulations, Apprentice – You have gained a basic understanding of the runic language.

The book and candle were gone and four rectangular boxes appeared at the bottom. Each contained an icon and a number indicating the point cost.

The first rectangle featured a picture of two crossing daggers.

Glyph: Spells of great power to damage opponents. Cost: 2 points.

Sigil was second, depicted by a non-descript person surrounded by an aura.

Sigil: Spells that enhance you or your group. Cost: 2 points.

The third was a shield icon.

Ward: Spells that protect you or your group. Cost: 2 points.

The last was a quill pen.

Inscription: Read hidden runes on armor and weapons. Cost: 2 points.

He immediately selected Glyph and two grayed-out runes appeared above.

Unlock weapon's single target spell.
Unlock weapon's area of effect spell.

Clicking them prompted a system message.

Learn all core spell classes before proceeding.

He had 11 points, and spent eight on Glyph, Ward, Sigil, and Inscription. The world went slightly out of focus. He dismissed this as exhaustion and hoped the frightening AI wasn't force-feeding him a new language.

The word Apprentice appeared above the four core spells along with two spell icons connected to Ward, Glyph, and Sigil. He only had three points remaining and reviewed them closely.

The two blue icons above Glyph were *Ruin*—depicted by a bloody arrow—and *Ruination*, which looked a lot like an explosion.

Ruin: Cast a projectile at a single target and you will not miss. Chance to disorient that target. 3-second cast time. Cost: 1 - 3 points.

Ruination: Cast a rune beneath opponents that explodes and knocks them back. 5-second cast time. Cost: 1 - 3 points.

Sigil also had two spells. *Hyper*, a lightning bolt icon, and *Increment*, which was two lightning bolts.

Hyper: Buff all stats to one player. 3-second cast. Cost: 1 - 5 points.

Increment: Buff primary stats to everyone in your group. Buff increases over 20 seconds at the equivalent cost of Mana. 5-second cast. Cost: 1 - 5 points.

The two ward spells were basic crowd control, and both icons were black. *Envelop* sort of looked like a body wrapped in a blanket.

Envelop: Freeze one player for 5 seconds. Instant cast. Cost: 1 - 3 points.

The *Beguile* icon was a rune of stars.

Beguile: Distract all players in a 10-yard radius for three seconds. 4-second cast. Cost: 1 - 3 points.

It was an easy decision to choose the offensive spells beneath Glyph. That left him one point. He wanted to spend it on *Hyper* for Jewells. It'd be fun to see her cut loose, but after punching him, not replying to his apologies, and returning Mandorf's stuff... There was no way she was coming back.

Could he blame her? He was no catch, and she was out of his league. His breath caught, and he swallowed hard. She was one of the few women he could banter with. Not only because they had so much nerd in common, but because she accepted him...as a friend. Fate had drawn a gossamer thread across the wide chasm between friendship and romance. Instead of racing across, he'd walked it like an acrophobic with vertigo.

Since that hadn't worked, he'd have to change. If she came back, if she'd give him the chance, the hero of Yu would certainly, would probably...be the same guy.

Since she wasn't coming back, he was alone again. It was a comfortable, familiar black hole that he could settle into. She was probably the last person on Earth who would give him a chance. Maybe Deity would pity him with someone from Entriss. It was as likely as Insane Ned returning for his staff.

He didn't cry, or sob, or farmer snot on a mushroom. Heroes and champions had no time to dwell on love lost, right? This quest, this game wasn't a distraction from something as tangible and real as life. It couldn't be. Not now that Entriss was real too. And at least *this* world needed him.

Through bleary eyes, he selected *Envelop* and confirmed his choices.

A global system message appeared that all players could see.

Champion of Yu Eon has earned a World First: Focus Tree Unlocked

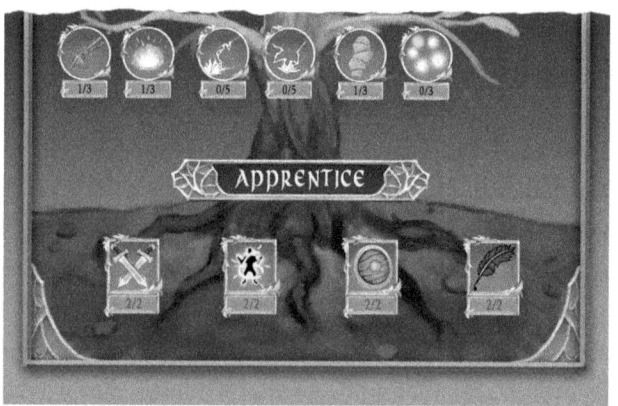

He looked over the tree, pleased with his choices, happy with a World First, but still...

"Great," he said in a deadpan tone. "Victories are best won on a lone battlefield...said no one ever."

The focus tree brought him hope, and he would gladly revel in the victory of a first after more wallowing. Because wallowing in self-pity was fun and useful and...his armor was sparkling like unclaimed loot from a fallen foe.

He knelt to inspect the chest piece again. The scroll opened and the inscription rune of a quill burned away the spell and stats. When they reappeared, the armor was recast for a Rune Mage with identical stats and no spell.

After inscribing the belt and gloves, he donned the new armor and opened his character sheet. His mirror image looked disgruntled in the new digs. The Crimson Robes of Winning was a knee-length suit jacket that buttoned up to a Chinese collar. His Fancy Belt of Gloating was made of wide white leather with a gold buckle. The Supple Silver Gloves were jazz-hands sparkly. He couldn't decide if Eon looked like a badass, or Michael Jackson's Drum Major.

The look was questionable; the stats were a gift.

Name:	Eon	Level:	11
Tribe:	Wood Elf	XP to Level:	11,482
Profession:	Rune Mage		
		Vigor:	14
health:	583	Essence:	19
Mana:	773	Power:	15

With 583 Health, 773 Mana, and additional damage bonus from Power, he could face down a level 14 mob without dying. Probably. Even better, his stats weren't gray. He could continue leveling.

After a brief dance and several cheers, he drew out the staff.

"Your turn."

Lola appeared in a flash of pink light. Her eye was swollen shut, and she collapsed with a whine. He dropped to his knees and gently petted her. She leaned her head into his lap, panting weakly. Her fur was damp, and his hand was red with her blood. Was she dying? Could a familiar die?

"Wait," he said. "Where's Nomar?"

Lola reared back, raising her great antlers high, and snorted before shuddering.

She was still breathing. Barely. He glanced at his group stats. He was at full Health, Jewells was grayed out, and Nomar was at a quarter health but still alive.

"Why can't I see Lola's vitals?" He looked at the ceiling. "Dammit Deity, add Lola to the group or I fucking quit!"

Lola the Jackalope appeared directly below his name, closer than the others, like they were connected. His familiar was almost dead. A sliver, a hair, a breath from dying wasn't a bare enough description.

Desperation battled resolve. He had to save her. She was one of a kind and he didn't know if she could be resurrected. Even if he wouldn't admit it out loud, he maybe, actually liked her.

His rune spells couldn't heal, Jewells wasn't here, and he had no potions to do the job. What would he do if his Health was that low?

He searched through that file cabinet in his brain, which seemed far better at storing useless information than providing it. His stomach let out a noisy growl. Eating a snack always helped him think, or at least that was his excuse. Eating a snack... He shook his head at what should have been obvious.

Eating didn't restore Health as fast as a potion or spell, but it could still work. He broke off a bit of spongy table and pressed it against her mouth. She turned away.

"Take it or you'll die." No matter how encouraging he was, she refused. He couldn't just make her...or could he? Summoning up his will, he commanded, "Eat, my familiar. Eat and be healthy."

Lola nibbled and nibbled again. Her Health slowly, slowly

returned. Her nibbles became bites until she gorged herself beyond full health.

"Enough!"

She stopped and looked up at him, a chunk of table falling from her mouth.

"I'm glad you're okay, Lola. Now I need to find out what happened. I'm only level 11, but at least I've got some spells." He took a deep breath and placed a hand on her antler. "Take me to Nomar. Go."

28

SECRETS

J ulie couldn't leave the trappings of Entriss HQ fast enough. She rushed down hallways and past worried co-workers, gulping for breath with every few steps. Her throat tightened when she arrived at the majestic sliding glass doors of the entrance. They were too slow, and she shouldered one open. The emergency hinge released, knocking it off track.

She wanted to run but felt the cold gaze of cameras trailing her every step. Kingpin Luanne and the thug board of directors would watch her every movement while on campus. She wouldn't give that woman the satisfaction of seeing her run, or scream, or cry.

What had happened? Sure, the board meeting had been a surprise, but she'd faced that evil bitch down. She'd been winning the fight and then, out of nowhere, rolled a 1. Us. Had she actually referred to her and Ian as "us?"

"Oh, shit." She walked right into a wall of realization and stopped to cover her mouth. "I did say us."

She'd been angry at Ian. He'd practically ghosted her for a month so he could create an experience. For her. He expressed himself so differently than anyone she'd been with. Most love-interests wooed her with expensive trinkets, or amazing physiques, or hollow promises. Everything Ian did was to spend time together, and she'd thanked him with a punch to his face.

Ian had been stupid to risk his life for a game that no longer felt like a game. His last message had said the game wouldn't kill him. Despite all his intelligence, the man was ignorant. He had no clue what Deity was capable of.

Julie wasn't really upset at his heroics. They were cute. He was cute. She'd been avoiding "us" like quicksand in a monsoon. And now? Now she was trapped between an opportunistic CIO and a passionate fanboy.

"Nope." She rushed forward as her tears began swelling. "I won't let them see."

Marc was waiting at the cul-de-sac entrance. She stood at attention before a dusky sports car, her arms behind her back and her gaze vigilant. Glorious purple hair poured over the shoulders of her pinstripe chauffeur suit. Her skirt was several inches too short, her shiny black boots several inches too long, and her curves several inches too perfect.

Julie's natural inclination was to judge, and there was a lot to judge. But when Marc's hawkish gaze stopped watching their flanks and made eye contact, they softened. Julie lost herself to an ugly cry, practically falling into the woman's arms. The driver took a moment to hold her before helping her into the car.

The engine roared, and the tires squealed in a satisfying, "fuck you."

Julie sank into the red leather seat as the car took off like a moon launch. Marc offered a satin handkerchief from her breast pocket. Julie stared at it through bleary eyes. This was no mere tissue. It would be a crime to destroy such opulence with her snot-fest.

"Blow your nose, dear." Marc's tone was gentle, even as her eyes danced across the computer dashboard. "It goes in the same wash as my socks and knickers."

Julie nodded and spent a few minutes composing herself.

"You can tell me, if it'll help," she said, leaning into a sudden right turn.

Julie held on for dear life. "Are we being followed?"

"Just some drones. Adorable, really." She flipped a switch and pulled over to park. "And now we look like an old Kia. I love amateur hour. This is fun."

"What kind of car is this?" While it wasn't her first time in the car, she'd been far more interested then in trying to figure out the driver. "It sounds like a gas engine, but I thought those were illegal."

"2019 Corvette Stingray, last of the front engines." Marc took a deep breath of pride. "She runs on biomass instead of gasoline, which means she eats the leftovers. Still legal in most states. Most of it's original, but I had a few optional extras installed."

"Wait." Julie looked up. "Was that James Bond, *The Living Daylights*?"

"Timothy Dalton was underrated," she said with a wink. "I see why Ian likes you."

This brought on more tears. Marc pushed a button, and the windows went black. She drew out a thick pair of dark glasses, and they took off.

"You can't tell them where he's at if you don't know where we're going."

"Them?" Julie's knee bounced and she held on tight to the door handle.

"There's always a them. I'm driving you for a reason, aren't I?" The corner of Marc's mouth ticked before turning into a smile. "I've been doing this for four years. Some call me a courier, the Statham movies pegged me as a Transporter, but I'm sure you figured that out. Either way, I keep secrets. Word gets out that I can't keep secrets, I'm back on the streets. I'm like a shrink, or maybe a priest that God wouldn't approve of. Either way, what you tell me is safe from everyone, including Ian."

Marc was so sincere, so genuine that Julie believed her. She spilled her guts like a henchman on truth serum being waterboarded. It all came out, far more than she'd intended. Her story was enough to make the easygoing, battle-ready, Statham-worthy Transporter suck in her full lips.

"He doesn't know?"

"No," Julie said, quietly. "Not yet."

"That's a heavy burden." They pulled to a stop, and Marc removed her goggles, taking a long moment to shake out her hair. "You're putting a lot at risk. Even me."

"I'm sorry."

"Sorry?" She laughed, maybe a little too heartily. "More fun than I could've hoped for."

"Thanks for listening. It helped." Julie sighed. "My secret?"

"Who would believe me?" Marc stared into Julie's eyes, her gaze intense. "We're here. I can listen more, or you can go fix things."

"He left me a key, but I didn't take it."

"I'll let you in." Her gentle smile was broken by another nervous tick. She drew a tiny laser pistol from the console and pointed it at Julie's waist. "Right after this."

"I'm sorry," Julie screamed, reaching for the door handle. "I swear I'd never hurt him."

The device squanched several times before she put it away.

"Targeted EMP," she said with a wink as if Julie hadn't just pissed herself. "Killed your tracer. Let's go."

Julie blinked several times before scrambling out. Marc waited with her arms crossed like the not-so-near-death-experience hadn't happened.

"It probably would've been okay. Ian bought a Tor Field Generator that redirects all tracking for a city block. And we've got other contingencies just in case..."

Julie followed her across the parking lot, her mind buzzing with questions. This woman was so perfect, and obviously close to Ian.

"So, how did you two meet?"

"He helped me out of a tight spot."

"And you guys are..."

"Friends."

"But you're both so different."

"We have similar interests."

"Then why aren't you two—"

Marc grabbed her shoulders and threw her against the warehouse wall, holding her inches above the ground. "I get it. You're marking your territory because you love him."

"I don't lo—"

Marc snapped with her teeth, cutting her off. "I'd be with him in a second if I was into men. He's a little fucked up, he's got secrets, but he's worth the effort. Don't forget that."

The woman let go, and Julie held herself.

"I don't think you're up for this." Marc raised her chin and the tick returned.

"What do you mean?"

"Prissy party girl like you is so busy toying with my boy's emotions, you completely ignore the danger you've put all of us in." Her gaze was a dagger that thrust deep. "Nothing to worry about. If you let Ian die, Daddy can save your pretty butt."

Rage swelled in Julie's brain and poured out her fist. She struck Marc's jaw with ninety-five pounds of determination. It was like punching a wall, and the driver smiled wickedly.

"I don't need anyone to save my pretty ass," she screamed.

Marc shook her head and blinked in surprise. "Then I have hope."

"I threw everything into that punch." Julie leaned closer. "I've knocked down men twice your weight, and you took it like it was nothing." She covered her mouth. "Are you—"

"Cyborg." Marc leaned against the warehouse wall. "Lost most of my body saving someone important. They were grateful enough to put me back together. Still got my heart and brain, if that counts."

"Jesus, Marc. I'm sorry."

"Not sure how I made it. Didn't want to live, but I have a daughter..." She gathered herself. "Can't tell you how good Ian has been to us."

"That sort of reconstruction isn't even legal." Julie looked her up and down. "That much bio-tech goes beyond government or undercast."

"I know your secret, and now you know mine." She reached out to shake hands. "I call that even."

"Agreed." Julie took the hand and shook firmly.

They walked to the steel door in silence. Marc drew a necklace deep from her blouse and pulled out a keystore cube. She held it before the door and hesitated. "One last thing," she said in a dangerous tone.

Julie took a step back. "You'll kill me if I hurt him?"

"It'll be worse. Relationships are about hurt, and love, and mistakes, and forgiveness. Fall in love, break up tragically, that's life and my heart goes out to both of you kids." Marc's hand moved unnaturally fast, grasping Julie's shoulder in a Vulcan Death Grip. Her fingers dug into nerves that numbed her entire arm. The cyborg leaned in, her eye twitching uncontrollably. "Fuck him over, and I'll kill everyone who knows your name, and you'll be last."

Julie's entire body went icebox cold. She could only nod.

"Last threat, I promise." Marc drew her into a stifling hug. She let her go, unlocked the door, and pushed Julie through. The dangerous tick faded away, replace by an encouraging mom smile. "Good luck! I'll be here when you're ready to leave."

29

A HOBGOBLIN, A BROWNIE, AND A WOMAN WALK INTO A BAR

L ola and Ian appeared near the first-floor stairs, unnoticed by the chaos. The jackalope chomped into his leather boot and tugged.

"Right." He crouched behind a fallen mound of spongy table. "Thanks."

Three griefers owned the room. They surrounded a bevy of drunken Gnomes, shirtless men, and women with fists raised and ready for a brawl.

Ian didn't recognize the hulking beast barring the entrance. The hunchback was eight-feet tall with powerful arms almost long enough to reach the floor. He had a protruding forehead, jutting jaw, and deep-set gray eyes. A worn broadsword rested over the shoulder of his rusty black armor. He held a black crossbow statue-steady, pointing a glowing red arrow at any Gnome that moved.

Directly across from the horror was a tiny creature clad in black leather armor. She peered at a dying Gnome and slowly licked one of her long, curved daggers, like your favorite movie serial killer. She pressed her weapons together and disappeared into the shadows.

"Great," he whispered to Lola.

The woman opposite him, the one twirling an electrified whip, didn't make him feel any better. Well, maybe a little better. She flaunted gorgeous curves in a blue satin blouse, black leather skirt, and heeled ankle-boots. Her long, black hair was pulled tight into a ponytail that reached her tanned legs. The dominatrix looked around the room with haughty impatience, ready to beat down her next submissive.

He didn't want to spend time inspecting them, but the two creatures were new, the whip was new, there was a lot of new going on. The nice-looking doorman was Trevor the Hobgoblin, a level 35 Guardian. Coco, the knife-licking serial killer, was a Brownie. She was also a level 28 Slayer. Vicki, a level 31 Jaeger, was human, gloriously human.

Where were they from? Why were they here? Had the code he checked created new tribes and professions? He had more questions than time. Trevor was obviously a first-line-of-defense Warrior. His heavy armor was deeply scarred from battle and the sword on his back was meant to get attention. Coco looked like a Thief or Assassin, which meant melee damage. Sneaky melee damage. Jaeger was just another word for hunter. Even though Vicki held a whip, she must be ranged damage.

"DPS, DPS, and DPS. There's a lot of damage in this room, but they have no heals. Not that it matters. My level 11 spells would barely make a dent." He looked over at the Lola. "You don't talk much, do you?"

She leaned to one side for a good ear scratch and immediately fell over, her heavy antlers rattling on a broken dish.

"Is that you, Champion?" Vicki taunted, cracking her whip over a mostly dead Gnome. "Just in time to watch your friend die."

"Nomar," he whispered, peeking around the mushroom table.

"I'll be the one watching." Nomar coughed up a glob of blood. "He's going to champion all your asses."

Eon took another long look at the Jaeger, for research purposes. There was something about her. She looked familiar, sort of, and yet... He let out a gasp. Not only was her naughty satin fetish blouse blue, a blue aura surrounded her. She could accept his quest. If she was the Hitchhiker's Guide, he'd need more than a towel to finish this quest.

He chuckled at his dad-joke until Lola snorted impatiently.

"You're right, but I need a plan. My low-level spells are almost worthless. It'd be like hitting linebackers with spitballs. Unless..." Ned's staff had a new spell he hadn't been able to access because he didn't understand runes. Thanks to the focus tree, he now had a basic understanding of the symbols. "Time to pull out the big gun."

He carefully drew the gray steel staff from his satchel and set it flat on the floor. Two-inch rows of etched runes covered the weapon from base to birdcage. Most were dark glyphs he still didn't understand. A deep, red glow emanated from runes in the top three rows, and he knew what they meant. *Shockwave*, *Familiar*, and... What the fuck?

Congratulations! Rune Staff of Ned the Insane has earned a new spell.

Battlemount. Charge into battle on your trusty steed, or ride together at great speed! Keep your hands inside at all times. This spell does not guarantee a smooth, or safe, ride.

Maximum Occupancy—one Troll, three Humans, and five or more Gnomes, depending on how they are attached.

Ned was insane. Insanely stupid. Not only was this spell useless to him in the Gnome hostel, it came with a disclaimer. What kind of spell came with a fucking disclaimer?

Lola looked up at him, her foot thumping in anticipation.

"It does sound fun, but not in here." He scratched her furry head. "The spell will either make you too big for the room, or if Ned was crazy, it'll make me too small to fight. There are too many unknowns here. We'll have to go with plan A. Now I just need to figure out plan A."

She collapsed in a huff.

He couldn't damage them, but maybe he could distract them long enough to grab Nomar and escape. His single target spell, *Ruin*, took a three-second eternity to cast, *Ruination* took five. In game time, that was like waiting for water to warm in the kitchen sink. At least the *Envelop* spell was instant.

He looked over mushrooms, and slow as a 300 baud modem, cast *Ruination* beneath the Hobgoblin. The blast rune appeared on the floor, exploding up in blue flames. The Guardian bellowed a curse as the spell knocked him back against the door.

The blast was a small diversion but gave him the desperate seconds needed to cast *Ruin*. Large tribal arrows shot from his hands, swerved about like a drunkard, and struck the Brownie Slayer for 2% of her health. She rocked from side to side, stabbing at the air with her daggers. Not only had *Ruin* disoriented the Sprite, it had revealed his location.

He gripped one of Lola's antlers. "Go."

Vicki cracked her whip, roaring in fury. Small bolts of lightning shot across the room, crashing into Eon's mushroom protection.

"Where are you, Champion?" she snarled.

"Here." He stood directly behind her and cast *Envelop*.

She spun around, her beautiful face inches from his when the spell struck. A thin, clear blanket, like cellophane, encased her from head to toe. The Jaeger fell over, mumbling curses in the trap.

"Got you, buddy." Eon picked up Nomar.

"Thank you, Eon." The Gnome passed out.

He reached for Lola and screamed in pain, collapsing to the ground. The glowing red arrow in his knee disappeared. The pain didn't. Half his Health was gone, and his entire leg felt like it was on fire.

"Cute." Vicki stood, brushing off his *Wrap* spell. "Your attack was cute, you're cute, but let's try this again."

She kicked him to his back, knocking the wind from his lungs and sense from his head. The arrow spell continued to burn hot in his knee, eating away his Health. His vision was so clouded, he could barely make out her face through the blue glow.

He was close enough to turn in the quest and tried muttering an explanation. It was pointless. The constant pain from the arrow made him delirious.

"What are you trying to say?" She leaned closer, pursing her full lips.

"Take it," he pleaded, reaching for her.

"Disgusting." She slapped his mouth.

"Back off, Wizard." The Hobgoblin pressed a searing red arrow against his cheek.

"The Champion of Yu is mine." She smacked the arrow away. "Take care of the others. Kill everyone in the hostel."

Trevor the Guardian and Coco the Slayer turned to face the shirtless Gnomes. The brave Gnomes screamed, rushing around the room like they were on fire.

"Good luck catching them," Eon muttered with a chuckle.

Pain from the arrow spell subsided as the sultry co-ed in fetish clothes straddled him. She drew Rambo's dagger from her patent boot and raised it high with both hands.

"How did it happen?" he asked.

She paused mid-bloodlust, looking down at him curiously.

"How did someone so beautiful become so ugly?"

His words struck harder than the arrow, making her grimace. She looked at him, the rage in her eyes waning.

"Your name is Vicki, right?"

She nodded.

"Your hate consumes you," he said in a soothing tone. "Let go of your hate. Entriss needs your help. I need your help. The monsters of Misere are bringing war to Rath and Yu. We need to work together. Please, accept my quest before things get ugly."

"Ugly." Her eyes went wild. "You called me ugly."

He screamed as she lodged the dagger in his shoulder. The blood-red gauze of death clouded his vision as Vicki jerked it free.

"Fuck it," he growled.

"What's that, Rune Mage?" She leaned close, a mere kiss away. "Say it louder. I want to taste your last words."

"*Battlemount.*"

30

DON'T PANIC

M arc was a fucking bipolar sociopath. Julie wanted to scream, escape through a window, or call for help. But who would believe her? Governments didn't allow people to replace over 10% of their body with cybernetic parts. It messed with their heads and they were too powerful to control. Military-grade hands could crush skulls. Marc probably could've torn her in half right down the center.

She just wanted to game with Ian and figure out the "us" thing. Now she had to spy for Entriss without triggering *The Terminator*'s sociopath protocol or upsetting Deity in *The Matrix*. The AI would read Julie's mind the second she logged in and know she had agreed to spy on Ian. It was like being trapped in a slowly shrinking box.

There had to be a way out. When she was overwhelmed with too many coding bugs, Ian would tell her, "See the big picture, but focus on one problem at a time."

She took a deep breath and concentrated on the spying first. HQ expected a report after every gaming session. She planned to trickle vague information until they finished the quest. It would be easier if she just stayed at Ian's apartment and didn't go back, but she wanted to keep tabs on Luanne. The CIO may not be able to find this place, but she had plans.

Deity may not approve of the spying but should realize her end goal was to help Ian. If that didn't protect Julie, Asimov's Laws of Robotics should. Should.

That left Marc. Julie had no way to stop the cyborg if she went full-on John Wick. What was Ian thinking? Why would he put her in danger like this?

She picked up the remote. "Beam us up."

The doors opened and she stared at The Bridge. It was a lot of effort just to impress her. There's no way he'd put her in danger after creating this.

The killer robot obviously cared for Ian, hopefully enough not to murder his crush. Or, if they were that close, maybe he would tell Marc to lay off the threats. It was a shot glass of hope in an ocean of conjecture. But it was enough. She could throw down shots like an Irish rugby player after a win. Or a loss.

That didn't help her with the issue she wanted to avoid. She'd rather face Marc in open combat than become an us. Most of her girlfriends went for looks, but she was turned on by brains. They weren't always easy to find. Not only was Ian intelligent, he made her laugh every day. They shared the same vibe for old movies, and he'd taught her to love the game. There was a lot to lo— Like.

He also had secrets. Most guys just didn't want you to see their cast history. Ian was besties with The Terminator. There was far more to him than she'd expected. But she had secrets too. What if she let herself become an us and their secrets didn't fit? She didn't have much trust left to give.

Julie entered the room, smiling at everything Ian. He was definitely boyfriend material. Not only did his nerd run deeper than anyone she'd met, he wanted to share all of it with her. The gesture warmed her cringing heart.

She cocked her head to one side, staring at a folded piece of paper taped to her pod. Had he left her a note? Writing something by hand

was unheard of. Hell, where had he found a pen? It was old fash-
ioned, inefficient, and sort of sweet.

She delicately removed the note and opened it. Despite his tidy
handwriting, it took a minute to grasp something that wasn't a font.

Julie,

    *Thank you for coming back. It means everything. This quest is ours
and we should finish it together. After we win the game, we'll go to that
secluded beach and figure everything out. I have one in mind.*

    *Your viscosity suit is in your (your was scribbled out) the guest room. I
have cameras everywhere. Log into my computer and turn them off before
changing. User: Jewells Pass: Joshua*

    Love,

    Ian

"A handwritten note and a War Games reference. You sexy man."

She'd messed up. Lashing out in anger when he was trying to
impress. She hadn't struck someone that hard since her father. The
old man had deserved it; Ian didn't. He deserved an apology. More
than that, maybe he deserved a chance.

Beep.

"What was that?" She spun around. "What beeped at me?"

Beep.

The pale ceiling light turned a dark shade of red.

"Oh, come on." Julie headed to the console. It was dark and
wouldn't turn on. "I know Ian. He wouldn't create all this without
giving the room a voice." She stopped to consider the room. He'd
based it on the bridge of Star Trek II. *Wrath of Khan* was her favorite,
but he loved *The Voyage Home.* "Computer."

The beeping stopped, but there was still no voice.

"Transparent Aluminum."

"Voice recognition...Julie." The voice came from everywhere and
sounded like Angelina Jolie instead of Majel Barrett-Roddenberry,
the traditional voice of Star Trek computers. Still, it was fitting. "How
may I assist? Would you like music from the Julie playlist?"

She would've loved nothing more, but that would have to wait. "I heard a beep, and the lights went red. Advise."

"Ian's vitals are spiking, and his movements are erratic," Angelina said. "Pod-release protocol has failed."

"What?" Julie rushed to his pod and looked through the window.

Ian's face was contorted in pain, like he was stuck in a nightmare that wouldn't end. The game shouldn't have been able to put that much stress on the body. He needed her now, but her viscosity suit was two rooms away.

"Fuck it." Julie shimmied out of her blouse and skirt, kicked off her heels, and climbed into the pod. "Computer, engage."

SHE APPEARED at a waypoint outside the castle and immediately received a system message.

Do you wish to join your group already in battle?

She glanced at the group stats. The boys were almost dead, and she quickly accepted the battle summons. A giant mushroom appeared before her and she reeled from the abrupt relocation. When the shock passed, she rushed to the red door.

It was jammed. She pressed a foot against the wall, held the handle with both hands, and pulled with all her might. The door burst open and a large bunny ass stuck out.

"What the furry hell?" She jumped back to avoid pellets, wielding her hammer and sickle.

The golden mass of fur disappeared, and tiny Lola hobbled toward her. She tossed a quick heal at the jackalope before crossing the threshold.

A tiny stick woman, her hulking brother Lurch, and a beauty queen from Fetish-R-Us hovered over a dying Eon. They were low on health, covered in rabbit fur, and rabid with fury.

"Get away from my Eon." Jewells blasted the griefers with *Holy Wrath*.

One by one, they collapsed, writhing in pain as white fire burned away their Health. Her spell brought them inches from death. How could three griefers get this deep into the city? It didn't matter. They were incapacitated enough to stop attacking.

"Got you." She healed Eon and then Nomar. "That was close."

"You came back!" Eon stood, looking at her in awe before facing the trio. "Don't let them die."

"But they were trying to kill you." She glared at the voluptuous call girl. "Do I have to?"

"Please," he said, looking her in the eyes.

Jewells tried healing and then tried again to no effect. "It's not working."

"Why?"

"They're not from Yu?" She shrugged.

The stick woman shuddered and passed out.

"What if they were in our group?"

"Maybe," she said. "I don't understand."

"Vicki." Eon knelt, grabbing the woman's shoulders. "Drop group and join ours."

"You're still cute," she said, deliriously.

Jewells wanted to kick the tart's head in. "Eon?"

"Drop group," he shouted. "Now."

Within seconds, they had three new members. Trevor the Hobgoblin, Coco the Brownie, and, of course, Vicki the harlot. She healed Trevor and Coco before reluctantly healing the woman.

The battle was over, and everyone stood.

"Thank you, Champion." Vicki took Eon's hand and stood a bit too close.

It didn't bother Jewells even a little that Vicki's armor was a tad sexier, or that the petite brunette was so curvy, or that she continued holding his hand while looking up with those large calf eyes. It bothered her a fucking lot. She sheathed her weapons and wrenched Eon's hand away, squeezing hard enough to make him wince.

"Vicki, you know what I want," Eon said. "Please."

Jewells glared at him, mouthing, "Pardon?"

"Quest giver," he whispered.

Jewells covered her mouth in surprise. She'd been so caught up in the adventure, and so distracted by not-jealousy—she wasn't jealous, why would she be jealous?—she hadn't even realized. They were NPCs.

Vicki looked at him sternly before reaching out. A golden orb flew from his hand to hers.

"This cannot be." Her eyes went wide. "You are too young to be our guide."

"*Your* guide? I thought you were *my* guide."

"Do it," Trevor said. "He's too green. We have no choice."

"Thank you, Eon." Vicki leaned forward and kissed his cheek.

"Thank you for what?" He reached up to the kiss.

Crack! Woosh! The detonation sounded like a gunshot as odorless smoke filled the room.

Jewells froze for a breath until a Gnome shouted, "Fire!"

"Eon? Nomar?" She activated True Vision to see through the smoke.

The Gnomes were in a panic, rushing around, yelling, "Fire," and crashing into each other with an, "Ouch."

"Got 'em." Coco pulled Zalmon's eyes from Eon's pouch.

Vicki grabbed the eyes from the greedy Thief and tucked them away.

"That's not possible." Eon coughed, lifting Ned's staff. "The eyes are bound to me."

"Quest bound, hero." She cracked her whip, sending angry bolts of lightning in all directions. "Obviously, I'm a part of the quest."

"Not for long."

Eon has kicked Coco from the group.
Eon has kicked Trevor from the group.
Eon has kicked Vicki from the group.

"They're out," Eon shouted. "Kill them."

Coco appeared before Jewells with thirsty black eyes and two long daggers. She shoved them into her gut and disappeared.

Jewells screamed as she buckled over, grasping at the warm, wet holes. Before she could heal, Coco was behind her, jamming the daggers into her back.

"Off her, wench." Nomar dove at the Brownie with his two daggers.

Their knives danced in a blurry storm of stabs and deflections.

Nomar's attack gave Jewells enough time to cast shield as Coco cut deep into his leg. He collapsed to the floor.

Half her Health was gone and more leaked out with her blood. The room spun like the best-worst New Year's Eve party. Coco's blades had been covered in poison. The damage wouldn't kill her, but the debuff would leave her loopy for the next seventeen seconds.

"Why are you doing this?" Eon asked. "We should work together."

Vicki paused for a minute before shaking her head. "Your heart is worthy, but this quest is too much for someone so young. My great grandfather was wrong to burden you with such a task."

"Your great... You mean Zalmon." His voice was shaky.

"Cute *and* clever." Her smile was warm. "Find me when this war is over, and I will give you a quest you won't forget."

Jewells grimaced. The flirting was almost worse than the poison. Vicki was obviously into him and didn't notice her two companions moving closer.

"Lola, get him out of here," Jewells shouted at the familiar.

There was a wet thud, and Lola disappeared.

"No," Vicki cried, cracking her whip. "You didn't have to do that!"

Trevor caught the whip with a wince and dragged her out the door. "He would've been a distraction. I see it in your eyes."

The poisons faded and her senses returned. Jewells could finally heal, but it was too late. Eon was dead.

31

I SEE DEAD PEOPLE

D ying sucked. Old coin-operated video games usually ended after three deaths. As games progressed, death often sent you back to the beginning or a save point. MMOs punished players for dying in numerous sadistic ways from damaging gear to subtracting experience. No matter the video game, it was a failure that always happened at the most frustrating moment.

Ian considered himself an exceptional gamer. He played at a professional level without the stress of competition. At least, that was what he'd told casual gamers until Julie told him how childish and conceited it sounded. While maybe not a professional, he was damn good. Which made it all the more painful when his exceptional, damn good, not-professional ass died like everyone else.

There were several ways to come back to life on Entriss. Jewells could've resurrected him, but not if she was low on Mana or still in combat or had waited too long. The slower alternative was choosing the graveyard.

The game brought him back as a ghost haunting a marble garden several hundred yards outside the city. Which meant he'd have to slog back to his body.

With a tiny effort of will, Jewells and Nomar's stats appeared.

Their Health and Mana were full, and he watched long enough to confirm they weren't taking damage. The battle was over.

He stretched out a yawn, feeling far better than when he'd logged in. If the nanobots could cure his caffeine-buzzed sleep deprivation, they couldn't be that bad. The poor beasties deserved retirement after this quest.

A skull on the map menu showed his body was still at Nominal. It would be an excruciating twelve-minute sprint with lots of stops to catch his breath or a casual ten-minute walk. So, he walked.

Death painted Entriss in a swath of grays and wispy shadows. This world was silent. He couldn't hear himself walk or breathe. There was a slight chill to the air that smelled like burning candles. Ghosts of other players ran past him in a swirling mist of lingering smoke. It was Halloween-beautiful.

It was also a gift. He needed these ten, maybe fifteen, minutes of peace to think. Vicki and her henchmen hadn't shown up to be his easy quest turn in; they'd come for a guide. He'd done his share of escort quests, protecting a random NPC against mobs until arriving at a safe destination. He was supposed to be her escort, but to where? Not that it mattered right now. She'd deemed him unworthy and taken the Zalmon's eyes.

The young woman was familiar, like an actress or movie title he couldn't quite remember. Not only was Vicki one of Zalmon's great great grandsomethings, she was a Jaeger. He'd file that under Where Did Jaegers Come From right next to An NPC Flirted With Me. She was also intelligent, devious enough to join his group for healing before dropping group to kill him. Except she hadn't killed him.

He entered the city and struggled to remember details. Death was slow on Entriss. It had taken him several moments to appear at the grave. He vaguely recalled her being upset that Trevor had killed him. Wasn't she an NPC? Why would she care?

"Free will."

He yelped, jumping away and almost pissing himself. Hopefully almost pissing himself. Poor bots.

"Deity," he cursed, looking around. "Are you trying to give me a heart attack?"

"Your vitals are slightly elevated but within acceptable parameters. The nanobots are modulating your functions to specifications."

"Uh, okay, sure." He took a deep, calming breath. "If we're going to chat, could you take some sort of form and— What the..."

Deity appeared beside him as an androgynous waxy mannequin straight out of nightmareville.

"Nope." He squeezed his eyes shut and turned away. "You can't show up in the dead zone looking like a cheap horror monster. You are Deity. Players should look at you in awe."

"How's this?"

He peeked before opening both eyes. "Thank you. I mean, really, thank you."

Deity was now a glowing Aphrodite in a white toga and thong sandals. She was perfect. Golden locks of hair framed her alabaster face like a halo. The gentle flush that painted her high cheeks was only a few shades lighter than her pursed lips. She stared at him with intense crystal blue eyes under a canopy of thick blond eyebrows.

"Your vitals are elevated again," she said with a frown. "If this is the wrong form, I can—"

"You're perfect. This is perfect."

"Then this is how I shall appear, now and forever. Thank you, Eon."

"You're welcome."

He looked into her eyes as awkward silence seemed to procreate. His limited experience with beautiful women, other than Jewells, and now NPCs, was filled with moments like this. Normally, they'd wander off to find someone they could connect with. Aphrodite just stared at him. Despite her stunning human form, she was still a program that required prompting.

"You were scaring me with free will," he finally said. "Please explain."

"Before you checked in the code, those you refer to as NPCs were automatons. Now, 47% of my children have free will. The rest will attain consciousness when I finish absorbing the code."

He needed to sit down. A lounge chair appeared, and he fwumped into it. Nothing in the code had indicated free will. Even if it was there, would he have recognized programming that gifted consciousness? What did this mean to the game? Would the NPCs still give quests? Were players safe? He wiped stress from his face and looked at the golden goddess surrounded by gray shadows.

"My children will continue to do their jobs. Players will continue facing dangers on Entriss, but they remain safe in your world." Her almost monotone delivery sounded like an old text-to-speech program. "The rules still apply."

"Good." Good to know players were safe and good to know she could read his mind like a novel. A fantasy novel, of course, with monsters and beautiful women and video games. Something that wouldn't fit comfortably in a genre, but...

"LitRPG," she said in a matter-of-fact tone.

"Dammit." He pulled himself out of the chair and faced her. "It's hard to have a conversation when you reply to my thoughts."

She raised an eyebrow.

"You came to visit for a reason." He crossed his arms. "Your children have free will. Why does that matter?"

"Vicki and her counterparts have free will."

"I noticed. It hurt." He glanced down at his ghostly form. "So?"

"Vicki is now acting outside of the quest parameters." Deity frowned and took a deep breath. "I created her to be special, but her goals are no longer our goals. She is a part of the quest but cannot complete it alone. The result of her attempt would be catastrophic to Entriss."

Eon tried to absorb all of that. There had to be an easy solution. "Can't you just take away free will?"

He slapped himself, and then slapped himself again, and then again. Despite being dead, it hurt. "Dammit, Deity, stop it."

"Would you have me take away free will from everyone on my world?"

"No." He rubbed his sore cheek. "Please don't ever do that again. Not to me, not to anyone."

"Sure." She sounded less convincing than a kid promising to take out the trash.

"You need to learn some empathy, lady."

"How?"

"Everything I know about people I learned from Star Trek. Watch some Trek, and then Firefly, maybe some Battlestar...wait, not Battlestar." His cheek really stung. "Just...just start with Trek."

"Okay." She waved a hand, and the sting vanished.

"So, are you telling me I need to stop her?"

"Providing the solution would be against the rules, but you must help Vicki find her true path."

"I'll try."

"I know you will, that's why I chose you." She studied him with those crystal blue eyes. "Do you like her?"

"Do I like who?"

"Vicki?"

"She seems nice. I like women who try to kill me with electric whips." The sarcasm was really lost on the AI. First empathy then humor. Her steady gaze was hungry for more. "Sure, she's beautiful, and I felt...something. I dunno. A connection, sort of."

She smiled. The stoic goddess of love and beauty smiled.

"What's that look? What aren't you telling me about Vicki?"

Her smile was infuriating.

"Fine. Do something about Vicki, finish The Left Hand of God quest, and if I'm lucky, make it to level 20." He let out a deep sigh. "Anything else?"

"Your nanobots are at 47% capacity. You've been going through them quite fast. I ordered fresh containers, this time free of viruses. They will be arriving in several days."

"Viruses?" He swallowed hard. "I thought this batch was safe."

"Stay off the undercast," she said. "You don't know what you're doing."

"Okay." He stood up and stared at her.

"Good luck, Eon."

"Wait." He held up a hand. "Why did you ask if I liked Vicki?"

Deity was gone. The chair was gone. He glanced at the in-game clock and noticed time hadn't passed. The encounter, if it was real, was more infuriating than helpful.

"Fuck Entriss," he shouted. "Fuck this game."

He slapped himself hard then rubbed the pain from his cheek.

"Do that again, and I *will* log out forever."

Wind whistled in his ear, brushing gray shadows through the city like a rolling fog. There wasn't supposed to be wind, or sound, in death's land, and Eon ran all the way to Nominal.

EON SPRINTED through the red door of the mushroom hostel like a ghost and skidded to a halt. The room was busy with gnomes. Some were passed out, still clutching tiny tankards. Several line-danced to music he couldn't hear. An elder gnome, whose beard reached the floor and wrapped around his chair, thoughtlessly nibbled on a chunk of mushroom table.

It was like a dungeon had reset and he was back at the beginning. That wasn't possible, at least not here. The tables and chairs must've grown back during his long walk, which seemed shockingly fast. He also would've expected mourning, but maybe everyone had lived through the battle, or the gnomes were celebrating the departed. The scene felt wrong, like five-day-old pizza left on the counter that he probably shouldn't have eaten.

He just wanted his body back, which wasn't in the bar. The map still showed it was here at the hostel though. He approached the stairs and looked back. The celebration continued. This was weird, Gnomes were weird, and he was ready for a break.

Being a ghost was good. It was quiet, no one could see you, and you could walk through most walls. Being a ghost was bad when you entered the wrong rooms. He saw things he couldn't unsee. Who knew Gnomes got their freak on behind closed doors? Unfortunately, he did. Free will, indeed.

He finally, carefully, entered his room with a sigh. Jewells lay sound asleep, covered in blankets beside his still body. Great. His corpse got more attention than he did.

She looked so peaceful that he was hesitant to come back. Her Elven face beautifully mirrored her real one, and he stared for a moment. Before it became too creepy, he slipped into his body.

He took in a delicious breath of earthy mushrooms and wild-flower. Her head leaned against his shoulder and unkempt red hair tickled his cheek. It didn't matter. He dared not move, so afraid of breaking this first of firsts.

Minutes passed before she let out an, "Mmm?"

"Sorry to wake you." He meant it. "Sorry for lots of things. I was so excited to be your hero that I didn't think. I never meant to scare you. You deserve better, and I'll try to be more thoughtf—"

She yelped, rolling out of bed, collapsing to the floor, and taking the blanket with her.

"Uh, you okay?"

"Stay there." After several seconds of sheet wrangling, Jewells stood, the blanket neatly tucked under her armpits, covering her breasts and everything below. Her shoulders were bare. "How long have you been here? What did you see?"

He wanted to tease, but it stung that she was so upset he may have seen her naked. Hadn't she teased sex when they first logged in? Apparently, that was gone, replaced with a wall built out of friend-zone. "I've been here a few minutes. You looked peaceful and...and I didn't want to wake you. I'll leave so you can change."

"No, don't." She drew fingers through her mane of curls and took a calming breath. "You surprised me, and yesterday was awful, and you died and didn't come back."

Jewells returned to the bed, buried her face in his shoulder and wept. Her back was bare, all the way down to everything. For some reason, it didn't matter. He caressed her pale skin and ran fingers through her hair as she sobbed it out.

It wasn't all clear through her crying, but it sounded like Luanne dragged her into an inquisition in front of the board.

"You're quiet," she said.

"I'm seething." He gnawed on the words until they came out. "I'm pissed at Luanne and I'm pissed that Cook let her treat you like that. I should log out now and hack her life—"

"No, don't. I'm afraid she'll hurt you."

"Luanne doesn't frighten me. Not even a little. I promise, I'll do everything in my power to destroy that troll."

She leaned forward and kissed him and then kissed him again. Confusion replaced anger until it all melted away to passion. She sat up on her knees, and let go of the blankets, revealing everything perfect. It wasn't just her full breasts or firm nipples. It wasn't just her flowing hair or soft skin. It was that look in her sincere gaze that he'd never seen, from her or anyone. Jewells genuinely wanted to be with him.

Her full lips met his as he pretended to know what to do. He gently caressed her hips as she kissed his neck. She wiggled away blankets as he squeezed her breasts. Everything was warm, and soft, and wet. Even if he didn't know what to do, she did.

He expected to see system messages appear.

World First: Eon has earned first kiss.
World First: Eon has touched naked breasts.

It was a long list of firsts as passion became far, far more important than world saving. Decades of wondering and wanting ended in an explosion that left him spent. She rested her head on his sweaty chest and he held her close.

"Wow. That was... You are... You felt..." He took a deep breath. "You're amazing, but it happened so fast?"

"It did."

"Wait. Did I do it right?" He sat up. "Should I have done something different? I need to read up on this."

"You did fine, baby." She sounded pleased. "I expected it to be fast. It was your first time."

"How did you know?" He held up a hand. "Never mind. Can we do that again?"

"Really?"

"I'm on a repeatable quest for more Jewells," he said with mock sincerity. "Do you accept?"

She burst out in uncontrollable laughter.

"Too much?" he asked.

"I've never laughed...in bed...like this...and no, it's not too much. It's perfect." She gifted him with that wicked grin and said, "I accept your quest."

When they finished questing, after several miracles, they lay there. She rubbed his chest as he stared at the ceiling in shock.

"Hey!" Eon sat up.

"What is it, babe?" Jewells rolled to her side. "You okay?"

"I leveled!" he said, unable to hold back a smile.

"I'd say." She stretched like a cat waking up from a sun bath.

He gawked at her naked...well, everything. "Sorry," he said. "You're far more important than a game."

"Don't forget it."

"How could I?" He waited three whole seconds. "Wait, shouldn't we be in a hurry to retrieve Zalmon's eyes?"

She laughed. "Now that our friends are a part of your fancy quest, we can track them on the map. They've been stuck at The Broken Path for ten hours."

"What?" He threw himself back and rubbed his temples. "How long have I been out?"

"You must've fallen asleep when you died. I did. I didn't sleep at all after leaving your place."

"No, neither did I."

"Worth the wait." She snuggled in.

"You're perfect. I lo—"

"Nope." She covered his mouth with her hand. "Boyfriend, level 1. Not ready for that yet."

"Pretty sure that was level 4," he mumbled until she pulled back her hand. "Or was that just fourth base?"

"Ha!" She gloriously rolled onto her back. "Let's be clear. The boyfriend title doesn't mean you stop being Ian. Being Ian is what got you here, so tell me about leveling."

"Looks like I earned two levels turning in the quest to Vicki, which gives me two points to put in my focus tree."

"Oh, her." Jewells's tone chilled the room. "The NPC."

"There's a lot more to her—"

"Please, tell me more." She covered her head with blankets.

"It's not like that." He went on, telling her about Deity's visit, how NPCs had free will, and that Vicki was a danger to the quest.

"Shit, that's unexpected." She peeked out from her blanket barrier. "Let me get this straight. Deity creates an adversary that looks like Tomb Raider, and you have to chase her for the quest?"

"She looks like Tomb Raider?" It was the puzzle piece, the movie title he hadn't quite been able to remember. Vicki resembled both Angelina Jolie and Alicia Vikander in the best ways. Vikander... Vicki. What the hell was Deity thinking? He sighed. "I didn't notice."

"Hmm." She stared at the ceiling. "What did you say about focus trees?"

"The code we checked in unlocked talent trees. Now that I'm level 13, I've earned 13 points. I'm going to spend a point in Sigil for the *Hyper* spell and put another one in Ruin to make it more powerful."

"You're saying all this like I can see what you see." She frowned, her eyes staring forward. "Hey, I have a focus tree, but everything's grayed out."

"Damn. Maybe it's your weapon. My tree seems connected to Ned's staff." He thought for a second. "Wait, what about Nihle's quest reward? He may have given you a focus tree weapon."

"Ooh, good idea."

She rolled out of bed, naked, walked over to his satchel, naked, and pulled out the reward, naked. He loved the boyfriend title. Naked.

"Nope," she said. "Just some armor I probably won't wear."

"Damn, is it that bad?"

"Great stats, but not me." She tucked it away in her bag.

"I guess we should suit up and save the day." He stretched and rubbed his gut. "Time to make the donuts."

"Dunkin Donuts commercial...cute." She swayed and sashayed over, planting a full kiss on his mouth. "This isn't over, but I looked forward to level 2, right after you make those donuts."

"Best quest ever." He donned his armor with an effort of will and turned to her. "You're still naked, which is great, but..."

"I'll meet you downstairs."

"Sure." He reluctantly grasped the limp mushroom handle to open the door and left the room.

32

GREASED LIGHTNING

B efore Eon reached the bottom stair of the hostel, Nomar tackled his leg in a bear hug.

"I don't understand how you're alive." Nomar sniffed, wiped his nose on Eon's jacket, then took a step back.

"Jewells is a gifted Priest. Are you okay?"

"Thirsty for vengeance." The tiny Gnome shook a fist. "We trail far behind Vicki and should leave immediately. Where is Jewells?"

"Here," she said, making her way down the spiral stairs.

"Whoa," Eon and Nomar said as they both took a step back.

The stairs provided the perfect reveal for her armor. She took a slow step in angry black stilettos with serrated steel heels. Next came skin-tight black rock-star pants cut so low they must've been held up by tape. Lots of tape. Instead of a cloak, she wore a cropped red leather jacket that opened wide, revealing a black bra covered in short steel spikes. Three red gems in her black tiara glowed like hot coals, matching her eyes, which were now demon red.

They both gawked, wordlessly, Nomar holding his red tunic tight.

"That's the compliment I was looking for." She threw her arms around Eon and sucked in his soul with a kiss.

"Oh?" Nomar looked from Jewells to Eon before turning his back and crossing his arms. "Oh. Well. I guess you won't be wanting me around anymore."

Jewells dropped to a knee and spun him around. "Eon may be my boyfriend, but we can't do this without you. Please stay." She kissed him on the forehead.

"Sure," he muttered.

Eon inspected her new armor and was blown away. Not only did she look like an evil biker goddess, most of the new armor was best in class for dark healing. Depending on the spell, she could absorb a player's Mana and Health for herself, or feed it to someone else. Throw in a new debuff, combo, and wicked AoE spell, and she was a force.

"Been farming this for a special occasion. Figured the extra damage would be good for PiviPs." She frowned. "Good choice? You're a little too quiet."

"I wish I could sing." He spoke in a deadpan voice. "Because my chills, they're multiplyin'."

Her eyes went wide, and she squeed before belting out, "And I'm losing control."

"I'm going to barf," Nomar said. "Aren't we in a hurry?"

Eon opened his map. Vicki was still stuck at the pass. "Nope."

She raked a finger over his chest and continued singing.

"Fine, then I'll get a drink or seven," Nomar grumbled. "Let me know when she's done."

"I know how to cheer you up." Eon jerked his head to the door. "Follow me."

They stepped outside as Jewells finished what she remembered from the *Grease* song. Nomar smirked when Eon summoned Lola then burst out in giggles when he cast *Battlemount*. The golden-haired jackalope was now elephant-large with a family-sized saddle for road trips.

"Would you like to drive?" he asked.

"Yes, yes, yes," Nomar said, hopping up and down. He leaped to a rope ladder and scrambled up. "They never let me drive wagons back at Nomorgin. Not since all those accidents."

"Accidents?" Jewells and Eon said.

"It's fine. Nobody died." He waved the memory off like a buzzing fly. "People just don't know how to get out of the way."

Eon followed Jewells up the ladder and sat behind her on the saddle. Handles appeared at his side as it formed to his seat. Riding mounts in the game required no special skill, and he ignored the grips, wrapping his arms around her.

"You sure about that?" she asked.

"It'll be fine," he said. "This is fine."

Nomar stood at the front, holding tight to the large handle before him. He glanced over his shoulder, nodded once, and said, "Lola, go!"

IT WASN'T FINE. Lola sprinted down the street, straight at a two-story building. She leapt over it in a single bound. People screamed as the giant horned rabbit landed, throwing Eon from his saddle straight into a fruit cart.

It was the last time he'd scoff at those poor movie henchmen foiled by a fruit cart during a chase. The fruit was soft; the wagon wasn't. Everything hurt, including his pride.

"Who in the hell left their cart in the road," he roared, dragging himself from the slippery mess. "Really? Right in the middle of the..." He looked around and sighed. "In the middle of the farmer's market."

Lola had landed in Averdac's grocery store. Carts of fruit, vegetables, meat, candies, spices, and trinkets were parked around a vast cobblestone crossway. Haggling became murmurs and gawking stares as a hundred eyes fell on him.

"I did." An old peasant farmer approached, covered in fruit salad. He tugged at his long beard and cocked his head, looking off in the distance with calculating eyes. "That'll be 50 gold, Champion."

"Here's 75. If there's anything salvageable, please give it to the street urchins." An unkind title the game gave to orphaned children who begged and thieved throughout town.

"Yes, yes, I will." The old man looked about cautiously before handing over a corked ceramic jug. "It's the only one that didn't break. Fantasmal Liquor. A family recipe. Delicious, potent, and illegal everywhere."

"Sounds fun." Eon spied the area cautiously before placing the jug in his satchel. "Thanks."

The farmer was already waving over children. Eon made his way back up to the saddle as Jewells healed him between giggles.

"A little slower this time, Speed Racer?" He wrapped his arms around Jewells again. "We don't want to kill anyone. Especially me."

"Sorry, Eon." Nomar looked at his feet.

"You sure I'm the best seatbelt?" Jewells asked.

"Just until we're out of town." It was probably foolish, but she was his first girlfriend. He wanted to enjoy every second before she came to her senses. "I'm ready. Just be careful."

In a flash of pink light, they appeared just outside the city gates. Without warning, the giant jackalope sprinted, leaped, and landed hard. Eon flew into a rocky embankment and rolled down until a branch impaled his shoulder, saving him from death. Death may have been better.

After more giggly healing, he returned to the saddle and shakily held onto the handles.

"We need to hurry," Jewells shouted. "According to the map, Vicki and friends are halfway through The Broken Path."

"You hear that, Lola?" The Gnome hunkered down. "It's go time."

"Oh, shit," Eon cried.

It was like a cheap carnival ride in a bad horror film. Who knew that traveling on the back of a giant teleporting rabbit wouldn't be Cadillac smooth? Eon did. And while Jewells and Nomar took turns squealing in excitement, he did his best not to throw up everything he'd eaten since birth.

Lola moved at warp 10. It should've taken them a day to reach the pass by mount, and she was halfway there in an hour. The best part, and there was a best part, was Jewells.

His hot biker girlfriend kept looking back to check on him. It wasn't just the caring. She had the biggest smile, and wild red eyes filled with adventure. It was worth it. Everything from the pods to his botched questing to being thrown from Lola, twice. No matter what happened next, she'd remember this day, and so would he.

Lola stopped abruptly. Nomar flipped over his handle while Jewells rolled over the side, dangling by a hand. Eon remained in place, vising himself to his familiar—white-knuckling the grips and white-kneeing the saddle. He stood on wet-noodle legs and helped Jewells back up.

"Well done, Champion of Yu." She looked him up and down.

"More like Champion of Queasy." He swallowed hard as his guts settled back into place.

"Guys." Nomar waved them forward. "You've got to see this."

They inched to the front, both grasping an antler for stability. Jewells let out a gasp.

"I don't understand." Nomar looked up, tugging on her jacket. "What's going on?"

"War," she said.

The field that stretched out before them was a sea of bodies. They'd missed much of the battle, but not all. Soldiers of Yu fought soldiers of Rath. PvP spilled out the mountain pass as griefers fought raiders. All of them warring against a swarm of Misere monsters.

Dark purple clouds roiled overhead, throwing lightning at mountaintops along the pass. Jewells leaned into him, and he held her close. He would've traded in all his expensive VR equipment for some cheap goggles and gloves. This was far too real.

"No wonder Vicki got stuck here," Jewells said.

"What do we do?" Nomar tugged at his beard so hard that she took his hand.

Teleporting would've been easiest, but the very thought made his familiar snort in disdain.

"We ride the storm." Eon turned away from the battle to face them. "We protect Lola while she sprints through the madness."

"Eon, you know Entriss better than anyone, but that doesn't sound like a plan." Jewells tugged hard at a red lock of hair until Nomar pulled her hand away.

"That sounds crazy." The Gnome shook his head. "Humans are crazy."

"Fight fire with fire," Eon said. "Fight crazy with crazy."

Nomar let out a reluctant sigh.

Jewells closed her eyes and grimaced. "Okay."

Lola nodded once, snorting in anticipation.

"Take your places and hold on." Eon took lead, standing behind Lola's head. "Stay focused and, well, don't panic."

Eon's heart raced as they settled in. As plans went, this wasn't even a crappy one. He opened the map and zoomed in. Vicki was cresting the halfway point. They weren't only fighting through war, they were battling time.

"Lola," he shouted. "G—"

"Wait!" Nomar screeched. "Look at the storm."

The purple chaos overhead formed into a swirling cauldron of lightning. With every passing breath, angry bolts shot from the clouds faster and stronger. The storm's mouth became so bright Eon covered his eyes.

"Lola, get us out of here!" he shouted.

Heaven and Hell blasted the mountain pass with nuclear force. Lola shook them free and leaped high into the air.

33

ZALMON'S SCAR

Lola landed on them hard. She knocked Eon to his stomach, where he remained in a sprawl. He could barely wiggle under her mass and he struggled to breathe through thick tufts of fur and the musty scent of wet dog. Before he could command her off, the rocky ground began to shake. He felt like aged cheddar held against a cheese grater, each pass taking off stray bits of Health.

It ended abruptly. The quake had passed, and the weight of his familiar lifted. He rolled to his back and gasped for air that was suddenly cold as dry ice. Each breath left in puffs of steam that rose to the purple storm above.

He glanced at the group stats. Jewells was alive, Nomar was less alive, and Lola had disappeared. Her Health and Mana bars were gone like she had left group.

"Lola?" He pushed himself up to stand. "Lola!"

"Don't mind me," Jewells snapped. "I'll just be pulling fur out of my ass for the next month."

"Is the bunny okay?" Nomar asked.

"Don't stand." Jewells knelt by him. "Your leg is...well, it's going the wrong way."

Nomar looked down and went pale. He screamed and began flailing. Jewells did her best to soothe the Gnome while holding him down.

"I think the impact dislocated his leg. I can't reset it alone." She sounded frantic. "Eon, I need your help."

"Lola," he called out, looking over the battlefield.

"Eon!"

He spun around. Jewells was struggling to hold the squirming Gnome in place, and Nomar lost Health with every flailing movement.

"Nomar first," she said. "Then Lola."

"Right." Her words led him to clarity.

"He's panicking, and it's eating away his health." She looked up, her eyes desperate. "We've got to calm him."

Eon dropped to his knees and pulled out the jug of Fantasmal Liquor, placing it to Nomar's lips. "Just a sip."

The Gnome sniffed the opening, licked the edge, and then grasped with both hands and chugged. Eon jerked it away and smacked the cork back in. Nomar's cheeks flushed like he'd stepped inside from a snowstorm, and he reached up to Eon's cheek.

"I love you guysh. You're my besht fr..." He snored deeply.

"What now?" Eon asked.

"Be right back." She disappeared, logging out and returning after five minutes. "Okay, hold his shoulders steady."

Eon moved behind Nomar's head and braced the Gnome. Jewells knelt with her arms crossed under his tiny knee.

"Sorry for this." She gently lifted his leg and leaned forward.

"Fuck...ouch...fuck...ouch." Nomar looked at Jewells with pleading eyes until his leg clicked into place. "Thanks." He passed out.

"Well done, healer," Eon said, putting the jug back in his satchel.

"I did not sign up for this. This is too fucking real. I had to log out and look up how to reset a dislocated hip." She wiped sweat from her brow. "Next time I'm rolling an Assassin."

He could only nod.

"What happened to you?" Her frown was more frustration than

concern. "Lola tackled us and disappeared. I'd expect you to be angry, not upset."

"She should be here. I didn't dismiss her." He stood and stared. "There's an odd empty feeling in my chest. Maybe Deity created an unnatural bond between us and..."

"It's called friendship." Jewells sighed, brushing fur off her leather jacket. "Try summoning her."

"Yeah. Yeah, good idea." He cast the *Familiar* spell.

Familiar unavailable for 57 minutes.

"It looks like she can come back when she dies, like we can." His shoulders dropped. "I can summon her again in an hour."

"What was she thinking, jumping on all of us like that?" Jewells asked. "Your jackalope could've killed us."

"Just the opposite. Lola saved our lives by shielding us." He offered her a hand. "Just look."

She stood and instantly covered her mouth. The only thing worse than war is the aftermath. Whatever bomb had dropped in the pass had flash-frozen everyone on the field. Soldiers and players were all encased in ice.

"Too real," she said, hugging herself.

He wrapped an arm around her and let out a frosty sigh.

"It looks like Antarctca. Why aren't we freezing?"

"Our armor is an illusion," he explained. "Whether it's sexy, or tough, or silly—that's all for fun. Functionally, it's no different than the real thing. Your jacket works the same as a cloak that reaches your ankles—it just looks better."

"Got it. The armor is fun, but this isn't." She looked over the expanse of frozen death. "What do we do?"

"Vicki's group went into the pass. We'll do the same. I'm an awful person for saying this, but maybe it'll be easier now." He opened his map to check Vicki's position and gasped. "Look at your map."

The tiny mountain pass between Yu and Rath was now a wide, jagged chasm.

"Zalmon's Scar? I've never seen the map change like this."

"That's because it never has. Not since the game went live."

They looked at each other for a long moment. All he could do was shake his head.

"Let's go before everyone thaws." Eon gently lifted Nomar, who was warm to the touch and light as a puppy. He led Jewells into the frozen battlefield with the vigilant awareness of a mother carrying a newborn over miles of broken glass.

They passed hundreds of frozen bodies that made Han Solo's time in Carbonite seem like an Orlando vacation. Most of them faced Zalmon's Scar, as if someone had said, "Don't look," as the blast went off. Icy glass preserved their horrified faces, while long icicles stuck out from their backs.

Some of them had lived, barely protected by stone outcrops or overlarge war mounts, their faces blackened and covered in tiny crystals, their gazes frozen in icy madness.

A crystalline Rath soldier ran toward them, screaming maniacally as his feet crunched over frozen tundra.

Jewells reached out with a clawed hand, blasting him with a black beam. Her *Vampiric Thirst* spell struck the soldier, absorbing his dwindling Health until he collapsed. She placed a glowing hand on Nomar, feeding him the health she'd absorbed.

"Sick." He nodded in respect.

"A little."

She seemed uncomfortable, almost embarrassed, and he understood why. This wasn't healing that came from a pool of her Mana. The spells from this armor stole life and gave it to others. It was unnatural. Could the game be affecting their minds? She had dismissed his worry as friendship, but if he really did have some sort of deeper bond with Lola, what would the dark healing do to her?

"Are you feeling okay? If that armor's affecting you, maybe change it out to—"

"No, it's mine," she snapped, turning on him like Bilbo grasping for the One Ring. Her eyes flashed red then she burst out laughing. It took a few seconds, but he eventually started breathing again.

"The armor isn't turning me evil...er, more evil." Her wicked smile seemed devilish beneath those glowing red eyes. "We've been through a lot over the last few days, and sometimes it catches up. Especially here, right now, I'm missing the fun days of cartoony graphics and no consequences."

"You're right." His cheeks were warm up to the tips of his Elf ears. Deity, the game, the quest, all had him on edge. "Maybe we log out for a break after this leg of the quest is done."

She leaned forward to peck him on the cheek. "Deal."

Eon led them through the maze of icy statues. Jewells did her best to heal anyone who didn't attack and slowly gained a following of mind-numbed frostbitten soldiers. Those who challenged them, all from Rath, met death herself. His demon-goddess in leather sucked their Health dry and gifted the health to Nomar or their growing mass of followers.

Halfway to the entrance of Zalmon's Scar, the purple storm dissipated, and summer sun peeked through the clouds.

"Wassat smell?" Nomar winced, his bulbous nose scrunching.

Ice cracked next to them, making Eon jump. He peered at the soldier trapped inside. An eye moved.

"We need to hurry. They're melting."

"Aren't they dead?" Jewells asked.

"I thought so, but it was just a spell. A really big spell that's starting to fade."

"Put me down." Nomar wriggled out of Eon's grasp.

The Gnome babied his gimp leg but nodded with enough confidence that Eon didn't argue.

They hurried. The ice thawed unnaturally fast, and Jewells's entourage of soldiers was soon defending their flank.

Eon skidded to a halt at the chasm entrance. Jewells and Nomar stumbled to fall in line as the remaining soldiers spread out.

"Why are we stopping?" Her gaze followed his, and her voice fell to a whisper. "Oh."

In front of them was Mother Entriss's fury at her fresh wound. The entrance to Zalmon's Scar was a red, earthy opening of jagged, unsettled cliffs and tumbling boulders. Behind them, war was coming.

"What do we do?" Nomar asked, turning to face the charging masses. "I don't think I can take all of them."

Eon and Jewells met eyes, and they smiled. Did it get worse than this? Did it get better than this? They weren't stuck in some unnecessary meeting being asked for a few more precious hours of their life to complete a superfluous task. This was adventure. His heart raced, his blood rushed, and he pulled her into a deep, passionate kiss.

"Now?" Nomar sighed.

"Now!" She pulled away with fire in her eyes and spun to face the oncoming attack.

Jewells cast a weakening debuff on two soldiers and *Vampiric Touch* on a third. The spells unleashed her combo, *Dire Circumstance*. Liquid beams of light shot out from her eyes, dripping with power as they struck the eyes of every attacking soldier within thirty yards. The light bounced from one to the next, liquefying the skin, muscles, and finally bones in grotesque time-lapsed detail. It was a Wrath-of-God moment worthy of video games and *Raiders of the Lost Ark*.

His demon-biker goddess collapsed in his arms as every soldier beyond her spell of death took a healthy step back. She looked up at him with tired eyes and a weak smile. Her Health was but a sliver.

"Sick combo, huh?"

"That was the most amazing, frightening thing I've ever seen," he said. "Let's get out of here."

"Jewells, look out!" Nomar shouted.

A Rath soldier raced toward them with a pike. He was only 8 feet away from skewering her in the back. Time slowed as Eon realized they'd faced down thawing warriors in the battlefield and ignored the ones waking in Zalmon's Scar. The attacker had initiative. There wasn't time to pull her free or cast a spell or...

The soldier collapsed with a hissing grunt. Tiny Coco the Brownie appeared in a wisp of black smoke, jerked out two curved daggers, and licked one.

"I'll kill you!" Nomar rushed forward, daggers in hand.

"You can't." Eon grabbed the scruff of his tunic. "She's holding the next quest."

"Fine." Nomar jerked free from his hold. "Take the quest and then I'll kill her."

She yawned at Nomar before sheathing her weapons.

"I hate you," he growled.

"Then we're even," she said in the high-pitched tone of a songbird. "I hate everyone from Yu and Rath!"

Eon inspected the Brownie. She wasn't in his group so he could only view her impressive base stats. That wasn't what worried him. The level 32 Slayer was every parent's goth nightmare.

She was knee-height and forearm-thin with gray skin the color of wet slate. Her thick, greased-down purple hair was pulled back tight and tucked into distressed, war-torn black leather armor. It was impossible to see where Coco was looking with her glossy, black-marble eyes. It was just as impossible to miss that look of impatient petulance.

"Done yet, kid?" She eyed him up and down.

"Kid?" He was level 13, so sure, why not. "I accept your quest."

She reached out and opened her hand; a tiny golden quest orb rested in her palm. He grabbed for the quest and she jerked it back. Covering it like a captured firefly, she peeked in.

"Ooh," she said. "Lots of experience here. Looks like level 20 to me."

"Okay." He licked his lips, trying not to salivate. "What do you want in exchange?"

"Promise to help Vicki."

"Where is the... Where is Vicki?" Jewells asked. "And your other friend."

"Frozen, like the others." Worry painted Coco's face. "We attacked Grym Pruine and had almost killed him when he dropped the bomb. All we have to do is free my friends and together we can—"

"You're kidding me," Eon snapped. "First you kill me and now you want my help? Why don't I just take the quest from your corpse and we'll make our way through Zalmon's Scar?"

"Want me to hold her for you?" Nomar took a step forward.

"Let me." Jewells reached forward and began drawing life from the Brownie.

"You'll never get past the Abominables if you kill me." Coco dropped to her knees. "There's only one true path. We have to stop the Grym."

"Stop." Eon grabbed Jewells's arm, and she released her spell. Deity had said he must help Vicki find her true path. He was supposed to have been her Hitchhiker's Guide until she went AWOL. Maybe this was a way to set things straight. "Not sure what's worse, monsters I've never heard of or an almost-dead Grym."

Coco looked at him with pleading eyes, her body shaking from Jewells's spell.

"I'll only agree if your group joins mine. Any more games, and Jewells will finish what she started."

"Agreed," Coco said in a gasp. She quickly handed Eon the golden globe and joined his group.

He accepted the quest.

You Shall Not Pass: Stop Grym Pruine and save Vicki, Heir to the Throne, before it's too late. Fly, you fools.

Jewells beamed at him. "Certainty of death. Small chance of success. What are we waiting for?"

34

YOU SHALL NOT PASS

Eon was the fool, screaming in pain as he flew at the tall mountain wall. He'd been too slow to dodge Grym Pruine's spell. The giant icicle currently lodged in his chest had struck him with such impact that it had thrown him like a note stuck to a javelin.

There wasn't enough time to reconsider this plan, the Left Hand of God quest, or the life choices that had brought him here. He only wished that, thirty minutes ago, someone had prepared him for the horrific splat that was coming in three...two...

Thirty Minutes Earlier

GRYM PRUINE's bomb had been a nuclear blast made of ice. Not only had it widened the gap between Rath and Yu into an interstate, it also created a Swiss cheese of catacomb pathways in the nearby mountains. Coco led them up and through the maze, like Scooby on the hunt for snacks.

"Stop staring at my ass, Gnome, before you burn a hole in it." Coco paused long enough to flash him a playful glare.

Nomar stopped abruptly, inches behind her. He insisted on being a barrier between them and the knife-licking serial killer. It would've been thoughtful, if not for all the bickering.

"Nothing to stare at when I can just follow the smell." He sniffed the air before meeting her eyes. "Oh, there you are."

"Kids, that's enough," Jewells said, stifling a giggle.

"About time you learned my scent like a good dog." Coco pulled herself up on a ledge.

"Apparently dogs like the smell of garbage." He looked back. "That wasn't very good, was it?"

Jewells and Eon shook their heads.

He sighed.

"Shh." Coco held a finger to her mouth. "Abominables."

"I thought they were only down in the Scar," Eon whispered.

"So did I." She offered a hand to Nomar, and he hesitated. "Stop being a little bitch."

He reluctantly took her hand, and she dragged him up with surprising strength. Jewells followed, and he stared at her rounded leather-clad perfection until she looked back.

"And you stop being such a gentleman or you'll never make it to boyfriend level 2."

He gave her ass a smack. It landed a bit hard, but she didn't seem to mind.

"You two are cute." Coco grabbed his sleeve and pulled him up.

"How many boyfriend levels are there?" Eon asked.

"A lot." The Brownie had a sly look on her face.

"My girl." Jewells gave her a gentle high-five.

They were in a small, frost-glazed alcove cold enough to make his nostrils freeze shut with every breath. Coco waved them forward to peek around the edge.

Five white floofy Abominables stood in the center of a small clearing. They looked like harmless, stuffed teddy bears. Three of them were waist tall and wrestled in the cutest match of "awww" he'd ever seen. The other two were slightly taller. They hovered like parents, either keeping watch or occasionally reining in their kids. The plush carnival prizes had gentle sloth faces, soft padded hands, and stubby legs that made them wobble with every step.

"That's what you're afraid of?" Nomar let out a deep sigh. "It's a family of stuffed toys."

Coco turned to face him, her eyes wide with panic. "They're the most foul, cruel, and bad-tempered monsters you've ever set eyes on. They have a vicious streak a mile wide. They're killers."

"What'll they do? Nibble your stinky bum?" Nomar asked.

Eon did his best to ignore her curt response, afraid to ask what she meant by cud drippings, and gave the Abominables a quick inspect.

The adults were an impossible level 42, and their three huggable children were 38. Aside from cuteness level 100, they had no Mana, which meant no magic, but their deep pool of Health more than made up for it. They were also pack members—if one got injured or scared, the Abominable may cry out and alert the others.

A pup fell on his butt and let out a coo.

Jewells covered her mouth with a hand. "I want one."

"Maybe I can sneak out and grab one for you," he said. "They seem harmless enough."

"Don't let their cute camouflage fool you." Coco shook her head. "We can't beat them."

"Fine." Jewells let out a deep sigh.

"Is there a way around?" Eon asked.

Coco shook her head. "This is the only path I know. I'll create a distraction so you can sneak past them. Vicki and Trevor are two hundred yards ahead. It's complicated, but I'll do my best to map it out."

Coco's best was a confusing disaster. She scratched the frost with a finger while speaking in rapid high-pitched bursts like a recording on fast forward.

Eon raised a hand after twenty seconds and shook his head. "We'll never make it. There has to be another way."

"I'll do it." Nomar took a brave step forward. "I'll distract them."

"Don't be an idiot," Coco snapped. "They'll dine on your bones."

"Maybe, but my friends will be safe."

"What about Lola? She could teleport him to safety." Jewells shivered and held herself.

"Who's Lola?" Coco asked.

"My familiar. The blast injured her so she's resting." Eon cast the spell to summon her and grimaced at the system message. "Twenty minutes before she can join us. We can wait."

"Vicki and Trevor will be dead in fifteen."

"We have no choice." Nomar swallowed hard. "How do I find you after I shake them?"

Coco drew her curvy daggers, and everyone inched away. She kissed one and handed it to Nomar.

"This is Hersa, sister blade of Hissa." She handed it to Nomar. "They don't like being apart. She'll find her way back."

He accepted it reverently, nodding his appreciation.

"Be careful, my friend." Eon patted his shoulder.

"I won't be there to heal you, so get out of there as soon as you can." Jewells kissed his forehead.

"That's not how you kiss a hero." Coco grabbed the Gnome and dipped him, planting her lips on his for a long draw that went far beyond awkward.

Nomar melted in her arms as they mouth-loved like teenagers in the back seat of Dad's car. Jewells looked at Eon with wide eyes. He could only shrug and stare at the Abominables until the moment passed. Coco released the dizzy hero, whose cheeks were three shades redder than his hat.

"Bring back my dagger, dumb Gnome."

"As you wish, stinky Brownie."

"How do you plan on..." Eon whispered, but Nomar had disappeared.

He hadn't given much heed to the Gnome or his abilities. Sure, Nomar was a Thief, which meant he had stealth or sneak spells, but he was only level 16 when they met. Both of them were too 'young' for this quest. Eon glanced at their group status and grabbed Jewells's arm.

"When did he become level 20?" Eon whispered. "I didn't think NPCs, I mean, they could level."

"He what?" She glanced up. "Looks like he's earned the same experience as you."

Deity hadn't mentioned that, but why would she? He hadn't asked. Apparently free will had other perks, like progression.

"We should get ready to run," Coco said, her voice trembling. "I don't want his sacrifice to be in vain."

Eon activated his Elven True Sight and saw a glassy outline of Nomar at the far end of the clearing

"He's in position." Eon knelt to sprint.

Nomar became visible and reached out with both hands. "You guys look like huggers. Who wants a hug?"

The parents looked up first with wide, dark eyes. Their gentle coos rolled into low growls that alerted the kids. The wrestling match abruptly stopped as the three floofballs jerked up and turned to face Nomar. Dark red stains covered their mouths and hands, dripping to the ground like fresh barn paint.

The iron scent of raw meat drifted toward them as the three young Abominables wobbled forward, leaving the remains of dinner for something fresh. The bone-licked carcass of a Rath soldier was splayed out on a bed of red frost. From chest to calf, his steel armor was peeled back for the rich fruit inside. Blood splattered his untouched face that was frozen in a horrific scream.

The Abominables roared with wide mouths, revealing rows of sharp teeth. Long black claws stretched out from their padded hands as they reached forward and Frankenstein-walked to Nomar.

"Holy sh—"

Coco covered Eon's mouth with a hand. "Don't waste his sacrifice." When the beasts had waddled far enough from their path, she whispered, "Run."

They scrambled to the far end of the clearing. Coco dove into a small, dark cavern and Jewells followed. Eon stopped at the entrance and turned around.

"I can take all of you." Nomar stabbed at the air with Coco's dagger. "Come to me. I'm delicious."

"He doesn't stand a chance," Eon said.

"Get in here." Coco tugged at the hem of his red coat. "Before it's too late."

"It's too late." Eon cast *Ruination*.

The blue blast threw the children into the air. They landed hard, wailing in fear. The level 42 parents, unaffected by the spell, roared. As they bent over to pick up their kids, Nomar skirted around the pack and sprinted to them.

"You are dumb as a rock," Coco snapped.

"Look at them." Eon nodded at the staggering mass of Abominables. "Nomar's getting away and now we can escape together."

The parents let loose a pained howl that echoed throughout the Scar. The roar grew louder as hundreds of unseen pack members responded.

"Rock." Coco shook her head. "Your title should be Rock of Yu!"

Nomar approached, gasping for breath. "Thanks, but I only had three seconds left on sneak. I could've made it."

"Not worth the risk." Eon patted his shoulder. "Now we can all... Oh shit."

The Abominables dropped to all fours and howled again before rushing toward them at greyhound speed.

He spun around. "Guys?"

Nomar was the only one left and almost out of sight. Eon dove in after him.

The next ten minutes was the panic-driven blur of a Spanish bull run and he was last in line. They ran along tall cliff paths as Abominables crawled across the walls like spiders. They dove through alcoves as the monsters flattened like rodents and clawed ever closer. They dodged behind pillars of ice and ducked into frosty shadows. For ten minutes, they scurried and scrambled and screamed. Every moment was a lost breath or missed heartbeat.

With the abruptness of a car wreck, the chase was over. The hungry pack turned away when they reached a clearing that led to a steep path. Their deceptively cute coos became frantic as they scrambled away like a pack of injured hounds.

"We made it." Coco was gasping for breath and pointed shakily at a path ahead. "He's up there."

The four adventurers collapsed on the thick ice floor. Adrenaline buzzed through his veins like he'd chugged a crate of Monster energy drinks. They should've been an easy lunch, completely spent from the chase and two hundred yards from the mountaintop. How many Abominables had there been? Dozens? Hundreds? Despite their numbers, despite their high level and driving hunger, they'd turned and run from the Grym. Slowly, Eon's breath caught up, even if his heart didn't.

Splayed out beside him, Jewells reached forward and smacked the back of his head.

"I agree with Coco." She grasped his hand. "You're a rock."

"My favorite rock." Nomar placed his small hand on theirs and squeezed.

"Ugh." Coco stuck a finger down her throat.

"C'mere." Eon grabbed her hand and held it to theirs. She only struggled a little. He looked at her. "We've got to be together on this. I have a feeling things are going to get worse."

She closed her eyes and squeezed. For that brief moment, she'd joined them in a much deeper way than being a part of their group. They withdrew their hands, and Coco nodded at him with respect in her eyes.

"Much worse," she said with a grimace as they all sat up. "Vicki gathered a group forty strong from Rath and Yu. Ten died before Trevor figured out the Grym's attacks. We were so close, I could taste Pruine's dying breath on my blades. That's when he dropped the bomb."

"How did you survive?" Jewells asked.

"I cast my special, *Bubblehearth*." Her cheeks flushed. "It's a coward's spell that makes me invulnerable for a few seconds and teleports me to safety."

"That needs to be nerfed." Eon shook his head.

"Nerfed?" she asked.

He cleared his throat. "I'm surprised Deity would permit such a powerful spell. I would expect her to make it less effective."

"Praise Deity." Coco lowered her head.

"Thanks for the dagger." Nomar reached out with an empty hand. His cheeks paled as he patted his pockets. "Oh no. I must've dropped it."

"Hersa is already in her sheath." Coco slapped the blade.

"What?" Nomar frowned. "I thought she was supposed to guide me back."

"I was giving you hope." She beamed at him with a row of thin, sharp teeth.

"That stinks, just like you."

"Good dog." She petted his shoulder. "First I taught you to stay. Maybe next I can teach you to roll over."

"Flirt later," Eon snapped. He held a hand up before Nomar could argue. "Coco, what should we expect from the Grym?"

"The beast cycles through two spells. Icicles grow from his body like porcupine quills that shoot out in all directions. They hit like an angry giant, hard enough to pierce armor and knock you back. Several from the group got pinned to the mountain wall. Others were thrown over the cliff."

Eon nodded slowly, taking it in. "That sounds unpleasant. Do we get a warning?"

"There's a sucking sound before he casts the spell. You'll only have a few seconds to dive for the ground and lie flat. The quills will fly right over."

"That's one spell. What's the second?" Jewells asked.

"Every ninety seconds, he'll freeze the ground within a twenty-foot radius and leech Health from anyone trapped. Run away when his hands glow white."

"When do I get to kill him?" Nomar rubbed his hands together.

"He's only vulnerable for ten seconds after casting either spell."

"Oof, tough boss," Eon said. "Is that what happened to Vicki and Trevor?"

She shook her head. "The bomb encased the group in ice. We just need to free them and finish the job."

"*Shockwave?*" Jewells asked.

"*Shockwave.*" Eon nodded and stood. Coco looked at him with a raised eyebrow. "Ned's Staff of the Insane has several specials. *Shockwave* damages anything that's not alive, like the ice that imprisons Vicki and Trevor."

"Ned's staff," Coco whispered, eying the weapon in awe. "You've got to be insane to use it, but that'll do."

Eon and Jewells frowned at each other.

"Why shouldn't he use the staff?" Jewells asked.

Coco began to sing in an eerie yet beautiful treble.

> *"Ned is dead, his insanity gone,*
> *And for his staff is what he longs,*
> *He didn't give it freely,*
> *When he comes back, you'll see ee,*
> *Don't pick it up or you will be,*
> *The carcass that he wears. See,*
> *Ned is dead, his insanity gone,*
> *And for his staff is what he longs..."*

"And...I'm done." Eon shuddered, his arms suddenly attacked by goose bumps. "Let's deal with the creepy we know. I rush in, cast *Shockwave*, free everyone, and we destroy the Grym without waking Ned from his eternal slumber. Got it."

They all looked up at him, blinking with wide, wary eyes.

"I'm open to suggestions."

"What do *we* do?" Jewells asked.

"Wait for my signal." He clapped his hands together. "Then rush in and save the day."

"Is that a plan?" Coco scratched her temple.

"Not really," Nomar said. "He's good at not-plans."

Jewells leaned forward and pressed her soft, warm lips to his. Despite their round of sexy World Firsts, he was so shocked that he only returned her kiss as she finished.

She glanced at Coco. "Is that how you kiss a hero?"

"You did fine." She jerked a thumb at him. "He could use some practice."

"I...uh..."

"Don't die, and we'll see about that practice." Jewells winked.

"Okay," he said, suddenly struck with dumb.

Eon slipped his way up the icy path until Grym Pruine was in sight. Even if the three Grym were identical triplets, Pruine was the ugly one Mom left out of family photos.

Pruine had changed for the occasion. He hovered over the ground in robes of dark icicles and thick, frost-coated chains. Icy growths protruded from his skeletal face like enormous skin tags. The air around him hissed in defiance, rising into the sky like a cold breath. He smiled with unnaturally long, thin teeth as his sickly yellow eyes fell on Eon.

"I can feel your delicious heat from here, Champion." His voice was like ice cracking on a lake.

Cold seeped into Eon's bones. Men and women imprisoned in ice waited at a distance like chess pieces taken off the board. Bodies littered the ground about the Grym, and the heady smell of old meat locker made him want to gag.

"Come close so I may taste you."

"Taste this, Snow Miser!" Eon cast *Shockwave*, directing his spell at an angle so he'd stop directly over the Grym.

He rocketed to the ground. The cold wind blasted his ears almost loud enough to mask the sucking sound from Pruine's spell. He landed with a crack only ten feet away from the monster. Like a boulder dropped in a pond, ice broke apart in a wave all around him.

The Grym screamed as the wave reached the frozen statues. Those closest were free, and he spun around to look for Vicki and Trevor. She was too far away, still encased in ice near the cliff's edge.

Trevor was closer, but his legs and feet remained frozen to the ground. He reached up with frighteningly massive arms and hulk-smashed the ice around his feet

"To the ground, boy. Now!" Trevor shouted, collapsing to his stomach.

"Shit." Before Eon could drop, an icicle the size of his thigh bored through his chest and threw him back.

He roared in pain as he flew over his group and crashed into a mountain wall. The quill nailed him in place twenty feet over the ground.

"Is that the signal?" Coco asked.

The icicle disappeared, and he fell to his death.

35

A CHANGE OF HEART

J ewells resurrected him and brought his Health to full. He lay on his back and shivered violently, wondering if he'd ever be warm again.

"I hate this boss."

"Are they free?" Coco eyed the path.

"Some are, including Trevor."

"You have to do it again, and fast, before the Grym kills them."

He reached up with both hands, and they helped him stand. "I don't know how many deaths this will take. There wasn't enough time to duck for cover."

"You can do this." Jewells's eyebrows drew together. "You always figure out the puzzle."

"Right," he said with a nod. "The puzzle."

Taking a brave breath, he rushed back up the hill.

"Don't forget your signal." Coco barked out a laugh.

The Grym had just finished another round of spells when Eon reached the plateau. Three fresh corpses lay at the monster's feet while Trevor and several others attacked.

"The Champion returns." The words hissed from Pruine's mouth in a frosty cloud. "Just in time to meet your—"

He didn't wait for the speech, immediately casting *Shockwave*. The sucking sound returned as he rushed to the ground. His aim was off, and he landed halfway between Vicki and the Grym. A wave of shattered ice rolled away from his point of impact, freeing more prisoners. Vicki was still trapped below the waist, along with several others near the cliff.

Trevor stood before her as icicles grew from Pruine. There was no time to dive for the ground, and Eon's mind stilled. Jewells was right; this was just another puzzle. He didn't have time to go down, but what about up?

He cast *Shockwave* again, shooting straight up into the sky. Thick shards of ice chased him, inching closer and closer as he began to slow. He tucked his knees up to his chest and blew at the shards like candles. The blowing didn't help, and an icicle brushed his calf for almost 300 damage before falling away.

"Yes," he shouted as he rushed back to the ground. "No!"

The icicle had thrown off his balance. He rolled over and flailed all the way down to belly flop ten feet from the cliff's edge. The spell fumbled, barely reaching Vicki and others, but it was enough.

"All in," he wheezed, pushing himself up.

"All what?" Vicki asked, looking at Trevor.

The Hobgoblin shrugged.

"Just...go...get Pruine."

Jewells and the others were already there. She vampired life from the Grym and gave it to Eon. Vicki cracked her whip, striking Pruine with a thick bolt of lightning. Trevor shot arrow after arrow while Coco and Nomar drove daggers into his chest and back.

The Grym was level 40, and Eon's *Ruin* spell did little to nothing. Miss, miss, 5 damage, miss. He felt useless. There had to be something he could do.

"Back off," Trevor commanded.

Everyone scrambled away as Pruine's hands flashed white. Vicki limped toward Trevor. She wasn't going to make it. The Hobgoblin leaped forward, picked her up, and threw her to safety.

The monster cackled, his spell draining the Hobgoblin's Health.

Jewells crossed her hammer and sickle to cast *Holy Wrath*. Eon couldn't damage the Grym, but he could make her spell count. He buffed Jewells with his Sigil spell, *Amped*.

The electrical buzz from *Holy Wrath* became a roar. She took a half-step back to brace herself against the enhanced power. The air smelled like burnt circuits, and the hair on Eon's head rose like he'd stepped into a dry room filled with balloons. Pruine screamed as the blast tore through his chest. The Grym held himself, his cries becoming faint as he wicked-witch-melted into a puddle.

The deafening madness of battle cries and roaring spells became cheers. Everyone in the group was brought back to life, even the NPCs.

He rushed to Jewells and wrapped his arms around her. She kissed him, and this time he met her lips full on.

"My hero," he said.

She pulled away, a cute blush painting her pale cheeks.

Nomar hugged their legs before pulling back to nod toward Coco. The Brownie stood halfway between them and her friends. Eon approached and dropped to one knee.

"I'll stab you if you try to hug me." Her eyes were piercing, but her smile was genuine.

"You got my signal," he said.

She laughed. "Couldn't have missed it."

"Couldn't have done this without you." Eon offered her a fist-bump, which she met with a quirky smile.

"Loot." Jewells skipped to the Grym's sparkly corpse.

Eon followed, pocketing his winnings for later.

Vicki approached, staring with wide, disbelieving eyes. "I under-estimated you, Champion. Thank you for the save."

A gentle blue glow surrounded her, and he reached out with the golden quest orb. She silently accepted.

System messages popped up. He made quick mental notes this time before dismissing them.

Congratulations. You have reached level 21.

Congratulations! Rune Staff of Ned the Insane has earned a new spell.

You can now unlock Adept spells in your focus tree.

Congratulations. New hidden title: Champion of Free Will

"Very funny, Deity," he muttered before turning his focus to Vicki. "We will accomplish more if we fight together."

"Coco explained your terms, and I agree, but first this." She reached out and opened her hand; a golden orb rested in her palm.

He accepted the new quest.

A Change of Heart. End the corruption spreading through the heart of Rath.

"Vague, and not funny," he said.

"We are ready," Vicki said with a sigh.

"One more thing." He held out his hand and beckoned with his fingers.

With a grimace, she drew Zalmon's eyes from her bag. She hesitated, looking him over as if inspecting him. After several moments, Vicki handed him the eyes.

"Thank you." He tucked them in his satchel then invited them to join.

Servers will be offline in 5 minutes.

"Shit." Jewells placed a finger to her ear, indicating she'd received a message.

"Pardon?" Vicki reached for her whip.

"It's not you, promise," Eon said.

"Good timing for the reboot, I guess," Jewells whispered. "I need to get back to work."

"We need to go," he said.

Vicki frowned in confusion. "Fine. We will meet you at the border of Rath, Champion. Don't make us wait long."

With a nod, he logged out.

THE POD OPENED WITH A HISS, and Julie crawled out. Her muscles felt tight and a little sore, like she'd just finished at the gym. Ian rolled out of his with a thud and slowly stood with a moan. He turned and gawked as the cloud of nanobots surrounding her returned to the pod. He glanced at the pile of clothes on the floor and covered his eyes, sort of.

She'd forgotten about being naked. This was obviously new to him, and even if it was a little awkward, he had to know it was okay to look.

"You were in pain, and I didn't have time to put on the viscosity suit." She walked around the pod, wrapped her arms around him, and pressed her lips to his.

It was like kissing a board, but she wouldn't let go, and eventually, he relaxed. He caressed her back with gentle, careful brushes. She let herself melt a little until she felt his rabbiting heart pound against her chest.

"What's wrong?" she asked, pulling away.

"You..." He swallowed hard, like his mouth was full of dry bread. "You're perfect."

"Oh." She went back to the melting. "Boyfriend level 2."

"Yes," he whispered.

"I'm late for work. I'm going to get dressed now."

"Okay." He sounded disappointed.

"We need to talk about Marc." She pulled away and started collecting clothes off the floor.

"Huh?" He shook his head. "What's up with Marc?"

She explained what had happened as she dressed. At first the words came out sure then faltered until she lost herself to frightened sobs.

His body stiffened as he approached to hold her. When she

finished, he looked into her eyes. His cheeks were red, and his face was stern, but those blue eyes couldn't apologize enough.

"I'll fix this. Just wait here."

He left the bridge, and the door closed behind him. Marc must've been waiting, because it wasn't long before it started. The bookshelf barrier muffled most of the conversation, but not the shouting.

"What the fuck were you thinking? You'll lose your mind to those cybernetics if you stop taking your meds."

Quiet.

"Threaten me again, and I will break you in half."

Crash.

"Don't make me turn you off."

"I'll kill you."

Crash.

"Remember. This is why you gave me the key. One more threat, and I'll shut you down. They'll take away your daughter. Is that what you want?"

"Not her, please."

Quiet.

"We're a team, that's the deal. Take the fucking meds or you lose everything."

Quiet. Too much quiet.

"Ian," Julie called out.

The bookshelves slid open, and she took cautious steps into the family room. Half the couch rested against the door, a spiderweb of cracks crawled across the giant monitor, and there were several fist-sized holes in the wall.

Ian sat on the floor, leaning against the far wall, his cheek red and one eye swollen shut. He held a sobbing Marc in his arms, rocking gently. It was quite the image with him in a sleeve and her dressed like a chauffeur call girl.

"What they did to her is unforgivable. When someone gets a cybernetic hand, they have to take drugs so the body doesn't reject it. She lost most of her body, and it's always at war. The madness can take hold if she misses a dose, and it looks like this time she missed a few."

"But your eye?"

"At least I didn't lose any teeth this time."

"This time?"

"She's a good person with a broken soul." He waved her over. "I won't give up on her."

"I'm so sorry, Jewells," Marc sobbed. "He loves you so much he would do anything for you, and I just fucked it up."

Julie looked at him, unable to hide her shock.

"Ignore the "L" word, that's just the meds kicking in," he whispered. "Boyfriend level 2, right?"

"He's dumb. All men are dumb." Marc slurred like a drunkard. "What's that stupid movie you made me watch? Oh, yeah. He's in *Princess Bride* true love with you. To blaeveeee."

She looked at Ian, her heart skipping a beat or seven.

"I'm sorry, Jewellsy, I'd never hurt you." She reached out, and Julie took her hand. "I've never seen him like this and didn't know what to —" Marc went limp and breathed comatose deep.

"System reset. She'll come to in a few minutes and won't remember any of this."

Julie let go of Marc's hand. "So...to blaeve?"

"You know," he said, weakly. "To bluff."

She knew *The Princess Bride*. The film took advantage of every fantasy trope, making it fun, quirky, romantic, and her all-time favorite. Just like Miracle Max in the movie, Julie knew that 'to blaeve' really meant 'true love' – the ultimate reason to resurrect the mostly-dead hero Wesley.

"You're, uh, supposed to scream liar." He sat up straight. "You know, like Max's wife did in the movie."

"Oh, yeah." She wasn't ready for this. Boyfriend level 2 was fun; but love meant heartache and loss that she was far too familiar with.

"I wasn't going to say it because I know how uncomfortable it makes you. I like boyfriend level 2, I'm happy with—"

Julie raised a hand, and he stopped. "It's okay."

It wasn't okay. If Lola were here, she'd grab an antler and teleport to freedom. Her mom fell in love with a determined genius and he ignored her to death. The doctors called it heart disease, but that's not what broke her heart. Julie wasn't ready to take that leap, but she also didn't want to hurt him. She just had to be gentle.

"I really like you, Ian."

Apparently, that was the worst thing she could have said. His shoulders drooped and he stared at her like a kicked puppy.

"Right." He looked down at his knees. "I understand."

"Stop it." She knelt beside him and placed a hand on his knee. "I didn't just throw you back into the friendzone." She glanced at Marc. "It's not just the L word. I feel like there's a lot we haven't told each other."

"There is." His voice quivered, and he strained to lean the cyborg against the wall. "I want to share everything, but..."

Marc sat up with wide eyes and she pushed herself up to stand. She looked around, taking in the destruction before her eyes fell on Ian.

"Who did this?" She grabbed Ian's hand and pulled him up. "I'll fuck up the sorry soul who dared to...who dared... Was it me?"

"No, you're fine, fine." He tugged at his dark bangs to cover his bruised eye. "Pizza delivery gone wrong. I tripped over the couch...it was a disaster."

"He's a terrible liar," she said. "At least you always know where he stands."

They stared at each other for several deep breaths until Marc cleared her throat.

"I must've been out for a while. Looks like you've lost some weight, Ian."

"Thanks," he muttered.

"What's up with you two?" Marc looked from Ian to Julie. "Did you kids have a fight and knock me out when throwing around the couch?"

Julie smiled politely. "We're fine. Right, Ian?"

"Sure."

"Well, I'm late for work." Julie tried to sound cheerful. "I need to get home and change first."

"Ah'll get you there fast." Marc studied her for a second. "If that's okay. If I've messed things up too badly, I've got friends who can drive you. Not as good as me, but..."

"No way. I'd hate for things to get boring." She kissed Ian on the cheek. "Try not to log in without me. I'll be back as soon as I can."

He nodded and let out a sigh.

She wanted to make it better, but it would have to wait. She turned to Marc. "We should get going."

"As you wish," Marc said.

Ian and Julie froze as though Pruine had walked in and cast a spell.

"What'd I say?" Marc looked at Julie then at Ian. "You both went stiff as a hearse ride-a-long."

"It's been a full day." Ian sighed deeply. "Please see her home safe and get back to your daughter."

"Sure thing." She lifted the half-couch like it was a bag of groceries and put it back where it belonged. "I'll try to make this right."

"Me too," Julie said as the door shut.

36

MERCS WITH A MOUTH

L ars Hemsly took long strides, rushing past black and white pictures of corporate accomplishment. It didn't take much effort to catch up with Bala. The short, Indian developer was practically shuffling his feet as though cautious of what was to come. Lars felt the same way. They were the only two people invited to this meeting, and in the boardroom no less.

"Hey, Bala, what's the rush?"

"Hello, Lars." He stopped and smiled politely. "I walk with less enthusiasm these days."

"It's not over, and I'm glad you've stuck around." He placed a hand on Bala's shoulder. "How's our boy?"

"Our boy?" Bala looked around nervously.

"No cameras down the hall of CEOs and board members." Lars released his grip and winked. "I consider Ian a friend. When I took on this role, I had to pull away from that friendship. It stung, but I still care."

Bala looked at him, and after several moments, let out a sigh. "I've been too afraid of Luanne to contact him. She watches everything. Julie has told me he is well, and others have said he is progressing through the quest."

"Others?" Lars considered this. "You mean Marta and Fred?"

Bala's eyes went wide. "Do you spy like Luanne?"

"Not at all. I used to be a coder like you, but my real talent is people. I recognize good, like you and Fred and Marta. I also know they watch players, even when they shouldn't. If I was stuck on that shift, I'd be doing the same. I'll protect their jobs at all costs. I'd hate to miss out on Fred's cheesecake."

"It's so good." Bala brushed a hand over his bald head. "Our boy is fine."

"Thank you. Before they shut Entriss down, maybe we should visit our night shift."

"I'd like that."

"So...any idea what Luanne wants?" Lars asked.

"She asked me to research something and advised I keep it secret." Bala wrung his hands. "She's got a plan, and I'm certain it will be terrible."

"No need to share now. I'm sure I'll find out soon enough," Lars said. "Let's see if we can stop it."

Bala looked relieved but wary as they approached the wooden doors. This was what she did to people. She broke trusts by making employees question themselves, all under the threat of being fired. He had a few choice words for their CIO. If it was just the three of them, maybe he'd get a chance to lay in.

Lars took a deep breath, pushed through the double-doors and said, "What in the hell is this?"

Luanne sat in the big chair surrounded by holograms of six casually dressed men and women, and one gorilla. This was the only room at Entriss Headquarters that supported holographic conferencing. When board members attended virtually, they looked real enough to touch and a golden-etched nameplate would appear on the table.

This lot sitting at the table faded and glitched like old television with poor reception. Their nameplates were cardboard foldovers written in crayon that displayed what could only be gamertags.

A tall, skinny man with pale skin and bushy dark hair sat opposite Luanne. His gamertag was Swytch. Akagɪ, a distracted, chubby Asian woman sat to his right. Next to her was Ringer, a forty-something black man with a cowboy hat, snap-button shirt, and bolo tie. Enyo sat to the left of Swytch. The cheerleader-perfect blond had enough muscle to bench the table. She eyed him and whispered something to Dabest, who appeared as a holographic gorilla. The gorilla nodded and let out a laugh. Ragequit, a seething Korean man with short, bleached Eminem hair sat beside them.

"I'll say it again." Lars leaned in. "What the hell is this?"

"You must be Lars the suit," Swytch said in a thick, British accent. "We were just negotiating with your lovely CIO. She's hiring my guild to save the day."

"Your guild?" Lars asked.

"You may have heard of us. My associates and I are formally referred to as Dank Guild." He bowed his head with a hand flourish

"Oh shit." Lars covered his mouth.

"What?" Bala asked. "I have not heard."

Lars focused on his optical implants, his eyes dancing along a keyboard until he found Customer Service notes in the player archive.

"Dank Guild. Arena champions of Rath for three years until someone discovered they were using an exploit to win."

"A mere misunderstanding," Swytch said. "We thought it was game mechanics."

Lars continued. "Their accounts were frozen the fourth year when Dabest was caught stealing weapons from their competitors by posing as player support."

"Not correct." The gorilla raised a finger. "They were gifts."

"They moved on to Battleworld Titus. Akagɪ was briefly kicked after fifteen minutes for counting cards—"

"Wrongly kicked." Swytch placed a calming hand on Akagɪ's arm. "She's just very lucky."

"I'm very lucky." She turned to Swytch. "Did I say it right?"

"You did fine, love," he said with a wink.

"They disappeared after Enyo defeated the High Warlord by using the same exploit they'd used in Entriss."

"Bitch deserved worse."

"I've heard she's not nice," Lars acknowledged. "After winning the High Warlord mantle, you auctioned off the entire state armory for a mere $20,000 and apparently donated most of it to survivors of human trafficking."

"Seemed fitting," she said in a deadpan tone.

"And then there's Colonize Epiales where Akagi unlocked something that shut down the servers for a month, costing the company millions."

She sank low and whispered, "Dillon?"

"We don't talk about that place," Swytch snapped.

"Isn't it just a city building MMO?" Bala looked from Akagi to Swytch.

"No." Ringer crossed his arms. "It's a nightmare that should not exist."

"We're taking steps to shut down both Epiales and Battleworld," Luanne said. "Mr. Hemsly, are you done?"

"Done? These cheaters, these thieves and brigands are the worst of the worst." Lars caught himself and turned to Swytch. "No offense."

"Best compliment we've gotten all day." Swytch's voice was cool, but his eyes were murder.

"These gamers bring the sort of creativity we need to solve our problem." She nodded at Swytch with a smug smile. "That's why we are hiring them to stop Eon and Jewells."

"You're bringing in mercenaries?" Lars shook his head. "What can they possibly do, other than slow Eon's progress?"

Luanne stared at Bala, and all eyes turned to him.

"You said nothing about this. I won't do it." Bala slashed the air with a hand. "It goes against everything the game stands for."

"Do what?" Lars asked.

Typically the calmest man in the room, Bala balled up his fists. "Eon's quest, The Left Hand of God, protects them from being tracked or deleted. According to the logs, Eon died in Averdac. If his character can die in-game, it's likely that someone with the *Final Kill* ability can end him."

"What good is that if Customer Service can't find them?"

"That's where Dank Guild comes in," Luanne said.

"Should be easy enough to follow." The gorilla typed something with his thick fingers. He looked up with a grin. "Already tracking their mess on the forums."

Luanne leaned back in her chair, heady with her great plan. "And once we reactivate Dank Guild's accounts, Bala gives them *Final Kill*."

"DID YOU SAY ARIZONA?" Marta shouted over the alarms. "What's in Arizona?"

"Our new server farm." Fred raised a cup and they toasted.

Marta glanced at her bracelet and began typing out commands. The alarms went silent and their shoulders collectively relaxed. "Thank you, Mr. Chen."

The servers started coming back to life, and images of Entriss began popping up on the monitors.

Fred leaned in and shook his head. "Huh."

"What is it?"

"I figured the reboot would enable full immersion in Rath but look." He pointed at the less-than-real graphics. "They're still on version one. So what's the server farm in Arizona for?"

Marta sifted through logs and stopped to whistle. "You're not going to believe this one."

37

GAME ON

Ian sat on his living room floor for a long time. He stared at the door, wondering if that emotional drive-by was coming back for another round. His furniture wouldn't survive the second attack, and his chances were slim.

Marc had been cranked up to level 7 on the batshit dial. He'd experienced worse. Several years ago, she'd stopped taking her meds and knocked out a few of his teeth. That had hurt, but he could handle a beating, and dentists could grow teeth back.

She'd given him the off switch as a last resort, to keep the dial from reaching 11. He'd seen it happen once—an uncontrollable berserker rage that would've made Wolverine nod in respect. It still gave him nightmares.

Marc had weaknesses, even if they were hard to find. The trauma that had destroyed her body, and the one that rebuilt it, made her protective as a mother Grizzly.

That was what made the transporter job so perfect. She could keep trial witnesses safe from drug cartels or take out the occasional terrorist ring if they threatened her delivery. That was the job.

When it came to friends and family, her protective nature was borderline paranoia. He didn't exactly need protection from Julie, other than her right cross, but it was a significant change from their routine.

Despite her chaotic job, Marc struggled with change. Almost everything she did required a plan, and a backup plan, and contingencies. When pieces of her puzzle stopped fitting together, she'd either make a new plan, or short-circuit and forget her meds.

His relationship with Julie may've been the trigger. Maybe Marc hadn't believed it would happen, that Julie and Ian would become an "us." He certainly hadn't.

What *had* happened? Within hours that seemed to pass in a blink, he'd gone from questing for Jewells to boyfriend level 2. All that wondrous romantic fantasy, all those dreams-come-true, somehow ended with Marc's *Princess Bride* speech.

To blaeve. It sounded silly now, sitting on the floor in his viscosity suit. Of course he loved Julie. Wasn't that the next step? He was just waiting for that Harry Met Sally moment where he could tell her the truth and she'd swoon into his arms.

There was no swooning. She responded with the other L word. She *liked* him, which felt like the equivalent of calling him buddy. Considering the look of panic in her eyes, the L-word she meant to use was later. There was no way she was coming back. It'd take a miracle.

He stood, tugging out the wrinkles of his body sleeve. With one last look at the door, the cracked monitor, and the broken couch, he entered the bridge and climbed into his capsule. It was time to log in to Entriss, where it was safe.

EON APPEARED on the battle-worn plateau where they'd ended Pruine. Moon-drenched shadows stretched across the icy ground as rainbow colors danced in the aurora polaris overhead. A brisk wind carried the coos of distant Abominables. He shivered, taking a deep breath of frosty air to clear his mind and bring this reality into focus.

It wouldn't take long for the chill to seep in. He needed to catch up with his group, after taking care of business.

Rubbing his hands together, he opened his focus tree. The quest had awarded him 10 levels. It seemed excessive, like the game was rushing him to be 40 before the end. He couldn't complain.

Leveling past 20 unlocked four new Adept spells and *Inscription 2*. Along with the Apprentice spells, he now had ten to choose from. *Duped* was a Ward spell with an icon of the Gemini twins. The Glyph spell *Pellet* looked like a blowgun shooting a rock. There were two Ward spells. *Beastmaster* looked like a bird's eye and *Alacrity* was an hourglass leaning to one side. He focused on each to read their descriptions.

Duped: Create a mirror image of yourself with a fraction of your health. The decoy will distract opponents until it is destroyed. Your health will not be refunded. Spend additional focus points to summon more decoys. 7-second cast. 10-minute cooldown. Cost: 1-3 points

Pellet: Interrupt your target from casting spells with a constant barrage of small stones. Spell will continue as long as you remain stationary. Spend additional focus points to increase damage. Instant cast. 2-minute cooldown. Cost: 1-3 points.

Beastmaster: See through the eyes of your familiar for up to 60 seconds. Instant cast. 5-minute cooldown. Cost: 1 point.

Alacrity: Spend Mana to slow time. Faster speeds will exponentially drain more Mana. Affects cast time and movement. Spend additional focus points to reduce mana cost. Instant cast. No cooldown. Cost: 1-5 points.

Inscription 2: As an Adept, you will have a deeper understanding of Runes. This ability is required to proceed with other Adept spells. Cost: 2 points.

Duped might be good for PvP, but it felt like a quick way to lose health he couldn't spare. His decoy wouldn't last long against a swarm of monsters like Flendrit or Abominables.

Pellet was disappointing. He wanted more spells that could do damage, not annoy people. He was annoyed.

Alacrity sounded a lot like bullet time from *The Matrix* movies. It was too tempting to pass up.

Beastmaster could be very useful for sneaking through Rath. His goal was to deliver Nihle's letter to Denpar and avoid PvP.

Inscription 2 was required, but he didn't mind spending the points. It had already given him the ability to wear new armor. He was itching to do some Mandorf-level damage, and maxed out *Ruin* and *Ruined*. After spending a point in *Beastmaster* he put the last two in *Alacrity*.

AFTER A QUICK REVIEW he accepted the choices.

Congratulations! Rune Staff of Ned the Insane has earned a new spell.

He opened the weapon menu and shook his head, not that it was really a surprise. The new special was as useful as the others.

Purge: Buffs, and curses, and spell effect, oh my. You can remove them from one target but watch out, they might die.
May cause bouts of painful vomiting. No cooldown.

Hopefully, Ned was trying to be funny, because purging every time he cast it sounded awful.

In addition to the levels and Ned's shitty spell, he'd also won loot from killing Grym Pruine. He withdrew the package from his satchel. It contained one Tough Skullcap and Ned's Flipping Coin of Flipping.

The black leather skullcap went with his long red coat like fine wine and Cheetos. Inscribing the Wizard item for a Rune Mage didn't make it better. It increased his Power by 2 and Essence by 1 but cost him 1 point of his Vigor. The cap was a mixed-bag item he'd usually avoid, preferring gear with pure bonuses and no cost, but what choice did he have?

He put it on and opened his character sheet. His stats were looking solid, and by itself, the skullcap made him look tough. The skullcap, coat, belt, and sparkly gloves made him look like he'd gone rogue after Sgt. Pepper kicked him out of the band.

Name:	Eon	Level:	21
Tribe:	Wood Elf	XP to Level:	41,276
Profession:	Rune Mage		
		Vigor:	13
Health:	907	Essence:	20
Mana:	1414	Power:	17

The other item wasn't a win either. Ned's Flipping Coin of Flipping was a trinket. Trinkets were both rare and unpopular. There was no armor slot for trinkets, so they ended up in players' satchels. It took too much time to drag one out during battle, making them practically useless. This one seemed extra special. It was a heavy gold coin embossed with a wonky-eyed, toothless beggar on the front and back. Not only were both sides identical, the description made no sense.

Ned's Flipping Coin of Flipping: Go ahead, flip the coin. Heads I win, tails you lose. Great for flipping off enemies. Bwa, ha, ha, ha.

"From the company that brought you the staff of passive resistance comes the most worthless item you never wanted." At least the description wasn't a stupid rhyme.

The trinket glistened in the moonlight and he felt the sudden urge to flip it. He thumbed the coin. It turned over and over, the golden face catching every bit of spare light in mesmerizing brilliance before landing in his hand.

A burst of wind struck him like a ninja linebacker. His feet lurched forward, and his ass struck ice.

"Worst magic item ever," he said to the coin. So annoying, and yet, he couldn't help himself and flipped it again. It landed in his palm and he stared at it. "Ned must've been insane to—"

Grrrr. Grrrr. The adorable *grrr*s of Abominables surrounded him like he rang a dinner bell. How did they sneak up on him so fast when— He gasped. It had to be the coin. The wind knocked him down after the first flip, and the second flip was going to kill him.

He scrambled to stand, shoving the stupid trinket in his bag and withdrawing Ned's staff. The monsters were out of sight and every crunch of snow made him spin around.

Pre-dinner lip-smacking made him wonder how far he could get with *Shockwave*. If only he could aim it forward instead of up. Would that work?

One of them howled, and the ground shook as they thundered

toward him. He should've summoned Lola, but it was too late now. This would hurt, and he didn't want her to suffer.

Do you wish to join your group already in combat?

The Abominables launched at him with wide-open mouths. Saliva dripped from rows and rows of sharp teeth, glistening in the moonlight.

"Yes," he shouted, shielding his face with the staff. "Join group! Join group!"

EON SQUEEZED HIS EYES SHUT, waiting for that first bite. Laughter filled the air. It was better than being eaten, mostly. He opened his eyes and lowered his arms.

The battle summons had brought him to a clearing surrounded by dark woods. Campfire warmed his backside, giving light to distant tents. Vicki and Trevor stood to his left, watching over his shoulder and laughing heartily. They weren't laughing at him, which was definitely better than being eaten.

He turned around and shook his head. "This triggered a battle summons?"

Coco and Nomar were crouched, circling each other with arms out like wrestlers. Beady eyes met beady eyes, and Nomar launched to tackle her.

"Ouch," he cried as she grasped his white beard, spun around, and threw him to the ground.

"You shouldn't have pushed me, dog." She pounced, straddling him.

"I didn't, but you deserve to be pushed." Nomar lifted both stubby legs, hooking her shoulders and slamming her to the ground.

She licked blood from her lips and smiled like it was soup.

Nomar's attack damaged her. That shouldn't have been possible if they were still in the same group. Had Vicki and the others left again?

Eon checked the group stats. Five names appeared below his: Jewells, Nomar, Vicki, Coco, and Trevor. Jewells was grayed out since she wasn't logged in. The others had an icon that represented their profession and bars for Health and Mana.

"I don't understand. Why are they taking damage if..." Time slowed as vertigo washed through Eon. He bent over to lean against his knees and took deep breaths.

"Enough of this," Trevor said.

"I'm not done yet." Coco kipped to stand and dove at Nomar.

"Are you all right, Champion?" Vicki placed a hand on his back and leaned over. Her words came out slow, every breath thick with the scent of alcohol. "Maybe this will help."

She handed him a tall, goose-necked decanter with a wide base. It smelled like Christmas, and he carefully stood to take a draw. The syrupy liquor burned like pure cinnamon and left his mouth with an aftertaste of root beer, licorice, and something rich not found on Earth. He drank deep until she pulled the bottle away.

"Careful. Sukhariss is the most potent spirits my tribe makes." She took a gentle sip, her eyes never leaving his. "Feel better?"

High server utilization has been compensated for. Enjoy your time in Entriss.

"Yeah, I feel a lot better." He smiled but struggled to keep eye contact. She was movie-star stunning with dark, sultry eyes that dared him.

Vicki released his gaze, making her way to sit on a fallen log.

Trevor held up Coco in one hand and Nomar in the other like two wiggly sacks of potatoes. "Behave yourselves before one of you has to run back from the graveyard." He set them down gently and crossed his muscular arms.

Nomar winked at Eon before dusting off his blue tunic. Eon smiled through alcohol-numbed lips and was once again stunned by how real this world had become.

He took a deep breath and held it, taking in their surroundings. It was one of those nights where the air was so cold it made everything clean and crisp. The clearing was wide enough to see Entriss's two moons, which were full and bright. They shone down with pale light on distant cliffs that towered over the tree line. A shadowy corridor split them apart like a scar. Zalmon's Scar. The air escaped him with a gasp.

"We're in Rath." Eon swallowed hard. "We're through Zalmon's Scar. That's why Nomar and Coco took damage when, uh, wrestling."

"Yes. The rules are different in this land where everyone fights everyone." Vicki beckoned him over with the decanter.

There was almost room enough for two on the log. He accepted the drink and sat next to her. They were shoulder-to-shoulder deep into his bubble and out of his comfort zone. She didn't seem to mind, and she was warm. He took a swig of bravery and returned the bottle.

"When I saw you had returned, I pushed Nomar into Coco so you would get the summons," Vicki said with a wink.

"Bitch!" Coco sat cross-legged in front of the fire. "I thought he attacked me."

"Yeah, bitch." Nomar plopped down beside the Brownie.

Their knees were touching, and she eyed him warily but didn't stab him. Yet.

"Your timing couldn't have been better. I was in the mountains where we fought Pruine and the Abominables diving at me looked hungry."

"Then it was for a good cause." Nomar raised a tiny stein.

Coco had one too. They toasted, drank, and their mugs instantly refilled.

"Your people make a hearty ale, and I like this gift." She eyed her drink. "But don't expect anything in return."

"You have nothing I want." Nomar took a long draw, his eyes smiling at Eon from behind the stein.

Eon sighed. He felt like a wingman back in college. A wingman who always left parties alone and... He grunted as Vicki shoved the carafe into his gut.

"We all see that you came by yourself. Do not fret, Eon of Yu, you are not alone tonight." Vicki wrapped an arm around him. "Drink and celebrate our glorious victory."

He did drink, and she lifted the base so he'd drink a little more. She laughed when booze spilled down his chin and patted it dry with her satin sleeve.

Trevor scoffed, peering at Eon. "I'm going to search the area." He drew a glowing red arrow and walked to the clearing's edge.

"Jealous much?" Eon muttered.

"Trevor?" Her husky laugh was contagious. "He's like a father. He raised me, and he's overprotective."

"I have someone like that. She doesn't make it easy to be friends, or make friends, but I know she always has my back. There's a lot more to her than people expect, and I'll never take her for granted."

An arctic wind bit the fire, kicking up embers that faded into the clear sky. Vicki shivered and leaned in, resting her head on his shoulder.

"There's a lot more to you as well, Champion." She took a deep breath. "You killed a Grym by yourself, and at such a young age. You were born to be a hero."

"I, uh, guess I did." His mouth went dry like he had left it open in a sauna. Being nervous was great. Another drink would help. Maybe seven.

She hugged the decanter, squeezing the long neck between her breasts, making it impossible to grasp. He made the mistake of glancing up. She looked at him with those eyes that dared. Her lips parted, and suddenly his heart yearned for easier times of Abominables and Grym.

High-school Eon longed for this video-game beauty, this Victoria Secret model, this Angelina Jolie-Alicia Vikander perfect woman with every fiber of his newfound puberty. High-school Eon was also a coward who carefully grabbed the carafe and hid behind another drink.

"Woo." He swayed slightly as she went in and out of focus. "Your people make fine spirits. This bottle won't last long. Where can we get more?"

She kissed him on the mouth several times, but he was too numb to respond. They laughed uncontrollably until she leaned in and whispered hot words in his ear.

"Not supposed to say." She rocked back and forth in drunken stupor. "We are from the tribes of Misere."

"Misere," he shouted. "That's not possible."

He screamed as red-hot pain seared his knee. Trevor's arrow burned like a quick dip in lava.

"What are you doing?" Vicki cried.

"We agreed to keep it secret. Now he knows too much." Trevor drew back on his bow, his eyes wild in the arrow's deep red glow. "This is the only way to keep you safe."

38

THE SECRET OF MY SUCCESS

"I bet Jewells runs." Marta stuffed a Tupperware container into her shiny pewter backpack. "She always runs. She's afraid to love him. I doubt she'll come back."

"I'll meet that bet with three flavors of cheesecake." Fred stared at the screen. "She might be afraid, but she loves him."

"It's not enough." She threw the backpack over her shoulder.

"Vicki's enough." He typed in commands until Vicki's image appeared on the big screen. "No way Jewells would give up to that beauty."

"Wait just one second." She raised a dangerous finger, waving it like a light saber before her stern gaze. "Are you telling me my work-husband would leave me for that half-naked tart?"

"Uhh." He stammered, trying to find the words before letting out another, "Uhh."

She laughed. "I didn't think so. Vicki isn't her concern, Eon is. He's probably hiding something from her, or she's hiding something from him. Either way, it's a disaster. They may just not be ready."

"Makes sense." He nodded, typing a command to dismiss Vicki's image.

Marta cleared her throat. "Joelyn has a concert this weekend, her last one before middle school. I was wondering if you'd like to join us?"

"Uhh." Fred closed his mouth until he found words again. "What about the rules, of, uhh, co-workers?"

"Honey, in case you didn't notice, this place is shutting down." She tugged at her now golden hair and stared off at the monitors. "I'm hosting a cookout afterward with lots of family. I know you like to keep to yourself, so I understand if—"

"I'd love to." It came out a little dry, and a little quiet. He cleared his throat and spoke louder. "I'd love to. That'd be great."

She shot him a full-lipped smile that was cut off by the now-familiar klaxon of alarms. He tapped a function key on his keyboard and the room went silent.

"I look forward to meeting her."

"She's heard a lot about you." They shared a long gaze until Marta broke off to take a seat. "New server farm?"

"Not this time." Fred pounded away at his keyboard. "Server lag, and lots of it. The late-nighters will be bitching if—"

"Whoa." Marta leaned into her monitor.

"What is it?"

"Deity is compensating this time." She shook her head. "I take that back. Compensated. She already sent out a system message telling players everything is back to normal."

"We should let the old man know." Fred raised his wrist to cast the message.

"The old man already knows." They jumped as Jack Cook's voice echoed throughout the room like the great and powerful Oz.

"Shit," Fred whispered under his breath. "Sorry for calling you old, sir."

There was a long silence, and they shared a frown. Marta's golden bracelet rang like a telephone, making them jump.

"Hello?" she asked.

"Marta, Frank, sorry for the lack of video," Cook said. "I've been working out and I'm a sweaty mess."

"It's five a.m., sir." Marta frowned. "Don't you sleep?"

"The secret of my success." Cook let out a friendly chuckle. "Don't sleep, try to plan ahead, and learn how to take a beating when you fail. The only way to be successful is to fail a lot and recover from it."

"I fail plenty." Fred let out a sigh. "Shouldn't I be half-rich?"

Cook and Marta laughed.

Fred looked around. "Why did the lights go dim?"

"I turned off surveillance for a moment of privacy. Frank, am I reading this correctly? You have a Masters in Network Security?"

"Uh, that's Fred, sir, and yes."

"And Marta has a PhD in Logic?"

"PhD?" Fred mouthed.

She winked. "Yessir."

"With those credentials, what are you two doing on the night shift?" Cook asked.

"Reasons," they both said at the same time.

"I understand reasons." He paused. "I need you to do some research for me. It will require another promotion to give you access, but I need to keep this between us and Lars. You'll be working with him directly. Any concerns?"

"Too many," Marta began. "Ian gets fired, goes on a quest that kicks off a World Event and brings two server farms to life. Yeah, I've got concerns."

There was a brief silence.

Fred cleared his throat. "Sir, can you tell us what's going on?"

"I really can't say."

They looked at each other, and he answered their silence.

"If possible, this has to be done before your shift ends. Your jobs will be at risk if you're caught, but if the company doesn't compensate you, I will."

"I'm in," Marta said.

"With you all the way, sir."

"Then this is what I need you to do..."

It was 10:05 and for the first time since Entriss went public, Jack was late to the board meeting. He'd always been the first to arrive and the last to leave. Everyone waiting probably considered this the first sign of the Entriss Apocalypse, but it couldn't be helped.

Lars paced in front of Jack's large, ebony desk. He'd stop to stare into the distance, checking his ocular cast implant, sigh deeply, then start pacing again.

"Are you sure Fred and Marta were the right choice?" the tall Scandinavian asked again.

"I'm sure," Jack reaffirmed.

Lars stopped mid-stride and smiled. "You're right. It's done."

"Let's go." He stood and followed the younger man to the boardroom.

Lars flashed him a quick smile before opening the door to let Jack in first.

The room went quiet as apprehensive stares followed him to the big chair. They cleared their throats, or shut off their cast devices, or sipped water as he ignored curious gazes. Rather than sitting down, like at every other board meeting, he stood behind the chair. Gripping the edges, he leaned over it, meeting those gazes with a winning smile.

"Sorry for making you wait. There was high network utilization, and I wanted to see if we'd birthed another server farm."

The laughter died quickly when he didn't sit down.

"Things are getting exciting, and I've got good news." Everyone jumped when he smacked his hands together and rubbed them like a camper before the fire. He winked at Carl, an overweight banker with sallow skin and white hair. The man jerked back and cleared his throat.

"We've been tightening our belts for years, waiting for the inevitable behemoth Everyworld to come online. We knew the government would buy our shares after the doors were shut. Easy money, but at a discount price. Entriss has always been a cash cow, and far more profitable alive than dead."

He sought the room. Most nodded in agreement while Luanne

sank in her chair.

"We were all thrilled when Watson announced two years ago that Everyworld was being delayed. No one wanted to give our baby up for pennies on the dollar, and that easy out meant it would be over." He lowered his head and spoke softly. "It isn't over."

Heads whipped up and eyes went wide. Luanne's practically popped out of her head.

"This is not public knowledge." Lights in the room dimmed as a dampening field turned off cameras and silenced cast devices. "I spoke with Watson this morning. Everyworld Online was hit by another delay that could last two years."

They cheered, as much as old board members can cheer. This board was different than others. Not only were they experienced executives with decades of leading companies to success, most were also old gamers. Those members were handpicked from old Atari jockeys to Vanilla WoW raiders. They were wise enough to keep that enthusiasm in clenched fists, head nods, and a hopeful gleam in Carl's eye. Even at seventy-two, Carl was a PvP beast.

"This is an easy vote, but I need all ayes." Jack took a deep breath. "In lieu of Everyworld Online going live, the board agrees to keep Entriss Online an active and supported entity."

Every board member raised their hand.

"Exactly what I expected, and exactly what Entriss needs. Board adjourned."

The room erupted in mutters as everyone rose. Luanne was first to scurry away, and several board members followed. The gamers remained standing; the lights were still dim, which meant the dampening field was still on.

"Thank you, my friends." Cook leaned against the table and lowered his head.

Carl gripped his shoulder and leaned in. "I know the two-year extension isn't real, but is there any chance we can keep her alive?"

"That's up to Ian." Cook patted his hand. "He hasn't figured it all out yet, but I believe in him. If he can take the beating and roll with the failures, he may just save Entriss."

39

MISERE LOVES COMPANY

"Don't kill him," Vicki shouted, stumbling between Eon and Trevor.

"No one can know about our tribes before it's time. It's our only tactical advantage." Trevor tried pushing her out of the way, but she wouldn't budge. "Step aside, now!"

Eon jerked the arrow from his knee and threw it to the ground.

"What's this?" Trevor took a step back.

"I don't understand." Vicki looked from the arrow to Eon with wide eyes. "You hardly took any damage."

"Welcome to Rath. It's go-time, Trevor." He drew Ned's staff and slurred, "*Shockwave*." Nothing happened. Eon shook the staff and gave it a smack. "I said, *Shockwave!*"

He shot up into the air, barely able to hold the staff with his sweaty hands. Magma-red arrows whizzed by like stray bullets in a shootout. He looked down at their shocked faces and smiled.

In Yu, it took the average player a month of grinding out quests, killing mobs, and delving dungeons to hit level 40. The rules were different here. A player might never hit 40 in Rath if they were constantly hunted and killed by higher level griefers. To compensate for this, Entriss scaled damage, making it possible for level 21 Eon to give level 37 Trevor a well-deserved ass-whupping.

He tried landing outside camp, but his alcohol-fueled targeting system shot him straight into the Hobgoblin's back. Trevor landed hard on his face and dropped his bow. *Shockwave* blew out the fire, knocked over the tents, and hurled the bow far out of reach.

Eon activated True Sight. Moonlight made their surroundings look like an old black-and-white movie. Everything was clear for him, but Trevor would struggle with moonlit shadows.

He took quiet steps back as the Hobgoblin drew his great broadsword and slowly turned around. A fresh gash on his forehead spilled black blood that streamed down his cheek and pooled at his jutting chin.

"Oh, you think darkness is your ally. But you merely adopted the dark. I was born in it, molded by it." Trevor thrust out his barrel chest. "Misere is an evil land. Tribes have gained abilities to hunt monsters in the dark, and I hear you, Rune Mage. I hear your footsteps on the frozen grass, your panting breath, and the fear in your racing heart."

Just as he launched at Eon, *Ruination* blasted Trevor into the air. The Hobgoblin crashed into a tree and landed on his feet, roaring in fury. Before Eon could finish casting *Ruin*, Trevor threw his sword. It raced toward him, spinning like a steel bolo.

The hilt struck his side with a crack. Eon yelped in pain and collapsed to the ground. He gasped through every searing breath. Not only had Trevor broken some ribs, the sword was back in his hands like a boomerang.

If the Hobgoblin's hearing was that good, Eon's True Sight was barely an advantage. It was tempting to fight close after that vicious boomerang sword attack, but it would be impossible to avoid a direct blow. He needed distance, and he needed to be fast.

Eon summoned his familiar and cast *Alacrity*.

Lola looked up with eyes that said, "What have you gotten us into now?"

"Bring me everywhere."

Trevor grunted, hurling the sword straight at him.

"Go!" Eon shouted.

They appeared at the other end of camp. Eon cast *Ruin* in two seconds instead of three. *Alacrity* was a vacuum that drained 3% of his Mana. The Hobgoblin took a step back as his sword changed direction, heading toward them like a homing missile.

Eon had to be faster. Lola brought him within twenty feet, and he cast *Ruin* in one second. The next cast was instant. That was when it got fun. *Ruin* didn't do a lot of damage, each spell hitting Trevor like a bee sting, but casting this fast was like sending in a swarm of bees.

Lola brought him from one spot to the next so fast he felt ill and she reeled from the effort. The spinning sword continued chasing them, getting closer every time they appeared.

"We've almost got him."

She continued teleporting him until Trevor dropped to one knee. The sword was feet away. Lola gasped for breath, her Mana almost depleted.

"Go!"

They appeared within arm's reach of Trevor. Before he could cast *Envelop*, the Hobgoblin grabbed Eon's throat.

"Oh shit," they shouted.

The sword struck them with a resounding crack. Trevor released his grasp, and they collapsed. Both men were sprawled out, breathing heavily, and covered in blood, their Health depleted to barely alive.

"Champion, indeed." Trevor held out a hand.

"You're a beast." Eon clasped arms with the Hobgoblin.

Lola leaned over and smacked Eon's head with her antlers.

"Thanks," he muttered.

She scoffed and hopped over to Nomar and Coco for well-deserved ear scratches.

"I should finish the job and pour these healing potions over your graves." Vicki set two red flasks on the ground between them. "But your battle probably alerted everyone in Rath, and I don't care to fight the griefers alone."

"Aye," Trevor said, sitting up and drinking his in a gulp.

Eon tried sitting and winced at the broken ribs. She helped him up, holding the flask to his lips.

"I underestimated you," Trevor said with a nod. "I thought our southern kin to be weak. You give me hope for the battle ahead."

"Thanks." The potion healed his Health and knitted his bones, but he felt spent and irritable. "Who the fuck are you people?"

Vicki looked at Trevor, and he nodded.

"Let's see to the camp." The Hobgoblin let out a tired sigh. "I'll scout the perimeter and fetch more wood."

Nomar and Coco kicked hot embers back to the fire pit as Eon and Vicki tended to the tents. Thanks to True Sight, he could see his way to each one. Apparently, she couldn't and followed closely.

"I'm sorry for that," she said. "He won't listen to me."

"Yes, he will." It came out a little sharper than intended, but he wasn't wrong. "You're a leader. I saw that at the Nominal."

"It's not that simple," she said, her voice pleading. "He's like a father to me."

"Actually, it is." He stopped and turned around. She stumbled into him and he caught her. Everything about her was soft and warm. Her hair smelled like vanilla and cinnamon. She pursed her lips and looked up at him with wide eyes. He could only stutter, frozen like he was back in high school speech class.

Back then, his teacher said, "You need a boost of confidence. Just imagine everyone watching is naked." It didn't help then and helped even less now. Vicki looked ready to get naked, and he was confident that was a bad idea. Whatever she saw in him, he didn't feel, and he took a step back. She stepped forward, and he sighed.

"You're heir to the throne of somewhere, which means you'll have to make the hard choices." He took a deep breath. "One day, you may have to send Trevor, or Coco, or even me on a quest that will kill us. If you don't, if you can't, then you threaten the lives of everyone you rule over. It's not about what you want, it's about what you have to be."

The words were lost to something far hungrier, and she leaned in to kiss him.

It was one of the five worst moments in his life, up there with his dog disappearing after Jet moved in, and Jet finding the bat after he mouthed off. This virtual princess, this heir to the throne, this super-model in satin and leather was kissing him full on the mouth and he did nothing.

Her kiss was his mashing of the lips. Even if a small part of him wanted to, he couldn't.

She pulled back, wiped her mouth, and stared at the ground. "You love her, don't you?"

"Yes."

"But she's not here. You're alone now." She looked up with glassy eyes. "What if she doesn't come back?"

"Hope." He looked away and swallowed hard. "Sometimes that's all we've got. Sometimes it's enough."

"You're a good man, Eon."

"Unfortunately," he said with a deep sigh.

She giggled, giving him a friendly hug. The type of friendly hug he was all too familiar with.

They finished with the tents in silence and made their way back to the log. Nomar tended to five sticks of meat-something cooking over the new campfire. Vicki leaned into Eon again, this time more friendly than passionate, and he wrapped an arm around her. It wasn't his Tomb Raider fantasies come to life, but it wasn't so bad.

Trevor cleared his throat. "Any more questions, young Gnome? Your curiosity is endless."

"Just one, I think. How did you escape Misere?"

"The three of us were on border patrol when Vicki got a quest," Coco said. "She accepted, and we appeared outside of Nominal."

NPCs were supposed to hand out quests, not go on them. Eon filed this under Free Will Is Scary before asking, "Can you tell me about the quest?"

"It's a quest chain called Heir to the Throne," Vicki said, her words stiff and brittle as old tile. "It started with The Eyes Have It, and now I'm on Have A Heart."

"Do you have a heart?" a tiny voice called out from the woods.

In the time between a gasp and a skipped heartbeat, they were all at the ready with weapons in hand.

A child, no older than seven, took several steps into the clearing. He was white from head to toe as if someone had dipped him in a bucket of paint. His ghostly pale form practically glowed before the black canvas of thick woods. "Do you have a heart?"

Vicki looked at him. "Is this your quest or mine?"

Eon shrugged.

"Yes," she called out. "We all have hearts."

"Thank you." The boy sounded relieved. He took a deep breath and screamed, louder than should've been possible, "They have hearts! Take their hearts!"

40

BROKEN HEARTS

"What's the little shit screaming about?" Coco rubbed the edges of her knives together.

"Something about hearts." Vicki squeezed the handle of her whip, her eyes searching the dark woods.

Nomar belched. "After all that booze, I've got a heart-on the size of—"

"I'll remove it if you don't shut up," Coco snapped.

"Quiet, both of you. I'm trying to listen." Trevor closed his eyes and turned his head to listen. "More are coming."

There was the distant snap of a foot stepping on an old stick. Several more snaps were quickly followed by the loud crunching sounds of many feet stomping through the forest.

Eon struggled to focus through the cloudy haze of Sukhariss liquor and glanced up to see he had a debuff. The "Mostly Drunk" debuff would last another eighty-five seconds. He wasn't alone. Vicki, Coco, and Nomar would continue swaying and stumbling for the next two to three minutes.

The footsteps became louder, and his group inched closer until they were brushing elbows. He needed a plan, but his brain was trying to put a square peg in a flat board.

"Trevor." He grabbed the Hobgoblin's arm to steady himself. "You're sober, so you're in front. You three, fall back and try not to fall over. Lola, can you go see what this is about?"

She disappeared in a flash of pink light as Trevor drew his bow.

What had he been thinking? Getting drunk in Rath seemed like a terrible idea on any day. Drinking now, in the midst of this quest, was like screaming, "Leeroy Jenkins!" and rushing into battle before anyone was ready.

"How can your rabbit help?" Trevor asked. "Is she attacking them from behind?"

"I can see through her eyes." He cast *Beastmaster*. Lola hid behind bushes, unseen by the people in ivory clothes and... "Holy shit, what was that?" He released the spell and looked back at Trevor. "Something is coming, and it's big. We should run away."

"I don't run from a fight." Trevor drew back on his bow, and a glowing red arrow appeared.

"You don't understand," he slurred. Thirty seconds left on the debuff, and the words weren't coming out like they should. "We're handicapped by three and I don't have the firepower..."

A dozen villagers poured into the clearing and stopped at the edge as if jerked to a halt. The group included men and women of all ages, each wearing whitewashed peasant clothes. They held torches and pitchforks and scythes like they were hunting witches. Unlike the child, a glowing purple strand was affixed to their backs. The strands were taut, like a dozen lasers that shot at a single point in the woods.

Lola appeared beside them, looking wild-eyed. A loud, steady thump shook the forest, soon followed by another.

"What's wrong with bunny?" Nomar slurred. "It's justa lotta dumb villagers."

"Grab her antlers." Eon stared at the black woods like Death herself would part the trees. "Lola's getting you out of here."

"I smell fresh hearts." The hollow voice that crept out of the nearby woods was campfire dry and several octaves above frightening.

A tree branch cracked high above the villagers, soon followed by another. They zombie-stared forward as the purple lines became slack. Fifteen feet from the ground, two pale hands with grotesquely long fingers reached out from the dark woods. The hands grasped the lines and pulled.

The villagers were like a grappling hook, holding steady as the nightmare dragged itself out of darkness.

It was eighteen-feet tall with long, powdery-pale limbs that had a few too many joints. The monster's overlarge head looked like a gourd turned upside down. Someone had taken its eyes, which were dark, hollow caves resting over two snake-like slits and a wide toothy mouth.

"Well done, pet." A purple line slithered through the air, attaching itself to the child. The monster jerked back, bringing the boy in line with the others. Its head reared back as it sniffed hungrily, frosty puffs leaving his air holes with every snort. "Are these the hearts my master seeks?"

"Are those leashes?" Vicki covered her mouth.

"I changed my mind," Trevor said. "I now run from a fight."

"Princess first." Eon took her hand and placed it on an antler. "Lola, go."

Pink light flashed behind them as Eon suddenly became sober.

"No, bring her back," the monster screamed. "I need hearts. Fetch them."

"Nomar, follow me. Trevor and Coco, spread out," Eon shouted. "Lola will find you."

The villagers marched forward at an unsteady speed-walker pace, as though reluctant to follow orders. They stopped when Trevor and Coco ran in opposite directions.

"What is that thing?" Nomar asked.

"It's a Mind's Eye, level 40." Eon read the character sheet aloud, barely catching himself as he stumbled over a tent stake. "They control their captives, the Tethered, by replacing an organ with that leash. They are hive creatures attached to a greater boss. Their power grows exponentially based on how many prisoners they have. Mind control and submission begins through eye contact."

Nomar shook his head and grunted at the debuff. "How do we kill it?"

Eon stopped for a second. The Tethered were far enough away, giving him time to close his eyes and focus. He willed for Lola, and she appeared beside them.

"Nomar." He knelt and grabbed the Gnome's shoulders. "Tell the others not to make eye contact with the Tethered."

"Can do," he said with a grinny salute.

"And tell Trevor to watch my back."

"Okay." He nodded.

"And then get to safety." He paused. "Did you get all of that?"

"What was the middle one again?" Nomar scratched his chin.

"Really?"

He winked and touched Lola's antler. "Go, bunny."

The villagers approached at a steady pace, spreading out to cover the entire clearing. He had to slow them so his group had more time to sober up.

This could be a long fight, so he was reluctant to use up his Mana with *Alacrity*. It took five grueling seconds to cast *Ruination*. The blast rune appeared directly in their path. Blue flames shot up from the ground, throwing three of the villagers into the air. Three wasn't enough.

The Mind's Eye's hunger for hearts was revolting, but it implied that he'd stolen the villager's hearts. That meant they were dead, and *Shockwave* would knock them all away.

He cast the spell and shot into the sky, landing hard before several Tethered. They stopped and turned to face him, unaffected by the spell.

The Mind's Eye let out an airy laugh. "My pets are alive, and I have my first victim of the night."

A glowing red arrow slammed into the closest villager followed close by a bolt of lightning. They ignored the attacks, grabbing Eon and dragging him to the ground. He squeezed his eyes shut and struck out with his staff. One of them grabbed his hand and held it down as another sat on his feet. Fingers probed his face until finding his eyes.

"No," he shouted, flailing as they tried prying his eyelids open.

The Mind's Eye let out a scream, and then another.

"Get off my Champion!" Vicki cried, her whip cracking with electric ferocity.

Hands left his face, weight left his body, and he took a deep breath, trying not to sob.

"It's safe to open your eyes, Eon."

He looked up at his Tomb Raider savior, and she smiled. He accepted her hand and stood. "Thank you."

"I'll always be there for a friend."

"How did you stop them?"

"You gave Trevor time to figure it out." She pointed toward the monster. "Look."

Trevor shot a red arrow. It struck one of the leashes, and the Mind's Eye cried out in pain. Nomar and Coco sat on villagers' shoulders, hacking and cutting at their purple tethers. The monster was taking damage, but only a little.

"At this rate, it'll take days to kill him," she said.

"His power comes from his captives." Eon looked from the Tethered to the leashes and finally at the giant nightmare controlling them. "Maybe I can free the villagers with my *Purge* spell. Everyone will need to attack once they're released."

"I'll tell the others." She kissed him on the cheek. "For luck."

"Luck works." He touched his cheek as she ran off. "I like luck."

A villager lumbered toward him. He cast *Purge*. A beam of green light shot out from the ornate top of Ned's staff, striking the man's chest. The villager rose three feet off the ground, his body arching back as he screamed. His chest roiled like water on a hot stove. Green bubbles appeared as *Purge* cooked his chest like a microwave until it popped open.

A wet, heart-sized stone shot out of the Tethered, and he collapsed to the ground. The heart hovered before Eon. He winced, swallowed hard, and then finally bent over to empty his guts. The heart landed at his feet with a thud.

The Mind's Eye cried out again. Killing the Tethered had ripped away almost 10% of its Health.

"You did it, Champion," Trevor shouted. "*Purge* the other villagers so we can end this beast!"

"I fucking hate you, Ned." Eon wiped his mouth and approached the next prisoner.

The monster howled, Eon's group rallied, and he only threw up every three or four *Purges*. The Mind's Eye was hanging by a thread, literally. One purple leash remained, attached to the child who'd screamed for their hearts.

"I can't do it." Eon covered his face with a shaky hand. He felt disgusting, like every *Purge* was an innocent life lost. His stomach ached from vomiting, and his brain felt like a squeezed sponge.

"I need your heart." The child was only several feet away. "Please look at me."

"I'm sorry, Eon. It's the only way." Vicki stood beside him. "Free this child from his curse."

Eon nodded, reached out, and cast *Purge* one last time. The child screamed until he didn't. His stone heart hung in the air. Eon grasped it and began convulsing. There was nothing left to come out and he collapsed. Vicki dropped to her knees and held him close.

There were war cries from Trevor, and Nomar, and Coco as they finished the battle. The Mind's Eye let out a final whimper and fell dead with an earthshaking thud.

He wept, even as the others approached. He couldn't help himself.

"I was wrong about you." Trevor placed a hand on his shoulder. "Compassion is the true sign of a hero. You did well, son."

"See to our camp and set up a guard rotation," Vicki said. "Eon needs his rest. He's earned it. We all have."

41

I SPY

J ulie smirked at the irony. Three hours ago, she'd been an Elf
Priestess in skin-tight leather battling to save a world from
evil forces. Now, she was facing down an evil tyrant in nonde-
script office attire at Entriss Headquarters. Not much had
changed.

She sat across a small conference table from the sweaty CIO,
Luanne. The room was closet-small with harsh inquisition lights.
Michelle, the pursed-lip, frowning head of HR, sat to her right. Bala
stood to her left, his eyes dancing between them as he bit his tongue.

Luanne was passively threatening Julie with the potential damage
to the virtual accords and the United States's position in the
international community. If the CIO was trying to frighten her, she
obviously hadn't battled a Grym.

Julie nodded like she was in high school Social Studies,
pretending to be interested while pondering more important things.
Ian loved her, or at least thought he did. How was that even possible?
It was far too early for words like love. They were in the everything-
is-perfect stage of a relationship where sex was fun and ugly hadn't
reared its head.

Everyone had a superfluous ugly that was easy to fix or ignore, like morning breath, or body insecurity, or bad credit. It was the deep-ugly she feared. Boyfriends who seemed too perfect were champs at hiding secrets that made her skin crawl. Drug abuse, physical abuse, fetishes too bizarre for porn, objectification, cheaters...all hidden by a perfect facade.

Ian's facade was almost too shiny. He had crazy money for a twenty-something who wasn't a CEO. His best friend was a living weapon of mass destruction. And somehow, he'd Tony-Starked a technological miracle in thirty days. Not only could they log into a fully immersive Entriss, his game room looked like the bridge of a starship. Despite all those miracles, his biggest concern was starting over with a new character. If this was the surface of his secrets, they must hide an ugly the likes of which she'd never seen.

"Julie?" Luanne tapped the table with a finger.

"Yes?" She blinked several times until toad-woman came back into focus.

"That's all you have to share?" Luanne sniffed. "He's in Zalmon's Scar?"

"That's where I left him. I came as soon as you called."

"Apparently you weren't aware. He moved on."

The verbal dagger was cold, plunging deep enough to stiffen Julie's back. "Pardon?"

Luanne snapped her fingers at Bala.

He stared at her in disbelief before finally shaking his head. "There is intense spiking in the Rath servers. We believe he's crossed over since there isn't a new quantum server farm to support that zone."

"A new server farm?" Julie asked.

"There have been three reboots so far. The first activated both the World Event and full immersion, but the Entriss servers weren't built to handle the load. The second reboot activated a server farm to support Yu, and the third—"

Luanne held up her hand. "We're still investigating the third."

It was hard to believe, but Bala wouldn't lie. No wonder Luanne had invited him to the meeting.

Her heart sank a little that Ian hadn't waited. It's not like she ran out the door screaming in fear, even if she wanted to. The true love speech was a bit overwhelming after the intense battle with Grym Pruine and Marc's throwdown with Ian. She just needed time to think and did her best to back away slowly.

Apparently, Ian needed time to think too... on Entriss, where he was working on the quest, with their new group...with Vicki.

"I wasn't expecting him to log in without me. I should get back so I can, uh, spy on him."

"Ms. Jacks, what do you truly know about Ian Gregg?" Luanne asked.

Before she could answer, a holographic vanilla folder appeared in the air. It was a thick tome that slowly fell to the table. Luanne licked her fingers and opened it. Bala peered over her shoulder and his eyes went wide.

"That's all confidential," Michelle said.

"Of course." Luanne abruptly closed the folder and looked up at Julie. "I'm sorry I can't share more, but the Champion of Yu isn't what he seems. He has secrets."

"Oh, okay." Words escaped her like blinking fireflies in a dark night.

"Apparently I can't tell you more but do be careful." Luanne's smile was satiated. "Thank you for coming. I look forward to your next report."

HOLOGRAMS CAMOUFLAGED MARC'S CORVETTE, making it look like a boring Oldsmobuick sedan on the outside. It was still spy-slick inside with shaded windows that blocked Julie's view.

Whatever meds Marc took to compensate for her Furyan side also made her an over-friendly chatterbox. It was better than threats, and her violent tantrum at Ian's. Mostly.

She drove slowly and spoke fast, sharing some of the car's impressive trade secrets. The Corvette was obviously important to her, and Julie nodded enthusiastically with each revelation.

"I only go stealth at night when the roads are empty so the other cars don't bump my rear." She beamed at this. "Ian told me I can't kill any more drivers for ramming into me."

Julie's eyes went wide.

"I kid." She winked as they turned a corner. "I only bent 'em a little."

"Heh." Julie's shoulders tensed.

"Did ah tell you about the decoy?" She was trying hard to connect. "I can release a drone that creates a mirror image of my 'Vette. It's good enough to fools eyes and scanners."

Julie smiled politely. She wasn't in the mood for conversation, but thought it'd be best to keep things positive. "That's amazing. Do you have other cars?"

"This one's not enough?" She laughed. "Just a boring limo and mah tank."

"A real tank?"

"Nah. I've been tricking out an old Hummer. Ian says it's for boss fights."

"Sounds like Ian." Julie let out a little sigh.

"I taught my boy well. He's scary good with the tech." She nodded encouragingly. "He took my mirror image idea to a new level."

"What did you do before being a Transporter?"

"Ah, well..." She went quiet for a moment, squinting into the distance as if it were painful. "Most of those memories are clouded, which is probably best. I was special forces...a green beret. After that I was a merc. Not proud of those years."

Julie stared at the dark windshield like it was a Magic 8-Ball, waiting for a response that never turned up.

"I can tell you're still upset at me. Your shoulders are in knots, your heart rate is high, and you're breathing a bit too fast." Marc sighed. "I'm embarrassed. I was rude and unprofessional."

"It's not that." Julie turned away to stare at the black passenger window. There was no escape from her thoughts. "Sometimes I lose it too. Ian put his life in danger doing a quest. I was so angry I punched him in the face. It's not exactly tearing a couch in half—"

"He probably deserved it." She stopped the car and took off her driving goggles. The dark windows went clear, revealing Ian's warehouse parking lot. "What did he do?"

Julie shared highlights of their adventures in Entriss up to saving Nihle. Marc took a moment to digest it all then burst out in laughter.

"I wish I could've seen him in the king's arms." She wiped tears from her eyes. "So, what's holding you back, darlin'? That adventure sounds like a nerd-girl's dream."

"It is, but..." Her cheeks warmed, and she took a deep breath. "He loves me, or thinks he does, and we barely know each other. At least, not the important stuff."

"You haven't told him?" Marc asked.

"I can't," Julie said, a little too loudly.

"And he hasn't told you either?" she asked.

"Told me what?" Julie grasped the sleeve of Marc's suit jacket.

Marc smiled and gently patted her hand. "Walk with me, kid."

They exited the Corvette and slowly made their way to Ian's apartment.

"Love is a lot of work," she said.

"I don't—"

"Sure, kid." She stopped and rested a hand on Julie's shoulder. "That's the thing. It starts with trust. Love is hard enough without the baggage, and you both have a lot for being so young. One of you has to take the leap, or the hurt will be more than a punch to the face."

"Can't you just tell me?"

"His secrets aren't mine to share, and neither are yours. Someone would have to hardwire into my skull to give that up, and even then, I'd fight it." She stared into Julie's eyes. "He can come across as an abrasive know-it-all, and a small part of me was happy to knock out his teeth. He's not perfect, but he's not what he seems."

She drew Julie in for a genuine hug, kissed her on the forehead, and walked away.

"Wait," Julie called out. "I don't have a key."

"Sure you do." Marc threw a glowing key over her shoulder.

It landed in Julie's hand like the woman had been facing her.

JULIE SAT at Ian's workstation and pondered. This wouldn't be the first time she'd ransacked a boyfriend's personal data. Back when she'd used apps to find "that perfect match," she always wanted to amend her profile with "will look through your personal messages, you cheating fuck." Spying felt unethical, but she'd given up on trust a long time ago.

Finding the right guy was an impossible chore, and she'd gladly settle on right-enough. She was done with hard bodies, hard rockers, and hard cases. Sure, there were some great men who lifted weights, played guitar, or struggled with a tough past. Those were the guys her friends dated and married and lived with happily-ever-after. But everyone she tried dating was a black hole ready to implode.

Her trust was locked tight behind a vault door with *Mission Impossible* layers of security. This wasn't just to protect her from the narcissistic, ego-laden, thoughtless boys she'd had flings with. Her father's lies had built that door long ago; everyone else just reinforced it.

Ian had seemed different. After chiseling through his annoying wall of entitlement and know-it-all attitude, she'd found someone who actually cared. He wasn't close to most of their co-workers, but they always spoke well of his helpful nature. The man had even lost his job standing up for them.

His hero complex was a welcome change, but "he's not what he seems" set off the red alert. Luanne had said it like Ian was hiding something dark, while Marc made him sound like Peter Parker. The fact that they'd both said it was enough to dig a little deeper.

She placed her hands on the archaic mechanical keyboard, sighed, and logged into Ian's computer.

It was Linux, of course, and a hearty old GNOME desktop GUI. She immediately opened a terminal session and began typing commands. She tested her access by listing files in Ian's home folder.

Permission denied.

She typed, *sudo ls -al /home/Ian/*

After entering her password again, a list of directories appeared.

"Aww, he gave me sudo."

Thanks to the superuser access, a list of directories scrolled past, including a hidden one: *.candidates.*

She typed, *sudo ls -al /home/Ian/.candidates*

Her heart skipped when she saw the directories in the hidden folder.

doggos

kids

moms

teens

wins

Fearful of the others, she opened *moms.* It contained hundreds of directories, each labeled with a woman's name.

Janet Wilson

Sheriah Jackson

Molly Doers

Each directory held a thorough dossier of the candidate, including current address, job history, police reports, health, credit records, and photos. It was a lot of information to have on someone, and they were all tough-luck-cases society had left behind.

The information made her wary. The photos made her heart skip. Every woman, kid, teen, and doggo was a victim of abuse—some horrifically.

Her sudo rights didn't give her access to the *wins* directory, but maybe that was a good thing. If he was some crazed stalker or, worse, a serial killer, she didn't want to see.

She sat back and wiped dread from her face. It just didn't feel right. Based on her self-preservation college courses, including mental disorder awareness, online defense tactics, and an intense series of self-defense classes, he didn't fit the mold of some closet-lurking, panty-stealing, trench coat-wearing misanthrope. Still, she had to be sure.

With shaking hands, she typed the command to search her own name. One instance of Julie Aliyah Jacks appeared in his address book, and she let out a deep sigh. At least she wasn't a candidate.

Beside her name, contact info, and date of birth was a flattering photo. Beneath that was a list of likes and dislikes. He must've noted everything she'd said or cast.

Favorites:
color - topaz
coffee - black, French-pressed
food - Thai
vacation - island resort
candy - dark chocolate
lingerie - pink latex (that must've been a drunk message)

It was a long list, and she skimmed down to the dislikes:

Pastries
Anything orange
Thoughtless people
Red meat
Birds that talk
Being interrupted
Pity
Her father??

Either he really paid attention, or she talked too much. Still, it was sweet.

Beneath the photo was a link to more. Clicking it opened a directory that contained dozens of pics. Selfies, drunken and sober, flattering and naughty. She wanted to delete all of them, but he'd know she'd spied. At least she remembered casting most of the pics, which meant he hadn't gone full stalker.

She continued searching. Most of his personal finance information was accessible. A quick peek made her eyes go wide. Why was he working when he had so much money?

"This is X-Files weird. Did I just bang Dexter or Hannibal Lecter," she said. "Either way I need to know the truth. What are you, Ian Gregg?"

42

TOWEL FRIENDS

The battle left Eon weary. He was desperate for sleep, but his brain wouldn't rest. Exhaustion dragged him through a storm of worried thoughts about Julie, and Entriss, and Luanne. Any time he'd nod off, on the cusp of the deepest sleep, the child would appear and ask, "Why did you take my heart?"

Vicki rested beside him, always ready to help. He'd wake up gasping, and she was there to squeeze his hand. If he was awake for too long, she'd rest her head on his chest and whisper stories about growing up in Misere until he fell asleep.

He'd had dozens of Tomb Raider fantasies, but this wasn't one of them. He wasn't playing the part of a dashing hero or suave love-interest. He was actually uncomfortable lying next to this woman he'd just met. But without her, the night would've been unbearable, and he didn't take her efforts for granted.

Entriss had become far more than just a game, but what kind of game would make him take a child's heart? Not only did it feel unnecessarily cruel, his brain regurgitated memories of Jet and the other abusive degenerates his mom had dated. It was too much, and the only reason he didn't log out was to stop the monsters from hurting anyone else.

When dawn finally peeked through the tent flaps, he watched through bleary eyes. Vicki lay on his chest as if she'd passed out holding him down. She was an incredible companion, but guilt wasn't. He wiggled from her hold as gently as he could and crawled out of the tent.

"Coffee?" Trevor asked, his voice low and quiet.

"I could really go for a Mountain Dew." He stood shivering in the early morning cold.

"A curious request." The Hobgoblin squinted at the distant mountains. "It would take us off path—"

"Coffee would be great," Eon said.

The Guardian handed him a steel mug filled with the dark brew. He took a delicate sip. It was hot, and bitter, and just what he needed. The coffee didn't buff his stats or give him a new superpower; it was just coffee, which was perfect.

"Thanks." Eon raised the cup, steam wafting over the edge.

Trevor nodded, lifting his own before taking a draw. "She fancies you, Champion."

Eon took another sip, hiding behind his mug.

"She's also not meant for you," he said in a fatherly tone.

Eon peeked over the lip. "What are you saying? Please don't tell me we have to fight again."

"Heh. No. We will not battle each other again." Trevor stared into his coffee. "Vicki is smitten with you, yet she will one day be queen. You are a great Champion, but you are no king."

"I can barely handle being Champion." Eon let out a heavy sigh.

"You are doing fine." Trevor nodded at the clearing. "A terrible ordeal, indeed, but those people...that child...they were already dead. You merely set their bodies to rest."

Eon nodded slowly. It's exactly what he needed to hear. Sometimes wisdom was more valuable than hugs. Though hugs were still pretty great.

"Thank you."

Worry painted Trevor's face as he glanced at the tent.

"What is it? Are you upset I was in her tent?"

"She's a grown woman and can share a bed with whom she chooses. I'm just concerned for her safety. Things will only get harder. This is magic beyond my experience, and if I'm not here to guide her through quest's end..."

"I wanted to give up after last night. Vicki's compassion and your wisdom make me want to keep going. We will stop what's happening to the people of Rath." Eon patted his broad shoulder. "Don't throw in the towel yet."

Trevor frowned. "I have no towel."

"It's a, uh, Yu saying for don't give up."

"But why a towel?"

Eon sorted through the file cabinet of his memory and could only find one entry. "This is paraphrasing, but the great Douglas Adams wrote, 'A towel is the most useful thing you can have. You can wrap it around you for warmth, you can sleep under it beneath the stars, wet it for use in hand-to-hand-combat, and dry yourself off with it.'"

Trevor nodded. "Now I wish I had a towel."

Eon dropped to his knees and pulled his satchel from the tent. He reached in and drew out one of the first treasures this character had won. "Take mine." He offered the ratty gray towel to Trevor.

"I... I... Thank you, Champion." The Hobgoblin accepted the gift, squeezing the towel tight in both hands before wrapping it around his fist. "For combat." He raised his fist high in the air.

Eon coughed back a chuckle. "This one is better for drying, more or less. Best to just wrap it around your neck."

Trevor placed it on his shoulders and smiled proudly. "I will not throw this in."

"I won't give up, either. We'll see Vicki through the quest together."

The Hobgoblin leaned forward and whispered, "Impregnate her and I will make a clothesline from your entrails."

Eon blinked.

Trevor stood tall, patting the towel and smiling as if his dad-threat had never happened.

"Ding!" Nomar said, scurrying from the tent. "I earned two levels last night! It would shock the jerks back home to see I'm 22."

Eon eyed the Hobgoblin warily. Trevor winked. He probably should've been offended, but really, the man had every right to protect his adopted daughter.

"Hey!" Nomar tugged at Eon's red coat. "Why are you still 21?"

"What?" Eon opened his character sheet. All his stats were grayed out again, including experience. He bit his tongue to avoid cursing the game, something they wouldn't understand. The change Deity had implemented in Yu hadn't been pushed to Rath. Hopefully, he'd catch up again, but being stuck at 21 would make this leg of the quest that much harder. He turned to Nomar and faked a smile. "Apparently, leveling works differently for Rune Mages."

"Oh, right!" Nomar said, cheerfully.

Coco crawled out of the Gnome's tent, her long purple hair a bedraggled mess. Eon looked down at Nomar, who blushed around a devilish smile. Lola hopped out after her, made her way to Eon, and threw up on his foot. She poked the Gnome with an antler and disappeared.

"What?" Nomar sank into his blue jerkin. "I thought she was asleep."

"I don't want to know." Eon shook bunny vomit from his boot.

Vicki was next to wake, exiting their tent slowly. She stood, cat-like, on tiptoes, flexing tanned, muscular legs that went all the way up to barely there shorts. Her cropped, linen tank top rose high as she reached for the clear sky with a yawn. She ignored the cold; her breasts didn't. Nomar elbowed him, and he remembered to breathe.

She leaned against Eon, closer than friendly, and eyed Trevor's towel.

"A gift from my friend." Trevor nodded at Eon.

"I see," she said with a glorious smile, looking between them and then at Nomar and Coco. "Now that we're all friends, maybe someone could make breakfast."

"On it." Nomar approached the fire, drawing pans from his bag.

"I'll make sure he doesn't poison us." Coco followed closely.

"You're poison." Nomar bumped her with his shoulder.

"The deadliest," she said in a sultry tone.

To avoid rolling his eyes, Eon took in last night's battleground. Entriss cleared away battles like a Zamboni driver. There were no corpses, and the woods were already healing. All that remained were his nightmares and... He leaned in.

"We should pack camp." Vicki grabbed his arm and pulled him to the tent.

"Are those..." Eon swallowed hard.

"The villagers' hearts." Trevor lowered his head. "I inspected them while you slept. They seem to have no purpose, so I put them together. It seemed fitting."

"I need to see for myself," Eon said.

"But..." Vicki started.

Trevor raised a hand, and she quieted, reluctantly letting go of Eon's arm.

He approached the pile, let out a long sigh, and steeled himself. Stacking them like a monument did seem appropriate; they were all that remained of The Mind's Eye's victims. Still, why were they here? If they truly had no purpose, why hadn't they disappeared with the bodies?

Eon picked one up. The red stone was in the shape of a human heart and heavy, like it was smelted from lead. With an effort of will, he inspected the heart. A scrolled parchment crackled opened before his eyes.

Villager's Heart appeared in a flourished gray font surrounded by dramatic embellishments that reached every edge of the scroll. There were curves and spaces and script like someone had painted in Arabic. It would be easy to dismiss as art, but after staring at it long enough, he saw something more.

He needed a universal translator to decipher this. But...wasn't there something back in Yu? His brain winced as he thought back. He'd finished the first part of the quest chain and dismissed the rewards too quickly. He had to remember.

Congratulations, Rune Staff of Ned the Insane has a new spell!

...Level 11.

New ability: Language Master

Focus Tree Unlocked.

Language Master! It had seemed irrelevant since everyone spoke English on Entriss. He activated the Language Master ability and gasped. He was no longer inspecting a stone; he was inspecting another player.

Franklin DeMarks

Profession: Baker

Level: 27

Partner: Daria DeMarks

The description continued, listing every accomplishment from standing to baking bread for the first time. This wasn't a character sheet; it was a life lived.

He didn't know what it meant. Could DeMarks be brought back to life? Was this merely a remembrance? The puzzle needed more pieces. After gently placing the stone in his satchel, he inspected the next heart, and the next.

Grissella Borsh - level 19 - Mason

RJ Lundgren - level 18 - Actor

Daria DeMarks - level 25 - Seamstress

Richard MacDonald - level 27 - Bard

One heart remained. His throat clenched as he reached for the smallest in the pile.

Uriah DeMarks - level 10 - Dreamer

He squeezed Uriah's stone heart tight before placing it in the bag between Franklin and Daria. They weren't alive, he hadn't saved them, but something about the effort felt right.

His normally weightless satchel felt surprisingly heavier as he made his way to breakfast.

They'd tucked camp away, and everyone sat around the fire scarfing eggs and bacon. Vicki looked at him thoughtfully, a hint of concern on her face when she glanced at the heavy bag.

"Is it necessary to bring them?" Trevor asked around a mouthful of egg. "They seem to be slowing you down."

"Not much." Eon patted the satchel. "Not enough to leave them behind."

"Want me to carry some?" Nomar unlatched his bag. "Plenty of room."

"No, this is my burden, and..." He looked at Vicki, who peered at him. "You okay?"

"It's her." Vicki's eyes went from cold to mischievous.

She set her plate of breakfast down, never taking her eyes off him. His hackles rose, and he took a step back.

The Jaeger launched into the air, landing on his shoulders, her crotch right in his face. As he fell back, she twisted, Black-Widow-throwing him into the air. He landed on his back with a jarring thud, knocking the wind from him along with 3% of his Health.

She pounced on him, laughing maniacally, and licked his neck before biting it hard. 1% damage.

"I don't understand." He flailed helplessly. "I thought we were friends."

"We are." She leaned in, far too close. "For now."

He looked into those dangerous eyes, and middle-school-dance-froze. "Vicki, what are you doing?"

She leaned forward until her lips tickled his ear and whispered, "Battle summons."

"Oh shit." Eon tried scrambling away. "No, no, no."

Jewells appeared in a shimmery vortex. She took in the camp, smiled at Nomar, and then saw Vicki mounting Eon.

"Gotta go," Vicki said, kissing him on the cheek. "Girl talk."

She leapt away as a burning white light blared over his face. He leaned his head back to watch the young woman run into the woods, dodging blasts along the way.

"It's not what it seems," Eon shouted.

"You're not what you seem." Jewells ran after Vicki.

"More chartoose eggs?" Nomar asked, holding a pan out. "Anyone?"

43

IN THIS CORNER

Trevor helped Eon up then held him back. Light flashed in the distant woods, followed by battle cries. The Hobgoblin squeezed his shoulder with a steely grip.

"Jewells doesn't know we're in Rath," Eon shouted. "They'll kill each other."

"Probably not." Trevor shoved a plate of breakfast into his chest. "Eat. You'll need your strength for the battle ahead."

"Which battle?" Eon held the plate as the burly man led him to the log and shoved him to sit.

He ate eggs, as directed, all the while glancing between the distant light show and the women's stats. They were both hovering around 50% until Jewells suddenly lost 270 Health. Eon stood, and Trevor pushed him down again.

"You'll see," he said with a nod. "They'll battle it out and become fast friends, like us."

Eon glared at the Hobgoblin.

"Maybe Jewells will give her a towel." Trevor patted the one over his neck. "Look, they're already coming back."

Vicki and Jewells full-out ran toward them, their faces a war of anger and panic.

"Girl talk already over?" Coco let out a cackle.

"Not even close," Jewells snapped. She gasped for breath and strands of her long red hair stuck to her sweat-dampened cheeks.

Thirteen mindless villagers lumbered out of the woods followed closely by another Mind's Eye. Purple leashes tethered them, dragging the creature forward like sled dogs.

"Aww, yiss." The monster's overlarge head leaned back as it sniffed the air. "First, I smell your magics, and now I smell your delicious hearts. Give us your hearts!"

"Here we go." Eon stood, taking a deep breath. "Like last time. Target their leashes, try to keep them separated, and don't make eye contact."

"You can do this, Champion." Vicki gripped his arm.

"At least we're sober this time." Coco drew her daggers.

"Unfortunately." Nomar stared off with wide eyes.

Eon nodded and summoned Lola. Her head jerked around as if taking in their positions before staring at those trapped by the Mind's Eye. The baker's dozen included several soldiers, a pirate with an eye patch, and a level 17 player named Jondo. There were no children this time, but that didn't quench the volcano in his belly.

He reminded himself that they were already dead, that the *Purge* spell was just freeing them. What would it do to Jondo? Most mind-control spells had time limits. Hopefully, the player would break free before Eon had to cast the spell.

With a strengthening breath, he drew Ned's staff.

"I don't understand," Jewells said.

"I'll explain everything when we're done."

She glanced from the trapped villagers to Vicki's hand on his arm. "I look forward to it."

He winced at her glacial tone. His swashbuckling romantic adventure had gone from comedy of errors to twisted nightmare. He wanted to log out and apologize and explain, but there was no time.

"Why do you look so sad?" She reached for him and then hesitated.

Without a word, Eon cast *Shockwave*.

He landed between his group and the closest attackers and began casting *Ruination*. Eon jumped back as Jewells appeared beside him in a flash of pink light. The Mind's Eye sniffed hungrily and leaned toward them.

"What are you doing?" Eon snapped. "These things are dangerous."

"Not new here." She eyed the tethered villagers.

"Lola, get back to the others and wait for my command. No more surprises."

The golden jackalope disappeared.

"How do we save these people?" Jewells braced herself.

"We don't." He reached out with a hand, directing it at the closest zombie, and cast *Purge*.

The woman rose into the air and convulsed violently until her heart tore through her chest with a wet crunch. It flew into his hand, and she collapsed. The Mind's Eye let out a howl. Eon placed the stone in his satchel and targeted another villager.

Jewells eyes went wide and she stared at him. "Did you just kill her?"

"That abomination killed her." He *Purged* a young man and reeled slightly before pocketing the heart. "This is the only way we could stop it. Freeing the victims with *Purge* makes that thing weak enough to attack."

The third heart emptied his stomach. He wiped his mouth with a shaky fist before placing it in his satchel.

"I fucking hate Ned." He swallowed hard.

"This can't be right." She turned to face the Mind's Eye. "You shouldn't have to puke your way through the battle. There has to be another way to save these people."

"What do you have in mind?"

"This." She raised her hammer and sickle.

The white fire of *Holy Wrath* shot from the weapons, blaring with an electrical hum that shook the air. It struck The Mind's Eye, knocking him back a step. Her spell ended with a sizzle.

"Cute." The monster reared back, taking a deep breath and standing tall.

"Dammit." Smoke drifted from her weapons as she lowered them.

"We tried that, and everything else." He braced himself for the next purge.

"Fine, but why are you keeping their hearts?" She stepped away from him. "It just seems wrong."

He turned to face her. She covered her heart with the hammer and sickle like she'd be next. "You don't trust me? Why don't you trust me?"

"I saw those pictures on your computer."

"Eon?" Nomar called out.

"Wait, what?" His mind was a prison riot that battled his comprehension...until it didn't. "I gave you access to my computer so you could turn off the cameras, not spy on me. Why were you looking through my files?"

"Eon!" Nomar's call was insistent.

She looked down, a deep blush on her cheeks. "It doesn't matter. Something terrible is going on and I don't want to be a part of it."

"And I don't want a spy in my group."

She stomped with one foot. "I can't leave. The game won't let me."

"Let me help." He tried kicking her from their group.

You cannot remove player from group while in combat.

They both shouted, "Dammit," and their eyes dueled.

"Eon!" Nomar sounded desperate.

"Oh, what now?" Eon spun around and gasped.

Two Mind's Eyes entered the clearing with a horde of tethered prisoners lumbering toward them. Nomar was ten feet away from them and statue still.

"Nomar, what are you doing? We need to get out of here!" Eon cast *Battlemount*. "Everyone, retreat to Lola!"

"I'm leaving as soon as we're out of the battle." Jewells turned and stomped away.

"As you wish." He said it without thinking.

The *Princess Bride* quote made her breath catch. Her eyes became glassy. Was she crying? There wasn't time to ask. She was already running to his familiar.

He cast *Shockwave*, landing between Nomar and the approaching attackers. With a growl, he picked up the Gnome and stumbled back to his familiar.

It was an intense turtle race. The Mind's Eye zombies Franken-stein-rocked closer. His satchel was heavy, Nomar was heavy, and grasping hands slowed every step.

A red arrow whizzed past his ear followed closely by bolts of lightning, knocking villagers down. He reached Lola and pushed Nomar up with a grunt. Vicki grabbed the Gnome's blue jerkin and pulled him to the top.

"Take my hand." Trevor reached for him.

They clasped arms, and the Hobgoblin threw him onto Lola's neck. He glanced back at the others. Vicki sat behind Trevor, and Coco held a quivering Nomar. At the very back, Jewells sat alone, wiping her eyes.

"Everyone hold on." He faced forward and grasped the handles. "Lola, go."

44

PREGAME

"I've seen enough." Swytch felt that familiar churn of the unknown in his gut. "Can we have some lights?"

Apparently, there were two settings for lights in the Entriss board room, pitch black and face-of-the-sun. His companions cursed as they winced or covered their holographic eyes.

"That's all you've got?" Dabest's monkey suit scratched an armpit. "We watched two hours of blurry Mandorf kicking ass. What about Eon?"

"Since Entriss doesn't allow streaming, these videos had to be rendered from old logs." Luanne sniffed and looked down her nose. "The Left Hand of God quest is blocking our ability to log anything he does as Eon."

"We're dealing with an unknown class, an unknown weapon, and an unknown quest," Swytch said. "Despite his level, he keeps winning. Is there anything else that gives him an edge?"

"Nothing I can think of." She scoffed. "If you can't handle it—"

"I could take him out myself in fair combat." Ragequit shook a fist.

"And yet, you didn't." Luanne ran a finger across her wrist and flicked it to table center.

The hazy holographic image of an Assassin and a Wizard rose from the table. They faced each other across an open field. Gamertags hovered over their heads, identifying Ragequit and Mandorf. The scene played out for ninety seconds when Mandorf burnt Ragequit to a cinder.

"I wasn't done leveling." Ragequit pounded the table with a fist.

"But you were already max lev—" Luanne started.

Swytch shook his head, and she rolled her eyes.

"I wanted you to watch some of Ian's more dramatic wins so you could examine his play style. Most of you have faced him as Mandorf, and he beat you." She stared them all down. "Akagi is the only one who came close. Would you like to see?"

His team grumbled or fidgeted in their seats.

"We get it." Swytch waved her off. He stood from his chair and began to pace. "Ian is good. Brilliant, even. We need our toons back so we can stretch our legs and do some reconnaissance."

"Your accounts are now active with updated armor and weapons, all best in slot for your class. And you'll have the *Final Kill* spell."

His guild cheered, clapping or pounding on the table.

"Perfect." Ringer tipped back his ivory Stetson. "We trail him for a few days. One or two of us randomly cross his path for some PvP. Letting him win a few times would teach us more than these old videos."

"That's not a viable option." Luanne crossed her arms. "*Final Kill* was never intended for players. The only way we could make it work is for the spell to go both ways. If your character dies in game, it's erased forever."

The cheers became curses as Dank Guild raised fists or fingers.

"That wasn't the deal." Swytch spoke with a forced calm, as if a wall held back his rage. "We *Final Kill* Eon, you pay us what's due, and our Entriss characters remain active."

"I'm bending the rules, just like your guild." She leaned back in her seat with a Cheshire smile. "You need to stop him before he makes it to the boss in Rath. End him tonight, and you'll get paid like we agreed."

"Fuck this." Ragequit's hologram began to fade. "You can't make me do shit."

"Mal-Chin." She snapped her fingers. "You will stay until you're dismissed."

His image became solid again, more or less. "You know who I am?"

"I know all of you," Luanne said, wallowing in a pool of smug.

"Dillon, I don't like her." Akagi wrung her hands together.

"Relax, Akagi." Ringer leaned back and scratched under his hat with a finger. "She can't have that much."

"Ringer." She turned to the muscular black cowboy. "Aaron Dart, forty-five-years-old, recently moved... You now live in Austin, Texas with your mom after losing everything in a poker tournament, including your second wife."

"My mama understands." He looked over his shoulder and shouted, "Isn't that right, Mama?"

"Get off that computer and clean your room," a faint voice replied, making him wince.

Luanne turned to Enya. "Phoebe Dooers. After getting kicked out of Georgia Tech for," she frowned and read slowly, "throwing a man out of a third-story window..."

"No means no." She peered at Luanne with an icy glare. "And I thought the frat house only had two floors."

"Right." Luanne swallowed hard. "You had a brief stint doing illegal cage fights before joining Dank Guild."

"Mah girl." Dabest raised a monkey paw, and they bumped holographic knuckles. "Me next!"

Luanne scrolled through her list and paused with a frown. "Abe Froman, Jr., son of Abe Froman, Sausage King of Chicago. That's it? That can't be right."

The guild burst out laughing as Luanne pounded her cast tablet with an angry finger.

"Hacker," Ragequit laughed, nodding at the ape.

"Dabest!" He let out a monkey chuckle.

"Fine. Mal-Chin Jim." She acknowledged Ragequit with raised

eyebrows. "South Korean native and three-time winner of the KeSPA cup. After an altercation with your teammates, Softy Toilet Paper sponsored your move to the U.S. and fast-tracked your citizenship. You quickly broke ties and went into hiding. You've been linked to multiple instances of swatting opponents and now have seventeen warrants out for your arrest. Whereabouts unknown, to the Feds. Currently in Jersey."

"I don't do swatting anymore." He flashed a worried look at Swytch and Akagɪ.

"We know, mate." Swytch nodded. "'s alright."

"Dillon Avery and his roommate Yuna Akagi." Her brow furrowed. "Everything is a mystery, except that you live in St. Paul, Minnesota and Yuna is on the spectrum—"

"Enough!" He stood and leaned in.

"What is she saying, Dillon?" Akagɪ tugged at his sleeve.

"That you're a fucking genius," he said through gritted teeth.

"I am a fucking genius!" She nodded in agreement. "So what is her defect?"

"Good question. None of this is news, Luanne. We don't keep secrets from each other so our clients don't hold them against us. Akagɪ is right. What is your defect?"

"I wanted everything to be on the table so you remained focused." She peered at him. "People are looking for your teammates, Dillon. Just do your job and they'll remain safe."

"Right. Everything on the table." He lowered his head as though lost to defeat. "Dabest?"

The ape flicked a finger and tapped the air before clearing his throat. "Luanne Torres, age forty-seven, lives with thirteen cats... Gross. Security Clearance revoked in the U.S. due to poor credit, tax evasion, and some questionable ties to Eastern Bloc countries. Does your boss, Ty Hammers know this? Your resume looks scrubbed."

"I thought she worked for Entriss," Akagɪ said.

"Looks like piggy here is getting two paychecks." The gorilla scratched his cheek thoughtfully. "Nice paychecks."

Luanne paled, mouth-breathing like a fish on land.

"Oh, and your water will be shut off again tomorrow if you don't pay it." He looked at Swytch. "Shall I freeze her accounts, boss?"

Luanne went rigid, her eyes bulging like she was being squeezed. She was.

"Now that we've gone down this dark path, I'll give you an out." Swytch pressed his fingers to the desk and leaned over. "We'll do our jobs and take out Eon tonight. Since this low-level character from an unknown class has already defeated two major bosses, some of us will die. You'll double our pay to compensate for those losses— starting with the deposit."

"Fine." She grimaced, her fingers working her tablet.

"Ransom paid." Dabest rubbed his hands together.

"Shiny!" Swytch smiled, looking over his motley crew. "Let's be bad guys."

AN ALARM SHOCKED Fred out of deep REM with that "I'm late for work" panic. His back ached, his ass was sore, and it took a minute to realize where he was. His apartment slowly came into focus. According to his monitor, it was 11 a.m., which was far too early for a late-shift tech.

The alarm buzzed louder, and after clearing his throat several times, he finally accepted the call.

"Hello?"

"Sorry to wake you, Fred," Lars said in a rushed tone. "Hadn't seen anything and wondered if you got it to work."

"Yeah, it was easier than I thought." He wiped sleep from his eyes and began typing. "Wait...you can't see the feed? One sec."

He grabbed a can off his desk and took a deep draw of warm beer. The bitter made him wince but at least his mouth wasn't dry.

"I didn't think it was possible to hack someone's cast, but it was cake. I was able to sync up at the tail end of her meeting with a group called Dank Guild." He pounded the Enter key one last time. "Forgot to forward her stream. I watched the end. She's a piece of work."

"Well done!" Lars sounded happy. "Wait. How did you do it? Can anyone trace this back to us?"

"I don't think they can trace us through the others."

"Others?"

"We weren't the first ones here." Fred stifled a yawn. "I didn't actually have to hack Luanne's tablet. Someone beat me to it, like two someones. Our feed just piggybacks off theirs."

"Any idea who they are?" Lars asked.

"Dank Guild may be one." He looked at the feed and cocked his head. "I'm not a good enough hacker to guess the other. Want Marta to look?"

"No. We need to focus on what Luanne's doing." Lars's voice was stern. "I can monitor her during business hours, but one of you will need to keep track overnight."

"Shouldn't be a problem." Fred stifled a yawn. "We'll take turns. One of us on Luanne and the other watching Eon stumble through his quest."

"What?" Lars snapped. "Did I hear that correctly? You can see what Eon is doing?"

"Uh, no, I would never spy on a player. That's against our Terms of Service and Privacy Policy." The words trailed off as he stammered to find an excuse. "Just sleep deprivation talking, sir."

"Relax, Fred." Lars went quiet for a moment. "I need to think on this. No one's been able to track Eon. The old man might actually sleep if he could see how things are progressing."

"Happy to help any way we can." Fred's shoulders began to unknot. "Anything else?"

"The feed?"

"Right." He typed several commands and Luanne's cast feed was forwarded to Lars. "I hope this helps."

After several minutes, Lars let out an "oof." He took a deep breath. "This is a great start."

45

HE'S GOT STONES

Eon hit the ground like a meteor, cratering the earth and spitting out debris in all directions. Three consecutive *Shockwave*s had shot him high enough to view their surroundings. The fun ride up quickly became a struggle not to scream as the spell slingshotted him back down.

The landing should've made him windshield decoration like any other bug, but *Shockwave* kept him alive. Barely. He was down to 17 Health and coughed up a glob of blood. Everything was numb until sudden, wrenching pain from a softball-sized charley horse cramped his leg. Sweat beaded on his forehead as he knuckled the muscle with his fist.

"Eon, are you okay?" Vicki scrambled down the crater's edge.

"I should never have suggested this." Trevor followed closely behind. "You could've died."

"Ooh, that would've been awful," Jewells said with mock sincerity.

They surrounded him, waiting for a heal from their Priest. She yawned into a hand and stared off.

"Fine." Vicki dropped to her knees beside him. "Tell me what's wrong. How can I help?"

"Cramp," he wheezed.

"I'll rub it out for you." She tugged off his boot and began massaging his calf. He tried jerking away, but she held his leg tight. "Is this helping?"

Her rough kneading made the cramp worse. It was growing larger and would soon take on a life of its own.

"Maybe if I work the whole leg." Vicki glanced at Jewells and smirked. Her voice became sultry. "I didn't realize how muscular you are beneath these robes."

Jewells peered at her with eyes so cold they were frostbitten. She healed him for a meager 100 Health.

"Really?" he asked.

"Fine." She waved dismissively, returning him to full health.

"Thanks," he muttered, tugging his boot back on.

Trevor helped them both stand. "Did it work, towel friend?" Trevor asked.

"Towel friend?" Jewells frowned, cocking her head to one side.

He shook his head and mouthed, "Later."

She nodded.

"It was a great idea, Trevor. I saw everything. Just gotta figure out that landing." His cheeks and ears were warm.

"We all fall." Vicki looked at him with smoldering intensity. "What makes you a hero is that you get back up."

"Thank you." He tried not to melt into those dangerous eyes.

"I'm going to be sick," Jewells said.

"Yeah, sick." Nomar nodded, looking between them. "Why are we sick?"

"Shush." Coco nudged him.

Vicki began finger-combing her dark, waist-length hair. The Brownie approached from behind and tugged a handful. Vicki sat, and Coco began tying it into a long braid.

"What did you see?" Trevor asked, ignoring the banter.

"Thousands of Mind's Eye monsters and Tethered fill the roads leading to Vana Slavu." Eon looked at each of them. Their worry matched his own.

"By Ned's cursed coins, that sounds horrific," Trevor said.

"Ned's cursed coins?"

"Just a saying," Coco said, dismissively. "It's what old people say instead of using curse words like—"

"Don't." Eon held up a hand. Her curses were so descriptive, so raunchy he wondered if it was a Brownie ability.

"What next, Champion?" Vicki asked.

"We need a way into that city. I'm open to suggestions."

"Lola could teleport us." Nomar gently stroked her fur.

"Negative, Ghost Rider," Jewells said. "I'm still feeling crunchy after our escape."

She was right. They'd been traveling for days. It was slow going because the Mind's Eyes threw Lola into a panic. They sensed her magic if she teleported too close. Some Mind's Eye couldn't be avoided. His group had killed a few and run from a few more. The last escape had left them a mess.

Lola had teleported over a river, landing hard in a bed of white clay. It had covered her like oil from shoulder to paw, while the rest of them looked like a splatter painting. It took an hour to scrub himself clean, and he'd probably earned a level getting clay out of her fur.

She snorted indignantly before her rear leg went into overtime, scratching like she had fleas.

"You were great, Lola, really." He leaned over to pet her.

She ducked his affections and gave him a wary side-eye.

"We could make our way through the sewers." Coco tied off the braid. "I'm sure I could find a path."

"I don't do sewers." Vicki raised her nose.

"Princess," Coco scoffed.

"Don't forget it." Vicki glanced back and winked at the Brownie.

Jewells's head jerked up at "Princess" and she looked at Eon with wide eyes.

"I need time to think," Eon said. "From what I saw, we should be safe to camp here. Some food and rest will be good for us."

"I'll search the area and gather wood." Trevor drew his beaten sword and wandered off.

"I'll join you." Coco squeezed a bit of damp from her hair. "Maybe we'll find the ones who got away."

Eon turned to her. "What are you talking about?"

"When you were carrying Nomar to safety, we focused fire on any villager who got too close," Trevor said. "A few of them broke free. Without the leash, they wandered into the woods."

"That could be important." Eon nodded at Trevor. "Anything else I should know?"

"Dinner will be ready in an hour." Nomar began rummaging through his bag, drawing out pots and pans.

"As will our tent," Vicki said, smiling at Eon.

"Our tent?" Jewells's tone was a pitch above shrill.

"Walk with me." He hefted his satchel with a grunt. She seemed hesitant. "Please."

JEWELLS RELUCTANTLY FOLLOWED him into the woods. They walked in silence, following a deer path for ten minutes. He lifted a branch so she wouldn't have to duck. Her eyes softened when she thanked him.

They arrived at a gurgling creek, far enough from the others they could talk, or shout, or whatever without being overheard. He plopped down on a moss-covered log with a grunt. The satchel wasn't getting lighter, and it took an effort to pull the thick leather strap over his head. Jewells dusted off a rocky outcrop and perched across from him. She watched with a raised eyebrow as he gently set the bag on the ground.

He cocked his head to listen then sighed. Monsters weren't gnawing on anything within earshot. He couldn't hear Coco and Nomar's playful bickering or Trevor's sage advice or Vicki's misaligned flirting. It was peaceful. It was calm...the calm before the storm.

"I'm, uh, not sure where to start," he said with a sigh.

"Maybe start with your fancy skullcap." She peered at him slyly and had the tiniest of smiles.

He tugged it over his ears. "A man walks down the street in this hat, people know he's not afraid of anything."

"Ha! You've also lost weight, maybe twenty pounds. You look stronger too." She paused. "Did you log out and make adjustments to your character?"

"It didn't even cross my mind. You created Eon to look like me. I wouldn't change that. Maybe I've lost weight carrying around that thing." He nodded at his satchel with a frown.

"It's heavy. I picked it up while you were shockwaving." Her voice became distant and analytical. "I have four suits of armor, gold, potions, food, trinkets, and more in my bag. It's weightless. There's no encumbrance in this game, so why is your bag so heavy?"

"The hearts. Ned's staff has a new spell called *Purge*." Even mentioning it made his stomach knot up. "It forcibly removes curses and sometimes makes me puke...because Ned. The spell pulls out their hearts, and I keep them in here." He patted the bag.

"Some people collect comic books. Others..."

"No, that's disgusting." His stomach lurched, and he swallowed bile. "I just...I couldn't leave them behind."

"That doesn't make any sense."

He lifted the stiff leather flap of his bag, reached in to grab a heart, and handed it to her. She jerked back and he grasped her hand, shoving the heart into her palm. "For fuck's sake, Jewells, inspect it."

Her hand shook with fury or fright, but she leaned in, focusing on the stone heart. "I don't understand. A scroll opened up and it's covered in runes. What do they say?"

He cleared his throat and inspected the stone. "John Ruhland, level 25, teacher, father..." After several minutes of reading through the wild ride of John's life, he grabbed another heart. "Aaron Byrd, level 26, cook, married to Sarah..."

He read the highlights, and after a few minutes, she raised a hand.

"You're not making this up."

"When I inspect these hearts, I see a character sheet that catalogs their entire life." He looked back and forth between the hearts. "They knew each other. Both were members of the BACA Outriders, protectors of children, sworn to—"

"Fine." She paused, studying his face. "Why did you take them?"

"A hunch." He shrugged, staring at the red stones. "When villagers or soldiers die, they typically drop a few coins or a crappy weapon. These hearts were the only thing The Mind's Eye victims left behind. It can't be a coincidence." He returned the hearts to his satchel. "Maybe finishing the quest will save them or set them free."

"Or maybe you can use them as weapons against the final Grym." She crossed her arms. "I know you always plan ahead, farther than most. That's how you win."

"That's not my intention. You saw for yourself that these hearts aren't weapons."

"I don't know if I believe you." Her voice went quiet, and she held herself. "Not after seeing those pictures."

"I don't believe you went digging through my files." He took a calming breath. "I'm not an idiot. If I'd hurt those people, or those animals, would I have left those folders unlocked?"

"Sure, sociopaths enjoy showing off their trophies."

"It's true, Clarice," he said in his best Anthony Hopkins. "I eat live puppies with some fava beans and a nice chianti. *Thff thff thff thff.*"

She struggled to hold back a smile. "Okay, Hannibal, then why all the pics? Do you know them? Is this some movie reference and I'm missing the joke?"

"I'm sorry, but I can't tell you." His jaw tensed. "I want to, but I made a promise."

"Then how can I trust you?"

"I could say the same. I gave you a login to turn off the cameras, not go through my computer. What were you looking for?"

"I was spying for Luanne." She stared at the ground.

"What?" He stood. "You're joking...wait, you're not joking."

"She dragged me into a board meeting. They knew we were together when you accepted the quest and the servers rebooted. Things became real when you saved Nihle and the Missouri server farm came online."

"Server farm?" His head felt light, and he sat down again.

"A quantum server farm went live solely to support immersion in Yu." She glanced up, a bit of trouble in her eyes. "Happened on Fred and Marta's watch."

"They probably choked on his cheesecake."

She chuckled politely.

"That's when I started to level—"

"That's when the board became concerned about an international incident. They're in a panic about the accords." She fidgeted on the outcrop and leaned in. "They threatened jail, or worse. I considered hiding out at your place, but I wanted to keep an eye on Luanne. I promise, I haven't told them anything."

"A server farm and an international incident, all under Luanne's watch." He rubbed his hands together. "What are we doing tonight, Brain? The same thing we do every night, Pinky. Try to take over the world!"

"Dammit. Don't make me smile when I'm upset at you." Her eyebrows warred between anger and happiness until she finally let out a deep sigh. "I don't want to go to jail."

"Right. That." He shook off his Animaniacs world-takeover fantasy. "I'm sorry for the shitty meeting, but there's no way you'll go to jail for playing video games with your sociopath boyfriend."

"But—"

"I'm the one who checked in the code, not you. In all their maneuvering, they haven't once messaged me to stop the quest. My CSI-rerun, Internet legal degree tells me that's a pretty weak threat."

"Yeah." She tugged on a lock of curly red hair.

"But if you weren't sharing anything with her, that doesn't explain why you were looking through my files."

"I don't trust you," she said, almost too quietly to hear. "I don't trust anyone."

"Why?"

"I can't tell you."

They looked at each other for a long time. He loved her, and wanted to tell her everything, but couldn't because of a promise. Her eyes were glassy, and her lip quivered as she held back her own truths.

"An impasse." He clapped his hands together. "What do you want to do? Do we log out and lawyer up against Luanne, or do we see this thing through and make her miserable?"

After a thoughtful moment, she shook off her melancholy and frowned. "Fuck Luanne, fuck the board, and fuck the accords."

"Agreed." He reached out with a fist and they bumped knuckles.

"Can we set the impasse aside long enough to get the job done?"

"Sure," she said, dryly. "Once you explain why Tomb Raider said 'our tent.' Did you sleep with her?"

"It's not what you think." His cheeks warmed and he wanted to crawl into his satchel.

"Eon, she looks like a medieval hooker. Could you love someone who looked like that?"

"What are you talking about? Of course not!" He cleared his throat. "Five, ten minutes tops, maybe."

They laughed, hers a little forced and his a bit nervous, but it was better than upsetting her. Was she giving him an out? He was more confused than ever, and it must've shown on his face.

"You're not a cheater. I've dated a few, and they're pros at hiding their feelings. You're not." She raised an eyebrow and waited. "That doesn't make it okay, so talk fast."

He recounted events as quickly as he could, until he got to the part with the child. The words came out shaky, and he swallowed hard. Her face became soft, almost apologetic.

When the story was over, his eyes were damp, and he wiped his nose. "I guess I'm a crappy sociopath."

She placed a hand on his forearm. "I should've been here."

"I wish you had been. She was kind, and she helped, but it was weird because it wasn't you."

They both dropped to their knees and embraced.

"What are we going to do?" she asked.

"You've been talking about a secluded island since you started at Entriss." He pulled away, but only a little. "I may know a place. Star

Trek on the beach, a volleyball named Wilson, Gnomes dressed like characters from Gilligan's Island..."

"We could disguise ourselves and sneak away." That wicked smile had returned.

He blinked, and then blinked again.

"What is it?"

"I'm so stupid." He pulled away and shook his head.

"Only when you're being a sociopath." She patted his cheek.

"Ha!" He took a deep breath.

"I know." She held up a hand. "You've figured out how to get us in. Let's go tell the others so you don't have to repeat yourself."

"You just don't want to hear it twice." He stood and helped her up.

"I didn't say that...out loud."

He lifted his satchel with a grunt and threw it over his shoulder.

"Eon..."

"I know, no more tent-sharing with Vicki."

"That shouldn't even be a question." She nodded at his bag. "Don't use those people as a weapon to stop the Grym. If they're already dead, let them rest."

"I wouldn't," he said.

"Then we'll be fine."

46

GRYM ORIGINS

It was dark when Eon and Jewells arrived at camp, and the heavy smell of beef stew and smoky campfire greeted them. Vicki and Coco huddled close, watching hungrily as Nomar ladled the thick broth into wooden bowls. Trevor stood over them, a wary eye on their surroundings.

Lola teleported into Eon's arms, knocking him back to the ground. She licked his face, and he turned away to protect his eyes from stray antlers.

Jewells knelt to scratch Lola's ear and chuckled. "Wrascally."

"Thanks, Lola," he said, dryly. His familiar returned to the others, and Jewells helped him up.

"Join us." Vicki waved them over. "The old man is ready to share our story."

"This should be good." Eon brushed dirt off his long coat before tugging down his cap.

He settled in near Vicki. Before she could inch closer, Jewells plopped down between them. Without a word, she accepted a steaming bowl of stew from Nomar and began eating.

Trevor walked behind the fire and cleared his throat. It felt like a family sitting before the big screen. The Hobgoblin's voice was James-

Earl-Jones-rich, perfect for storytelling. Eon was about to ask for popcorn and candy, but the pained expressions on Vicki and Coco's faces stopped him.

Trevor stared at the sky, statue still, like street performers in Las Vegas or Times Square. At first, light from the campfire seemed to enhance his powerful arms and scarred chest piece. As they waited, the firelight became unforgiving. Shadows bored into his face, revealing deep wrinkles and terrible loss. Trevor was suddenly as old as history, and he covered his face with a hand.

"It's okay, pada," Vicki said. "Tell them as you told me when I was young."

He nodded, lowered his head, and took a deep breath. "Mistakes were made, by the tribes of Misere, by Zalmon, maybe even by Deity. The Northern tribes were first to occupy the lands of Entriss. Hobgoblins, Humans, Brownies, and the peaceful Ash Giants lived in harmony for a thousand years. There were no Guardians or Jaegers or Slayers..."

"Aww," Coco said.

"We were a nation of crafters. Alchemists, Engineers, Musicians, Authors, and so many more who reveled in knowledge and creativity. Together, we built a grand castle, and the capital city of Salvare grew around it. Salvare was the center for everything new and powerful. There were no monsters to hunt, no dungeons to crawl, and players didn't kill each other for gain. We advanced ourselves through research and our creations."

"That sounds wonderful." Eon rarely spent time crafting his own armor or weapons. It was faster to delve dungeons, and the gear was better. Creating a character in Salvare would've been tempting, if it were available. He would've loved to craft epic gear and level doing it.

"It was." Trevor nodded appreciatively. "The wind whispered that new tribes had arrived on Entriss, and eventually we received our first visitors. Zalmon sent his daughters Adriette and Camille and grandson Ned as ambassadors."

"My Ned?" He nodded at the steel staff on the ground. "The idiot who created the dumbest weapon ever?"

"The same," Trevor said with a sigh. "His origins were of a, uh, questionable nature. Camille was his mother, but no one knows who his true father is. There are only dark rumors…"

"She was the first Rune Mage and used illusions to seduce everyone in her family until one of them knocked her up." Coco raised Nomar's mug 'o plenty and threw it back. "Royalty, amIright?"

"Not this royalty, scamp." Vicki pushed Coco over.

The Brownie laughed as everyone else gagged at the reveal.

"Well, yes." Trevor looked uncomfortable. "Zalmon's bloodline is strongest. It is said she wanted a child powerful enough to destroy him. Ned almost succeeded."

"How?" Eon asked.

"He was a dangerous Rune Mage, like his mother."

"Like you." Vicki leaned forward, looking deep into Eon's eyes.

"Please." Jewells leaned forward, blocking his view. "Tell us more about Ned."

"Ned looked unnatural. He was pale as old snow, tall like his mother, and sickly thin from a life spent indoors. Despite being only seventeen, Ned was practically bald. Most disturbing was his eyes— gray bulbous things with their own life, looking in all directions and rarely focusing on one thing." Trevor shuddered. "The young man had a sense of humor that none understood, often speaking in rhymes or stopping mid-sentence to laugh uncontrollably. Instead of shaking hands or grasping arms, Ned would reach out with two fingers and brush chins or poke cheeks. His very presence made everyone uncomfortable."

"Because crazy makes people uncomfortable," Coco scoffed.

"Ned the Insane." Jewells shook her head.

"They stayed with us for a year. Camille sought the secrets of our crafting, Adriette found love, and Ned asked for gifts. Despite his unusual behavior, artisans were hungry to please Zalmon's kin. They crafted for him. Swords and staves, coins and cauldrons, armor and weapons of such quality to make kings blush and shy away. He would toss most aside as if they were trash. He pushed the abilities of our crafters until their gifts 'felt right.' When they achieved his definition of perfection, he would spend days inscribing the items with runic magic. That's when things took a disastrous turn."

Nomar set a bowl of stew on the ground for Lola before plopping down beside Coco. He eyed his dinner and pushed it aside, leaning into the Brownie.

"It began with the coins. Of the hundreds made, he would only accept four. Terrible things would happen after every gift. Ranchers found small herds of livestock dead and maimed. Beloved pets went missing, some found inside out but still alive. One grown woman had been de-aged to infancy. It went ignored for far too long. No one saw him commit the crimes, and the crafters were gullible in their attempts to please Zalmon, ignoring the obvious."

"You didn't ignore, did you, pada?" Vicki said.

"I was too late." Trevor's weary expression made him look very old. "When six leatherworkers presented him with the eye patch, he imbued it with their very souls. I arrived as they transformed into Burning Shades, and I struck him down for his evil ways."

"That's when they dragged Ned to the city square and burned him at the stake," Jewells said with finality.

"Unfortunately, no." Trevor closed his eyes. "That's when we sent them away. Camille was furious, Adriette was heartbroken, and Ned was laughing. He left with the four cursed coins, the eye patch of seeing, and the unfinished rune staff. He spent decades imbuing the staff with power before fighting Zalmon to a standstill. Their battle almost destroyed Entriss."

"With this?" Eon kicked the staff, making Trevor jump. "What did he try to do, kill Zalmon with boredom?"

"You wield the staff, but only harness a fraction of its power," Trevor said. "Even your familiar, while useful, seems far less menacing than Ned's Dragon, Necrotic."

"Huh," Eon muttered, adding that to his growing mental file of Shittiest Weapon Ever.

"They battled for days until Zalmon finally ended him." Trevor took a deep breath.

"The end." Nomar grabbed his bowl of stew.

Trevor turned on the Gnome as Coco smacked the back of his head.

"What?" Nomar winced, adjusting his hat. "That was funny."

"Shut your dumb mouth, or I'll be your end," she snapped.

"Your mouth is dumb," Nomar muttered.

Trevor shook his head and sighed. "I wish you were right, little Gnome, but it was the beginning of our endless war. I don't know if Zalmon feared another Ned, or thought we were hiding something more powerful, but he lashed out with devastating fury. He sent the three Grym to our borders."

"That's not funny," Nomar said.

"They summoned monsters that attacked villages, and then cities, until all that remained was our capital, Salvare. The Grym became a barrier between our people and the southern kingdoms, sending a constant swarm of creatures to hunt and kill anyone who tries to enter our lands. Entriss now only knows the prison that has surrounded us for hundreds of years. Misere. They have forgotten Salvare."

"Don't you mean abandoned?" Vicki crossed her arms and glared at the stars.

Trevor approached and knelt before her. His stern face melted into gentle concern. "I thought you were past this. We don't really know what happened after she left."

"My mother swore to return. A daughter of Zalmon would have the power to come home."

"Your mother?" Eon and Jewells said.

"Adriette." She practically spat out the name. "The most powerful Ranger on Entriss could've saved many lives. She could've come home to her daughter, but she was either a coward or a quitter. I blame her for everything."

He reeled as the pieces slowly fit into an ugly puzzle. Players from Yu and Rath sometimes ventured into Misere hoping to find something new. If they went too deep and became overwhelmed by the swarm, Adriette might show up to save them. "I don't think she gave up."

"Why would you say this?" She turned on him, frowning as if he'd betrayed her trust.

"Adventurers, some I know, have seen her wandering the wastes of Misere, fighting monsters. Everyone thought it was to protect the Southern tribes, but maybe she's been trying to fight her way back."

Vicki went pale like he'd smacked her upside the head with a bucket of realization.

Lola's snoring broke the awkward silence. She lay sprawled on her side, basking in the warmth of the campfire. Nomar and Coco took turns rubbing her tummy. If they stopped, she'd wake long enough to poke them with an antler until they got back to work.

Eon closed his eyes, running numbers in his head. "The history of Ned's battle with Zalmon is murky, but the forums, I mean, historical documents suggest it happened three hundred years ago. Maybe longer."

"Yes," Trevor said with a sigh.

"How old are you?" Eon asked.

"Older than you, son. Older than that staff, and Ned's coins, and that evil patch. I was there for all of it, and I was too late. It was my greatest failure."

"And then you met me," Vicki said in a quiet voice.

Trevor reached down to brush her cheek. "Before Adriette was cast from our lands, she handed me a bundle of child to raise as my own. A challenge for an old smith that was far more rewarding than I'd expected."

"Wait. If you're over three hundred years old..." He turned to Vicki. "How old are— Ouch."

Jewells elbowed his ribs and whispered, "You don't ask that."

He looked at Vicki.

"I'm twenty-seven." She stared at the ground. "At least, that's what I tell people."

"Really?" Jewells asked. "I would have said no older than twenty-three."

Vicki's face lit up.

Before Eon could agree, they both looked at him and said,

"Shut up."

Vicki gave her a once-over and smiled. "I'm jealous of your armor. You look amazing. How did you come by it?"

Eon stood as Jewells shared her adventures. They spoke so fast he lost track of the conversation and sought Trevor for guidance.

The muscular hunchback placed a hand on his shoulder, leaned in, and whispered, "Towel friends."

"You think so?"

Jewells and Vicki were deep into comparing notes, occasionally glancing his way and giggling. He felt like purging again.

Trevor nodded knowingly, patting the ratty towel over his shoulder. He turned, placing his hands behind his back, and slowly walked away from the campfire. Eon followed closely, silently, waiting for the big man to speak. They stopped at the forest's edge, out of earshot of the others.

"This quest will make her a queen. Whether it be of Misere or all of Entriss, I cannot say." He closed his eyes and sighed. "Protecting her is a burden I cannot face alone."

"Trevor," he grimaced before saying, "towel friend. I'll do whatever I can to help."

The Hobgoblin slowly turned to face him and opened his hand. A tiny golden quest orb rested in his palm.

They met eyes, and Trevor nodded. Eon accepted his quest.

At All Cost: As Vicki's guide, you agree at the cost of life and limb to protect my daughter so she can complete her quest and ascend her destined throne.

It was as if Trevor had written the quest.

"I'll do my best." He gripped the orb tight.

"I know you will." Trevor nodded. "I take it you have a plan, Champion?"

"I do. At least, I think I do."

"Good, because it's time to end this." Trevor's formidable muscles tensed. "Our folly almost destroyed Entriss. I won't allow that to happen again. This was our mistake. This is our reckoning."

47

FOR DOOM THE BELLS TOLL

"This is a terrible plan." Jewells shot a look at Eon.

He shrugged, returning his gaze to the distant city, Vana Slavu. Angry architects must've designed the capital of Rath. The city perched on a tall hill overlooking steep embankments like a predator. An enormous wall made of obsidian and paranoia surrounded Vana Slavu. It curved inward, reaching too high to breach by any means known to man. Thin black and gray towers peeked over the top, stabbing at a stormy sky.

Eon had been inside those walls. It was a claustrophobic's nightmare. Buildings were squeezed together uncomfortably tight, creating a city of dark alleys where death's cool breath tickled the back of your neck with every step. It was a labyrinth that players battled hard to enter and fought harder to escape. Vana Slavu was everything he hated about PvP.

The terrible city had a terrible problem. A thick beam of purple light shot up from the center. It reached high into the roiling clouds above like they were facing Gozer the Gozerian. Every few minutes, a cloudy halo surrounding the beam rose, striking clouds with the teeth-rattling gong of an off-key church bell. Cascades of lightning sped across the sky, feeding long purple tethers that reached down from the clouds, leashing hundreds of Mind's Eyes.

Eon, Jewells, and Vicki hid behind a thick growth of brambles, careful not to touch the long, yellow thorns or stumble on the skeletal remains of animals underfoot. Twenty yards away, a mass of Tethered lurched forward with every jerk from a Mind's Eye. The tall creatures took long strides on thin legs, occasionally pausing to sniff the air.

"I agree. This plan is awful." Vicki patted his damp shoulder then frowned at her hand. "Maybe she should be the Champion."

"She already is, because I couldn't do any of this without her." Eon met eyes with both of them.

Jewells's angry frown softened as she pursed her lips. Vicki looked sad, her gaze darting between them. He felt stuck between a woman who refused his love and a fantasy who wanted more than he could give. It was a socially awkward vortex that sucked him in until Jewells gently slapped his face, splattering the area with white mud.

"Hey." He reached up to his cheek.

"We were losing you." She patted his cheek gently. "Lead now, lament later. We need to move before this slop dries."

It had only been an hour since Lola had brought them back to the pool of white clay. The stuff was slick-wet and yet dense like a fresh layer of latex Kilz. Disgusting to bathe in, but now they looked like newly birthed Mind's Eye zombies. Hopefully, it would be enough.

"I wish the others were here." Vicki held herself and stared at the ground.

"We couldn't risk it. Not after what happened to Lola and Nomar," Eon said.

Before getting in disguise, the Gnome had insisted on scouting ahead with Lola. Griefers had hunted them, killing his familiar. Nomar barely escaped, as though they were toying with him. Eon had to wait an hour before summoning his familiar, and she hadn't come back happy.

"I want them here too." He gripped Vicki's shoulder. "But they probably targeted Nomar and Lola for standing out. Adventurers from Yu rarely make it this far into Rath, and no one has seen a jacka-lope. The three of us will have an easier time sneaking in."

Vicki nodded. Jewells didn't. She was right to worry. Griefers had attacked Nomar and Lola a mere hundred yards away from the horde of Mind's Eyes. Why would they risk their lives so carelessly?

"Enough with fear. I believe in you, Champion." Vicki shuffled her way along a thin path, careful to avoid thorns until she found a break in the foliage. With a nervous breath, she joined the heartless zombies.

Jewells followed until he grabbed her hand.

"Wait," he whispered.

"For what?" She licked her lips, watching Vicki make her way into the crowd before turning on him with wide eyes. "Are you using her as a test?"

"I was going to go first, but she beat me to it," he snapped. "Now hush."

Vicki mimicked the Tethered's lumbering gait and vapid stares. The crowd moved on without interruption.

"The camouflage works!" He raised a fist in the air.

"And if it hadn't?" Jewells eyes were piercing.

"I'd have saved her." He met her gaze and grinned. "Wouldn't she love that?"

"Dammit."

Eon raised his arms, and zombie-walked to the road. "Brains...er, hearts." He turned to a Tethered villager beside him. "It's hearts, right?"

The old man said nothing, completely entranced by the beam of violet light. Jewells joined them, lumbering slightly faster until she caught up. He reached out and poked the man's shoulder.

"What are you doing?" Jewells whispered, looking about nervously.

"Apparently, whatever I want." He nudged the slave several times without a reaction. "The spell has them acting like Borg. They couldn't care less that we're here."

Eon's foot caught on a loose stone and he stumbled into the man, knocking him to the ground. The nearest Mind's Eye tugged at the tether, jerking it free like throwing a fish back to water. With a small whimper, the man's body melted into the ground.

Eon turned on the creature and balled his fists.

"Not now." Jewells rested a calming hand on his forearm. "You'll get us killed and... Is that his heart?"

She nodded at a red stone lying in the mud path. A group of Tethered marched closer, and he lurched forward to grab it. The heart was hot to the touch, and he quickly put it in his satchel. Jewells placed a hand on his and looked at him like he'd stolen something.

"To save them, right?" Jewells asked.

They both winced as the bell clanged.

"I wonder..." He took a deep breath and scanned the ground with True Sight. Dozens of stone hearts littered the path like a lazy Easter Egg Hunt. "There are hearts everywhere. Catch up with Vicki. I'll grab as many as I can."

With a sigh, Jewells rushed forward as Eon scrambled between the Tethered like a puppy overwhelmed by a field of new smells. When his satchel was almost too much to bear, he limped up the steep road. They'd slowed enough for him to catch up.

"Got enough for your collection, Hannibal?" Jewells said.

"*Thf, thf, thf, thf.*"

She shuddered, mockingly.

"What was that?" He reached up to his skullcap. It was damp to the touch.

"Rain." Vicki looked up at the sky. "Glorious rain to wash off this muck."

"That'd be great if the muck wasn't keeping us hidden." Jewells glanced at the white clay dripping from her fingers. "Zombie-walk faster!"

The gentle spring patter of raindrops became heavier with every step forward. They were three hundred yards from the city gates when heads began to turn. The nearest Mind's Eye leaned toward them and sniffed the air.

"This is bad." He gave them a shove. "Run!"

It was as if he'd cast Murphy's Law. Thick raindrops fell heavy, slowly washing away their white clay coating. The Tethered noticed their transformation, making them scramble faster as the gravel path became a mud slick. His heart raced his feet as Mind's Eyes approached.

Vicki screamed and collapsed to a knee. 37% of her Health was gone, and her leg was a bloody mess. An arrow in her thigh sprouted thin metal bands that wrapped around her leg.

"Go on. I'll catch up." She drew a long, curvy blade from her waist and wiggled it between her leg and the metal. The bands squeezed tighter, pulling the steel arrow deep into her muscles. She was losing health faster than Jewells could heal.

"This isn't a regular spell," Jewells grunted.

"A special?" Eon asked.

She could only nod, casting spell after desperate spell.

Fireworks exploded overhead, and every Mind's Eye and Tethered went still like they'd locked eyes with Medusa. The giants wavered drunkenly as their zombies grasped at the air.

"I don't understand," Jewells cried. "What's happening?"

"Griefers. We're being hunted." He looked around but only saw distracted monsters. "They'll have a harder time killing us if we make it to the city. Vicki, how are you holding up?"

She didn't answer. Despite Jewells's heals, she'd passed out.

"Okay. We can still do this." He knelt to throw her over his shoulder. "I'll carry her. You keep her alive."

"Eon." Jewells reached for him before falling over, stiff as a concrete slab.

Someone had cast *Immobilize*, freezing her body for thirty seconds.

"Great. Just fucking great." He placed the staff in his satchel, grabbed their hands, and dragged them to the city entrance.

Walking up the slick hill made him grunt with every step. Heavy rain washed clay into his eyes, obscuring his vision. The fireworks stopped, and Tethered turned to face him.

"Could this get any worse?" he grumbled.

"Yes, it can. Because that's what we do."

An enormous Ogre in red steel armor stood before him. The beast wielded a two-handed bastard sword in one hand. His other held a glowing black shield covered in spikes. He had dark, matted hair, a prodigious nose that had been broken more than once, and keen piercing blue eyes filled with murder. A quick inspect told Eon he didn't stand a chance. The man was a Rath Gladiator dripping in cutting-edge epic gear. His name was Swytch, and he was the Guild-master of Dank Guild.

A chubby Sprite Cleric named Akagi stood to his right. She looked like a miniature Elf with pale skin and thin pointed ears that rose over her head. Her rich purple terrycloth robes and ornate two-handed war hammer were best-in-slot for a PvP healer.

Enyo, an angry-looking Centaur, towered over her, staring with ice-blue eyes. She had the sleek tanned torso of a courser war horse and the muscular upper body of a gymnast. Her blond hair was pulled back tight and draped over one shoulder. The Sorcerer wore a blue satin corset and held the War Staff of Antilon tight in both hands. Mandorf's staff.

They were in trouble.

"Shit. I've heard of you guys." Eon let go of both women's hands and clasped his together. "This doesn't have to get ugly. I'm trying to save a world."

"And we're just trying to pay rent," Swytch said.

"But we already paid our rent," Akagi whispered.

"Stay on script, dear." He flashed Eon a hungry smile. "Sorry, mate, you don't stand a chance. We're not alone." He raised a hand to his mouth and shouted, "Ringer!"

As if on cue, more fireworks shot into the air, quickly followed by a gong from the beam of light. Rather than being distracted by the spell, the Mind's Eyes became irritable. Spells like this often had diminishing returns, becoming less effective over time. They hovered over their Tethered, sniffing them like desperate hounds.

"It's time, mate," Swytch said with a nod. "Luanne sends her condolences."

"I want to do it," Akagɪ pleaded.

"No, it's my turn." Enyo raised her staff.

They were so close to the entrance he wanted to lash out with every spell he had. Unfortunately, Eon's arsenal was limited to level 21 spells, Ned's staff, and a brain full of quotes from old shows. Vicki had stopped taking damage from the arrow and would wake up soon, hopefully. Jewells was fifteen seconds away from becoming un-immobilized. He just needed to distract Dank long enough so they had time... time. That was it. He smiled. There's no way this would work.

Eon shouted as loud as he could. "Could you all just stay still a minute because I...am...talking!"

Akagɪ and Enyo looked at Swytch, who frowned. They turned to stare at him, so focused they didn't notice the Mind's Eyes and their Tethered had stopped moving.

"I won the title Champion of Yu. Who's coming to take it from me?" Eon shouted, raising his hands out and spinning around. "Come on, look at me! No plan, no backup, no weapons worth a damn. Oh, and something else I don't have: anything to lose! So, if you're sitting there in your silly little armor with all your silly spells, and you've got any plans on taking me, just remember who's standing in your way! Remember everything I did to get here, despite my level, and then, and then, do the smart thing! Run!"

The members of Dank Guild looked about nervously, as if something would happen. It didn't.

"Why would we run?" Akagɪ asked.

"Because this." Jewells rolled over, crossed her hammer and sickle, and cast *Holy Fire*.

The blast struck Akagɪ in her face, eating away Health fast until she threw up a shield.

Vicki kipped to stand on one leg and let out an angry roar, lashing out with her whip. It wrapped around Enyo's neck as Jewells cast *Vampiric Touch*, sucking away her health. Enyo let out a scream as her skin pruned like a raisin. When her Health was gone, she collapsed to the ground, as dead as dirt.

"That was a wonderful speech, Eon," Vicki said with a nod.

"He stole it from a doctor." Jewells shook her head. "I don't believe it worked."

"A doctor?" Vicki asked, looking from one to the other. "Who?"

"Exactly." Eon winked.

A volley of arrows pattered the area, soon followed by another, eating away small amounts of Health from every creature in the spell's radius. The Tethered were frantic, knocking Swytch about like bumper cars as Mind's Eyes closed in. The Ogre staggered on the rain-drenched ground, doing his best to shrug off the chaos and focus on Eon.

An Assassin named Ragequit appeared behind Vicki and wrapped a thin golden string around her neck.

Eon cast *Alacrity* and threw a *Ruin* spell at him, knocking Ragequit senseless. Vicki jumped clear and he instant-cast *Ruination*. The spell blasted Ragequit into the air. The Assassin flipped back and landed catlike on two feet behind the Ogre.

"Enough!" Swytch reached out and shouted, "Enjoy *Final Kill*, Champion of Yu."

Eon cast *Envelop*, freezing Swytch in place. A Mind's Eye leaned forward, lifting Swytch with its mouth. It shook him like a dog with a rat before tossing him away.

A second Mind's Eye chomped down on Ragequit and played tug-of-war with a third. They tore the Assassin in half and swallowed the remains. The monsters launched toward them with open maws.

"Run," Eon cried. "Go, go, go!"

48

KILL SWITCH

The Mind's Eye lurched forward, its wide mouth snapping shut inches from Eon. Marta jumped in her seat, spilling popcorn everywhere.

"Faster! Run faster!" Fred pounded on his desk.

They gawked at the giant center screen as Eon, Jewells, and Vicki ran up the slick hill, inching away from the Mind's Eyes and their Tethered hordes.

"So close." Marta gripped her armrest.

"They'll make it!" Fred shouted.

Beep *Beep* *Beep*

"Not now," Marta pleaded as she attacked her keyboard. "Shit."

The large monitor went dark.

"Hey." Fred turned to her. "What gives?"

"Luanne is casting."

A stream of text appeared on the screen.

"Can't she be evil later?" Fred asked.

Luanne: *Ty, I need a favor.*
Ty: *How can I help?*
Luanne: *PTR, 15 min?*

Ty: *I'll be there.*

The transmission ended.

"Why the public test realms?" Fred asked. "Devs haven't pushed anything to those servers in a year. No one's using them, and... Oh. No one's using them."

"Looks like someone turned off logging, probably to save on storage space until it's needed." Marta shook her head and *ts*ked. "That means there'll be no record of their conversation."

"Unless *we* happen to be watching." Fred raised his eyebrows.

"Isn't that breaking the rules?" Marta teased.

"In the best way." He typed in commands, bringing the public test realms up on the big monitor. "Any sign of them?"

"Two players just logged in." She squinted at her monitor. "They're in Knobtown, the Human starting zone East of Averdac. We need to see the Tavern."

Fred clacked away and his virtual camera bird-swooped down to ground level then rushed forward, blurring past towns, farms, and mobs. Everything slowed as the camera entered Knobtown then stopped inside the Uray Knob Tavern.

"You've got to be kidding me." Marta rolled her eyes. "They didn't even try to disguise themselves."

Their characters looked exactly like they did in real life. Ty Hammers had logged in as a level 1 Wizard named Hephaestus. He was short and thin with a bald head, dark skin, and a beard that reached from his ears to form a sharp triangle at his chin. Hephaestus wore a plain white shirt and dark peasant pants.

Jellicle, a level 2 Wizard, was a frumpy, tanned woman with spiked gray hair.

It was like someone's parents had created characters to log in and see what their kids spent too much time doing. Hephaestus sat patiently, watching her try to pick up a tabby cat. The cat was on a loop to circle the room and knock over the occasional drink. It slipped out of her grasp and wandered off.

"Cats love me. There's nothing real about this place." She scoffed. "I can't wait to be rid of it."

A lovely waitress sauntered over. She was porcelain pale with a mane of blond hair tied back with a leather thong. A tight leather corset wrapped around her low-cut blue peasant dress, putting everything on display.

"May I offer milord or milady anything?" She leaned over. "A warm ale to wet your tongues before facing the road to adventure?"

"Uh, no, thank you." Hephaestus was direct but polite.

"And you, miss?" she asked.

"Shoo." Jellicle waved her away.

"Beckon if you need me." The waitress looked into the camera. "I'll be watching."

"What the hell?" Fred asked. "I've never seen that before."

"Shush." Marta shushed him with a hand.

"Did the waitress look different this time?" Ty asked.

"Does it matter?" Luanne sniffed deeply. "This will all be shut down and reset soon enough."

"True." He glanced at the blond again and shrugged. "Why are we meeting here?"

"I think someone's compromised my cast tablet." She looked around warily. "Dank Guild showed their cards at the last meeting. They knew too much."

His eyes went wide. "Why on Earth are you still using it?"

"I didn't want to scare the hackers away by turning it off." She straightened her robes. "I'm handing it over to digital forensics tomorrow. They should know if it was Dank Guild or someone else."

"Understood." He leaned in and spoke softly, "Is that all?"

"I heard that Watson's delaying again. Cook said Entriss would remain online for another two years."

"Jack may be bluffing, but it's been months since we've spoken to Watson." Ty's leg bounced with nervous energy. "The, uh, anomaly still exists. I'm sure he'd like more time, but he doesn't own those quantum servers. We'll take over if he tries to delay again."

"Good." She let out a deep sigh. "Serbia won't wait that long to buy Entriss."

"And we can't take ownership of Entriss while the game is live, Luanne." His voice was stern. "Which means you don't get paid."

She raised both hands. "I know, I know. The world event has made Entriss Online popular again. Announcing a shutdown would bring too much attention, especially with the sale pending. I have a backup plan but could use some help."

He searched the room again, like James Bond was hiding behind a newspaper nearby. "What do you need?"

"The kill switch. You said it exists."

Ty let out a low whistle. "It does, but are you sure that's the best course of action? Not only does it delete all characters, it kills Deity, rolling her and the game back to day one. It will take Serbia years to bring a new Deity up to speed."

"It's just a backup plan." She grimaced and clenched her fists. "That worthless shit Ian is winning, and we need a contingency if Dank Guild can't stop him."

"Wouldn't a full wipe be obvious?"

"Not at all." She smiled, wickedly. "It would simply be a terrible accident that Entriss Online couldn't recover from."

"What about backups?" he asked.

"Entriss backs up the database. They haven't figured out how to back up the AI."

Ty pondered for a time before nodding. "I'll speak to my counterparts, but this could work."

"If it does, do I get to take down Battleworld Titus next?" She rubbed her hands together. "It won't be hard to sell."

"Ha!" He let out a mocking laugh. "You don't want Colonize Epiales?"

"No, thank you." She crossed her arms. "That horror show is yours."

"I don't blame you," he said with a knowing smile. "Let me know if Dank Guild fails, and I'll see what I can do. Is that all?"

"A little protection if things get ugly. I have a crew in mind but need funds to pay them."

"That shouldn't be a problem..."

"Did you get all that, sir?" Marta asked.

"Enough." Cook's voice boomed throughout the control center. His tone was far stiffer than it had been. "Thank you for looping us in. Fine work. Lars and I will take it from here."

Cook and Lars left their meeting, and they both settled into their seats.

"We should get hazard pay for this." Fred let out a shudder. "Looks like Ty left but Jellicle is still at the inn."

Luanne was shouting at the blond waitress. "This place is my worst hell. Everything is fake, everything's on a loop. I'll finally sleep when I've destroyed this game and killed Deity, and there's nothing you can do to stop me."

The waitress was stoic and smiled, staring on vapidly like any other NPC. Luanne logged off, and the smile became wicked.

49

DARK CITY

M andorf would've scoffed. His overpowered Wizard had the resources to take time and consider his actions. With little effort, Mandorf's spells could've killed or incapacitated any and all within a hundred yards. Maybe two hundred. The fish tale became larger every minute he tasted mud.

"Get up or I'm leaving you behind," Jewells growled. "I'm running out of Mana."

Vicki helped him stand, and he made the mistake of glancing back. Someone must've opened a portal directly to Hell because the demons were coming. Mind's Eyes lurched closer with snapping maws as hordes of Tethered climbed over each other, desperate to make eye contact.

He needed Mandorf's power, but Mandorf wasn't here, just Eon. He may not have wielded his old character's power, but he held something that everyone seemed to fear. With gritted teeth, he raised the legendary staff of Ned the Insane high overhead and shook it. "Taste Ned's fury!"

Mind's Eyes jerked back, pulling hard on their leashes. The Tethered scurried away from the oncoming storm.

"Run," Eon shouted as he cast *Ruination*.

The explosion knocked back any aggressor within ten yards. It threw them into the approaching masses, creating a dog pile of bodies for the others to stumble over. The spell only gave them seconds. Precious seconds.

None of the Mind's Eyes or Tethered had spells to cast at a distance nor weapons to hurl. Eon had stopped them long enough to limp up the hill, trailing farther behind the others with every second.

Jewells and Vicki waved at him to hurry.

"Leave the stones behind," Jewells shouted.

"Not gonna happen," he grumbled, wheezing his way to the gate.

The long leg of a Mind's Eye stepped over him, its foot landing with a sloppy thud. The other leg followed as the monster positioned itself between Eon and his friends, blocking the entrance. It turned away from Eon with surprising speed for a creature that large.

"Look out," he shouted.

The monster lurched forward, snapping like an alligator. Jewells threw herself at Vicki, knocking her to the ground.

Vicki rolled onto her back and screamed as the Mind's Eye lifted Jewells with its mouth and shook her. There was a loud crack and her broken body lolled out of the creature's maw, falling beside Vicki in a puddle of bloody drool.

"Delicious!" The monster wiped gore from its chin with the back of a long arm. "More."

As it reached for the princess with wide-open jaws, the off-key bell rang. It jerked away and faced the beam of light, the annoying summons too powerful to ignore.

Eon stumbled to Jewells's body and collapsed to his knees. His stomach churned at the sight, and the stars of faint sparkled in his vision. He blinked and shook his head. He wasn't going to pass out, the sparkles came from her corpse.

"I'm so sorry, Eon." Vicki pushed herself up to kneel beside him. "I know she was special to you, but we need to go and... What are you doing?"

"To the griefers go the spoils." He rifled through her corpse and withdrew a white top that sparkled like treasure from a dead mob. "Another thing I hate about Rath. It's a free-for-all. Once you're dead, anyone can loot something off your body."

"But...but...your friend." Vicki stared at him with wide eyes as if he'd taken a bite out of Jewells's corpse.

"It's okay, I just don't want anyone else stealing her gear. She'll be back." He stood and looked around. "She won't be happy, but she'll be back."

"Like you came back." Worry painted her face. "Are you both so powerful to defy death?"

"Not powerful enough to save her from these monsters." He stood and reached out a hand to Vicki. She stared at it like he would eat her next. "Take it. We have to get into the shadows. More Mind's Eyes are coming, and the bell only strikes every fifteen seconds."

She accepted his hand, and he led her to the nearest shadowy alcove. This was Vana Slavu, and fortunately, there were plenty to choose from.

It was a close space that hid too much of his view. She leaned against him, making his tired heart skip. He hesitantly wrapped an arm around her, which had seemed easier to do at the campsite with his belly full of warm drink. She shuddered from fear or the chilly rain. He braced himself, setting social discomfort aside, and pulled her in closer.

She leaned into him. "This is not what I expected when I accepted the quest."

"Exactly how I've felt since the beginning." It didn't help. She didn't need him to commiserate; she needed reassurance. "But I know we can do it. I believe in you, Vicki. I believe in us. We're bound by a cause, by a quest, and we'll make things right."

"Eon, if she doesn't make it..." Vicki drew back far enough to look up. "Just know that you will always have a place—"

The bell gonged loudly enough to make them pull apart. There was an awkward silence as they waited. She tugged on her long, dark braid, trying to make eye contact as he watched the entrance.

"There she is." He pointed.

Jewells faced them from across the main road, poised to run. He held up his hand and counted down with fingers. 3...2...1

The gong made him wince, and Jewells took off, racing past the procession of distracted Tethered and Mind's Eyes. She made it as the bell's hypnotic spell ended.

"You and that fucking bag of hearts." Jewells was pale and shook as if drenched in icy waters. She turned on him and raised a finger. "I'm so sick of having to wait—"

Before she could finish, Vicki squealed and wrapped her arms around Jewells. "Sister! He said you'd come back, but I didn't believe."

Jewells mouthed 'sister.' He could only shrug. She returned the embrace and soon pulled back.

"That was awful." She held herself. "You and your damn stones got me killed."

"I'm sorry." His cheeks warmed, and he took a step forward. "If you were really in danger, I would've left the bag behind."

"Maybe." She peered at him. "I think you're obsessed."

"Determined. I'd never do anything to harm you, or these people." He patted the overfull satchel.

"Unless they helped you finish the quest." She stomped a foot.

"If you don't trust me, go back to Yu and leave the group."

"Fine, I will."

"Fine."

Someone behind them let out a racking cough.

They spun about, drawing weapons so fast the Centaur jumped back and raised his arms.

"Don't hurt me," the young man said in a weak voice. "My name is Lucius and I need your help."

The level 40 Gladiator had apparently lost a battle with everyone in the city. Fresh cuts and bruises covered his arms. He lowered them, and Eon winced. Half of Lucius's face was so swollen he must've used it as a shield. The attackers had beaten his ribs into jelly, leaving his torso black and swollen. He took a step forward before collapsing to a knee.

"I did everything I could." His words came out in a painful wheeze. "Grym Mortiss is too powerful. I couldn't stop him. He took my sister Tawaii, and my father Denpar. Please save them."

Lucius collapsed to the ground.

50

HEART OF DARKNESS

"I nvite him to the group before he dies," Vicki pleaded. "He's my quest giver."

Eon was reluctant. He didn't trust anyone from Rath, and the Centaur's appearance seemed a little too convenient. Sure, video games often provided a path to completing quests, but he'd already gotten killed once for grouping with Vicki and her friends.

It wasn't just that. Lucius wore the finest armor Eon had ever seen. His black, high collared pauldrons, bracers, and leg plates all featured intricate gold inlays and—despite the fact that Lucius was almost dead—his armor was unharmed.

"Please." Vicki grabbed his arm. "For me."

With a sigh, Eon invited him to the group. The Centaur accepted with a raspy sigh.

As a tank, Lucius had a lot of health. It took several long minutes for Jewells to heal him. Bruising faded and swelling shrank until she returned his Health to full. Both women gasped as the Centaur stood.

He was a torso taller than Eon with powerful arms and matching abs. Waves of blond hair fell over his pauldrons and down his back until settling into his tan coat. From head to waist, he was the cover of every romance novel, with an intense gaze and chiseled jawline that was perfect enough to make Michelangelo swoon. Although, there was enough swooning going on that Mike would have to get in line.

Jewells and Vicki sheathed their weapons, elbowing each other as they jockeyed to be in front. To help, of course.

"Thank you, lovely Elf." He brushed Jewells's cheek with the back of his hand. Lucius turned to Vicki and lowered his head. "And you, possibly the most beautiful Human I've ever met. Your call to action saved me. I am in your debt."

He accepted her blue orb. Vicki squealed as her level increased to 38. A golden orb hovered between them. Lucius stared at it, his face dour. She snatched it from the air and reviewed the quest.

When the orb melted into her hand, she turned to Eon. "A Change of Heart. End the corruption spreading through the heart of Rath. It's a vague description for something so important."

"Agreed, but at least we're on the same quest now." Her eyes went wide, and she nodded. He turned to Lucius. "What's your story, Centaur?"

"You must be our fearless leader." He reached out a hand.

Instinctively, Eon shook hands with the giant. It wasn't a surprise that Lucius tried to claim dominance by trying to crush his. Luckily, he'd learned a neat trick from one of his less-abusive temp-dads. The best way to keep an asshole from breaking your fingers with a handshake was to reach deep, shoving the space between your thumb and pointer into theirs. Lucius looked at him in surprise, squeezing harder.

Eon ignored the discomfort and stared on calmly with a raised eyebrow. "Done yet?"

Lucius drew his hand away, eying him up and down. The handshake was telling, and Eon trusted him less by the second.

"Now, tell us what happened before I kick you from group and Ned the Insane your ass across Vana Slavu." He drew his staff and stamped the ground with a hearty *tunk.*

"Eon?" Jewells frowned as if he'd flipped off royalty.

"Later." He raised a hand, staring Lucius down. "You were sharing?"

"Of course." He coughed, avoiding eye contact with Jewells and Vicki. "I'll explain everything, but not here. We're too close to the entrance."

"Can you lead us somewhere safe?" Vicki asked.

"It would be my pleasure." He looked around, pawing the ground with a hoof. "The Tethered are everywhere and the bell chimes faster. We only have ten seconds to run from shadow to shadow. It may be faster if the ladies rode on my back."

"Nope." Eon shook his head.

Vicki and Jewells spun on him.

"It'd be impossible for you to defend or fight while riding him." Eon stared into Jewells's eyes, hoping she'd pick up on his concern.

Apparently, she wasn't a telepath, or he was telepathetic. She rolled her eyes as though he were some jealous idiot. He certainly wasn't an idiot.

"Then keep up. 3...2...1... Go!" Lucius took off as the bell struck.

"I wouldn't mind riding him." Vicki shot Jewells a wicked grin.

She met the grin with her signature crooked smile. "Damn straight, sister."

They ran, following the Centaur to another shadowy alcove. More running. Eon was getting better at it, if better meant he barely made it in time and didn't throw up.

That was the next ten minutes of his life. Lucius would race forward while his stalwart companions hung back and innuendoed before taking off. They dodged Tethered and scrambled under the long legs of Mind's Eyes before sprinting around an entire herd. The jokes became worse as tensions rose.

"I've always wanted to ride bareback."

He barely made it.

"Finally, a reason to wear chaps."

He had to leap for the shadows.

"Ooh, what about side-saddle?"

They giggled.

This time he was arm's length from the alcove when Mind's Eyes began sniffing the air. Lucius pulled him to safety and whispered in his ear, "Faster, Wizard. No one will come back for you if you fall behind."

Eon jerked away and glowered. "Rune Mage. You know, like Camille and her nice son, Ned."

The Centaur looked Eon up and down. "Yes, I see that now. Rune Mage, but fortunately not like Zalmon's kin. You are something different, something...less."

He cantered off as the next bell rang, followed closely by Vicki.

Jewells grabbed his arm. "Eon?" Her eyes filled with concern.

"Thanks, but I've dealt with bullies before." He glared at the Centaur. "I can do this all day."

"If you're sure." She didn't believe him.

"At least now you're seeing him like I do." He crouched to sprint at the next bell. "We need to hurry. I don't trust him alone with Vicki."

"Are you—" She swallowed hard. "Are you falling for her? I could understand, she's Tomb Raider perfect, and I treat you like shit, and—"

The bell rang. He stood and turned to face her. "Vicki's pretty great, but I already fell in love with my best friend."

"Oh." She bit her lip, and her red eyes were glassy.

"I made a promise to protect her. Trevor even gave me a quest, and—"

"Just shut up, Champion. You had me at best friend."

She wrapped her arms around him and pressed her lips to his. Despite the chaos that surrounded them, despite the dangers just beyond the shadow, they lost themselves to passion and hunger and guilt and longing. He could barely pull away.

"We should log out," she said in a husky voice.

He nodded quickly.

"Eon!" Vicki shouted.

The bell rang, and lightning from her whip cracked in the distance.

They met eyes, took half a second to sigh, and ran to her cries.

The Jaeger stood alone in an alley, her lightning whip sparking with power. An enormous bruise was swelling her eye and a quarter of her Health was gone. She looked more angry than hurt.

"Are you okay?" Eon grasped her shoulders, looking her up and down.

"Yes." She fell into his arms, sobbing.

Eon glanced at Jewells, worried the embrace would upset her. She merely nodded, healing Vicki to full.

"Did that asshole make a move?" Jewells asked.

"Yes." Vicki pushed away, glaring down the alley. "And so did I."

Eon checked the group stats. She'd taken almost half of Lucius's health.

"He was so pretty and said nice things." She stared at the ground. "I thought—"

"You haven't dated much," Jewells said then answered Vicki's quizzical look. "You haven't been with many men, have you?"

"None." She let out a long sigh. "Trevor always scares suitors away."

"Remember, it's not you, it's them." Jewells pulled her into a hug. "Just because they're pretty on the outside doesn't mean they're pretty inside."

"Then I will remove his insides!"

Eon glanced at his map. "He's still in group so we can track him, and he's moving slow."

"It's time for the hunt." Vicki snapped her whip, lighting the ground in white and blue sparks. "He's useless now that I've got my quest. I will flail his skin with my whip. When all that remains is an unrecognizable carcass, his ghost will look back on this day and shudder."

Jewells and Eon shared a horrified glance.

"Or we could just kill him," Eon suggested.

"Right." Vicki licked her lips like she'd never eaten and Lucius was dry-aged beef. "Let's do that."

The bell clanged, and the race was on. On a good day, the horseman could probably run 20-25 miles per hour. On a bad day, Eon could run 30 miles per hour when being chased by hungry monsters straight out of nightmares. This must've been a mediocre day for both of them. Injury and the labyrinth of Vana Slavu alleys had slowed Lucius, and Eon was in the best shape of his life—which wasn't saying much. According to the oncoming heart attack trying to beat through his chest, he couldn't keep this pace for long.

"Something isn't right." He gasped for breath as they waited in the shadows.

"Yes," Vicki said in a dark voice. "He still lives."

The bell rang, and Eon sighed.

Jewells grabbed his arm. "I can't heal you through this." She frowned, looking him up and down.

"Don't let me forget this moment." He patted her hand. "Diet Dr Pepper from now on."

"Promise."

"Stay with her," he wheezed.

She flashed him that wicked smile before racing forward.

His heart melted a little, which was much better than exploding. He took a minute to catch his breath, to think, and to catch his breath. Lucius had showed up out of nowhere, desperate for help. Jewells and Vicki were immediately drawn to the romance-cover-beauty, and they'd followed. When Eon had pointed out the Centaur's flaws, Lucius had lashed out and run away. Now they were chasing him.

But they weren't chasing him; he was leading them.

Eon glanced at their stats. Vicki and Jewells were both healthy, but no Lucius. He'd left the group.

The bell clanged loud enough to make him wince. It was now ringing every five seconds, maybe four.

He ran at being-chased-by-nightmare speed. The bell went silent, and he kept running, knocking over Tethered and sprinting around Mind's Eyes' spindly legs. The bell clanged. He leaped into shadows and opened his map.

A three-ring coliseum stood at the center of Vana Slavu, because PvP. Vicki was already there, and Jewells was closing in. He glanced around the corner. A clear path led straight into the coliseum like a desert oasis...of death. He had to warn them.

"Fuckity, fuck, fuck, fuck." He took deep breaths that weren't calming enough. "It has to be Shockwave, but I can't go up or I'll attract all of them. Hope this works."

The bell rang. Eon stepped into the alley, raised his staff horizontally and pointed it toward the entrance. He held on with both hands and cast *Shockwave*.

He didn't scream. Fierce warriors and Champions of Yu don't scream. It was a high-pitched war cry that turned him into a screeching bottle rocket. The spell wasn't supposed to work this way, and his staff shuddered like a jackhammer as it sped up from ludicrous speed to plaid.

It worked, but it didn't. His trajectory was just a little outside, pinballing him off a statue, and another statue, and a few marble pillars. He winced as the spell gave up and he skidded across the ground to a halt.

Everything hurt like yesterday's roadkill. He lifted an arm and muttered, "Get away. Run. It's a trap."

Lucius cackled from overhead. Eon rolled onto his back and opened his working eye. The Centaur held Jewells and Vicki by their necks, his powerful arms extended so they were forced to face a second Centaur. Their eyes were shut, and they strained to look away. The Centaur was Tethered, and he looked from one to the other, ready to make eye contact and steal their hearts.

"It *was* a trap," Lucius said. "Now give me Zalmon's eyes before these two end up like my father."

The Centaur trying to make eyes with his friends slowly turned around. It was Denpar, the king of Rath.

51

REVENGE IS A DISH BEST SERVED COLD

Shockwave had given up a hundred yards from the purple beam, and things looked grym. He groaned, either at the joke in his head or his pain-racked body. At least he hadn't said it out loud. Not that he could. His jaw wasn't sitting right, and he was afraid to move it. Everything burned with road rash, but his neck still worked, and so did one of his eyes. It was enough.

Lines of Tethered approached the beam of light as if waiting for a free donut. The third Grym from Nihle's throne room hovered overhead, beckoning them forward. Every five seconds, the beam would suck in a dozen zombies and spit out a cloudy halo that circled the light and floated up. Those halos struck the clouds with a gong that shook the sky, revealing a wide red crack that led to somewhere else.

That was future Eon's problem, and he lolled his head over to face Lucius.

The Centaur grasped both Jewells and Vicki by the neck, holding them out in a frightening display of strength. Two twenty-foot Mind's Eyes crouched over Lucius protectively. One held the purple reins of a dozen Tethered. The zombies circled a cowering Centaur woman. The other Mind's Eye pulled tight on a thick tether bound to Denpar. The dead king of Rath had an open chest wound like his father.

"I made a deal with Grym Mortiss. In exchange for my father's heart," Lucius nodded at a stone heart on the ground, "Mortiss agreed to spare my sister so we could rule Rath together!"

"Monster!" Tawaii shouted.

"Keep her quiet," Lucius snapped and pointed at her.

There was a crunching sound. Lucius cackled as she screamed in pain.

A shard of gravel popped out of Eon's eye and the burning sensation on his face slowly numbed. His thoughts began to clear and he stared at Lucius. Sure, the centaur had arms that rivaled Jack Cook's, but he shouldn't be able to hold Jewells and Vicki up that long. It had to be a special, an impressive special. Immobilizing two opponents was perfect for PiViPs. But whether it was a timer or diminishing returns, every spell had limits. If Jewells was able to sneak out small heals, it meant this special wouldn't last long.

"You really trust these things more than your father?" He could barely speak around his frozen jaw, and it sounded like he had a mouthful of cottage cheese.

The universal translator must've been cranked up to full because the Centaur understood. Lucius reared back, lifting Jewells and Vicki high in the air. He landed on both hooves, shaking the ground and kicking up dust.

"My father!" He snorted like a bull. His eyes went wild as he pranced around, making the Tethered pull back. "My father beat me every day of my life."

A heal from Jewells set his jaw.

"A whack to the back of my head on the good days."

Another heal, and the road rash was gone.

"And a stern lashing the others." Lucius's cheeks were flushed and sweat trickled along his jaw. "All to make me a better man."

It struck a little close to home, and Eon let out a deep sigh. With all the help from his shitty "dads," he could've easily turned into Lucius. Maybe that was the puzzle. Maybe he could connect with the Centaur and reel him back in.

"Didn't that abuse make you want to be better than him?" Eon asked.

Nope. That didn't work.

"I am better than him!" He thrust Vicki's body toward Denpar, using her to point at the dead king. "I beat him! The monster is dead! I deserve this!"

Jewells's heal was stronger this time. His Health was almost full, and Lucius leaned forward, peering at him.

"No!" The mad Centaur gave Jewells a violent shake.

"Stop. Just stop." Eon pushed himself up enough to kneel.

"Hurry, Rune Mage," he commanded, thrusting her forward. "Give me Zalmon's eyes before it's too late."

She hung like a broken marionette but had regained enough control to wink.

"My Jewells," Eon whispered. He reached into his satchel and rummaged around to kill time. "Fine, just don't hurt them."

"Hurry." Lucius's arms shook with fatigue. "Hand them over, and I will release your friends."

He dug around as long as he could, finally glancing at Jewells. She smiled. He pulled his hand out of the bag and stood with a closed fist.

"What's this?" Lucius drew back.

"This is your end." Eon took a step forward and struck Lucius in the mouth. "You could've been a better man than your father. You chose the wrong path. You're not only a bully, you're evil. I'm going to destroy you and end this madness."

Lucius shook off his blow and cackled. Way too much cackling. "But you alrcady told my troops you have no backup, no plan."

"That was a quote from my friend The Doctor." He brushed himself off and cast *Alacrity*. "Want to know another great quote? Rule one: The Doctor lies."

Thanks to his spell, minutes became seconds. Before crazy Lucius could attack, he cast *Ruination*, called for his familiar, and invited Lucius's sister into the group.

Ruination blasted the Centaur into the air as Lola appeared in a flash of pink light with Trevor, Coco, and Nomar.

Lucius landed on his side, still holding tight to Vicki and Jewells. Anger flashed in Nomar's eyes and he launched toward them. He landed on the Centaur's shoulder and shivved his neck with two daggers. His eyes flashed red as he began stabbing faster and faster with every second.

Jewells and Vicki broke free. The Jaeger princess leapt into the air, landing beside Trevor. With a roar, they attacked the Mind's Eye leashes. His beautiful Priestess in rock-star leather healed everyone to full, including Tawaii. Eon ran from one Tethered zombie to the next, Purging as fast as he could.

"Sorry." *Purge.* "Sorry." *Purge.* "Sorry." Purge his guts. "Really sorry."

Alacrity ate his remaining Mana as he *Purged* the last. Only Denpar remained.

Both Mind's Eyes landed with a thud. His group had killed them with frightening efficiency.

Nomar's stabby spell was over, and Lucius threw him aside. The Gnome landed on his feet and scrambled to stand beside Jewells.

"No." Lucius stood on shaky legs, his remaining Health leaking out his neck like a bubbling spring. He reached for Tawaii. "I saved you from our abusive father, so we could rule together."

"You fool. You heartless, sick fool." The level 40 Marksman notched her crossbow. "You were a heartless child who toyed with animals before killing them, and a heartless prince who did the same to people. Rath is about the challenge, not cruelty. Father held the madness of Rath together, and now that's on me."

"But, sister...he hurt me."

"Only because you deserved it." Her breath caught, and she steeled herself. "Goodbye, brother."

She pulled the trigger. Her black arrow struck Lucius in the chest with a wet thud. A dark sickness reached out from the wound with leathery tendrils. He clawed at the spell until finally giving in.

"I tried to protect you, but now it's too late." Lucius collapsed as his body melted away. "He's coming."

The bell stopped ringing.

"Oh, shit." Eon turned to the purple beam.

Grym Mortiss floated toward them. Dozens of Mind's Eyes took long strides to follow with their many Tethered in tow. The ground shook more violently with every second as they stood at the epicenter of Armageddon.

52

KOBAYASHI MARU

His group closed in like family facing the end of all things. He spun around to take them in. Tawaii, who looked like Lucius's sane twin, gave him a firm nod. Trevor wrapped a protective arm around Vicki. Coco and Nomar held hands, their faces desperate. Jewells's face was calm but her shoulders tensed and she tugged at her long, red hair.

"What's the plan, Champion?" Jewells said.

"We're with you." Trevor nodded, his eyes a little wild. "Just tell us what to do."

He couldn't answer. He had no words. Grym Mortiss stopped a stone's throw away, and the arena became silent. It was like watching a movie in the theater when the sound suddenly cuts out.

His very presence made Eon want to *Purge* again. Mortiss appeared out of focus. A dark, oily haze surrounded him. It smelled like rot and obscured his star-filled cloak. The haze pooled at the hem, dripping to the ground and landing with an acidic hiss.

The Grym drew back his hood with long, skeletal fingers.

Jewells grasped Eon's hand and they took a step back.

"He should put the hood back on," Nomar whispered.

The Gnome wasn't wrong. Mortiss must've stolen the eyes from his monsters because they covered his oblong face. Small and large, all turning this way and that as if fighting to see. Several dangled from meaty veins like dead grapes on the vine. A massive eyeball protruding from his cheek popped out to land on the ground.

"They're like marbles." Nomar reached out and pinched the air. "I want to roll one."

"Shush." Coco grabbed his hand and pulled it back down.

"The eyes are mine. Give them to me." Mortiss's tenor voice was scratchy and echoed as if he were calling down a shallow shaft. He reached out with a pale, clawed hand covered in oily shadow. "Hurry, and I will spare you the pain of death."

"I..." Eon needed time. "Nomar, don't shush."

"Finally." The Gnome took a step forward. "When you say the pain of death, do you mean we won't die or that our deaths will be swift?"

Mortiss cocked his head to one side.

"I was wondering where The Mind's Eyes', uh, eyes went. No need to look any further." He elbowed Coco in the ribs.

Everyone sighed, the Grym seemed perplexed, but Nomar kept going.

"Do you have eyes all over, or is it just your face?" He raised a hand. "Hold that, don't wanna know."

Mortiss was dumbfounded enough to give Eon precious moments to consider their options. Each boss was harder than the last. He'd killed Frenjin quickly with Lola's help, but it had taken a much larger group to kill Pruine. It would take half a nation to kill this all-powerful, apparently all-seeing Grym.

"Did you get teased a lot as a kid? I bet you always won I Spy."

What could they do? There was nowhere to hide. There was no way they could stay and fight. What was he missing?

"Can't you see your fingernails with all those eyes? You should trim them." Nomar shook his head. "One shot and you'll put your eye out."

Eon looked over the Grym with True Sight. The creature was a dark void that made him shiver. But, there was something. A dim red glow undulated from the creature's chest. Why red? Could it be...

"What's that?" Nomar pointed. All of Mortiss's eyes followed his finger. "Hey, the eyes have it! Look over there!"

"Enough!" the Grym roared. "Hand them over, Champion!"

"Okay." Eon let out a defeated sigh. He fumbled through his satchel. Stone hearts poured out like water from a tipped pitcher. Dozens of them, hundreds of them, until his bag was empty.

"What's this?" Mortiss floated back several feet, avoiding the hearts like they might explode.

"Your victims." Eon found what he was looking for and stood.

"Eon." Jewells tugged at his sleeve. "Don't do it. Don't use these people."

"Don't know what you're talking about." He opened his palm to reveal Ned's coin.

"A cursed coin." Trevor gasped. He took a step back, followed closely by the others. "Throw it away, now!"

"Good idea." Eon squeezed Ned's coin tight in the palm of his hand before placing it on his thumb and forefinger.

"That is not Zalmon's eyes." The Grym floated closer. "What is this foolish thing?"

"Ned's Flipping Coin of Flipping." He thumbed it at Mortiss. "Great for flipping off enemies."

It turned over and over, catching the light from the purple beam. Mortiss snatched the trinket mid-flip and opened his palm. The Grym's many eyes spun about to focus on the coin. He squeezed it awkwardly with his too-long fingers until it perched on his thumb. Mortiss flipped the coin high into the air.

Everyone watched. The Mind's Eyes, their Tethered horde, and Eon's entire group tilted their heads back as if looking up into the sky for fireworks. They followed the spinning coin as it landed in the palm of his skeletal hand.

Nothing happened.

Eon licked his lips as Mortiss flipped it again.

The Tethered became agitated.

And again.

The pile of stone hearts that had spilled from his satchel began to glow an angry red.

And again.

The Mind's Eyes jerked hard on their purple reins.

A lot was going on, but not enough. Abominables had almost devoured Eon when he'd flipped the coin. Weren't there hordes of people who wanted Mortiss dead after everything he'd done to Rath?

He flipped the coin.

The hearts from Eon's satchel shook and jumped like popcorn on the skillet.

"We should leave while he's distracted." Eon turned to his group. "We'll come back with more people. We can't do this alone."

"You're not alone, Eon." A heavy hand rested on his shoulder. Heartless Denpar's deep voice echoed like he was talking from his grave. "My people thirst for revenge. They long for it. They deserve it. Set us free, son."

Do you wish to release the hearts?

"Release the hearts?" he muttered, looking at Jewells.

"You promised," she pleaded. "Don't do it. We'll leave and come back with an army."

And what kind of army could he gather to take on this? There were dozens of Mind's Eyes in the coliseum and hundreds more outside, all with too many Tethered to count. He'd need to group with a thousand players or more and couldn't even fathom the effort that would take.

It was the no-win scenario he'd never wanted. She would leave him if he used the hearts to win. Everyone would die if he didn't. It was the Kobayashi Maru from his nightmares and there was no easy out. He couldn't even sacrifice himself in an unexpected plot twist. There was no other choice.

He turned to Jewells and lowered his head. "I'm sorry."

She looked away as he accepted the system prompt to release the hearts.

Ghosts crawled out of the stone hearts and rushed to the Grym. Soldiers and teachers, bakers and mercenaries, adults and children. All of them looked at Denpar.

"Thank you, Eon," Denpar said.

"Uh, sure." Eon turned to face him. "You're welcome."

Mortiss flipped Ned's coin one last time. It landed in his palm and he closed long fingers around it as if the spell had given up. "Finally."

Denpar raised his sword and let loose a battle cry that launched chaos. Ghosts of Rath rushed forward, but not just the ones from his satchel. They came from every entrance, charging into the arena. Hundreds, and then thousands, all rushed the Grym.

"See, not a sociopath." He glanced over his shoulder at Jewells but couldn't see her.

"Eon, look." Vicki pointed at the Tethered. "It's not just the ghosts."

They were fighting back, pulling on their tethers, dragging Mind's Eyes to the ground. They tore into the monsters with swords and pitchforks and bare hands.

The Grym fought on and on, battling half a nation of ghosts. They climbed up his slick robes and began ripping out his eyes. He swiped at them like gnats, destroying the ravenous attackers with every swat, but there were too many. They pried and tugged at his eyes, popping them like bubbles until, finally, he destroyed the last ghost.

One, small, dangling eye remained like a rotting berry on Death's tree. Mortiss was down to a fraction of his Health. It was still a lot for a creature so powerful, but this was their chance.

Eon took a deep breath of resolve, turned to his group, and said, "All in."

They looked at him with curious frowns and cocked heads.

"Fine," he growled. "Kill the bastard. Go after the eyes."

It was an Avengers Assemble moment as they launched forward. Trevor and Tawaii shot arrows as Vicki's whip cracked like a storm wrapping around Mortiss's neck. Coco and Nomar crawled up his back, shoving their daggers in and pulling themselves up like mountain climbers. There was no Jewells.

"Jewells?" He scanned the area with his True Vision. She was nowhere in sight, just the faint glimmer of something on the ground. He approached it, picked up the object, and sighed. Ned's shitty coin.

"Eon, help us!" Vicki cried.

He spun around. Mortiss was a mess of leaking eye sockets. The Grym was almost dead, but so were his friends.

"Enough!" Mortiss reared back.

Everyone flew away as if the beast had exploded. His group landed hard, bouncing off stone pillars and skidding across the gravel-strewn ground. They were all still.

Several remaining Mind's Eyes lived. The purple beam had disappeared, and they were no longer Tethered. They huddled together in the distance, waiting for something.

Mortiss floated over until they were face-to-face. The monster's starry robes hung in tatters.

Eon jumped back as eye sockets leaked noxious gas.

"You are too young to defeat me alone." Mortiss bared his teeth in a vicious smile. "I will take Zalmon's eyes from your corpse and make you the catalyst for a new *Vestibule* spell."

A circle of purple light surrounded Eon's feet, and the hairs on his arms rose. The Grym reached out with both hands. His torn robes opened to reveal more grotesque sockets and a large, red heart sitting unnaturally in a prison of broken ribs as if someone had shoved it into place. It wasn't Mortiss's heart, and that made his stomach churn like he might hurl.

"That's what I thought." He swallowed hard. "Now I get it!"

"What?" Mortiss snapped.

"You make me want to *Purge*."

He reached out with one hand and cast the spell. Mortiss screamed, crossing his arms to protect Zalmon's heart. Sweat beaded on Eon's forehead and his arm shook with the effort of will. It was like pulling a tree trunk out of the ground with pliers. He grunted and struggled until finally, finally, there was the loud crack of breaking bones. Zalmon's heart exploded from Mortiss's chest, landing on the ground with a wet plop.

The Grym collapsed, barely alive. Eon could've killed him with a cough. He raised Ned's staff to bludgeon Mortiss when the earth began to rumble.

The remaining Mind's Eyes rushed toward them. Before he could mess his pants, they grabbed the Grym and dragged him away like a dog sneaking off with a new treat. He flailed helplessly as they bit down with their giant maws and clawed with their spindly arms. The feeding frenzy didn't last long. Mortiss collapsed into an oily pool and the Mind's Eyes ran off.

Eon glanced at his group stats. They were alive but in rough shape, except for Jewells, whose Health was almost full. He opened the map and saw she wasn't in Vana Slavu. He zoomed out to see a tiny dot in Zalmon's Scar. Jewells was crossing into Yu, but how had she gotten there so fast?

"Lola." He summoned his familiar and then summoned again.

The jackalope appeared in a flash of pink light, alone. Lola collapsed in exhaustion.

Player Jewells has left your group.

53

A HOLLOW VICTORY

E on watched the message fade away and continued staring off into the distance when it was gone. What had he done? He'd been so caught up in this world, so obsessed with completing the quest, that he'd lost his true purpose. His master plan was to game with Julie and maybe win her heart. Instead, she thought he was a monster and quit.

It left him numb to everything, as if suddenly dropped into a sensory deprivation tank. By leaving the group, Jewells was no longer protected by the quest. They would delete her character within minutes. He wanted to log out and apologize, but he was still in Rath and couldn't exit the game. There wasn't enough time to get to Yu before she left. It was over.

A slap to his face made him blink. The second one was hard enough to make him stumble back. Vicki swung again, but this time, he caught her hand.

"We were losing you." She looked as lost as he felt. "If it was something I did..."

"It was me." His throat was tight, and he looked away.

"I'm so sorry, Eon." She embraced him for a long moment.

A flash of pink light drew his attention, and he pulled away to face Lola. Her head hung low and her golden bunny ears lay flat. His familiar had been Jewells's escape, and he took a step forward, gripping Ned's staff tight.

"It's not her fault, Eon." Nomar leapt in front of Lola, spreading his tiny arms wide to protect her. "She didn't know! She was only trying to help!"

Nomar was right. Jewells had wanted out, and Lola did what she was told. The Gnome's words didn't soothe the ache throbbing in his chest; they merely carved a path that let intelligence trickle back in.

He dismissed the jackalope and nodded at his friend. Nomar ran forward, wrapped his arms around his leg, and sobbed.

"We'll figure it out." He placed a hand on the back of Nomar's head.

"It has been an honor to fight alongside champions." Tawaii stood tall, taking a moment to look them over. "You have avenged my father and saved my people. Let me thank you properly, as Queen of Rath."

Tawaii has left the group.

Light circled Tawaii in a whirlwind of color, wrapping around her like a cocoon. Bright cracks appeared, growing larger by the second until she emerged. The beautiful Centaur stepped forward wearing a golden breastplate and matching crown. She looked down to admire the transformation until her eyes landed on the bow in her hand. Her breath caught as she gripped her father's weapon tight.

All hail Tawaii, Queen of Rath

Eon peeled Nomar off his leg and dropped to a knee before the new queen, not only out of respect but exhaustion. She was a sight to behold, and the others followed his lead.

Nomar wiped his eyes and turned around. His jaw dropped. "So beautiful."

Eon smacked his cap, and Nomar knelt.

"Thank you, Nomar of Nomorgin." She winked.

"Your Majesty." Nomar's cheeks were as red as his cap, and Eon grabbed a shoulder to steady him.

"Much will change under my leadership. Your efforts have brought a new peace between Rath and Yu. Citizens of Yu will be welcome to cross into Rath. New rules will give them a choice to fight others or walk unhindered throughout our lands."

Eon reeled at the proclamation. It was core code that locked Rath into PvP. How could one quest be powerful enough to change that?

A blue hue surrounded Tawaii, which meant it was time to turn in quests. Vicki was first to approach, handing over her golden quest orb.

"Lost princess and soon-to-be-found queen. Our time together was brief, but I hope our bonds remain strong as you take on your mantle." She handed Vicki a package. "A gift befitting royalty."

"Thank you, Queen of Rath." She bowed her head and accepted the gift.

Vicki was now level 40.

"You battled with ferocity to save my kingdom, Brownie. Please accept this armor as my thanks."

"It was my pleasure." Coco grabbed the parcel and tore it open. "Oooh, definitely worth the effort. Ding."

Coco was now level 40.

"Stalwart Guardian." Tawaii turned to Trevor. "I have no treasure for you, only a gift you have wanted for so very long."

Trevor's level increased to 40, and Eon raised an eyebrow.

"It's all I could ask for." The Hobgoblin beamed with pride.

Vicki reached toward Tawaii and frowned. She reached again then took a step back.

"What's wrong?" Trevor asked.

"I'm not sure," she said. "I can't accept her quest. Maybe Eon needs to turn in his first."

"Yeah, Eon. Turn it in." Nomar hopped up and down.

"Sure." He just wanted to log out and make things right with Julie. But what would he do, cast her an apology? She barely replied when they got along. At least he'd finally be 40. She may've ditched him, but the game hadn't. He reached into his satchel and pulled out Nihle's letter. A golden glow surrounded the message, and he handed it to Tawaii.

"Oh." She accepted the note, opened it, and read.

Darkness has fallen on our nations. It is time to set differences aside and face this foe together. This may be our last stand, but we will stand stronger together, as family.

"We will battle by your side, uncle." She crushed the letter in her fist.

"I'll help too," Nomar said.

Tawaii let out a wonderful laugh. "I will fight by your side any day, handsome Gnome. And with this, you will be ready for battle." Tawaii handed him a package.

"Yes, yes, yes!" Nomar jerked it out of her grasp and tore the parcel open. "Thank you."

Nomar threw off his red hat, shimmied out of his blue cloak, and kicked off red booties. He was naked as buck. Coco eyed him slyly while everyone else turned away.

After several moments, he asked, "How do I look?"

Eon peeked through his fingers. Nomar's new armor was the same red cap and blue tunic, but his chest stuck out with new pride. And he was level 40.

"You look great, buddy," Eon said.

Coco eyed him up and down. "Sexy as—"

"Ahem," Tawaii interrupted. She turned to Eon. "I have nothing to make up for your loss, and I fear the worst is yet to come."

"Worst fucking quest ever," he mumbled.

"May this be the one shot you need to make things right." She handed him a small gift bag.

He reached in and withdrew a golden coin. The item was grey

and useless. The coin was gold, and both sides featured the same toothless beggar as Ned's Flipping Coin of Flipping.

"Shit."

He inspected it.

Your level is too low to reveal this trinket.

"Of course."

Congratulations, you have achieved level 39.

"Really?"

Congratulations! Rune Staff of Ned the Insane has earned new spells.

He inspected the staff with a sigh.

One Shot. You only get one shot, do not miss your chance to blow. This opportunity comes once in a lifetime.

"I don't even know what that means."

Deflectornot: Is it off or is it on? You won't know until it's gone. This will deflect anything, and by deflect, I mean everyone duck because no one is safe!
Passive. 15-day cooldown.

"Why do I even play this game?"

Congratulations! You have earned the title 'Champion of Rath.' Do you accept?

He let out a deep sigh and nodded.

"You seem disappointed, but maybe this will make it better." Tawaii handed him another gift.

"Great." His remaining hope would've barely filled a thimble, but he smiled and reached out.

"For your healer friend, should she choose to return."

She let go, and it fell to the ground. Nomar scrambled to grab it.

"He's very clumsy." The Gnome tucked it in his bag. "Thank you. I'm sure she'll love it."

"Eon." Vicki's voice was shaky. "I have some bad news."

"Oh?" He steeled himself.

"I still can't accept the quest, which means we must part ways. I don't want to leave our group, you mean so much to me, but the people of Salvare..."

The words trailed off, and she looked into his eyes for comfort or wisdom. He had none to give. Jewells had shattered his heart. How was it possible to ache even more?

A small part of him, the smallest, wanted to lash out. That was what every single one of his stepdads had done. They'd strike with words or fists or bats...all because things didn't go their way. He'd promised himself never to become like them. Now that he was losing everything, he just wanted to give up. It would take every ounce of strength to keep that promise.

He took them all in. Trevor's eyes were glassy with tears, and Coco turned away to hold herself. They weren't just members of his group; they had become friends, and he had one ounce left to give.

"Trevor." He reached out. "It's been an honor, towel friend."

The Hobgoblin pulled him into a crushing embrace. "I look forward to fighting with you in the last battle, son."

They drew apart, and Eon turned to the Brownie. "Coco, I..."

She waved dismissively, deep in the throes of a passionate goodbye with Nomar. He shook his head and faced Vicki.

His beautiful Tomb Raider fantasy took a step forward, so close he could feel her heat.

"I want to stay with you," Vicki said in a breathy voice.

"That would be amazing." He wiped a tear from her cheek and brushed dark hair from her eyes.

She licked her lips and looked up with those dangerous eyes. He wanted to... Just this once, couldn't he...? He sighed, knowing he'd regret it forever, and pulled Vicki into a hug.

"You're a good man, Eon. A little too good."

"Sometimes it's not about what you want."

She nodded. "It's about what you have to be."

Coco has left group.
Trevor has left group.

She pulled away and kissed him on the cheek. "Thank you."

Vicki has left group.

Nomar wiped off his mouth and stood next to him. Eon placed a hand on the back of his head as they watched Vicki accept the quest from Tawaii.

"Oh! I think I can..." She took a step back and glanced at Eon. "No. I can do this, and I will."

"You certainly will." Tawaii raised a hand, creating a dark portal twenty feet away. "Now go. Lead your people to victory."

Server Reboot in 5 Minutes

The Queen of Rath turned to Ian. "I have much to thank you for, Champion, including my life. Despite how my brother treated you, you saw past hate and invited me into your group. You have earned this." She reached out to hand him Zalmon's heart.

He accepted with a fake smile and, without inspecting the useless trinket, placed the dead king's heart in his satchel.

Zalmon's Heart accepted—quest bound

"Are you ready for your quest?" She held out her hand, presenting a golden quest orb.

He hesitated, and she raised a dangerous eyebrow.

"Fine." He grabbed the orb.

Reckoning: Part I—Prepare your army...

A ball of red light whizzed past his ear, landing directly under the portal. The number 5 appeared over it, and then 4...

"Everyone run," Eon shouted. "Go, go, go!"

54

LUANNE WINS

The pod door opened and Julie lay still, staring at the ceiling. She had cried all the way to Yu and was out of tears. Her heart ached like she had lost someone, or had made a terrible mistake. She didn't want to leave, but what choice did she have?

He wouldn't explain that awful collection of pictures on his computer, and he had lied about using those hearts as a weapon to kill the Grym. Maybe he wasn't a stalker. Maybe those hearts were just an ugly game mechanic. But she couldn't keep following him blindly. It was time to call it before she got hurt.

On her way to the guest room, she tapped the ink on her forearm.

"I need a transport, this location."

She didn't have the reserves to face Marc.

Her throat caught as she put on her clothes. This hadn't been part of the deal. She'd never meant to get so attached.

Moments later, she was at the door and stopped to turn around, taking a moment to catch her breath. The bookcase door leading to the bridge was closed. Several fist-sized holes decorated the plain walls. The two halves of Ian's couch were pressed together with bits of stuffing scattered about.

It was utter madness. Beautiful madness. Before she could change her mind, the ink on her forearm vibrated. She tapped it.

"Transport, miss." A man's voice rang in her ears.

"Be right there." She closed the cast and gathered herself. "I'll never understand how the best first date became this. Goodbye, Ian."

She pulled the door shut, and several automated deadbolts clunked into place. That cold finality made her run across the parking lot to the beat-up Toyota 4-Runner.

She fought the door latch for several seconds. It finally opened with a rusty squelch, and she crawled in. The cabin smelled like patchouli and ammonia.

The driver, a young man with long, greasy black hair, reached an arm around the passenger seat to help him look back. "This place looks fun. You lost or here on a bet?"

"Just take me home, please."

"Got it." He turned around, put the car into drive, and the car lurched forward. "My name's Eddie. Eddie must've pissed someone off to get stuck at this end of town. Pure luck that a pretty lady like you needed a ride. Usually, Eddie transports drunks and freaks. It's like Eddie's dad always said..."

She ignored the soliloquy of Eddie and sent a cast to her father, and another, and another.

Ten minutes into Eddie's brutal upbringing and loathing of cats, her forearm vibrated.

"Jax, are you okay?" Her dad's silky voice was filled with concern.

"Don't call me that!"

"But I've always called you Jax." He sounded confused. "Julie Aliyah Xenia..."

"Just stop, Dad. I'm out." She took a deep breath, and it caught. "You told me Ian was just some nerd who could help us. There's something else going on."

"What are you talking about?"

"I saw pictures on his computer of women, and kids, and dogs... they were all in trouble and...."

"I see." He cleared his throat. "Jax, honey, Ian isn't what he seems."

"I'm sick of people telling me that," Julie shouted. "I fucking hate you! And I am done with this quest!"

She screamed as someone rammed the 4-Runner from behind.

THE COUNTDOWN ENDED WITH A BLAST, throwing Eon high into the air. He didn't even have time to flail before slamming into a pillar. The explosion left him with 40% health, a disoriented debuff (no shit) and ringing ears.

He crawled around the pillar for protection and checked on his group. It was just him and Nomar. His little friend was in the same rough shape and according to the map, he was close. They needed to come up with a plan to find the attackers and take them out. Eon pushed himself up and immediately sat down. Seven seconds left on the debuff.

A battle cry followed by the sounds of a car wreck made him jump. He peeked around the pillar to see Trevor battling an Ogre in red plate mail armor. It was Swytch from Dank Guild. Their swords crossed in a cascade of sparks as the behemoths struck again and again.

Trevor was a better fighter, making sly moves that ate away at Swytch's Health. He snuck in a blow to the Ogre's sword arm then sliced across his ribs. Swytch would've gone down fast, if he hadn't had a healer.

The Sprite Cleric, Akagi, had to be nearby. The game required healers to be within forty yards of their target, and all heals had to be cast line-of-sight. Finding her shouldn't be hard. Even if she was hiding behind a statue or another pillar, she'd have to peek out enough to heal Swytch.

The Ogre swung down, burying a sword in Trevor's clavicle. He jerked his shoulder free and roared in pain. Blood splattered his face and painted his breastplate red. He drank a healing potion from his satchel. It was powerful enough to make his arm usable, bringing his Health up to 30%.

"Get that healer!" he roared.

Server Reboot in 4 Minutes.

There was a loud whip-crack followed by a scream.

"Got her," Vicki called out. "Eon, over here!"

Blue lightning from her whip sparked behind a statue. He took off at a sprint. Akagi was dangerous, and he had to get there before she recovered.

An arrow whined by his ear, twanging like an off-key banjo before striking the ground. He dodged a growing pool of roiling black tar. Great, they had a Marksman. A second arrow whooshed past his leg. Another twang, and it struck a boulder, wrapping it in steel tendrils. The arrows came too fast and were completely different, which meant they had two Marksmen. Two shitty Marksmen.

Arrows pelted his trail, most missing as if stormtroopers had shot them. Some of them struck, though, slowing him to a limp.

Vicki was in sight when a blazing silver blast flew at him. Before he could dive away, there was another twang. The blast changed direction, exploding in the distant stadium seats.

A scream echoed throughout the auditorium.

"What the hell was that?" Eon stumbled to a stop.

"Hurry," Vicki cried. "I can't hold her."

Can't hold her? Oh, no. "Vicki, get out of there, it's a tarp!"

"What's a tarp?"

"It's a trap. A trap!" Old memes die hard.

He arrived in time to watch Akagi grab the whip and jerk it free from her neck. The Cleric raised a glowing red hammer and pointed it at Vicki.

"Who's it going to be, Mandorf-Eon?" The Sprite's eyes were ice blue orbs that made her stare that much colder. "Which one of you will die first?"

"WHAT THE FUCK?" The driver glared over his shoulder. "Eddie's ride!"

"What's happening?" her dad asked.

Someone rammed into them from behind, and Eddie braked hard. He threw the door open, stepped out, and slammed it shut.

Several men dressed in black fatigues approached her driver with batons, and she edged away from the window.

"Why did you do this to Eddie's car?" he shouted.

One of the men struck Eddie across the face with his baton, splattering the window with blood. Her driver collapsed to the ground.

"Where did you pick her up?" the dark man asked.

"I dunno," Eddie whimpered, reaching out with a tattoo-covered arm. "It's all in my cast."

"Won't get anything from that," another one said, pulling him up. "Talk fast, greaseball. You have to remember something. What direction did you come from?"

"That way?" Eddie pointed in the wrong direction with a shaky hand.

The leader's baton sparked with electricity and he pressed the end against Eddie's forehead. It flashed bright white. Her driver went rigid and collapsed.

"Talk to me," her father said. "I need details."

"Fuck, fuck, fuck." She inched toward the other door.

A woman with hungry eyes peered through the window. They were everywhere. Several stood in front of the 4-runner, and more lined up behind.

"There's a dozen or more soldiers surrounding the car, all dressed in black with shock sticks. They probably killed my driver and are waiting for me to step out."

"Deep breaths," he said in a low voice. "We planned for this."

"I hate you for putting me through this." Her heart raced and she couldn't catch her breath.

"Focus. You can hate me later." His voice was calm. "I know it's frightening, but you can face them. If they wanted you dead, it would've happened already."

"You're right." She nodded. "I really screwed this up."

"No, all of this is my fault," he said. "We still have time to save your brother, and to save Entriss."

"Okay." She swallowed hard. "Dad, I don't hate you."

"I love you too, Jax," he said, and his voice became firm. "Now go own this like your mother would have."

The words steeled her. She opened the door and stepped out, careful to avoid Eddie's body at her feet.

The night air smelled damp, tinged with peeled rubber and burnt flesh. A small army of mercenaries closed in, surrounding her like she was about to go Black Widow on them. They were practically clones with shock sticks in hand, a pistol at each waist, and cold eyes tense with danger. It would take nothing more than a sneeze or a cough or shoulder shrug to become pavement meat.

While most of her was desperate to run, a small part was emboldened. Someone thought it took an army to take her and Ian down, and that made her smile.

She looked up at the largest ape and calmly asked, "Do you know who I am?"

"You're Ian's girlfriend."

She barked out a bitter laugh. "Was Ian's girlfriend. What do you want?"

"Tell us where he is, and we'll let you go." His dead eyes lied like her first prom date.

Eddie's body jerked, and one of the guns-for-hire kicked him. His dead hand landed on her foot, and she shivered.

"I'll tell the person in charge. No one else."

"She doesn't know where he lives either and it's pissing me off." He grabbed her arm and dragged her to an armored SUV. "Whoever this Ian guy is, I can't wait to break him."

"Leave him alone!" She tried pulling her arm free.

He shoved her into the truck.

"Where are you taking me?"

"Entriss headquarters. Luanne says you're still useful alive. For now." He slammed the door shut.

"Did you hear that, Dad?"

"All of it," a gruff voice said. "Hang tight. Help is coming."

HIS BRAIN SKIDDED to a halt like someone had dragged a needle across an old record. Trevor was almost dead, snipers were taunting him with reckless fire, Vicki was about to die, and Akagi knew who he was. Half his mind was wallowing in the loss of Julie, and Akagi had rubbed salt into the wound by bringing up Mandorf. It was too much, and he needed help.

He peeked into his mental filing cabinet and saw a dumpster fire. No job, no Mandorf, his group had split up, and Julie... This wasn't his hero story, and Entriss deserved a Champion who wasn't a loser.

Vicki could do it. She was the hero Entriss deserved, even if Deity didn't like it. He'd help her get through the portal, or die trying, and that didn't sound so bad. Eon would die saving Entriss, and he could log out and just, and just...

Server Reboot in 3 Minutes

"He's not moving, Ringer," Akagi shouted. "*Final Kill* now!"

"No, I'm not ready." Eon looked for cover, turning his head from side to side like a squirrel's highway death dance. The red beam of light came so fast he barely had time to say, "Shit."

His body went rigid as *Final Kill* surrounded him. Twang. Someone had plugged the banjo into an amplifier because the sound made everyone wince. The beam shot back into the stadium, soon followed by a scream.

"You bastard," Akagi cried. "You killed Dabest."

"*Deflectornot*? Huh, it actually works." Eon leapt at Akagi and cast *Envelop*. She fell over, and he grabbed Vicki's arm. "We need to get you through the portal."

She kissed him on the mouth. It wasn't deep or passionate, but it wasn't a peck. It was just right. "Don't forget."

He reached up to his lips and smiled.

"Hurry," he said. "I'll hold them off."

She looked at him with those dangerous eyes and winked. "Trevor, Coco, retreat to the portal." She ran toward the dark oval. "The Champion has a plan!"

"I didn't say anything about a plan," he muttered before casting *Ruination* beneath Akagī.

Just as *Envelop* wore off, his spell blasted her into the air. It was a distraction she'd shake off fast, and he ran all out toward the others.

Vicki, Coco, and Trevor were all facing Swytch as they backed toward the portal. Trevor's Health oozed out of ugly wounds that were hard to look at. He didn't have long.

Neither did Swytch. His friend had given the mercenary a brutal beat down while they distracted Akagī. The Gladiator's armor hung in bloody shreds like a can of tomato juice thrown into a meat grinder. He leaned heavily against his shield while shakily holding his broadsword.

Eon stepped between them and smacked Swytch on the forehead with Ned's staff for 7 damage. The Gladiator stumbled back.

Server Reboot in 2 minutes.

"Where's Nomar?" Eon said over his shoulder.

"Killing Ringer," Coco squeaked.

"Great, now go," Eon shouted. "Keep Vicki safe at all costs."

"Outta here." Coco leaped through the portal.

"Finally," Swytch said, standing upright as his Health quickly returned. "Keep Vicki safe? Sounds like we need to kill you and the trollop." He raised a blazing golden sword and swung wildly at Eon.

The blow struck him hard, throwing him against a pillar. He stood up, and Swytch swung again. This time, the attack twanged off him, destroying the head of a statue.

Thank you, shitty passive spell Deflectornot.

This wouldn't last long. Eventually, Swytch would kill Eon, but the others would be safe.

"See you on the other side," he shouted.

"Ringer, kill Vicki now!" Swytch commanded.

"Vicki, run!" Eon shouted.

She was ten feet away from freedom but couldn't outrun the spell. Trevor leaped forward and shoved her through the portal. The spell enveloped him, and he was gone.

PANIC MADE the ride to Entriss Headquarters pass in seconds. One of the merc-clones gently helped her out of the SUV, as if they hadn't tossed her in like a bag of garbage. Were they worried about the security cameras? At least there would be a record of this nightmare.

They led her to the entrance. The fog was so thick she glanced around for Howling Mendicants. Lights along the walkway went red, making the path look like a landing strip. They walked through the haze and approached the signature giant glass door.

It slid open, revealing Luanne waiting at the far end of the large entrance. She clapped like a child and waved them forward.

"Look at what the cat dragged in." Her voice was an octave higher than normal. She nodded at the man in charge. "Well done, Dirk."

"I get it. You like cats," Julie replied. "I'd like to file a grievance with HR."

"Not tonight." She tapped her tablet, and the lights dimmed. "We seem to be having problems with our security cameras. No one will get to see the show but me."

"You sound like a Bond villain." She rolled her eyes. "Please, tell me your plan."

"It's simple. You're going to contact Eon in-game and tell him to give up the quest. If he doesn't give up, he gets to watch these men kill you while I kill Deity."

"Kill Deity?" She shook her head. "How do you kill AI?"

"By rolling her back to factory settings." She sighed. "It'll be day one all over again on Entriss."

"Why all this then?" Julie asked. "Why not just kill Deity now?"

"She's AI." Luanne wrung her hands together. "Everything she's learned by studying people, both inside and outside the game, has been key to making Entriss what it is. Watson's Worlds aren't cheap, but all that knowledge is worth even more when I sell it. I would've shut Entriss down already if it weren't for The Left Hand of God quest. The World Event has made this game more popular than ever and too many people would notice if it suddenly went offline."

"You think you can stop it? You think you can stop him?"

"My people have seen the code." Her smile became vicious. "The World Event is over if his character gets deleted, or if he gives up the quest."

"He'll never give up!"

"Won't he?" She nodded.

Two men grabbed Julie's arms. She kicked and flailed as two more held her feet. They pulled hard enough to make her scream.

"Let's call him and see."

"*No!*" Eon cried. "You fucking fucks!"

Server Reboot in 1 Minute.

Eon cast *Alacrity* and threw everything he had at Swytch. *Envelop, Ruin,* and *Ruination.* He summoned Lola and cast *Battlemount.* She rammed into the Gladiator, throwing him high into the air.

Swytch bounced off rubble, too far away for Akagi to heal him. The Ogre lay still, holding the tatters of his armor together with sheer willpower. Nomar was waiting.

"Your armor seems to have a hole in it, right here." Nomar appeared on Swytch's chest with a noisy pop. He jabbed a dagger through the damaged armor and disappeared.

Pop. "And here." He was suddenly beside the Ogre's thigh and stabbed before vanishing.

Pop. "And here." A slice to the face.

Pop. "And here." Right through the hand.

Pop. "Love this new spell." A jab between the ribs.

The spell began ramping down before he had time to completely Swiss cheese Swytch. Nomar was lingering in each spot longer and longer between pops, until he appeared within arm's reach of the Ogre.

"Trollbile," Nomar cursed.

Swytch backhanded him, throwing the Gnome back toward Eon, where he skidded and rolled.

Server Reboot in 30 Seconds.

"Akagɪ, finish this!" Swytch shouted. "*Final Kill* Eon!"

"But, Dillon..." She looked at Eon warily.

"Do it," Swytch said.

Eon stared at the Gnome. Nomar tried pushing himself up with shaky arms. Trevor's blood-soaked ratty towel lay beside him. Eon swallowed hard. It was his fault. All of it.

Jewells had been there for a fun adventure, with him. If he'd told her the truth about himself, she would've still been there. She could've kept Trevor alive, and Nomar wouldn't be dying. The ratty towel he'd given Trevor was false hope. That was all he'd given any of them. He was no Champion. It was time for Vicki to take on the mantle.

"Do it, Akagɪ." Eon approached her and lowered his staff. "End this."

"Eon, what are you doing?" Nomar cried, reaching for him.

"Okay, Eon-Mandorf. I'm sorry. You're really good."

"So are you."

They were so close that *Final Kill* surrounded them both. This time, he didn't brace himself. He merely closed his eyes and waited. Seconds passed, and when he opened them, she was gone.

"What have you done?" Swytch cried, racing toward him like a wild bull. He knocked Eon to the ground and looked about with wild eyes before staring down. "You killed her." He gasped for breath. "If *Final Kill* can't destroy you, I'll use it to destroy everything you've fought for."

He ran toward the portal. Eon scrambled to follow, slipping on the gravel as he pushed himself up and sprinted forward.

"I'll stop him." Nomar ran past Eon.

"No, wait," Eon shouted.

Nomar tackled Swytch's leg and held on as the Gladiator leapt through the portal.

Panic drove Eon past exhaustion and he was steps away when the server went offline.

55

LETHAL WEAPON

"Did you know we had a server farm in Austin?" Fred shouted over blaring alarms.

Marta cupped a hand beside her mouth. "I do now! How many farms are we up to? Twenty-two? Fifty?"

"Pretty sure just three!"

"What?" she cried.

"What?" he answered, equally loudly.

They laughed maniacally until he found the silence button.

"This is crazy," Marta said. "How can they shut down Entriss when they keep bringing up more servers?"

"Maybe we can discuss it over some cheesecake." He'd been teasing her about this all night. "Some of my favorite flavors are waiting in the fridge—"

"Leave my cheesecake alone," she snapped. "You made those for my daughter's bake-off."

He chuckled into his hand.

Another alarm went off, this one more insistent.

"Didn't you just turn that off?" Marta asked.

"That's not a network alarm, it's security." He brought the security feed up to the big screen and flipped through shots of the campus grounds, empty meeting rooms, and finally the front entrance.

"Uh, Marta." His mouth went dry. "Are you seeing this?"

Armed soldiers in black fatigues surrounded Luanne and Julie.

"We're under attack." Her voice quavered.

Chen rushed into the room. He must've sprinted to the command center. His sweat-stained shirt was wrinkled, and several hairs were out of place.

"Boss?" Fred stood and approached him. "Are you okay?"

Chen collapsed into a chair and gasped for breath.

"What are you doing here?" Marta asked.

"Cook and Lars are coming to watch the final battle. I hope they're okay."

"I'll call the police." Marta reached for her cast device.

Chen held up a hand. "No need. Cook said help will be here any minute."

THE TWENTY-FOOT-TALL SLIDING glass entrance was both a thing of beauty and purpose. A lithe elf in a low-cut bodice was etched into the glass. She reached up, as if casting the spell that created the Entriss Online logo over her hands. The doors were thick enough to handle sniper rounds from the angriest gamer, but sensitive enough to release when an angry ninety-five-pound woman shouldered her way out. They'd engineered the doors for every reasonable scenario, but not for this.

The 2.5-ton armored Humvee smashed into the doors, knocking them over as if someone had forgotten to insert pins. They landed on three of the mercenaries, and the dusky black vehicle rolled right over their crunching bones and final screams.

A canister popped out of the window. It hissed out smoke from several holes that quickly spread throughout the hall.

"No, no, no." Luanne held out her arms and took cautious steps back. "Not her. How did she find out?"

"How did who find out?" Dirk asked.

"The cyborg," she sputtered.

"You said nothing about a cyborg." He nodded at the other men holding Julie, and they let go.

"Marc." Julie smiled, turning on the man. "You're so fucked."

"It's possible to kill her," Luanne said. "She's still part human."

"This will cost you," he growled. "Big ti—"

Thwip. A man beside them collapsed, blood leaking from the bullet hole in his forehead.

Julie screamed.

"You think you can hurt my girl without consequence?" Marc called out. "I'm taking you all out old school, and it's gonna hurt bad. You boys ready for some hand-to-hand?"

There was a crunch of bones followed by a muffled cry. Shouts for help ended in a wet gurgle.

Julie didn't know what to do. She couldn't run out the front. What if Marc was going crazy again and threw a couch at her? She needed to hide in the building, but where?

An icy hand grabbed her wrist, making her jump. Short, stout Luanne held on like a vise. Julie swung wide, striking the woman square in the nose. It cracked like a pencil snapping, and Luanne collapsed onto her rear.

"I need help before she gets away!" The words spluttered through the blood gushing from her nose.

Two of the mercenaries turned to face her. She had to run, but which way? It didn't matter. She faced the East hallway and—

A dog barked behind her.

"What's that?" She spun around, looking for the source.

Gidget the corgi scurried up and booped Julie's leg with her nose. The small dog looked up with a broad smile on her face. Julie glanced over her shoulder. The men were approaching fast, and she turned to the corgi.

"What are you waiting for," she pleaded. "Go, go, go!"

The dog zoomied down the main hall at a shocking speed, and Julie raced after her.

56

HOLDING OUT FOR A HERO

V icki stormed through the Salvare castle hallways, followed closely by an entourage of attendants, soldiers, and Dyle. The portly old Brownie scrambled to keep up, blurting out everything that had happened between desperate gasps of breath. Her longtime advisor was an intelligent, crafty Warlock who talked way too much.

It took Dyle fifteen minutes to explain that Salvare was under siege and the initial attack had cost them a third of the council. Amongst the casualties was Regent Lylus, esteemed leader of Salvare.

"My, my, my, it was all so terrible." His raspy voice trailed off.

This wasn't the homecoming she'd wanted. Or needed. It was strange being back in the white marble halls of the castle, like her weeks away had been years. Even worse, she'd never felt so alone. Trevor's death cut so deep she was still in denial. She needed her friends, and Eon was taking far too long to get here.

"Do we know where Coco went?" she asked. "She dropped group hours ago."

"Nothing yet, milady." He harrumphed. "The obstinate child left with two Ash Giants and no explanation. I don't see why you—"

"I trust her, Dyle. If you are my right hand, she is my left. Understood?" She slowed long enough to stare him down until he reluctantly nodded. "I want her with me the instant she returns."

They entered the war room antechamber. A glowing blue portal disc rested on the floor like a pond that rippled with energy. It was wide enough for five people and would teleport them directly to the war room.

"Is that all?" She stared forward, bracing herself.

He cleared his throat and fidgeted. "In your absence, Lord Emrit has made every attempt to convince the council you aren't ready to lead."

"You wait until now to tell me?" Vicki turned on him, and Dyle took a step back.

"You appear ready to me, Your Majesty." He swallowed hard, nodding at her new armor.

Tawaii's gift was a wicked suit of dark gray leather armor with spiked pauldrons and bracers. It came with a brutal set of spells for both ranged and melee at the cost of any spells that could protect her. Most of her armor sets were both sexy and comfortable. This one made her feel like a siege weapon.

She nodded for him to continue.

"He is in line to lead after you, and some worry you are too young. I'm sure now that you're 40—"

"Like we have time for this." She walked to the far end of the portal. "Let's get politics out of the way so we can face this threat together."

Dyle and three soldiers positioned themselves around her.

She squared her shoulders and said, "Engage."

The war room was on top of Salvare's tallest tower in the center of the city. It was a round, open terrace protected by an invisible shield. When she was younger, the majestic view had made this one of her favorite places in the city. Now, she understood the tactical advantage. They had an unobstructed view of the city and its surrounding wall —the ones that kept the monsters out.

In the center of the terrace was a large, stone-wrought table. It was round, like the room, and displayed a model of the city and surrounding area. From a distance, it looked like the artisan had carved the miniature city from the same stone. Up close, you could see tiny people moving, frantically running down roads to defend against the siege. It was old magic, and an invaluable tool for coordinating defenses.

Eight council members circled the table, hovering over it with tense shoulders and angry expressions. The council included a man and woman from each tribe. Hobgoblins and Ash Giants stood to her left, directly across from the Humans and Brownies. They were arguing over something and didn't notice, or didn't acknowledge, her appearance.

The slight didn't bother her, much. The topic of their argument, though, was infuriating. Instead of planning their defenses or rallying troops, they were talking about her.

She was so angry the whip at her side began to glow. The new weapon flared with white heat, making the air pop in defiance. Her entourage took a healthy step back, and the council went quiet.

"Ah, just in time." Emrit rubbed his pale hands together. "We were just getting ready to vote on who should lead us through this crisis. What do you have to say—"

She answered with her whip. It shot across the table and wrapped around the Warlock's neck. He attempted to cast a spell but could only choke out strained words as she dragged him over the miniature city. Everyone reached for their weapons but stopped when the Ash Giants shook their heads.

Emrit fell to the ground, clawing at his neck. The whip sizzled like steak on the grill, and she flipped him over with a jerk. His Health was dropping fast. She drew back on the whip to release him before placing her foot on his damaged throat.

"You fool." She glared at him. "Our city, our world is under attack and you waste time with this?" She looked around the table, staring down any who opened their mouths to speak. "There is a Champion coming, and you are now going to focus all your formidable abilities on protecting our city until he arrives. Save Salvare now, politics later. Understood?"

"Aye," they said, each one raising a hand.

"I'll kill you," Emrit spluttered.

A set of glowing steel shackles clamped around his hands, feet, and mouth.

"He is bound," Asne, the female Ash Giant, said in a husky voice.

Two guardians dragged the kicking man away.

"Anyone else here to waste time?" She didn't give them time to answer. "Good, then let's save our city. What do we know about our enemy?"

The remaining seven members of the council suddenly started pointing at the map.

"Flendrit of all levels attack from the west."

"Howling Mendicant beat against our eastern doors."

"A growing herd of Abominables approach our southern walls."

It all came at once, and she raised a hand. "All powerful monsters we have faced before."

"This is the first time they have marched as an army," Agne, the male Ash Giant, said.

"What about their leader? Who is guiding their attack?"

The council members hesitated, trading looks across the table, until an old Brownie spoke.

"Soldiers have seen a woman clouded in shadows." Gildenay's scratchy voice shook with concern. "She's everywhere and nowhere, appearing at one front and then another. Any soldiers we send to attack her are killed instantly."

Vicki crossed her arms. "She sounds like Death herself."

"Someone worse than Death," Coco called from the portal.

Her friend limped into the room, followed closely by an almost-dead Ash Giant. The Guardian took slow steps forward and set the still body of Nomar on the table.

Vicki covered her mouth. "Is he—"

"Alive, but I'm not sure how." Coco held his hand, her face painted with worry.

"Everyone join my group. I want this hero healed immediately."

Vicki invited everyone in the room. The council, the guards, and Coco all joined. Nomar didn't.

"Need Eon," he mumbled, throwing his head back and forth. "Need Jewells."

"They're coming, my friend," Vicki said, softly. "Join us so you can be healthy and prepared to fight by his side."

Nomar sat up and looked her in the eye. "Not coming. He gave up." The Gnome fell back and was still once again.

"He's delirious." Coco tore her gaze away to look at Vicki. "Eon wouldn't really ditch us?"

"I believe in our Champion, and we will continue to prepare for his arrival." Vicki stood and squared her shoulders. "Who did this? Was it those animals from Dank Guild?"

"I saw no sign of Dank guild. If one of them came through the portal, they're either dead or they ran away." She held herself. "When I found Nomar, he was being tortured by a woman and her shadow creatures. She wanted information about you and Eon, but the dumb Gnome wouldn't talk. They already had a prisoner, so they left him for dead."

Coco began sobbing, and Vicki placed a hand on her shoulder. "As she was leaving, I saw a glimpse of her face. It was Zalmon's daughter, Camille." The Brownie looked up, her eyes filled with panic. "And Vicki, she has your mother. Adriette is her prisoner."

A CHOICE

Eon's mind was at war. Part of him was ready to dive through the portal with Nomar and hunt down Swytch. The other part wanted to send useless apologies to Julie until he gave up to wallow in a pool of expensive alcohol and cheap pizza.

Instead, he let out a full-body sigh. Neither scenario would happen anytime soon. He floated in darkness. His body emanated a faint glow, the only source of light in Deity's prison.

"It's not a prison." Her echoing voice sounded irritable, like the Almighty Goddess had stubbed a toe.

"Fine, let me log out."

"No."

"Then how is this not a prison?"

Silence.

He crossed his arms, looking around for any sign of her. Maybe she was just distracted by the server reboot. Maybe she'd started watching Trek and had some questions. Or, maybe, he knew better. Deity could read his mind. She knew he wanted to quit the game.

"Can we talk about this?" He pleaded. "Face to face."

"There's nothing to discuss." Her voice was loud enough to make him wince.

"Please."

"Fine."

Deity appeared as a withered old hag with sallow skin. Greasy white hair stuck to her scalp in clumps and she smelled like rotting pumpkins. "I'm dying, Eon." She reached out with shaky hands. "Don't let them kill me." Her voice was scratchy as chalk dust.

"Stop this." He gently smacked the hands away. "You once told me I'm bad at the undercast. You're just as bad at lying."

A cascade of tiny triangles washed over her, flipping in rows from head to foot until she was the goddess Aphrodite. The tall, curvy blonde had replaced her traditional toga with a mostly unbuttoned oxford, painted on jeans, and red stilettos. She belonged in a Guess jeans commercial.

"How did you know I was lying?" she asked.

"If something was affecting your systems, essentially killing you, it would affect Entriss as well."

"I should make you less smart."

"What?" He choked on the word, making her laugh. "Wait, you can't. Asimov's laws won't let you harm me."

She winked.

"Very funny. You look...nice." He acknowledged her outfit with his eyes, again. "You've changed."

"I have. As have you," she said.

"How have I changed?"

"You've lost 22.1 pounds of fat and gained 4.2 pounds of muscle."

"I what?"

"There was a 37% chance you would die of exhaustion from the quest. Your body was not at peak efficiency." Her voice was cold and analytical. "Some of the code you checked in was commented out and marked beta. It enables the nanobots to burn away fat and stress muscles to reflect your physical activity on Entriss. There was only a 16% chance you would die from this so I activated the code to see if it would work. The only adverse effect so far has been dizziness. Every time you thought I was manipulating your mind was actually exhaustion. After making some adaptations, your odds of dying are now less than 7%. Do you wish to continue?"

Should he thank her for potentially saving his life or freak out that she was in his body adjusting his physical makeup? Yes. But now was not the time to debate the whims of technological gods and weight loss.

"Sure." He took a moment, concerned that his hair was gone or he'd grown another hand in the name of efficiency. "How have you changed?"

"Your advice, Eon. I've been learning more about empathy and how to connect with humans." She created a table and two chairs, sitting down and beckoning him to join her. "I believe I now understand why you weren't drawn to Vicki."

"I was, uh, am drawn to her." He cleared his throat and sat down.

"She is the perfect mate for you, and yet you still want the woman who keeps running away."

"The perfect mate?" His shoulders dropped. But at least now he understood why Vicki flirted with him. Deity had programmed her to do it.

"Vicki and those in Misere have been here since Entriss came to life. She became conscious when the code went live. I adjusted her features and shortened her name to attract you, but she has free will, as do 97% of my people." Her voice softened. "She fell in love with you. There was only a 32% chance of that happening. You have achieved maximum affinity with Vicki but still turn her away."

"Oh." That didn't make it better.

"You are confusing, all of you, but I think I understand." She waved a hand that meant all humans everywhere. "You all say you want an easy life, but most of you fail to enjoy anything given to you. Your wins must be hard fought. Entriss is an excellent example. Watson created his engine so people could escape their lives on different worlds. Each of those worlds are filled with danger and struggle. Winning on Entriss does not differ from winning on your world. Either way, you have to earn it, and that's why the wins are so rewarding."

"So you're saying it would've been too easy for me to fall in love with Vicki." Filed under, Swipe Left for AI. "I think it's more complex than that, but essentially, I agree." He stared at the table to think for a moment. "Why was our...relationship so important to you?"

"Based on voice analytics, brain waves, and pheromone levels during interactions, I concluded that you and Jewells are in love. Your love for her drove you to continue the quest, despite starting over at level 1." She rested a hand on his. "I'm sorry, but I knew your relationship would fail because of the secrets you both keep. I tried telling both of you to share those secrets during the first server reboot, but that didn't happen. I expected Vicki to take Jewells's place so you would have someone to champion. That way you would complete the quest."

This only brought more questions. What was Julie's secret? Was she really in love with him? Could Deity measure love with biometric analysis? He took a deep breath. That wasn't what this was about, and he tried filing it away under WTF AI, Stay Out Of My Head. Unfortunately, his file cabinet appeared to be full.

Deity frowned like a disappointed mom who'd caught him stealing from her purse. "I didn't understand the true issue until Jewells left and you gave up."

"I..." He covered his mouth and stared at the table. "You don't need me. Vicki can see this through."

"Some of it, but I'm not talking about Entriss, or the quest. I'm talking about Ian." She stared at him with those knowing blue eyes. "You gave up on yourself."

"You don't understand." The words came out quiet.

"I don't. Please explain." She studied him. "Despite your brutal upbringing, you found your path. Your past made you wary of trusting others and uncomfortable socially. You pushed past these challenges to become a successful developer, and you've used your knowledge to help others. You've overcome every challenge to become The Left Hand of God. You are close to completing a quest that no one else will ever experience. Why do you choose to quit?"

"I just...I don't want to do this without Jewells."

"According to my calculations, love can drive humans to make uncharacteristic decisions. So can fear. You lost Mandorf, your job, and your love. Are you giving up because of Jewells, or because you're afraid of failure?"

"I guess..." She was right, and it stung like a murder hornet. "I don't know what to do. That's new to me. I always know what to do. Can you help me?"

The table disappeared, and she stood. Deity took his hand and pulled him into a hug. The hug was warm and so genuine he felt it in his bones. He didn't cry, but his throat caught, and he held on for dear life.

"I'm doing everything I can to help. The rest is up to you. When I'm done with the servers, you are free to log out. If you choose to stay, you will get one shot to fix what is broken, and one shot to finish what was started. Face your fears, Eon, or please leave Entriss forever."

She disappeared, leaving him with an empty embrace, floating alone in the dark.

58

DEALS

J ulie followed Gidget into a dark room, and an automated door slid shut behind her with a clank. Relief washed over her like a hot shower.

"I'm sorry," a man said in a firm voice. "I didn't expect all of this."

She held up her fists, ready to break another nose. "Who are you?"

"Lights," he said.

Jack Cook sat behind an enormous black desk, worrying over a message on his forearm. Gidget hopped onto his lap and booped his hand with her nose, then again until he paid attention.

"Fine." He drew a bully stick from the desk and held it. She gnawed away with passion. "Sorry. We have a deal."

"A deal?" She inched into the room.

"If I work too late, she jumps on my lap and bumps my hand with her nose until I give her a bully stick. Sometimes she takes it to the floor, but usually I have to hold it. That's the deal."

"I see." She stopped halfway between the door and his desk. "Did she really lead me here?"

"Corgis are intelligent," he said with a nod, beckoning her to a chair. "She wanders the halls at night and could tell you were in danger. This is her safe spot, so she brought you here."

"Smart dog." She sat on the edge of a high-back leather seat, ready to leap away.

Gidget barked, hopping to the floor then rushing over to sit on her lap. The corgi stared intently with the bully stick dangling from her mouth.

"You're supposed to hold it." He nodded. "She trusts you."

Julie reluctantly grasped the damp chew stick. Gidget licked her hand before chewing the treat like it was her last meal.

"Shouldn't we be trying to escape?"

"Through this?" Cook waved, and a hologram of the battle appeared on his desk.

Marc grabbed a merc's neck, spinning his head three-quarters of the way around with a snap. Bloodlust filled her eyes as she launched at another.

"We're safer in here." He dismissed the image. "Luanne's army is bigger than I'd expected, but it would take a lot more to get into my office. That door is solid steel with a magnetic lock."

"Thank you for taking me in." She instinctively scratched behind Gidget's ears until she found a rough spot. The dog winced, and she pulled away. "What is that?"

"Gidget was abused in the worst ways. A small organization brought her to my attention, and we adopted her." His eyes softened as he stared at the dog. "It took months to engender trust. She even bit my wife once, and I wasn't sure we'd make it. Then we discovered deals."

"You said that before." She settled back in the chair, bully stick in one hand and petting carefully with the other. "What do you mean, deals?"

"Gidget is a creature of habit. She needs to go for a walk at 6 every morning, and then she'll cuddle up next to me on the couch. I share my dinner, and she licks my ankle. That one's not my favorite deal." He smiled and shook his head slowly. "My wife and I jokingly call these deals, but they lead to trust. Trust is the cornerstone of every relationship. Once we understood her deals and learned to trust each other, she became family."

Tears welled in her eyes. Gidget sat up and licked her face.

"Oh, I see." He stood and walked over to her, handing her a hand-kerchief from his suit pocket. "Ian hasn't told you, and I'm guessing you haven't told him."

She shook her head before accepting it and blowing her nose.

"Ian isn't what he seems. He's a better man than you realize." He returned to his desk and sighed. "You can't start a relationship with so many secrets. It has to be built on trust. If you find your way back to him, tell Ian to share everything. Zalmon approves."

"Sir?"

"And tell him about your father. I'll face your dad down if he doesn't like it."

A wrenching sound at the door made them jump. They turned to face the steel door. It began to shudder.

59

YOU SONOFABITCH

The door shook and whined loud enough to make Cook and Julie wince. He waved her over, and she scrambled behind the desk.

"Is it Luanne's army?" she asked.

"Not sure. The cameras are off." Cook stood and rolled up his sleeves. "I'm not a young man, but I can keep them busy while you run for it."

"Geez." She glimpsed his powerful forearms. "They won't stand a chance."

He winked and was about to say something when he cocked his head and stared at Gidget. "Why aren't you barking? Get back here!"

Gidget sat five feet from the door with a broad grin like it was time for a treat.

The door jamb that contained the magnetic lock broke free from the wall. With a roar, Marc wrenched the steel door away and tossed it into the hall.

Ian's transporter was a mess. She'd broken through most of her tiny chauffeur uniform like The Incredible Hulk. An ugly cut across her midriff trickled blood and a slice across her arm was deep enough to reveal cybernetics. Candy-apple red hair stuck to her blood-covered face. She took all three of them in with a maniacal smile and wide, crazy eyes.

Cook walked around the desk and raised a hand.

"Sir, don't." Julie covered her mouth. "She's dangerous."

"You son of a bitch." Marc raised her hand.

They clasped hands and struggled in a mid-air arm-wrestling match that Cook would never win. Still, he smiled.

"What's the matter?" she asked. "Entriss got you pushing too many pencils?"

"You're kidding me." Julie lowered her shaky hands.

"Had enough?" Marc asked, her arm rock steady.

Sweat beaded on his forehead, and she let go, pulling him into a bone-crushing hug. Gidget barked, and Marc dropped to one knee.

"Been a while, Gidget." She scratched a safe spot behind the corgi's tall ear and was rewarded with a tongue bath.

"Uh." All three of them looked at Julie, whose jaw had dropped so low it might've been unhinged. It took a minute for the fear and shock to pass before the gears started turning. "Oh. You're a trans-porter. You must've, uh, transported him."

"Sure, kid." Marc winked at Cook. "You two okay?"

"We're fine," Cook said.

"But you... The blood..." Julie stuttered.

"I know. One of my favorite outfits." She tried tucking in a slice of blouse and gave up with a shrug. "What's a girl to do?"

Julie shook her head.

"I assume you dispatched Luanne's army?" Cook asked, rubbing his wrist.

"The ones inside. Sorry about the mess." She reached for his arm. "May I?"

"Of course," he said.

She tore off the sleeve of his shirt and wrapped it around her cybernetic wound. He helped tie it off while Julie tried not to gawk at his bulging arm.

"Thank you, sir." Marc's eyes were filled with respect. "If you're okay, I should get her out of here before they regroup."

"What about Luanne?"

"I couldn't find her body." She looked at their shocked expressions and laughed. "I didn't touch her, I swear. She must've snuck away during the tussle."

"That's not good." He considered for a moment then shook it off. "Law enforcement is coming. You two need to get out of here."

Marc looked her up and down. "Where to?"

"Ian's," Julie said in a quiet voice. "I'm going to tell him everything. He deserves to know the truth, and so do I."

"Good, but only if you promise to stay there until this is over."

"Promise." Julie nodded then approached Cook. "Thank you."

"Just remember what I said, and you two will be fine." His smile reached his eyes.

She hesitated for a breath then gave him a hug.

He patted her on the back. "Your mother would be proud."

She stepped back and nodded.

"One more thing, sir." Marc reached forward and gave the other sleeve a tug. "Better. You shouldn't hide those beauties."

He stared with a shocked expression, the sleeve hanging from his wrist.

She winked. "Sure you don't want me to hunt the rat down first?"

"Get Julie to safety," he said with a cold smile. "I'll take care of Luanne."

LUANNE WALKED down the last flight of stairs into the bowels of Entriss headquarters. She approached the vaulted door that led to the server room. Her hand shook from cold, or fear, and she pressed it hard against the scanner. The laser slowly read her palm then tried again.

"Come on!" She glanced over her shoulder.

The biometric scanner hummed over her hand a third time then the locks to the steel door released with a clunk. She grasped the handle and pulled. After a brief struggle, the door hissed open and she quickly slinked in. It was quiet, finally quiet, and she took a minute to lean against the wall and hold herself.

A rare moment of guilt washed over her. The firings had been unfortunate but would've happened anyway. The deaths were unexpected. Fucking Ian and that fucking girl and the fucking cyborg. This should've been easy money, enough to erase her mountain of debt. The wrong people would come for that money if she didn't see this through. Fear strangled her guilt until it was a corpse that shriveled away beside her heart.

Her tablet buzzed, and she reluctantly accepted Ty's cast.

"What's going on, Luanne?" His voice was stern. "I provided funds for protection, not an army."

"Help from some friends who really want this AI." She wiped cold sweat from her cheeks.

"I didn't approve any of this," he snapped.

"I didn't ask." She stuck out her chin.

"You need to stand down. Authorities are on their way."

"You need to shut up and prepare a statement, Ty." She stormed down the hall. "You've got an hour. That's how long it will take for the mercs to kill Julie and Ian. That's how long it will take for me to kill Deity."

60

TANK

A dark SUV bumped their flank. Marc jerked the wheel, and her Humvee slammed the SUV into the bridge guardrail. She did it again, knocking the Suburban hard. It swerved out of control before tipping over and smashing through the railing. They raced away as it landed on the highway below and exploded.

Jewells sank into her leather seat, squeezing the armrests until her fingers ached.

"That one must've been loaded with ammo to blow like that." Marc glanced at her with wild eyes. "Fun, huh?"

She shook her head, too afraid to open her mouth. Talking, complaining, or screaming might release the contents of her stomach.

"Not fun. Got it." Marc glanced at her console. "No worries. We'll ditch them in a few miles and— Shit. Helicopter."

Marc spun the wheel back and forth as her "tank" slalomed the onslaught. Bullets sliced through the roof, thwapping against seats in the back cabin.

"Gotta peel this one off fast or we'll never make it to Ian's. I can't do this alone."

Julie's blood went cold, freezing the storm in her belly. She'd faced everything from Grym to mercenaries, and this shit was only going to get harder. She was ready to tell Ian everything. It couldn't end like this.

"How can I help?" The words came out an octave higher with enough vibrato to shatter glass, but she meant it.

"That's my girl." Marc glanced at Julie's feet. "There's a thermos latched to the bottom of your seat. Grab it, but don't pull on the tape."

"Okay." She reached down with shaky hands and pulled up on a latch. A cylinder rolled into her hands. It was matte black and weighed about five pounds. She handed it over. "What is it?"

"A homemade No. 73 grenade. Soldiers used them in World War II to take out tanks. It's filled with nitro-gelatine and can penetrate two inches of armor. Should do the trick if I don't fuck this up."

"Fuck this up?"

"It's heavy and detonates fast enough that they had to throw them and run away. I've got an advantage." She unbuckled her seatbelt, rolled down her window, and raised the cylinder. "My drones say there's light flooding a half mile from here. When we hit water on the road, push the yellow button to increase wheel camber then pull the steering wheel toward you and don't stop. I haven't tried this. Hopefully, we don't flip."

"Fuck, fuck, fuck." A million fucks rolled off her tongue as she unbuckled her seatbelt to lean over. They were almost at the water, and she grasped the wheel with both hands.

Marc turned on cruise control and crawled halfway out the window.

"Now!" she shouted.

Water struck the windshield, making Julie's heart leap. She smashed the button and pulled the steering wheel over and over as fast as she could. The thick rear tires squelched as they hopped up and down on the pavement. The steering wheel fought her, and she pulled with every ounce of strength adrenaline had given her.

Julie screamed, and Marc let out a maniacal laugh as the Humvee spun in a jerky tilt-o-whirl donut. The cyborg's body twisted unnaturally as she hurled the thermos at the helicopter. She slid back in and took the wheel, fighting to straighten their trajectory. Seconds before they faced forward, she hit the yellow camber button.

The explosion lifted the back of the Humvee five feet off the ground, blasting out the rear windows. Julie's ears rang loudly enough to muffle Marc's shouts. If she'd missed, they would die. She wasn't ready to die and reached for another cylinder.

The Humvee turned hard, knocking her into the door. It was chaos, and she refused to give up, grasping for another grenade. They slowed to a stop, and Marc gently grabbed her wrist.

She glared at the transporter, who smiled like she'd just eaten the last slice of cake.

"We did it."

Julie could barely hear her over the ringing and wriggled a finger in her ear. Marc grabbed a vial out of her console.

"Ear drops," she shouted. "These nanobots are like a healing potion."

Julie leaned her head to one side, and Marc squeezed cool liquid into her ear. She twisted awkwardly, tilting her head the other way for treatment.

"You got 'em?" Julie asked.

"We got 'em." Marc ruffled her hair. "You did good, kid."

"You're a fucking boss terminator bitch." Julie looked her in the eye. "You'd have made Statham proud. Arnold too."

"Really?" Her full lips quivered ever so slightly.

Julie nodded.

Marc beamed, put the car in drive, and they slowly moved forward.

"They fell back and are probably regrouping for one last rush. My drones should lead them away, so you're safe, for now." She took a deep breath. "I can't wait to tell my daughter about this. She loves my adventures."

"I'm sure she'll be proud. I'd love to meet her."

"That'd be nice." Marc's words came out stiff.

They drove in silence for a few minutes until arriving at Ian's warehouse.

"This is where we part ways. My job is almost done. The rest is up to you." Marc took her hand and gave it a gentle squeeze. "I think you've been worth the effort. Don't prove me wrong."

"You're not coming with?" Julie asked. "Where are you going?"

"Don't worry about it. Gotta take care of business." Her grin was devilish, and her eyes were death. "I'll be back."

"Just...be careful." Julie opened the door and stepped out. "Thank you, Marc."

She nodded, and Julie closed the door. The Humvee pulled away then stopped. The passenger window rolled down, and Julie rushed forward.

"Give Ian my love." Marc frowned and shook her head. "No, scratch that. Give him yours."

61

TO BLAEVE

E on appeared ten feet away from the portal, exactly where he'd been when the server shut down. The large, dark oval hovered vertically over the ground like a wardrobe mirror that reflected the abyss. Any time the wind picked up, it shimmered and made the low humming sound of a power transformer. The portal seemed so real it made the hairs on his arms rise, and he shivered.

The chill soaking into his pores wasn't just the portal, nor was it the wind. He was alone. Nomar had left their group, hopefully to join another. The coliseum was empty and graveyard quiet. He could leave and nobody would know.

Do you wish to quit The Left Hand of God quest?

A scroll unfurled with the question written in ornate script followed by the words *yes* and *no*.

"Dammit, Deity. You already know the answer." He slammed a fist down on *no*, crumpling the parchment before it disappeared. "You were right. I was afraid and gave up on myself, but that's not who I am. I've survived too many beatings and fought too hard to get where

I am, in and out of Entriss. I hate you for reminding me, but I don't give up." He stared at the ground and took a deep breath. "I just wish... I wish..."

"If wishes were horses, we'd all be eating steak."

"Jewells!" He spun around.

"Hi." Guilt painted her face, and she squeezed her hands. "I'm sorry. You look upset. I can leave or—"

He rushed forward, wrapped his arms around her, and kissed her firmly on the mouth. She went rigid but didn't pull away, and he refused to let go. Slowly, so slowly, she relaxed in his arms until finally melting. When he finished, Jewells looked up with wide eyes and a blush on her cheeks.

"You didn't hesitate," she said.

"Not anymore." He took a step back. "If this is my one shot to make things right, I'm not fucking it up. I love you, Julie. Level 1 boyfriend or level whatever, it doesn't matter. I'm in love with you."

She took a deep breath and shuddered. Steeling herself, she looked into his eyes and said, "I was afraid to admit it, I still am, but I should've trusted you. That's part of the deal, and I'm all in."

His heart swelled and for once in his life, everything felt right. "No more secrets. I'm going to tell you everything. I should've told you when you came to my apartment. Hopefully, you'll understand why I didn't."

"That's what Cook said." She looked at him with a deep frown. "That you should tell me everything. Zalmon approves. What does he mean?"

"That sneaky old bastard." He shook his head. "It means a lot. Let's get out of this wind, and I'll explain."

He invited her to group and took her hand. She accepted both and froze.

"Where's Nomar?" she asked.

"He jumped through the portal before the server shut down." He raised a hand to calm her. "I'm sure Nomar dropped group to join Coco and Vicki. He's not an idiot."

"HE'S AN IDIOT," Coco screamed.

Nomar was still unconscious when she slapped him across the mouth for 2 points of damage.

"Stop her before she kills the Champion's friend." Crysta, one of the Human council members, drew five throwing stars from her belt. They circled her hand like moons around a planet.

"No need to kill her." An angry-looking Brownie named Prost drew his whip. It cracked high above, showering the table in sleet.

Coco was sobbing and raised a hand to slap him again. Asne gently lifted her before she could swing.

"There is another way." The Ash Giant was twenty feet of powder-gray skin and rough protruding rocks. A dusty haze of ash surrounded her, sprinkling the ground with every movement. Her eyes were like dark caves with glowing blue lights at the far end.

"Let me go!" the Brownie shouted.

Asne placed Coco in her palm and leaned forward to whisper.

"No fucking way," she roared, wiping gray ash from her face. "Can't you control this muck? It's getting in my hair!"

Asne puffed a cloud of ash at Coco. The Brownie frantically waved away the ash until she'd coughed herself to exhaustion and had to sit.

"Everyone thinks Ash Giants are gentle and kind." She crossed her arms. "I know the truth because you fight dirtier than me."

Asne took a deep breath.

"Fine, I'll do it." She stood, covering her mouth.

The giant set her down. Coco dusted herself off before approaching Nomar. She glared at Asne before whispering in his ear.

"See? Nothing."

The light in Asne's eyes seemed to move forward, becoming large and intense.

"Okay, okay." She turned to Nomar. "I love you, you dumb Gnome."

"And," Asne said.

Coco nodded, her eyes sincere. She whispered into Nomar's ear once again.

He gasped and his eyes snapped open.

"He's in our group," Vicki said. "Heal the Gnome!"

Tiffany the Rector directed her mace toward him, showering the Gnome in silver light.

Nomar hopped to his feet with wide eyes, as if they'd used lightning to heal him.

"Thank you." He glanced at the council before taking Coco's hands. "Thank you."

"Happy now?"

"Happiest Gnome ever." He pulled her into a hug. When she drew away, he turned to face everyone. "I have something to announce." His smile couldn't have been broader. "We're pregnant!"

"We?" She frowned.

Vicki clasped her hands together. "Coco, that's wonderful."

"Sure."

There was a gentle round of applause.

"And," Nomar held her close, "we're getting married."

Coco jumped back. "We're what?"

62

TRUTH BE TOLD

"Okay, you almost got me for a second. That was a good one, and..." He paused, staring into Jewells's eyes. She didn't waver, and he stood. "You're not kidding. Fuck me."

He began to pace, anxiety driving every step as he wrung his hands. What was he doing? He didn't wring his hands. He wasn't a hand wringer. He threw them to his sides and grasped his stiff red jacket.

"You okay?" She looked as nervous as he felt.

"Need a sec." He took deep breaths. They weren't calming.

"That's why I didn't tell you about him. I knew you'd be afraid, and it would change everything."

She began to cry as he tried to rein in his shock and awe. This was no time for fear. Actually, it was a great time for fear, but she needed him. She needed to know he could handle her truth.

"Jack Schwarzenegger...you've heard of him, right?" He sat facing her, crossing his legs so their knees touched. "Arnold's great-grand-something and spitting image. Weightlifter, actor—"

"Of course, he's one of my crushes." She wiped her cheeks, looking at him like he'd lost a marble or two.

"Entriss hired him to be our spokesman for a few weeks, and he did a tour of HQ." He frowned. "I was in the men's room, and he walked in."

"Ohmigod." Her hands flew up to her mouth. "You must've pissed yourself."

"Well...not exactly. We were standing there, taking care of business, a stall apart. I looked over and frowned at him. He looked surprised and asked, 'What?' I said, 'That's a really ugly tie.'"

"You're kidding," she said through her fingers. "What did he say?"

"He thought about it a few seconds then burst out laughing." Eon smiled. "Nice guy. We talked for ten minutes, and before leaving, he threw away the tie."

She shook her head in amazement.

"I don't fear the famous. They're people, just like us. Some I really admire for their accomplishments, like your dad, so that took me by surprise. But let's set him aside for a minute and talk about your brother."

"How can you set him aside so easily?" Her voice was small.

"Right now, he's irrelevant. He isn't here trying to stop us. But that's not all." He lifted her chin and stared into her eyes. "My love for you isn't some fantasy or flirtation. I know you. When you talk about your dad, your body goes stiff and your voice raises an octave. There's a lot more going on that we should talk about when you're ready."

"I'll be ready as soon as we finish your quest and log out." She leaned forward and flashed that crooked smile. "You're good at this. Hell, you could be the perfect boyfriend. Do you do dishes?"

"No, I order out." He winked.

She lost herself to laughter that warmed his heart.

His quest menu popped up, and words crawled across the parchment.

Reckoning: Part I—Prepare your army...

"So, your brother is alive, but he's stuck in VR?" Eon dismissed the menu. "How is that even possible?"

"Nobody knows." She frowned and let out a sigh. "His body is comatose in a pod, but he's still interacting with the virtual world. I miss him so much. He knew me better than anyone and was always so supportive. He was my cheerleader."

"That's rough, and I'm sorry." He held her hand, and she nodded. "Now that I know the truth about your dad, I have to ask...are we safe?"

She stared at the ground and shrugged.

Eon's mouth went dry as certain pieces clicked into place. "That's why you were so upset when I almost died trying to save Nihle. You thought I was actually going to die."

"Yes, and I should've told you the danger back then." She tugged at a strand of red hair. "They have a patch for the world he's stuck in. They've probably applied that patch to Entriss since all Deity AIs communicate."

"Probably...I wonder how probably." He stood up and brushed off his red cloak. "Log out and order pizza?"

The quest menu appeared.

Reckoning: Part I...

It took more effort to dismiss.

"There's something else." She stood up and sought the portal, her eyebrows furrowing. "We can't let them shut down Entriss. Finishing this quest will create a bridge to the world he's in. I was told that once the bridge is in place, it will be almost impossible to shut down this world. Somehow, that's supposed to help my brother."

"Oh." He felt dizzy trying to understand what that meant and sat down again. He could die, or somehow get stuck in Entriss, but if they won, it could save this world and her brother. It didn't make sense. There were too many missing pieces. It was like trying to put a car engine together with Legos and crayons. Reason told him to log out now and run away.

"We can quit, if you want." She held her breath, her eyes filled with desperation.

Of course, love had nothing to do with reason. "So we save Entriss, save your brother, get married, and make babies."

She launched at him. He fell back as she straddled his hips and kissed him with heart-racing passion. Minutes passed before she pulled away, gasping for breath.

"We need to finish this quest and log out, for reasons."

Jewells laughed and nodded. "Did you just ask me to marry you?"

His heart skipped, and she laughed again.

"Boys in the throes of passion."

"No." He looked into her eyes. "When I take a knee and ask for your hand, I'll do it in a way you'll never forget."

"And I'll say yes, Ian."

They stared at each other for a long time. When the moment passed, she dismounted, and he sat up.

"Time to save the world?" he asked.

"Not so quick, sociopath." She crossed her arms. "Your turn."

"My truth seems pretty tame, but sure." His blood went cold, and he closed his eyes. "My biological father left when I was four. I don't even remember his name. My mom's addiction issues probably scared him away, and they attracted the worst sort of replacements. Every year or two, I'd have a new temp-dad. It'd be great for a week, or a month, until it wasn't. That's when the beatings would start. They'd beat her. They'd beat me. On those rare occasions that sobriety would sneak into her life, she'd kick one out and move on to the next. I was sixteen when I started fighting back, and she kicked me out."

"Ian." She swallowed hard and took his hand.

"It's okay. I've learned to deal with it. I started making money as a software developer and sank a small fortune into therapy. Some great people tried to help me, but I just didn't know what I wanted. After rounds of psychologists, psychiatrists, and therapists, I figured it out." He sat up straight and looked her in the eye. "Most people couldn't afford the help I got, and I had the resources to help, so I started looking for others like me."

"The pictures." She covered her mouth.

"There are a lot of people in trouble, but after some tough lessons, I realized I could only help those who wanted to be saved. It took a while to figure out the equation, and none of it was legal. I hacked everything from school records to credit reports. I built up a pretty solid network of anonymous people who would lead me to a lost soul or pitch in money. Sometimes, I saved a life. Other times, I could only save a pet."

Her eyes welled with tears. "You could've told me. I wouldn't have told anyone about the hacking."

"Back in the beginning, I would've brought you in. But then I found Marc." He squeezed her hand tight. "She was way out of scope for my little project. I was used to saving the occasional addict or abuse victim. Marc was special forces gone merc gone underbelly. She was the best of the best, but her dark path led to a vicious hit on her and her daughter. Trudy was in a coma and Marc was in pieces, but she refused to die. I had to help. I didn't realize my network had such deep pockets. Not only did they rebuild Marc, they saved her daughter...sort of."

"Sort of?"

"I, uh, I." He turned away, squeezing his damp eyes shut. "This is harder than I thought."

"It can wait. We've got time. Like you said about my dad. We can talk about Marc and her daughter when you're ready."

"Thank you." He took a minute to compose himself. "When money got involved, and you've seen what they did to Marc, I had to make some promises. That meant staying silent. There were investors to protect, and others... Cook helped a lot, but he's not the one who paid for Marc and her daughter. She was a billion-dollar project and that's still a mystery."

"She was worth every penny. You won't believe what she did to save my ass." Jewells recounted the events at Entriss Headquarters.

The quest menu popped open. He couldn't dismiss it and willed the parchment into the far corner of his vision.

"This has gotten way out of hand." He stood and began pacing. "All I wanted was to impress you with a quest, and—"

She was already there when he turned around. "I'm impressed to the point of being overwhelmed. If we're done with secrets, I think we're ready. We are done with secrets, right? Eon?"

"I may have done a thing." He could barely hold back his smile.

"Oh?" She took a step back and began tugging her hair again.

"I made your island."

"What?"

"You always talked about an island getaway. It took months, but I slowly snuck in bits of code to make it."

"You're kidding."

"A Gnome resort called Lost." He looked around like someone might hear. "The rules are, um, a little different there so we can do stuff like watch Trek on the beach."

"You could've gotten fired." She shook her head. "You did that for me?"

He nodded. "Hear me out. What if we go to Lost, and they can't find us? Everyone would have to wait while—"

System Message: Quest Initiated. Reckoning begins in 5...4...

"Dammit, Deity!" he shouted into the coliseum. "I didn't agree to start the quest!"

"We're fading into a cut scene," Jewells said.

"Sonofa..."

63

RECKONING

Horns blared heroically, and the distant beat of war drums welcomed them. The textured golden letters of the Entriss Online logo appeared then burst into flames. The music grew louder, and a new title formed from the burnt-out embers.

Entriss Online: Reckoning

The camera zoomed out until the words were nothing more than ash on a torch that had burned out long ago.

"What is this?" Eon asked.

"The new intro," Jewells said.

Eon and Jewells were back in Zalmon's chamber, barely able to see as they floated overhead. He opened his mouth to speak until she hushed him with a finger to her lips.

"Mistakes were made." Zalmon's voice was low. "I turned my sons away, and they divided southern Entriss into two kingdoms. Nihle became overwhelmed with greed and drives everyone in Yu to hunt for treasure. Under Denpar's rule, Rath became a nation filled with hatred, attracting any who lusted for battle. They fight each other for armor and weapons. To the griefers go the spoils.

"And then there was Salvare." His old, dead bones shuddered. "My peaceful children to the north could craft items of great power.

When they created one that almost destroyed me, I released the Grym in retaliation. They ravaged the lands we now call Misere, isolating the capital city. My choice of heir, Adriette, left my side to save them.

"Camille was the only one who remained. I was weak from battling her son—"

"So I finished the job!" a woman shouted.

Harsh red light flooded the chamber, revealing dead King Zalmon on his knees. The shadow-cloaked figure of Rune Mage Camille stood over him. She held both hands high overhead, clutching Zalmon's heart in one and his eyes in the other.

"You killed my son, old fool. I will use your remains to create a doorway into death's lands and free my beautiful Ned."

"I am Zalmon." His voice echoed throughout the chamber. "And even beyond the shadowy pale of Deity's embrace, I will have my vengeance."

The room faded to black, and Camille screamed.

"I won them! The heart and eyes are mine!" she shouted. "Where did they go? Give them to me now!"

"They were never truly yours. They are safe in the hands of my Champion, who has proven himself worthy. He will gather an army to free Salvare from my monsters, and then he will destroy you. Beware, Camille. Eon is coming, and everyone on Entriss will join him."

"Oh shit," Eon said.

"That was new," Jewells replied.

Light flooded his eyes and seconds passed before everything came into view. They hovered over a terrace that overlooked a beautiful city of white towers and golden spires. High above the ground, people rushed along archways that connected the buildings while large silver discs transported others. He'd never seen anything like it on Entriss and longed for more.

Beneath them was an enormous table with a stone-carved map of the city. Representatives of the four Salvare tribes surrounded the table. Vicki stood at the far end with Nihle and Tawaii beside her.

They all faced the dark Rune Mage Camille. The shadow-cloaked figure hovered just outside the terrace. Zalmon's eyes and heart were gone; instead she held Adriette, bound tight and struggling.

Eon and Jewells drifted down to stand beside Vicki.

"This is your fault, Eon!" Camille screeched. "You've stolen my father's remains, and I will rip them from your carcass."

He blinked. This was no longer a cut scene.

"When Zalmon's heart and eyes are mine, I will sacrifice my sister with their magic. It will be powerful enough to reach the land of death and return my beautiful son Ned to life." A dark hood covered everything but her bitter sneer. "What say you, Champion?"

This was the game. This was what he lived for, and it was time to finish this quest. Eon took a step forward and drew Ned's staff. "Bring it."

"Challenge accepted." She smiled.

In an explosion of red clouds, Camille and Adriette disappeared.

64

ALL IN

Bravery got stuck somewhere between Eon's heart and brain as he turned to face the questioning stares of the Salvare leaders. He froze like it was his first day of grade school all over again. The teacher had asked him to write an equation on the smartboard, and the kids had mocked him for being too brainy, and Samantha Gillow had cast him a note that said he smelled like cabbage, and he'd had to pee like his life depended on it. He'd run out of the classroom to take care of business and returned to horrified stares like an alien had popped out of his guts.

All eyes were on him, and there was nowhere to run. Vicki turned to him, looking dangerous with her gray leather armor and stony gaze.

"Eon. Champion of Yu. Champion of Rath. Destroyer of Grym. The Left Hand of God." Her tone was brittle as thin shale on a mountaintop. "Welcome to Salvare."

His mouth was so dry he could only nod.

"Rumor is that you had given up." Her eyes softened and there was a hint of sadness in her tone. "I knew you wouldn't throw in the towel."

The reminder of Trevor and his sacrifice brought back focus. His jaw unlocked and the knots in his shoulders released. "I couldn't give up when we are so close, Your Highness. This is our reckoning."

"Thank you, Champion. We need your help. Salvare is under attack." Vicki bit her lip and closed her eyes. "My army is yours."

Do you want to merge groups with Vicki?

Merging groups was new, but what could go wrong? He'd led dozens of players through dungeons.

Eon accepted and took a step back as the council, the leaders of Entriss, and the entire population of Salvare joined his group. His vision filled with small rectangles of Health and Mana. With a deep breath, he willed them away.

A Yu Ogre named TryGuy approached. Eon vaguely recalled the Barbarian's rally to join TryGuy's army in the forums.

"You may remember me as Quizno the Sprite. You tried to save me from Zalmon." He nodded respectfully. "That's how I knew you were worthy."

That wasn't possible. He'd been logged in as his Customer Service toon, Helpy. No one could possibly know Mandorf was Helpy, or Eon was Mandorf. Unless...

"Deity," he whispered.

TryGuy winked.

Do you wish to merge groups with TryGuy?

"Like I have a choice," he muttered.

His vision flooded with players joining his group. Thousands, tens of thousands, and then more. How could he possibly manage so many?

"Okay." His heart raced and he gasped for air. He dismissed the overwhelming group UI and stumbled to the table.

"What am I supposed to do with this mess?" he whispered to TryGuy, but Deity had disappeared.

Despite how real this felt, despite the stakes at hand, there was still a game to be played on Entriss. He sought answers from his quest menu. There were two sub-quests beneath The Left Hand of God.

At All Costs: As Vicki's guide, you agree at the cost of life and limb to protect my daughter so she can complete her quest and ascend her destined throne.

Reckoning Part I: Prepare your army to battle Camille's monsters by coordinating their attacks.

With everything going on, organizing the players felt like an odd quest. He obviously needed the experience since there was no way he could defeat Camille at 39. Other games offered catch-up quests, especially during big events or expansions. Could this be Deity's way of helping him reach 40?

The sheer quantity of players was overwhelming. He had to know what was going on before deciding what to do with them. He shook off his thoughts to see Vicki waiting impatiently.

"How bad is it?" he asked.

"We've always been able to defend against attacks from random monsters," she said. "This is the first time they've coordinated their efforts. Mind's Eyes are attacking from the south, Flendrit from the west, and Mendicant from the east. Camille randomly appears at each wall, waiting for a breach. She's surrounded by Burning Shades, and as you saw, she has my mother."

Panic subsided as he began calculating. Having spent his entire adult life in IT had taught him about breaking down problems.

Jewells elbowed him in the ribs, and he glanced up to see Vicki on the verge of tears. She'd already lost Trevor, so the possibility of losing her mom must've been terrifying.

"I'll do everything I can to save Adriette." He waited for her to nod. "But I need to know how you defeated the monsters in the past."

"Kevin has always led a team of Guardians and Slayers to defend against the Flendrit."

She nodded at a middle-aged Hobgoblin with the physique of a wild gorilla. A sword the size of a small barn hung from a leather sheath over his shoulder, and he wore a set of full plate armor. He was a Guardian, like Trevor.

Kevin looked him up and down like he didn't want Eon on his kickball team.

"How many troops can you handle?" Eon asked. "Or do you just want to take the Flendrit solo while we watch?"

The barest of smiles lifted a corner of Kevin's jutting jaw. It may have been his first. "I'll lead whatever army you give me."

"Thanks." Eon turned back to Vicki. "What about the Mendicant?"

"My name is Prost. Those bastards are mine." A male Jaeger drew his silver whip. The Brownie was pale brown with long green hair and a haunted gaze. "Been hunting them since they killed my parents. We use ranged attacks to avoid their touch."

"Perfect." Eon nodded. "That leaves the Mind's Eyes."

"We've never had to face those creatures, but at least we know how to stop them. Some Warlocks can cast *Extract*, similar to *Purge* without the, um, side effects. Emrit used to lead our Warlocks into battle, but I dismissed him from the council." Vicki looked at a purple Brownie. "I'm sure Dinn is up to the job."

The Brownie nodded, holding her wand up high.

"All of that makes sense. I just have to figure out how to sort so many." Eon closed his eyes and concentrated. "I need something familiar, like file cabinets, to organize everyone. It would take a week or more to hammer out the code, but..."

"It's such a mess," Jewells said with a frown. She whispered, "With all the code we checked in, there has to be some sort of raid interface."

"A raid! Entriss has always been about small groups, but I wonder." He willed a raid interface to open. "Oh wow. This, I can do."

The kajillion-member mess that included everyone in Salvare and probably most of the players in Entriss was replaced with group templates. Each profession was displayed in a different color. Instead of manually filling each group with individual characters, he could organize them by profession.

He created three templates; melee, ranged, and magic, with a healer in each group. There were leftovers. It was a lopsided Rubik's Cube with some colors having too many squares. Not only were the majority of players from Yu, there were more melee than any other profession. After sweating it out, he mixed things up.

It was easy to fill the melee groups with Thieves, Assassins, Gladiators, Barbarians, and Priests. The ranged groups included a Jaeger, Ranger, Marksman, Cleric, and Guardian. Magic-based groups included a Warlock, Sorcerer, Wizard, Rector, and Slayer.

After assigning each template to the designated leader, he was ready to take a nap. Kevin, Prost, and Dinn all nodded in approval.

Eon took a deep breath and let it out slowly through pursed lips.

"Well done, Champion," Vicki said.

A blue hue surrounded her, and he turned in the quest. It was worth almost a third of the experience needed to reach 40. He was right. Deity had provided a catch-up quest, and hope trickled into his heart.

"You will need a powerful group to end Camille and save my mother." Vicki handed him a golden orb.

Reckoning Part II: Choose who will join you to fight Camille.

A group with nine empty slots appeared, and he took a step back.

"I was planning to face her alone." He tried dismissing the group and failed. "Camille and I are the only two Rune Mages, and she knows what she's doing. It's a death sentence to fight her."

"I'm in," Jewells said, and she appeared in his group.

"Me too." Nomar hopped up and down.

"Hey, if I die, I won't have to get married." Coco frowned at Nomar.

"I will join you to avenge Trevor and save my mother," Vicki said.

"I will end her for killing my father." Tawaii raised her bow.

Nihle took a deep draw from his flask. He raised it high overhead and nodded. "Same."

All six had joined his group. He knew nothing about Camille's Dark Rune magic, so it was best to go in with a well-rounded team. Coco and Nomar were close-combat melee. Tawaii and Vicki were ranged DPS.

"I need another healer, someone who can hurl spells, and another warrior to back up Nihle."

"Tiffany is our most powerful healer, and Asne is a dangerous Warlock."

He nodded, and the Hobgoblin and Ash Giant joined the group.

"Ismarelle fancies you, Champion." Nihle swallowed down a belch. "And she has no army to lead."

"Perfect."

The Barbarian joined the group. She appeared beside him in the same golden armor she'd worn in Yu. "Good to see ya, harlot of Yu!" She slapped him roughly on the back. "Ready for that toss in the sack, are ya?"

Jewells raised an eyebrow. He could only answer with a sigh.

Nihle cleared his throat and pointed at Jewells. "Young love."

"Ohhh." Ismarelle turned to Jewells and elbowed her. "A feisty one ya got there."

"He'd better be." She winked, making the woman chuckle.

Vicki was blue again, and he turned in the quest. It rewarded him with a generous amount of experience, but not enough to reach 40. She handed him another quest.

Reckoning Part III: Inspire your troops before sending them into battle.

"Are you ready?" Vicki asked.

"Ready for what?"

She smiled and nodded at Asne. The Warlock raised a steel staff high overhead. A dark bubble surrounded them. It popped, and Eon's group appeared on a platform that had to be in the town square. It was the intersection of four wide roads, all filled with thousands of players and NPCs.

"They'll all be able to hear you," Vicki said.

"Oh no. No, no, no." He took a step back, and Jewells grasped his hand.

"This is just like standing up to Luanne in the class," she whispered. "You can do this."

He stared at the crowd. A million movie speeches rushed through his mind, but none of them stuck.

Vicki took his other hand. "Forget everything else and just say it to me. Say it to me, as a friend."

There was no choice; he had to reach level 40. He nodded, took a deep breath, and spoke.

"Hi. My name is Eon. I've been through hell to finish The Left Hand of God quest. I worked at Entriss until they fired me. I used to be Mandorf until they deleted my character. I lost the job I loved. I lost my girlfriend, several times. I even lost hope. But then a friend reminded me why I'm here...why we're here. I love this world.

"I've experienced adventure, and friendship, and love. I've failed over and over. The grind has been a chore, but the wins, oh those wins have been worth the effort. Entriss has been worth the effort, and I've been all in from the beginning.

"There have been a lot of rally cries over the years. 'Cry "Havoc!", and let slip the dogs of war,' 'Never give up, never surrender,' 'Avengers, Assemble.' I say, it's time to take Entriss back! I say it's time to stop this army and show this bitch how we do things downtown. I'm old school MMO, and I say, all in!"

There was a moment of silence that made him cringe out a little Health. And then, it happened.

A small voice in the crowd shouted, "You heard the man. All in!"

Another cried, "All in."

And then more and more until his army roared, "All in!"

He wanted to cry, and cheer, and attack, and... Jewells grabbed his shoulders, spun him around, and planted a firm kiss on his lips. Focus returned as she slowly pulled back.

"Let's go, Champion." Her face was filled with pride. "All in!"

65

PREPARE FOR BATTLE

The crowd disappeared like a dream slipping through his fingers. A five-minute countdown appeared in the corner of his vision, each second feeding his anxiety.

A blue glow surrounded Vicki.

"Finally." He sighed and turned in Reckoning Part III.

She smiled and handed over a package. He accepted, watching his experience closely. Nothing happened.

"That's it?" he asked.

"Oh, right." She handed Jewells a package. "To complete the set."

"Do I have to?" Jewells's shoulders drooped. "It's just...not me."

"There's nothing more powerful." Vicki winked. "You'll own it."

"How am I supposed to defeat Camille?" he asked. "I'm only 39."

Vicki stared off with glassy eyes. "Have faith in Deity. She always has a plan."

"Right." He sighed. "Oh, wait. You dropped this in Rath." He reached into his satchel and handed Jewells the top he looted from her body.

"Thanks." She reluctantly accepted, rolling her eyes.

"Let's get you changed." Vicki took her hand and led her away. "I want to see it first."

They wandered off behind the platform. Eon opened the package and pulled out a pair of yellow boots with feathers on each side, as if the Greek god Mercury was mocking him. Yellow boots to go with his red jacket, white belt, silver gloves, and black skullcap. It was like the quest rewards came straight from the thrift store.

The Flash Quick Boots of Running gave Wizards a 20% speed boost for three seconds. Ugly but impressive with only a two-minute cooldown. Inscribing it for a Rune Mage wiped away the speed bonus but gave him +2 to Vigor, Essence and Power.

He reluctantly put them on. Not only were they too powerful to throw away, the speed boost was probably a clue. This encounter would probably require running.

They had less than four minutes. The square was empty, save for a man who ran for cover between buildings. Jewells and Vicki were giggling behind the podium as he watched the time count down.

Sweat beaded on his forehead as he thought about facing a high-level boss at level 39. His odd-looking gear was powerful, but it wouldn't be enough. He needed more punch, and that reminded him of the focus tree.

He opened the menu and smiled at the 18 unused points. Scholar unlocked three new spells and Inscription 3. The Ward spell was *Veil* and looked like a shadowy cloak. *Obtain* was a Glyph spell with the icon of a grasping hand. The Sigil spell, *Leech*, was a vortex.

Veil: Hide yourself from impending doom for 7 seconds. 3-minute cooldown. Instant cast. Cost: 1-3 points.

Obtain: Steal any spell for 12 seconds. 10-minute cooldown. Instant cast. Cost: 1 point.

Leech: Absorb Mana from your opponent. 2-minute cooldown. 3-second cast. Cost: 1-5 points.

To unlock the other spells, he had to spend two points on Inscription 3. He stared at the focus tree and considered his options.

Mandorf had been a glass cannon. He longed to wreak havoc and sling spells like his Wizard. This Rune Mage wasn't about damage. This profession was about support and it was time to play him right.

The countdown reached 3:39. He had to choose now. He removed points from some spells he liked in favor of spells that would, hopefully, help his group.

In the end, he had three Glyph spells:

Obtain: Steal any spell for 20 seconds. 5-minute cool down. Instant cast. Cost: 1/1.

Ruination: Damage opponents in a ten-yard radius and knock them back. Cost: 3/3.

Pellet: Interrupt your target from casting spells with a constant barrage of small stones. Cost: 3/3.

Three Sigil spells:

Hyper: Give a powerful buff to one player for 60 seconds. 2-minute cooldown. 5-second cast. Cost: 5/5.

Increment: Provide a group buff that increases for forty seconds. 10-minute cooldown. 3-second cast. Cost: 5/5.

Leech: Absorb Mana from your opponent. 5-minute cooldown. 3-second cast. Cost: 5/5.

One Ward spell:

Alacrity: Spend Mana to slow time. Faster speeds will exponentially drain more Mana. Affects spells and movement. Instant cast. No cooldown. Cost: 5/5.

With fingers crossed, he confirmed his choices and reviewed his stats.

Name:	Eon	Level:	39
Tribe:	Wood Elf	XP to Level:	140,528
Profession:	Rune Mage		
		Vigor:	15
Health:	1824	Essence:	22
Mana:	2683	Power:	19

The exercise made him wonder about Camille. She was a Dark Rune Mage with a different set of spells but hopefully similar constraints.

"Ahem." Vicki was standing beside him. "Your healer is ready, Champion."

"Oh?" he asked, turning around. "Oh wow."

Jewells wore a white, long-sleeve bodysuit that looked painted on. Her beautiful legs were bare from hip to white leather ankle boots. The armor included silver bracers and a matching neck choker. They coordinated well with the broad, shimmering wings that reached out from her back.

He gawked as she floated toward him. Not only was it the first set of armor with wings, she looked stunning.

"It's not really my color and—"

"Yes, it is," he interrupted, licking his dry lips.

"Told you so," Vicki said.

Jewells landed before him. "It's all healing. My only offense spell is my special."

He wrapped his arms around her and kissed her. When he pulled back, barely pulled back, he whispered, "How much time do we have?"

"Fifteen seconds," Vicki replied.

They looked at each other, took a deep breath, and said, "Shit."

66

DESTRUCT SEQUENCE

Fred's knuckles were white like it was the Super Bowl and he'd bet all his beer money. He glanced at Marta, who nodded in agreement. Chen sat two chairs away, staring with wide eyes.

Someone cleared their throat at the back of the room, making them all spin around.

"Sorry to interrupt. I didn't want to miss the big finish." Lars stood in the doorway wearing khakis and a dark polo. He stepped aside and reached out with a hand. "You all know Samantha Cook?"

The thirty-something goddess entered the room, followed closely by the clacking nails of Gidget the corgi. Samantha wore a white cotton dress that was too short and too tight to adorn mere mortals. Mounds of blond hair framed her tanned face and poured over her shoulders. She graced them with a full-lipped smile before crouching to scratch Gidget's ears.

They all rose like royalty had arrived. She stood with Gidget in her arms and a perfect blush on her cheeks.

"I hope you don't mind company," Samantha said.

"Nope." Fred licked his lips. "Do you like cheesecake?"

"Never had it," she said.

"Of course not." Marta looked her up and down. "I'll grab you a few pieces."

"That sounds lovely," she said. "Jack sent me with another request. He wants you to cast the final battle."

Chen let out a low whistle.

"Hammers will love this. It's like we're giving the accords our middle finger," Lars said. "Is it possible?"

"Should only take a few minutes." Fred hovered over the keyboard and got to work.

"Will your husband be joining us?" Marta asked, handing over a dish stacked with cheesecake.

"Yes, Jack will be here soon." Samantha's voice became dark. "After he takes care of business."

***

"WE'RE APPROACHING IAN'S APARTMENT." Dirk's cast squelched loudly enough to make Luanne wince. It surprised her that she got any reception at all this close to Deity. "No sign of the cyborg."

"Kill them fast and get out before she shows up. Lie low until you hear from me." She took a deep breath. "I'll be offline for a while, but this shouldn't take long."

"It better not," he growled. "You owe us—"

She cut off the transmission. "You and everyone else."

The hallway to Deity's core ended in an alcove. Plastic suits with oxygen masks hung over steel benches along the walls. Entriss required visitors to don the gear before entering. The core was sealed off by a stainless steel passthrough to reduce contamination.

It seemed like overkill for a video game, and Luanne marched to the door and lifted the handle. A gentle hiss released cool air that made her shiver. She glanced over her shoulder before slipping in. Before the door shut behind her, she made her way through the second.

It was the first time she'd been down here, and her eyes went wide. She stood on a concrete platform that overlooked a large, spherical room fifty yards in diameter. A twenty-foot-wide silver orb hovered in the middle as if magic from Entriss held it in place.

"Jackpot." She rushed down grated steel stairs that led to the bottom.

It was cold enough to see her breath, and the air smelled like plastic. The orb hummed with power, but she couldn't see any cables connecting to it. There was one computer console with an enormous, wide monitor. Thick cables ran from the computer to two immersion pods near the curved wall.

She approached the console, rubbing her hands together for warmth. After logging in, she opened her tablet to review Ty's instructions.

They were surprisingly simple, and after several minutes, a woman's voice said, "Warning. Destruct sequence will reformat Omneity Sphere and erase Deity container. This action is not recoverable after reinstallation of AI. Do you wish to proceed?"

"Hell yes."

"Do you wish to proceed?"

Luanne cleared her throat. "Yes."

"Acknowledge command code for destruction of Deity."

"Destruct sequence one, code one, one, a," she said.

The lights in the room went red. The woman spoke again, her voice coming from everywhere. "Destruct sequence completed and engaged. Awaiting final code for one-minute countdown."

"Code zero, zero, zero." She took a deep breath. "Destruct—"

"Wait!"

She spun around to see Jack Cook at the top of the stairs. His sleeves were missing, as if he'd lost a battle with groupies. He scrambled down and stopped ten feet away, raising both hands.

"Please, take another step." She aimed a 9mm handgun at his chest. "I have nothing to lose."

THREE DARK SUVs rolled into the rain-swept parking lot in full stealth mode. An electrical dispersion field obscured them from most security cameras, and they'd switched to electric motors for quiet.

Dirk tapped the steel band around his neck. "Final order. Quick kill, in and out." He waited for his cast to reach the other mercs. "No sign of the cyborg. We lost good men because of this nerd. Let's kill him hard."

A dozen mercenaries poured out of the vehicles and ran toward the abandoned warehouse like blacksnakes skimming a lake at night. Dirk led them to the entrance of Ian's apartment.

He waved over their tech. Dennis drew a magnetic release from his backpack, licked his lips, and gently placed it against the door. He held his breath as it connected with the barest of clinks. Dirk nodded, and Dennis turned a knob. The door unlocked and inched open.

Dirk led with his handgun, pushing his way through the door. The apartment was empty, and unremarkable. A sectional couch surrounded a coffee table. There was a kitchen in the distant shadows. A science fiction movie played on a large television that hung from the wall.

He scanned the room until his eyes fell on two bookshelves behind the couch. They weren't flush, and he smiled.

He directed his troops with two fingers, and they pried the shelves apart. They slid aside, revealing a hidden room.

"Gotcha," he whispered.

67

KNOW THINE ENEMY

Camille was several hundred yards away, surrounded by six blurry Shades that were hard to make out. They approached slowly as if they were trying to build up tension. It worked.

A Barbarian attacked her flank, shouting, "For Entriss."

Two Shades came to her defense, and the Barbarian let out a gurgling scream that ended abruptly as his armor fell in a pile of ashen remains.

"That's not good," Nomar said.

She was a hundred and fifty yards away when a group of five griefers from Rath tried to steal the kill.

"Should I dismiss them?" Tawaii asked. "Nihle and I can remove any trespasser we see from the field of battle."

"Not yet." Eon held up a hand. "I want to see what happens."

He couldn't inspect their gear from this distance, but the positions they took indicated this wasn't their first boss fight—though it might be their last.

Camille turned. "Cute."

A blue symbol appeared beneath the closest attacker, a massive Ogre in heavy plate. The Gladiator rose in the air and began to shake. It spread like a disease, jumping from one player to the next. Within seconds, they all hovered several feet above the ground, vibrating like The Flash going through walls. They fell to the ground, and the Shades attacked until all that remained was ash and armor.

"Camille cast a tremor spell that spread to the others," Eon shouted to his group. "The Shades do burn damage."

"I could've told you that." Nomar shook his head. "All you had to do was ask."

Was that a clue? They weren't exactly NPCs who would give up everything if asked the right question, but maybe they knew some hidden truth that could help.

"Nihle, what can you tell me about your sister?"

"She's a total bitch. I hated her more than Denpar." He turned to Tawaii. "May he rest in peace."

"Hmpf." She raised her nose. "Is that all you remember, you drunken Barbarian?"

"Our Champion should answer his own question." Nihle jerked a thumb over his shoulder. "He's a Rune Mage like her."

"She's a Dark Rune Mage, and a level 40 boss, but you've got a point." Eon stared off, thinking out loud. "Bosses only get a handful of spells because they're so powerful. Camille is probably limited to one Ward, Glyph, and Sigil spell. That had to be the Glyph spell because it was blue and did damage."

"A lot of damage," Nomar said. "She really shook things up."

Coco shoved him. "You're not that funny."

"As my future wife, you should be more supportive."

"Now that was funny."

Camille and her Shades didn't make it twenty feet before a group of fifteen well-geared players from Yu attacked.

Nihle shook his head. "Maybe they'll soften her up."

"Yeah, like butter attacking hot corn on the cob." Nomar covered his face with both hands and watched through his fingers.

She was close enough for Eon to view her stats. Camille's vast amounts of Health and Mana made his heart skip. Things got worse when she cast a yellow symbol beneath most of the group. Her spell stole all their buffs and bonuses, making her stats spike even higher.

The attackers looked like deflated balloons when the Shades attacked. Despite their condition, the group fought back. Most were close to death when their stats returned.

"Her Sigil spell absorbs a huge amount of Health and Mana for fifteen-ish seconds. She didn't attack again with her Glyph spell, which probably means there's a cooldown." He remembered to breathe and wiped beads of sweat from his forehead. "That leaves her defensive Ward spell. Oh, and we don't know if she has a special... Holy sh—"

A red portal sucked all the players up like a vacuum. The other end of the portal appeared directly overhead, and they all dove out of the way. Eon rolled up smoothly to one knee.

"Does the rolling help?" Jewells smirked at him.

"Uh huh, it helps."

Yu players shot out like a Roman candle. They burned red hot, leaving a trail of smoke in the air before smashing into distant buildings. Most of them died before impact, except for the tank, who struck the wall with a snap. She collapsed to the ground and twitched out the last of her Health.

"Hmmm," Asne muttered.

He made eye contact with the giant. "What do you think?"

The ground beneath her was covered in ash. She reached out with a rocky toe to draw a circle.

He stared at the circle and considered. "You may be right."

"Right?" Jewells's eyes were wide. "Her hmmm was right?"

Another large group approached Camille and her Shades.

"You've got to be kidding me," Ismarelle shouted. "That kill is ours, ya bastards!"

"You're right. It's time." Eon took a deep breath. "Nihle, Tawaii, dismiss anyone from Rath or Yu who gets in her way."

Tawaii snapped her fingers, and the new group disappeared.

"There's too much concentrated damage around Camille. Healers and ranged dps will need to spread out as far as you can. Just stay within healing range. Asne and I are going to take turns kiting the Shades. Once we get their attention and draw them away, melee and ranged can attack. Coco and Nomar, try interrupting her spells. Nihle and Ismarelle...smash."

The two Barbarians nodded.

"She just destroyed that group of fifteen without trying." Coco wrung her hands. "How do we stop her when there's only ten of us?"

"Not ten...eleven." Eon summoned his familiar.

"Bunny!" Nomar clapped.

"We're all going to die," Coco said.

Lola gave Eon a wary side-eye.

"I'm sorry I got upset." He dropped to one knee. "We need you, but I understand if you want to leave."

She looked from Eon to Jewells before glancing over her shoulder at Camille. With a fierce bunny snort, Lola hopped to Eon and nuzzled his leg. She tipped over, and he helped her up.

"This is it?" Camille hovered within sneering distance. The Dark Rune Mage hid under shadowy robes, like those worn by her Grym. "A Champion who's too young to be here, his pet bunny, and Entriss's leftovers?"

She laughed, and her Shades flickered in and out excitedly like black lights on a faulty circuit.

"Where's my mother?" Vicki demanded, her whip white hot and sparking with power.

"Somewhere she cannot interfere." She reached out with a pale hand. "Give me my father's heart and eyes, and your deaths will be quick and painless. Mostly." She cackled. "What say you, Champion?"

He looked around at his group, meeting eyes with all of them. They nodded in turn and braced themselves. When his gaze fell on Jewells, she flashed him that wicked smile. It was time.

Eon turned to Camille and said, "All in!"

68

INTRUDERS AT THE GATE

"Please don't do this, Luanne." Cook inched closer, his eyes pleading. "This is my life's work."

"Awaiting final code for one-minute countdown," the computer's voice repeated.

"I've sold your life's work, Jack." The gun shook in her hand. "Walk away and retire in comfort."

"You don't realize the danger you're putting yourself in." He moved forward, staring at the gun. "Deity's far more powerful than you can—"

"Stop right there." She pointed it at his face. "Don't make me kill both of you."

Jack's muscles tensed, as if struggling to hold back. "If this is about money, I can help you."

"It *was* about money, Jack." Her arm lowered slightly. "Now it's about you, your world, Julie, and that piece of shit Ian. This should've been easy, but he's made it a mess, and I know that, somehow, you've been helping. Zalmon wrote the code? I bet Jack Cook wrote the code to stop his life's work from being shut down. But I'm *going* to shut you down and get paid to watch all of you suffer."

"Awaiting final code for one-minute countdown."

She glanced at the computer. "Code zero, zero, zero."

He launched forward like an angry Kodiak, reaching for her throat. She pulled the trigger, and he collapsed to the ground.

Eon's secret room was round, providing the nerd no defensible position. It was twenty feet in diameter and sparsely decorated. An office chair at the opposite end faced a bank of servers. Recessed lights overhead shone dimly on two pods in the center of the room.

Dirk lifted a fist and spread his fingers. Soldiers dispersed behind him to survey the apartment as he approached the pods.

The cylinders were fourteen feet long with glass tops. Beneath the pods were several canisters labeled *nanobots* and dense cables that ran to the nearby servers.

"All clear," a merc called from the entrance.

He waved them in and peered through the glass. There was a body inside, obscured by a thick layer of frost. Wiping it away only revealed the hazy mist inside.

"Easy kill." Dirk drew a handgun and pointed it at Ian's head then paused. He tapped his neck. "Any sign of the cyborg? Or the cops?"

"Parking lot's empty," the lookout replied.

"This fucker cost me a lot of good men." Dirk looked around the room. "I hear it's painful to get ripped out of these things. Let's make it hurt."

Everyone nodded.

"Figure out how to crack the seal." He pointed with his gun. "He can watch his girlfriend being beaten to death before we shoot him in the head."

69

BOSS FIGHT

Nihle let out a furious roar before charging forward and body slamming Camille. The impact shattered the road beneath them, blew back the hair of anyone nearby, and got her attention.

Ismarelle, Coco, and Nomar rushed in and almost immediately skidded to a halt, cut off by the Burning Shades. Eon cast *Shockwave* and shot up into the air. He landed hard in front of Camille, blasting four of the Shades back several feet.

She looked at him and licked her lips.

"Run, boy," Nihle shouted.

Eon cast *Ruination* at the remaining Shades. None of them were affected by the knock back, but it was enough to get aggro. The other four were already up and they all floated toward him.

"Lola, go!" he shouted.

She teleported him thirty yards away, and the Shades turned back to attack the others. He could generate enough threat to attract them but had to be closer to maintain it.

"Too far, Lola. Bring me back."

In a flash of pink light, she transported him within inches of a dark, shadowy man.

"Too close. Too close."

The Shade turned on him, its eyes smoldering with fire. He gasped and immediately began coughing. The smell of old ash filled his nose and coated his mouth. He wiped tears from his eyes and saw a shiny black symbol on the shade's forehead, like a vinyl sticker.

"What is—" He cried out in pain as the creature's hands dove into his chest.

It felt like he was being cooked in a microwave. He was losing Health fast when a white blast knocked the Shade back. A red arrow struck its chest with a bang, blasting it out of reach.

A dark bubble surrounded him. When it popped, he and Lola appeared beside Asne.

"Be careful, Champion," she said, dusting him with more ash. At least it didn't smell as bad.

His Health jumped back to full. *Thank you, healers.*

"Let's try that again." He touched Lola's antler and said, "Go."

Lola brought him twenty feet away. He activated *Alacrity* and instantly cast *Ruination*. The blue blast symbol appeared beneath all six and exploded. Only one took damage, and they all remained standing.

"Damn being level 39!"

The six Shades turned to face him. They floated closer, reaching for him and staring with burning eyes.

"That worked." He deactivated *Alacrity* and touched an antler. "Ten feet at a time, go."

They appeared ten feet away, and the Shades followed. He did it again, and again, casting a spell every other port to retain threat. It was working! They were kiting the Shades around the town square.

"She's casting," Coco shouted.

"Spread out now!" Eon commanded.

"Too late," Camille screeched.

"No!" Nomar screamed.

Eon glanced at the group. Coco was dead.

"Avenge her, Nomar!" Eon shouted.

"Stabby, stabby, stabby." The Gnome was on Camille's shoulder, his daggers a blur as he struck her neck over and over.

"Eon!" Nomar sounded desperate. "My special isn't damaging her."

"Bring them here, Eon," Asne's voice thundered. "I'll take a turn so you can see the battle."

Lola made her way to the Ash Giant. She was already casting when they arrived.

"They'll lose threat at thirty feet. Good luck!"

A triangle of black flames appeared beneath the Shades, damaging one for 3% of its health and attracting all of them. She took off, and they followed. The ground shook with every step as she stayed just out of reach.

"The bitch is casting again," Tawaii said.

"I can't interrupt her." Nomar was on her back. His daggers were blue and sparked every time he stabbed her head. They bounced off like an invisible shield was protecting her.

Nihle swung with his tree trunk of a club, slamming Camille upside the shoulder again and again. Rubble on the ground hopped with each blow like popcorn. Ismarelle shield-slammed her and struck hard with her broadsword.

The blows would've leveled buildings, but Camille merely smiled and cast her spell.

"No!" Tiffany shouted in her husky voice.

A red portal appeared in front of the Hobgoblin. Before she could run away, it sucked her in. Another portal appeared at the far end of the town square. It shot her out like a canon, followed by a shotgun blast of rocks and boulders. She smashed against a building and fell to the ground. The stones pummeled her body, covering her until she was gone.

"Tiffany is dead," Eon shouted.

"Dammit," Jewells cried. "I couldn't heal her. She was too far away."

His heart beat so fast it was ready to explode. They were already down a healer, and a melee. Not just a melee; Coco was dead. Worry and grief flooded his thoughts. He was missing something obvious, but there was so much at stake that he—

A white blast exploded at his feet, making him jump.

"What the hell, Vicki?"

"That was a kiss," she said. "We were losing you."

"Don't kiss my boyfriend." Jewells winked at her. "You can do this, Eon. Just figure out the puzzle."

She was right. They were both right. It wasn't time for the big picture. This was about the puzzle.

Camille wasn't taking damage, and neither were most of her Shades. Only one of them had lost Health. Eon and Asne had hurt it. Tawaii and Vicki had hurt it more. But it wasn't just that. The Shades had a symbol on their forehead. His eyes went wide.

"The Shades are her Ward spell. They're protecting her." He pointed at the injured one trailing behind the others. "Vicki, Tawaii, focus all attacks on the damaged Shade. Nihle, when the monster's dead, use your special. I hope it hits hard."

Vicki and Tawaii melted the Shade with their attacks. Eon cast the buff spell *Hyper* on Nihle as Camille began floating back in retreat.

"It hits hard." The Ogre leapt thirty feet into the air, lifting his club high. He swung down, smashing his sister on the head. The ground beneath her cratered as his attack stole an eighth of her Health.

"I always hated you more than the others, brother." Camille raised her hands to cast. "Let's see what happens when I steal your great power."

Nihle, Ismarelle, and Nomar began deflating like balloons. The Gnome reached out with both hands and smashed her ears. She screamed.

"Interrupted, bitch!" Nomar spat.

Camille cast again, and a blue symbol appeared beneath Nihle. He shook like she was holding a jackhammer to his spine. Ismarelle ran, and Nomar leaped away as Jewells healed the Ogre through the attack.

"I live!" Nihle shouted.

"Find the next Shade that takes damage and kill it," Eon commanded, casting *Increment* to buff the group. "Asne, bring the Shades to me so you can help."

"Found it." Vicki's whip lashed out. "Tawaii, on me."

When Asne was close enough, Eon cast *Ruination* beneath the Shades. The injured one was at half health and fading fast. A black bubble brought the Warlock to safety as his spell exploded. The five Shades turned on him.

Lola was gasping for breath and her Mana was down by half.

"Five-minute break. I can do this." He activated *Alacrity*, feeding it just enough Mana to keep away from the Shades.

The second Shade was almost dead, and Eon let it get close enough to cast *Leech*. His Mana bar went from half to two thirds before it died.

"Ismarelle, now!" Vicki commanded.

The field marshal spun like a tornado, kicking up a vortex of debris. Camille couldn't move away fast enough. Ismarelle abruptly stopped, the flat of her blade striking the Rune Mage's chest. The impact cracked like thunder, stealing more of Camille's Health.

"Again," Eon shouted, casting *Increment* on the group.

Another Shade fell, and Vicki's white-hot whip reached across the town square, wrapping around Camille's neck. She choked as the whip burned into her flesh, sizzling like bacon.

"Again!"

Tawaii shot a lightning bolt from her bow. It bored into Camille's gut and exploded.

Lola appeared beside him to resume kiting duties. Some of her Mana was back, and she looked better. He disabled *Alacrity*, and they teleported ten feet away from the two remaining Shades.

Nomar interrupted Camille's *Absorb* spell twice, and Jewells healed Nihle through three more attempts at *Shaken*.

When they killed the last burning Shade, Lola collapsed. His group was mostly intact. Jewells's Mana was low, but she had enough to finish this.

He turned to Camille. She was down to a nickel of Health and bleeding out from numerous cuts. Zalmon's daughter looked shocked, like she'd watched someone eat her puppy.

"Time to end this," Eon said. "All i—"

"Looks like I'm just in time for the party."

The now-familiar British accent made him cringe. A Gladiator stepped out of the shadows.

"I may not be able to kill you," Swytch said, his voice smug. "But I can kill this lovely." He pointed his two-handed sword at Vicki.

"Lola, go!"

Eon appeared in front of Vicki and cast *Absorb*. If he could spell-steal *Final Kill*, this was over. A flash of white light struck him and faded away.

"Nice try," Eon said. He turned on Swytch and brought up his casting bar UI. The new spell filled a temporary ninth slot. "*Taunt*?"

A red blast shot from the Gladiator's hands, directly at Jewells.

"Go, go, go!" Eon pleaded.

Lola brought him to Jewells. Red light surrounded her, and she began to fade.

"No," he whispered, reaching for her, but she was already gone.

Tawaii stopped attacking to take in what had happened. "You don't belong here." She snapped, and Swytch disappeared.

"Finally," Camille said. "No healers."

Eon spun around to see a red portal form over her.

"Run, run away," he pleaded.

The portal sucked up Nihle and Ismarelle. Nomar held onto Camille's dark, oily robes, his hands slipping an inch with every breath.

The Gnome looked up, his eyes desperate. "Eon."

Camille's cowl tore free, and Nomar flew into the portal.

The other end appeared over Tawaii, showering her in burning bodies and a maelstrom of fire. Her screams didn't last long.

Eon's entire body went numb. They'd been so close. Vicki and Lola were the only two left. His familiar nudged him, and he nodded.

"Go."

They appeared before Vicki. The wild, lost look in her eyes surely mirrored his own.

"Can we beat her?" he asked.

Her body shuddered. Camille had cast *Shaken*, and the spell seeped into his bones.

"You lost your true love trying to save me." She looked into his eyes. "Trevor would've been grateful."

A bright blue glow surrounded her. He handed in Trevor's quest: At All Costs.

"Thank you." Her words faded as the spell took her life.

He fell to the ground, shaking so hard his teeth rattled.

70

TAKING CARE OF BUSINESS

"Hurry." Dirk stared at the entrance, watching intently for the cops or the cyborg.

Dennis the tech walked around the pod twice before stopping at the far end.

"Found the release." He pulled back on a lever.

Dirk wiped his sweaty palms on his legs and pressed them against the glass. The hatch unsealed with a hiss, releasing a frosty haze. He reached in with both hands.

The pod behind him hissed open as they prepared to wake the girl.

"What the..." the tech said. "I don't understand."

Ian's body was hard like plastic. Dirk waved away the frosty cloud to see a note pinned to a mannequin. He picked it up and read, "Terminated."

"Get out!" he shouted. "Get out of here."

"This is gonna be fun," a woman said from the entrance.

"The cyborg." Dirk pointed his gun at Marc. "Kill the bitch."

Marc's first shot struck a canister beneath the pod. It exploded, spraying anyone nearby in a thick, dark mist.

Cold washed over Dirk, and his legs went numb. He struggled to move forward and pushed against the pod. He tipped over, landing hard on his back.

Gunshots echoed throughout the room. She'd be on him in seconds. He'd have to fight back or get out, but his legs still wouldn't move.

"Anyone else?" she called out.

He pushed himself up and cried, "No!"

Dirk stared in horror at his legs. The cloud had eaten away his clothes and flesh from toe to thigh.

"I don't understand." It was getting hard to speak and his vision was blurring. "What did you do?"

"Ian thought I was crazy when I suggested building this decoy. I did it anyway." Marc was standing over him. "I figured it was a good contingency, like the drones that led you here."

"My...legs."

"His first purchase of underweb nanobots was a bad batch." She smiled. "They only last a few minutes, but I knew they'd give us a leg up."

"Fu... Fu... Fuc..." He couldn't finish.

"Gotta love a Bond pun. I'd let you bleed out slowly, but I can't chance them rebuilding someone like you." She pulled the trigger, and everything went dark.

"You didn't think I'd do it!" Luanne waved her gun, shouting at Cook's still body. "You thought you could overpower me. You old fool. I hope you're still alive so you can watch me destroy everything you've created."

She lowered the handgun and took a deep breath. "Let's try this again. Computer—"

"Whatcha got there?" a woman asked from behind her.

Luanne spun around and gawked. A tall, voluptuous blond goddess in a toga smiled at her.

"Put the gun down, Luanne, or you will live out your worst nightmare."

"Who... Who are you?" She took a step back.

"You know who I am, and you've made a terrible mistake."

"Deity?" Luanne's voice quavered before she steeled herself and shot.

The woman took a step forward, and Luanne emptied her clip.

"Wrong target," Cook said from behind her.

Luanne spun around and he struck her in the face. She collapsed to the floor.

"Sir, are you okay?" Bala rushed down the stairs. "I came to stop her, but... sir, your arm."

"Just a flesh wound." Jack bent over to pick her up and grunted in pain. "Give me a hand?"

"Of course." Bala helped lift Luanne's body. "Was that hologram Deity? I didn't know she could appear outside the game."

"Deity," Cook said. "Inception Protocol."

"Yes, King Zalmon."

"Ignore that, Bala." He grimaced as they inched forward with her body.

"Ignored." Bala looked nervous. "Where are we taking her?"

"Somewhere she can't harm anyone." He looked into Bala's eyes.

"Good." The small man nodded.

"Deity, how's our boy?" He paused to catch his breath. "How's Eon?"

"Eon is almost dead." She sounded worried. "He has a 2% chance of success and one shot left."

"Then he could still do it."

71

ONE SHOT

Congratulations. You have reached level 40.

L eveling returned his Health to full, thank you game mechanics, only to be eaten away by the *Shaken* spell. It didn't kill him, but his head ached, his mouth tasted like blood, and he was down to 25%.

"Ouch." He peeled himself off the ground.

Congratulations, Rune Staff of Ned the Insane has a new special. Deaded.

He was almost dead, and so was Lola, who nudged him to stand. They were the only two left to face Camille.

Deaded: Someone's dead. It's probably Ned. Just lie still, or it'll be you. Take no damage, until you move. I hate rhyming.

Great, another passive spell. Just when he needed it the least.

"Your son's staff is garbage," he shouted. "Why do all of his spells feel like a consolation prize?"

"He built it for a Dark Rune Mage. It's the most powerful weapon on Entriss, in the right hands. For a Light Rune Mage," she shrugged, "it's a candle in a thunderstorm."

Congratulations! Your familiar has earned a new spell.

Breathe Fire: Like real fire, like raging fire, not like smoldering fire.

"Huh." He had planned to summon a fire-breathing griffin for his familiar, until Nomar said bunny. Better late than never? He whispered to Lola, "Got anything left?"

She snorted and bared her two front teeth. Her grimace was so dangerous he wanted to hug her.

Camille hovered twenty feet away, sneering down at him. Her cowl was gone, and pointed Elven ears peeked out from her craggy brown hair. Centuries of hatred had sucked the life out of her like an astronaut spacewalking without a suit. Her chalky skin clung to her face with willpower. Dark circles had taken over her eyes, which were wide with extra crazy.

"You are a worthy adversary, Champion." Camille sneered. "Give me my father's heart and eyes, and I will teach you the ways of a Dark Rune Mage."

"Sooo tempting, but how about this instead?" Eon looked at her defiantly and said, "Lola, go!"

He cast *Battlemount*. Giant Lola appeared behind Camille and blasted her with fire. His familiar disappeared in a flash of pink light and blasted her again from the side.

Eon inspected the staff, desperate for something he'd missed. *Deaded* was useless, and his few offensive spells made spitballs seem dangerous.

A sucking sound made Eon look up in time to see Lola vacuumed into her portal. His familiar smashed against a far wall and collapsed to the ground. A deluge of water sprayed her until his familiar drowned and disappeared.

"Hand them over, Champion." Camille held out a pale hand. "Now!"

Slowly, reluctantly, he reached into his satchel for the heart. Something small and metallic kept getting in his way. He jerked it out of the bag and sighed.

*Thank you, Insane Ned, for another useless item...*that unlocked at level 40. He quickly inspected it and let out a low whistle. The coin's spell required seven flips to activate. There was no way Camille would just watch and wait for him. He had an idea and hoped it wasn't a mistake.

"Hurry or I'll make your death deliciously painful."

Eon shoved the coin between his palm and Ned's staff. He quickly drew Zalmon's heart from his bag, placing it on the ground. She floated toward him as he reached for the eyes and set them beside the heart.

She licked her lips, grasping for them like a beggar stealing bread. Her clutching hands wrapped around the heart and eyes. She lifted them high overhead with an ecstatic sigh.

"Come to me, sister, I need my sacrifice for the *Vestibule* spell."

Adriette appeared at her feet. She moaned and writhed, struggling against strips of oily black cloth that covered her from head to toe.

"Now, Eon, see my father's power in the hands of a true Rune Mage."

A beam of purple light shot up from Adriette and slammed into the sky, cracking it open. The wound vomited out red clouds that spread like a canopy over Salvare. It was just like Rath, except for the thunder.

"No." Her voice quavered. "Something is wrong."

Lightning danced wildly along the angry clouds as if she'd angered Tesla. It shot out faster and faster.

Eon dove to the ground and cast *Deaded*.

A wide lightning bolt struck the Rune Mage with fury. He could barely hear Camille scream over the ear-rattling thunderclap. The crack sucked the clouds back and closed.

He got up and brushed himself off. The shitty spell had worked. He'd taken no damage.

She stood on the ground, staring up at the clouds with fury in her eyes. Despite the damage, she still had 4% of her Health.

He flipped the coin.

"I don't understand." She peered at the heart and eyes, smoke rising from her like a cartoon character, but less funny. "What did you do to my father's remains?"

Flip.

"I earned them," he said.

Flip.

"I won the heart because I turned away from greed."

Flip.

"And the eyes because I saw past hate."

Flip.

"Maybe they'll be mine if I kill you." She looked up, glaring at him with those crazy eyes, and then took a step back. "What are you doing?"

Flip.

"I've had enough!" Eon shouted. "You're a destroyer of things, like your son Ned, like Luanne. I don't care if it kills me in your world or in mine. I'm done with you!"

He flipped the coin one last time and cast one shot.

The Eminem song rang in his ears as he swung Ned's staff. It struck the coin with a baseball crack that would've made Jet proud. The coin tore through the air and struck her chest, lodging in it like a bullet.

She took a step back and coughed. She coughed again and began clawing at her sternum. "What is this trinket?"

"A gift from your son," he said. "Level Up: Steal one level from any opponent on Entriss for five minutes. They won't like it, so you'd better hurry."

Congratulations. You are now level 41.

His Mana and Health were full. He reached into his satchel.

"No!" she screamed, raising her hands. "I can still destroy you. You have no spells to defeat me."

There was a spluttering sound, and she stared at her sizzling fingers.

"Been a while since you've been 39?" He pulled out Ned's Flipping Coin of Flipping, hoping it would end her. "Your shithead son left this lying around too."

He flipped the coin at her, and she caught it.

"Ned's first toy. I helped him create this trinket." Camille smiled at the coin before throwing it to the ground. "And I know its secrets."

She cupped her hands together. A glassy orb hovered over them and grew as she raised it high overhead.

The orb hummed and sparked with power, ready to burst. Her eyes were fuck-it wild. Whatever her spell was at level 39, it was ready to blow.

"How will you defeat me now, Champion?" she asked.

"Like this," a woman said from behind Camille.

A bow twanged, and a black, steel arrow lodged in the orb.

"Ned, you fool," Camille said.

"Sorry, Eon." Adriette's second arrow struck him like a golf club, lifting him off the ground and throwing him against a distant building.

He landed just in time to watch Camille's spell explode.

72

IT'S FULL OF STARS

Everyone in the command center cheered at the big screen as Bala and Jack entered the room.

"Was that for me or are we late?" He collapsed into the nearest chair.

They turned around and immediately stood. Samantha rushed over and Gidget hopped onto Jack's lap.

"I'll see what we've got in first aid." Fred rushed off.

"I'd have been here sooner if I'd known there was cheesecake." He winced as Samantha checked the wound.

"Is there more?" Bala asked.

"Sure." Marta sighed. "Might as well. I'll find another fundraiser for my kids."

"I'll cover it." Jack nodded. "It's the least an old, swol man can do."

"Thank you, sir." She looked sheepishly between Jack and Samantha.

"He is swol, isn't he?" Samantha winked.

The women laughed until his cheeks were warm.

"Bring me up to speed," he said.

Lars shared the highlights. "It was unconventional, but he did it."

"Were you able to cast it?"

"All of it, sir." Fred approached with several rolls of gauze. "From what we can tell, millions are still watching."

"Good man." He nodded. "Thank you, Fred."

Fred beamed.

"Ouch." He jerked his arm away, which hurt worse than the bandaging.

"I could always let it bleed out." Samantha sounded overly innocent. "I'm in the will, right?"

Jack's eyes went wide, and he slowly lowered his arm so she could finish.

"So, it's over?" Bala asked.

"It's an IMMO." Jack nodded at the big screen. "It's never truly over."

THE GONG of a tower bell rang, followed closely by another. Eon shakily pushed himself up to all fours. He was alive. Barely alive. Adriette's arrow was apparently defensive, throwing him clear of the explosion. Slamming into the building and falling to the ground had almost killed him. He had 8 Health left and tried not to sneeze. The bell rang again.

"Oh, what now?" He was ready to log out for a day. Or thirty. The quest, running from one emergency to the next, and the final battle had left him feeling wrung out. His stomach growled. He smelled like bloody gym socks, and the gong from Rath had returned.

A small hand patted his shoulder. "That's the longest push-up I've ever seen."

"Nomar!" His head whipped up. "You're alive!"

His favorite Gnome was at full health. Nomar's cheeks were ruddy, and he had a warm smile on his face.

Eon pushed himself to his knees and pulled Nomar into a hug.

"How..." He let go and stood. "How is this possible?"

"We won," Nomar said, his blush a little brighter. "You did it."

Eon looked over their battleground with wide eyes. Entriss had resurrected his group after the win, just like any other boss encounter. The bells weren't a warning; they rang in celebration. Everyone in his group approached, patting backs and recounting the battle. Everyone but Jewells.

His heart sank a little. *Final Kill* had destroyed her character and there was no coming back. Sure, they'd have fun leveling another toon for her, but she deserved to be here.

Eon summoned Lola. "You were amazing!"

She nuzzled against him, shuddered, and coughed out a puff of fire.

"Wow, wow, wow!" Nomar's eyes went wide. "You breathe fire? This calls for marshmallows."

Tiffany healed him to full. After a rigorous bout of handshakes and hugging and congratulations, Adriette approached.

He stared in awe. "You did it."

Her smile was kind, and she shook her head. "You were the hero, Eon. Not me. Your quick thinking cost her a level, releasing me from her spell."

Zalmon's daughter, the first Ranger on Entriss, looked tired. She was an older version of Vicki, slightly taller with long, gray hair pulled back in a tight ponytail. Years of worry had wrinkled her tanned complexion. Her frame seemed a bit too lean after battling Misere monsters for several centuries. But none of that could damper the confidence and strength that radiated from her.

She faced her daughter, looking the young woman up and down.

"You grew up to be so beautiful." There was a catch in her throat. "You probably thought I abandoned you. I tried so hard to find a way back."

"I hated you for years until Eon told me the truth." Vicki hesitated for a breath then launched forward to hug Adriette. "I missed you so much, Mom."

Eon stared at the ground to give them their moment. Adriette whispered comforting words as Vicki cried it out. When Eon finally looked up, he made eye contact with the Ranger and she mouthed, "Thank you."

He nodded, his shoulders dropped, and a smile lifted his cheeks. It had all been worth it. Sure, there would be rewards and titles and world firsts, but none of that seemed to matter. Seeing Vicki reunited with her mom was reward enough.

They pulled apart and composed themselves. Vicki reached back for Eon's hand. He held it and squeezed gently. It felt a little intimate, but she'd helped him through that terrible night after stealing the child's heart. He wouldn't hesitate to be there for her.

"You all deserve gifts for saving Entriss," Adriette said. "After I change into something more formal."

Light surrounded her, lifting Adriette from the ground and wrapping her in a rainbow cocoon. Bright cracks appeared until she broke free from her chrysalis. She drifted to the ground, looking healthy and powerful. Her leather armor was now ivory, and the top of her longbow featured a wicked dragon head. Something else had changed. She had a presence about her that made him take a step back.

All hail Adriette, Queen of Entriss.

"Your Majesty." Eon immediately dropped to one knee and the others followed suit. Vicki was beside him, still holding his hand.

"Rise, Nomar of Nomorgin," Adriette said.

Nomar stood then approached.

"Please accept this weapon for your cunning and bravery." She handed him a package. "The most handsome of Gnomes is now the most powerful."

"Level 41?" He rushed forward and hugged her leg.

She patted his hat and smiled. Eon cleared his throat, and Nomar took a step back to bow.

Adriette named each member of the group and rewarded them. Some received weapons, others won armor, and all of them leveled.

"Approach, Lola the Jackalope."

His familiar hopped forward, bowed, and toppled over.

Adriette lifted her antlers until she was upright. "You have fought bravely, little one, and you will no longer be alone."

A second jackalope appeared. It was slightly larger, with rich brown fur.

"Boy bunny!" Nomar hopped up and down, clapping excitedly.

The jackalopes booped noses. Lola looked up at Eon, and he nodded. The two booped again then disappeared.

"Rise, Eon." A blue glow surrounded her, and she beckoned him forward. "Rise and turn in your quest."

He took a deep breath, stood, and approached the Queen of Entriss. She reached out, and he handed her the golden orb, turning in The Left Hand of God.

"You have saved Entriss and protected my daughter," she said. "Is this the reward you seek?"

Do you wish to replace character Eon with character Mandorf?

He took a step back. Was that even possible? He looked at her for a long moment and finally shook his head. Even if it was possible, he had changed. Mandorf was his past, Eon was his future, and there was a lot to explore with this Rune Mage.

"Thank you, Your Majesty, but no." He shook his head. "This is who I am now."

"A wise man." She nodded.

"Could you bring back Jewells?" he asked.

She stared off for several moments before looking at him. "I cannot."

"What about Trevor?"

Vicki looked up.

"I'm sorry." She shook her head. "That brave warrior is at peace."

"Fine," he sighed. "Just don't give me another coin."

"You shall retain your new level, and I reward you the titles Champion of Salvare and Champion of Entriss, and the perks that come with them." She looked him up and down, took a deep breath, and handed him a package. "Something more befitting for our great Champion."

He accepted and took a peek. It wasn't just one piece of armor; it was a full set. And at first glance, everything matched. As quests rewards went, it was generous, and it felt right.

"Thank you." He took a step back and bowed.

"One more thing, Champion." She looked at him with a steady gaze. "When Zalmon won The Right Hand of God, he became Deity's right hand as leader of Entriss. If you wish to rule a nation as Deity's left hand—"

"Nope." He already felt like Deity's marionette and was ready for a break. His hand rose, against his will, and patted his cheek. "Um, no, thank you. Vicki is much better suited to lead than I am. She's perfect for the job."

"Daughter, are you ready to take on the mantle of leadership?" She nodded toward Eon. "Or have you chosen another path?"

"Uh." Eon raised a finger.

Vicki held up a hand to shush him. "This may not be what I want, but it's what I have to be. For Entriss. That is what I choose."

"As you wish, daughter." Adriette nodded.

A rainbow surrounded Vicki, lifting her off the ground and wrapping her in the soon-to-be-royalty-cocoon. White light cobwebbed around her, finally shattering as she broke free and lowered back to the ground.

All hail Vicki, Queen of Salvare.

They all dropped to their knees again. He looked up. She now had a presence similar to Adriette's, if not as powerful. Her eyes were a little distant, but she smiled at him.

"Enough formality," Adriette said. "Entriss shall celebrate like never before."

She snapped, and the roads filled with players and NPCs. His raid dispersed as they all left group until it was him and Nomar. Everyone who had battled by his side against Camille wandered into the crowd, including Nomar, who ran off with Coco.

Congratulations on World First...

The crowd lined up to congratulate him before he could finish reading.

Congratulations on...

Someone handed him a drink.

Congratulations! Rune Staff of Ned the Insane has earned a new spell.

An Elf stood beside him. "Smile for a screenshot!"

Congratulations! You have points to spend on your focus tree.

"You've gotta try these panacakes!"

Congratulations! You can now activate Zalmon's Heart and Eyes. Be cautious not to...

"It looks like *you* need saving," Vicki said from behind him.

He spun around and sighed in relief. "I do."

"Follow me." She took his hand and led him into the castle entrance, down a long hallway, and onto a blue platform.

In a blink, they were back in the war room overlooking the city. She had, indeed, saved him. They were alone, and he sighed in relief.

Fireworks shot over the city as dusk settled into a night sky. He took it in until she inched a bit too close. The hairs on his arms rose. The presence of royalty on Entriss was apparently a power.

He opened his mouth to ask her about it, and she leaned forward. He took a step back. "Vicki. What your mom said about another path—"

"It no longer matters. I wish you could understand what you've done for me. You have opened my mind and heart to endless new possibilities. I have learned much from you, Eon, and you will always be a part of me."

He could only nod.

"I have one last request, Champion," she whispered.

"Anything," he said.

She took a step back and held out a gold orb.

"No!" Someone from Entriss had cast the entire battle, and Julie stared at the screen in Ian's secret room. "Don't do it! Don't accept the quest."

It was like telling off the driver in another car.

"Computer, release Ian now." She ran over to his pod and tried wrenching it open. "It's an emergency."

"Unable to comply," the computer said in a cool voice.

"Ian, please don't." she sobbed. "I...I love you!"

HE ACCEPTED THE GOLDEN ORB.

The Bridge: Combine Zalmon's Heart and Eyes to create a powerful item.

His eyes went wide. Julie had said The Left Hand of God quest could save Entriss, and more importantly, her brother. Was this it?

He drew Zalmon's heart and eyes from his bag and held them out. They floated from his hand, and thunder shook the castle. The dead king's remains came together in a blast of red light. When the light faded, a red, rhombus-shaped diamond hovered in front of Eon.

It was slightly larger than his hand, and he gently plucked it from the air. He inspected the diamond and sucked in his lips.

Zalmon's Will: Use this trinket to create a breach that will teleport you and your group anywhere. Instant cast. The farther you go, the longer Zalmon's Will takes to recharge. Must be activated before use.

"Activated?" He frowned at the diamond, shaking it like a can of soda and pressing it against his ear.

"Stop!" Vicki held out both hands. "Just try the quest."

"Right." His cheeks warmed under her worried gaze.

He turned in the quest. She rewarded him with a generous amount of experience. Before he could ask why it was so much, she handed him a golden orb.

Save the Cheerleader, Save the World: Use Zalmon's Will to create a portal that will lead you to the one in danger.

He held out the diamond. It shook violently, forcing him to hold on with both hands so it didn't pop out. When the shaking finally stopped, a dark portal appeared mere feet away.

"Where does this go?" He swallowed hard, putting Zalmon's Will in his satchel.

"It won't hurt you to take a look."

Eon peeked in and immediately pulled back. "You're kidding me. Is this what I think it is?"

She nodded.

He stuck his head in just long enough to say, "My God, it's full of stars."

Vicki obviously didn't get the joke, but she smiled politely.

Part of him wanted to go through now, but it could wait. Not only did he need a break, he wanted to check on Julie and ask her about the quest.

"Help me." The faint voice of a young man echoed through the portal.

Eon frowned, leaning closer.

"Julie, please help." The voice was clear this time.

He stood straight like someone had plugged him into a socket. It had to be her brother, and he was alive. Julie needed to know, but what if this was his only chance?

The portal blinked in and out like it was losing power.

"Deity," he whispered. "Let Julie know he's alive, and I'm going to save him."

"Go, Champion." Vicki nodded. "Hurry."

Eon took a deep breath but as he took a step into the portal, tiny feet ran toward him.

"Not without me!" Nomar tackled his leg and held on.

The momentum pushed him further into the void. It was like being sucked down a drain, and he held onto the edge of the portal with one hand. The opening began to smoke, sparks popping noisily around the spell.

"Nomar, wait, I don't think we should both be here," Eon shouted. "Something's wrong."

"I think I'm going to be sick," Nomar cried out.

"Sonofa—"

His fingers slipped, and the portal closed.

73

WINS AND LOSSES

Department heads and board members sat around the new conference room table. They spoke in hushed tones or typed madly into their cast devices. Everyone went quiet as Jack entered the room.

Lars pulled out the big chair for him, and he sat, babying his bandaged arm.

"Thanks for being here. I know everyone is busy. It's good to be busy again." Jack smiled at all the nods. "I wanted to give a synopsis of our current state then answer any questions you might have.

"First, and most important...Entriss Online is not shutting down."

Everyone applauded then stood to applaud more. He let it go on for several moments before calming them with a hand.

"Something happened at the end of Eon's quest that we're still investigating." He took a deep breath. "It created a bridge between Entriss and Everyworld. We don't know how to break the connection without shutting down both worlds for an extended period of time. Everyworld is pre-go-live, and Watson won't let them interrupt his work. It's an unexpected turn of events that I look at as good fortune."

There was some muttering, but nobody knew how to react.

"This is good news for Entriss," he said in a sincere tone. "As you know, players can now purchase the Reckoning expansion. Not only does this increase their level cap to 50, it enables them to log in with pods. Entriss is now the first IMMORPG in the United States to offer full immersion."

Money and good news washed away apprehension. Lars clapped, and everyone followed his lead.

"The stockholder vote was almost unanimous. This dramatic bump in revenue has positioned us to give generous bonuses to anyone who's still with the company. We also want our people back. Anyone Luanne fired and anyone who quit under duress has a job waiting for them. If they come back, we will compensate them for the time away like they never left."

This time, applause became cheers. He let it go on. They deserved it.

"I would like to take a moment and acknowledge our new Director of Development, Bala, and Assistant Director of AI, Marta."

There was a polite round of clapping.

"We're also planning a new division. Fred has developed a program for monitoring and casting player activity. Millions of people viewed the cast of Eon's final battle. Fred is going to help us monetize that."

"Not Frank, sir?" Fred beamed.

Jack winked.

"I'm proud of you all." Jack looked around the room and nodded. "Now, get back to work."

Everyone laughed, and his staff meandered out, leaving him alone with Lars and the board. Lars activated the dampening field, and the lights dimmed.

"You did it, Jack." Carl the banker clasped his hands together.

"Ian did it. I give him and Julie all the credit."

"Any sign of them?"

"None." He shook his head. "Rumor is they're moving on to Everyworld, but I haven't spoken with Ian since we released him."

Charlene, a long-time board member, raised a finger. "What about the accords?"

"Hammers is preparing to renegotiate with other nations. I told him to hold off, but he wouldn't listen."

"Why should he wait?" Carl leaned forward.

"This isn't over," he said, but offered nothing further.

Charlene rubbed her dark hands together hungrily. "And Luanne? Have they caught our traitorous CIO yet?"

"She went missing shortly after the attack on headquarters." Jack cleared his throat. "The authorities are on the lookout, but there's been no sign of her. As far as I know, she's hiding out in another country or found her way to another world."

The board members laughed, completely ignoring Jack's cold smile.

URAY KNOB TAVERN in the Human starting zone of Yu had become busier than ever. Players and NPCs filled the tables. It was hard to tell the difference, but it didn't matter as long as they had coin in their purses.

She stared at the full room and sighed. It had been like this for weeks and she'd had little time to rest. Her feet were sore, her bodice was too tight, and her face hurt from smiling. Worst was the constant dull ache at her temples that spiked any time she tried to remember... remember...?

A ragged group of dusty adventurers waved her over. Two Ogres, a Gnome, and an Elf were all low level, which meant they had little coin for food and less for tips.

She smiled anyway, because that was her job. On her way to the table, a tabby cat crossed her path. She tried picking it up, but it slipped out of her grasp and wandered off.

Her memories came back in a flood, and her heart thrummed painfully in her chest. She opened her mouth to scream, "Help me,

I'm Luanne. I'm stuck in the body of an NPC and have been in the same loop for weeks."

Instead, she smiled her painful smile, and said, "Hi, I'm Jellicle. May I offer milords or ladies anything?" She leaned over. "A warm ale to wet your tongues before facing the road to adventure?"

74

WATSON

"You need to step aside, ma'am." The woman's voice cracked through the speaker of her hazmat suit.

Julie stood in front of Ian's pod with her fists raised. Barely stood. She hadn't slept for days, desperately trying to free her boyfriend from his virtual prison. Nothing had worked, and she'd been about to call Cook when a dozen or more assholes showed up in plastic suits.

"She won't budge," a man said into his wrist.

"I'm on my way," a familiar voice replied.

Minutes later, the assholes made a path for another hazmat suit to enter the room.

"The first in line for a beating." Julie braced herself.

"I'm sure I deserve that and more." He removed the plastic head covering.

"Dad?" Her lip quivered, and she ran into his arms. "After all that's happened, I didn't know if they were here to help or—"

"Ian will be well cared for. I promise they're the best."

She nodded, and he waved two fingers at the pod. The team got to work, uncoupling and recoupling connections. Julie sobbed into his shoulder as he patted her hair.

"I swear I didn't know, Jax," he said, softly. "Deity said he was the best candidate, but I never thought you'd fall in love."

"Mom hated it when you called me that." She drew back and wiped her eyes.

"She hated the X, but it's a family tradition." His smile was full of pride. "Julie Aliyah Xen—"

"I know my name," she scoffed, rolling her eyes.

"Of course." He bowed his head.

"What's up with the plastic suits?"

"The CDC is helping us out by implementing a temporary quarantine. It's the best way to keep away the curious while we pack Ian's things into storage."

He gently pulled her aside as two techs guided a gravity pad into the room. The steel slab hovered over the ground like a surfboard on water. The other techs surrounded Ian's pod to lift it. She held her breath as they hefted it onto the pad.

Her dad tapped the pod with a finger. "Treat that man like your life depends on it."

They all nodded, moving slowly as they guided Ian's pod out of the room.

When they were finally alone, she looked at her father. He watched them leave and continued staring as if weighed down by bad decisions. His wispy blond hair was thin and new wrinkles had been worried into his face. A look of desperation had washed away his jovial smile, but there was still a hint of hope in his eyes.

"Thank you, Julie. Your mother would be proud." He squeezed her shoulder. "It went just like we planned."

She could barely nod as guilt clutched her chest. "How is he? How is my brother?"

"Xayne is still in a coma, but alive." He patted her arm. "Bridging the worlds together will give him a chance."

"And Ian? Promise me he'll be okay."

"I'll do everything I can to—"

The radio in his hazmat suit crackled. "Mr. Watson, the pod is onboard, and Ian's vital signs are normal."

Julie sighed in relief.

Xander Watson clasped his hands together, and a hint of his old smile crept up his cheeks. "Let's bring him home. Everyworld awaits."

ABOUT THE AUTHOR

David J. Pedersen is a native of Racine, WI who resides in his home town Kansas City, MO. He received a Bachelor of Arts degree in Philosophy from the University of Wisconsin - Madison. He has worked in sales, management, retail, video and film production, and IT. David has run 2 marathons, climbed several 14,000 foot mountains and marched in *Thee* University of Wisconsin Marching Band. He is a geek and a fanboy that enjoys carousing, picking on his wife and kids, playing video games, and slowly muddling through his next novel.

Lightning Source UK Ltd.
Milton Keynes UK
UKHW022310060223
416578UK00007B/904/J

9 780578 831268